P9-CML-264

RED THUNDER

John Varley

ACE BOOKS, NEW YORK

RED THUNDER

An Ace Book
Published by The Berkley Publishing Group,
a division of Penguin Putnam Inc.,
375 Hudson Street, New York, New York 10014.

Text design by Kristin del Rosario.

First edition: April 2003

Library of Congress Cataloging-in-Publication Data

Varley, John, 1947–
Red thunder / John Varley.—1st ed.
p. cm.
ISBN 0-441-01015-6 (alk. paper)
I. Title.

PS3572.A724 R4 2003
813'.54—dc21
2002038231

PRINTED IN THE UNITED STATES OF AMERICA

10 9 8 7 6 5 4 3 2 1

To Spider Robinson and
Robert A. Heinlein
for the inspiration;
and to Lee, for that,
and everything else.

PROLOGUE

★ ★ ★

INSPIRATION IS WHERE you find it. You can't force it, and you can't predict when and where it will come. I had nothing to do with the inspiration that made our great adventure possible. But the inspiration that made it practical came to me while I was walking with my friend Dak through a railroad freight yard in my hometown of Daytona.

Dak is a string bean, well over six feet, and could hide behind a flagpole. African-American, though he doesn't use the term, and fairly dark. Dak is short for Daktari, which is Swahili for doctor, "A hell of a thing to wish on a newborn baby," he once said. He's my age, from the same graduating class but different high schools. We often took these long walks, often on the tracks. Here we sorted out the big questions of life. Is there a God? Are we alone in the universe? Is Britney Spears too old to stay on the Top Ten Babe of All Time list? Would Al Johnson switch to Team Chevy before the next 500?

"Does it look like rain?"

I looked around and sniffed the air.

"Sure does." Thunderheads were towering in the east, and what else is new? This was Florida, it rained every day. Today the temperature was only about eighty, but the humidity was 210 percent.

Two minutes later it started to pour.

We ran to a line of a dozen rusting black tank cars that had been parked on a siding for as long as I could remember, and ducked under one. No trains came through this part of the yard anymore, and the grass was thick where spilled oil hadn't killed it. I wondered if the EPA had heard of this place. You probably should have had a hazmat suit and a gas mask to even come here.

There wasn't enough room to stand under the tank car, so we sat on the gravel and listened to the rain pelting on it. I think rain is harder in Florida than anywhere else. I don't mean it comes down harder, I mean the *water* is harder. We didn't say anything for a while, just picked out suitable golfball-sized rocks and chunked them at a rusty old fifty-five-gallon drum about twenty yards away. My arm was better than Dak's, I was getting two hits to his one.

Not the worst way in the world to waste time. But we hadn't made any progress on the big question of the day.

"So, how do we go about building a spaceship on pocket change?"

That was the big one. Some question.

We had been round and round it over the last few days. We weren't going to get any help, we had been specifically told we were on our own. Neither of us had ever designed a canoe, much less a spaceship. My experience with rocketry was limited to a few illegal broomstraw-tailed squibs on the Fourth of July. Dak's was no better.

We had what we thought were some pretty good ideas on many aspects of the problem, all helped considerably by the fact that the central, toughest problem of space travel, propulsion, was pretty much solved. But now we had to build something, and what we kept coming back to was, *Where do you begin?*

"Pressure," Dak said, for maybe the five hundredth time in the last few days. "It's gonna be tough to build something that can stand up to thirty psi for two months."

It really only had to stand up to 15 psi, but everything about the ship had to meet double the necessary tolerances.

We listened to the rain some more, and Dak tossed another rock, which made the drum ring like a gong.

"We can't start from square one," I said. "Too much welding, and every weld we make is a place for trouble to begin."

Dak sighed. He'd heard it before.

"We need components. Things we can slap together quick."

"Where we gonna get them? Go to the NASA junkyard, patch up an old ship?"

"A pressure hull," I said. Something was tickling the edge of my awareness.

"A globe," Dak said. "Or a . . ."

"A cylinder. A metal cylinder."

I jumped up so fast I hit my head on the bottom of the tank car.

I ran out and stood in the downpour, looking back at the old, rust-streaked, greasy, flaky paint, birdpoop-spattered tank car.

"Knock off the wheels," I said. "Stand it on its end . . ."

". . . and there's your spaceship," Dak whispered.

Then we were laughing and actually dancing in the driving rain.

BUT OF COURSE that all came later. It started about a month earlier. . . .

PART ONE

1

I ALWAYS THOUGHT the VentureStar looked like a tombstone. When it was standing on end it was twice as tall as it was wide. It wasn't very thick. It was round at the top. For a night launch it was illuminated by dozens of spotlights like an opening night in Hollywood. It could have been the grave marker for a celebrity from some race of giant aliens. The stubby wings and tail seemed tacked on.

The VentureStar didn't spend much time flying, which was just as well, because it flew about as well as your average skateboard. Sitting on the ground it looked more like a building than an aircraft or a spaceship.

That's okay. In about thirty seconds it would leave every airplane ever built in a wake of boiling smoke and fire.

"Manny, a Greyhound bus leaves Cocoa Beach every day for Tallahassee. Why don't we go watch that some night? We could get a lot closer."

That was my girlfriend, Kelly, trying to get my goat. Her point being that VStars left Canaveral once a day, too. Point taken.

"Who wants to neck at the Greyhound terminal?" I said.

"Hah. The only thing you've necked with so far is those binocs."

I put down my binoculars and thumbed up the brightness of the little flatscreen on my lap. I got a view looking into one of the windows of the cockpit blister. The flight crew were on their backs, going through the final items on the prelaunch checklist with no wasted motion. A woman with curly red hair was sitting in the left seat. I could read the name sewed on her NASA-blue flight tunic: WESTIN. A younger man with a blond crewcut sat on the right.

"VStars are noisier, I'll give you that," she said. We were sitting side by side on the tailgate of Dak's truck.

"Ain't you got no poetry in your soul, woman?"

I used the tip of the screen's stylus to touch 7, then 5, then ENTER on the tiny flatscreen keypad. Camera 75 showed a view looking up from the massive concrete abutments that supported the VStar. Center screen were the long, pinched shapes of the six linear aerospike rocket engines that stretched across the ship's wide tail. Wisps of ice-cold hydrogen and oxygen escaped from the pressure valves and swirled in the warm Florida night air. Down in the corner were the words "VStar III *Delaware*," a mission number, and a countdown clock. In less than a minute camera 75 would be toast.

In a corner of the screen the countdown clock went from twenty-five to twenty. I pressed 5, then 5, then ENTER. A head-on angle of the cockpit crew, slightly fish-eye from a wide-angle lens. There were no more checks to perform, no more toggles to switch. They were almost motionless, waiting for the automatic launch sequence.

I pressed 4, then 4 again: Looking down the center aisle of the passenger compartment. It was built to carry as many as eighteen, but only seven chairs were filled, all of them toward the front of the module.

I knew those seven faces as well as an earlier generation of space nuts had known the faces of Al Shepard, John Glenn, Gus Grissom, Wally Schirra, Deke Slayton, Gordon Cooper, Scott Carpenter . . . the original Mercury astronauts. None of this seven looked particularly nervous or excited. The white-knuckle days of space travel were over, or so everyone said. Mom says they'll never be over for her generation, who saw *Challenger* explode.

I don't think they'll ever be completely over for me, either. I mean,

I didn't expect the ship to blow up or anything, but was I the only guy on the planet who thought this VStar launch was just a little out of the ordinary? Was I the *only* one who noticed the Ares Seven had discarded the standard NASA-blue coveralls for bright red ones?

Mars. They're going to Mars. The passengers in the VStar were the Ares Seven, the crew, on their way up to the *Ares Seven*, the ship.

Fifteen seconds.

3, then 1, then ENTER: The last gantry arm detached and quickly swung to the left, out of the way.

Eleven seconds.

5, then 4, ENTER: A view from a camera on a helicopter three miles away, vibrating slightly because of the long lens.

Nine seconds.

75, ENTER: I was looking up at the engines. The floodgates opened and a million gallons of water streamed down, to cool the launch pad and soak up some of the thunder that would kill an unprotected man before the flames vaporized him.

Five seconds.

The candle was lit, with a huge cough of orange flame that quickly moderated to an icy blue.

Two seconds. Camera 75 melted.

45 ENTER: A camera looking at the hold-down latches.

One second.

The latches fell away and the VentureStar immediately leaped into the night sky.

62 ENTER: This one was perched on the top of the tower. The deep blue body of the VStar roared upward, followed by a fountain of fire. Camera 62 melted.

The sound hit me, miles away. As always, I thought I could feel it blowing my hair, like an explosion. I looked up to see the line of fire arcing in the night. I could see the VStar accelerate.

55 ENTER: The flight crew were pressed back into their chairs, their faces distorted by an acceleration of two gees and growing. I looked up again. The ship was completing a roll maneuver, and turning down-range.

44 ENTER: The Ares Seven were all grinning like fools. Cliff Raddison held one hand out in the aisle, palm up. That took strength at 2.4 gees. Across the aisle, Lee Welles took up the challenge, reached out and slapped Raddison's palm. Then they got their arms back as the gee forces continued to mount.

39 ENTER: I saw four globular objects in a line. Two were very dark, the other two a much lighter brown.

What the hell? Camera 39 was supposed to be aft-looking, mounted on the ship's tail. It was one of my favorite angles, looking back to see light-spattered Florida shrink and vanish over the horizon. . . .

"Dak!" I shouted. "You bastard!"

I jumped down from the high tailgate, raced around the pickup, and was just in time to see Dak and Alicia straightening and pulling up their pants. I gave Dak a shove and he was laughing so hard he simply fell over onto the sand. Dak's laugh was a high-pitched giggle; Alicia had more of what I would call a belly laugh, and she was not in much better shape than Dak, leaning against the truck, holding her pants up with one hand. I turned away; I didn't want Dak to see me smile.

Kelly came around to the front of the truck in time to see Alicia collapse in the sand beside Dak.

"Can somebody tell me what's going on?"

I went to the front of the truck and pointed to the *O* in *Dodge*.

"There's a camera in there," I told her. "It's about the size of a postage stamp." Kelly bent to study it, but couldn't see anything.

"Television camera?"

"Just in case," Dak said, sitting up with tears streaming from his eyes. "Bad things can happen to a *Nee*-gro in the deep south. If the cops ever do a Rodney King on my nappy head, I'm not going to cross my fingers and hope somebody has a camcorder."

"I still don't get it," Kelly said.

I showed her the flatscreen, thumbed the backup button until I had the image Dak had pirated into the NASA data stream.

"Yes sir!" Dak shouted. "That rocket ain't going to Mars, it's going to the *moon,* baby!"

There was barely enough light for me to see the smile on Kelly's face as she realized what she was seeing. I looked at the sky, where the VStar had now dwindled to a very bright speck to the southeast. A white vapor trail, barely visible by starlight, was twisted by the high-altitude winds.

"You've got a big zit on your ass, Dak," Kelly said.

"Huh? Let me see that."

She held it out of his reach, then tossed it back to me. Dak realized his leg was being pulled. He helped Alicia to her feet. The four of us stood together a few moments, watching the VStar's light dwindle and vanish below the horizon.

"Say hi to John Carter, swordsman of Mars, when you get there, guys," Dak said.

"Or Valentine Michael Smith," I added.

"Just so it isn't those H. G. Wells Martians," Kelly said.

It was a pleasant Wednesday night in the spring, one of those times that almost makes up for the heat and humidity in Florida most of the year. We were standing in a shell parking lot in Cocoa Beach. At the north end half a dozen cars clustered under the flashing neon of the Apollo Lounge. It advertised nude table dancing, pool, no-cover-no-minimum, and "World Famous Astroburgers." We had the south end of the lot to ourselves. Before us was a sand dune, the beach, and the Atlantic Ocean. Not far behind us was the Banana River, which isn't a river at all but a long, slender bay cut off from the sea by the barrier island that contains Indian Harbor Beach, Patrick Air Force Base, Cocoa, and Cape Canaveral, just a few miles to the north. There were places to get a little closer to the launch complex without a visitors' pass, but none that offered us a better view of the downrange flight of most VStars.

"So, are you satisfied with the flight, Captain Garcia?" Dak asked.

"Everything looks nominal from here," I said.

"Don't know what those folks at NASA would do without you to help get 'em in the air every night," Dak muttered.

"It's not every night, it's more like—"

"Couple times a week."

"Yeah, okay," I said. It was about that often, at least when I could convince Dak to fire up *Blue Thunder* and take me out there. "Anyway, this one's taking the crew up to the Mars ship."

"What's your problem, Dak?" Kelly asked.

"No problem. Just restless, I guess. Manny likes to come out here, look at 'em take off. Way I see it, it's just one more ship taking off without me on it." Dak looked at the horizon where the rocket had faded into the black sky. He looked hungry. At last he looked back at us.

"How about it, Manny?" he said. "Go back to the heartbreak hotel and hit the books? Or do a little off-roading first?"

"Is that one of those rhetorical questions?"

So me and Kelly piled into the back of the truck and Dak and Alicia got in the cab, and *Blue Thunder* roared to life. I've never asked just what Dak has under the hood, but I figure NASA would be amazed if they could take a look. Put wings on *Blue Thunder* and it could probably catch up to the VStar. Dak flipped switches on a dashboard only a little less complicated than the ones in airliners, and the lights came on in groups. There were headlights and taillights and searchlights. Yellow fog lights hung below the front bumper. Tiny running-board lights could be made to crawl around the truck, like the sign for a Miami casino. More headlights were mounted on the big chrome roll bar that Kelly and I clung to, standing up in the pickup bed. And right behind a thick Plexiglas spoiler on the hood was the truck's crowning glory: a blue neon scrawl spelling out *"Blue Thunder."* Cuban gangbangers in immaculate low-riders, not an easy group to impress, had been known to drive into ditches in amazement when Dak rocketed past. As more and more lights came on, the color became visible, a blue so rich the only place on Earth you could duplicate it was deep in the ocean, and of a transparency you could only get with dozens of coats of paint and endless hours of buffing. *Blue Thunder* was more a work of art than a vehicle.

Which is not to say it wasn't a hell of a vehicle. We bounced over the dune, me and Kelly holding on to the roll bar in the back, and then all four of the big off-road tires bit into the loose sand and we were off.

I knew as well as anyone that we should have gone home and done a few hours of studying. But if we had, Dak would never have run over the ex-astronaut.

IT'S NOT STRICTLY legal to drive on the beach in Florida.

Okay, it's against the law. Would you believe they used to have car races right out on the sand, not very far north of where we were that night, until they built the big track at Daytona? It's true, I've seen the video. Now they worry about every quart of oil that might make its way into the Atlantic. I'm not saying that's a bad idea, but if anyone thought *Blue Thunder* would leave so much as a drop on the clean sands of Cocoa Beach they didn't know Dak very well. You could cook and eat your dinner right off the engine block, assuming Dak would ever let you do such a messy thing to his baby.

Dak would be spending hours tomorrow hosing off the worst of the salty sand. He would remove wheels and brakes and shocks to clean them with a toothbrush. If you think I'm kidding, you don't know Dak.

Kelly and I hung on tight as Dak steered through the packed sand and foam, and every time he hit a wavelet spreading across the beach we'd get a fine salt spray in our faces. Looking down through the open moon roof I could hear the throbbing drums of some new South African group Alicia had discovered. I could see the dash lights, including the fuzzbuster unit I'd helped him install. It was supposed to alert us if there was a cop transmitting anywhere within two miles. We knew the cops had seen us out there, we'd heard them talking about us. They were even pretty sure of who we were, and so far hadn't been able to do a damn thing about it. They had to catch us first, and there wasn't a police vehicle in the whole state of Florida that could keep up with *Blue Thunder* in the sand.

Kelly had one arm around my waist and one hand on the roll bar, and that felt great. I had my arm around her, too. The wind and the spray blew through her hair and she looked great in the moonlight. Dak was staying close to the water and far from the dunes, because the soft, rolling sands were where nighttime lovers liked to spread their blankets.

Life seemed just about perfect. And that's when we ran over the guy.

He looked like a piece of driftwood when I first saw him. He was lying on his back looking up at the stars, or what few stars you could see with all the lights of Cocoa Beach behind us. I saw him turn his head and squint against the bright headlights.

Kelly saw him the same time I did, and she shouted something and started pounding on the roof. I looked down.

Alicia straightened up—

Dak glanced up at me—

Kelly hit the roof even harder—

Dak looked forward . . . mouthed an obscenity . . . slammed on the brakes.

Blue Thunder 's wheels locked and we began to skid sideways. Dak corrected. He had us straightened out again when we ran over the man's legs.

We came to a stop. The truck's engine died and for a moment there was only the sound of the surf. Then everyone started shouting at once.

I don't remember what anyone said. It wasn't anything terribly smart, I know that. We were scared.

Kelly and I jumped out of the pickup bed and hurried around to the side of the truck. Dak had his door open, but that seemed to be as far as he could go. He had his arms over the steering wheel and his head buried in his arms. He was shaking.

Alicia hadn't been able to get out over Dak, so she came around the front. Dak's running-board lights dazzled our eyes so we couldn't see in the darkness beneath them. Alicia shined her flashlight down at the sand, then made a little squeaking sound and backed up a few paces.

"We cut off his legs," she whispered. Kelly turned around and made a gagging sound, then turned back. I knelt close to where Alicia was shining the flashlight beam.

I could see that the man's legs ended a lot sooner than they should have. *Blue Thunder* had thrown up some big ridges of wet, heavy sand. I couldn't see where his legs ended because the sand covered most of them below the knees.

But I saw his shoes easy enough. They were a good five feet away from his kneecaps and three feet away from the truck.

Dak stepped out of the cab, took one look at the disembodied feet, staggered into the surf and vomited.

I felt like doing the same . . . and then I realized what had happened. I went over to them and prodded one with my own shoe. It rolled over. There was no foot inside.

Alicia knelt and shined the light under the truck. Kelly knelt beside her and worked her hand down into loose sand.

She pulled up a bare foot, holding it by the little piggy that stayed home, or maybe the one who had roast beef. A leg came up with it, perfectly well attached to the foot. There weren't even any tread marks on it.

First you feel a wave of relief. Then you get angry. I wanted to kick him. What sort of jerk lies in the surf line in the dark?

But I could almost hear my mother's voice. *Oh, yeah? What kind of jerk goes joyriding on the beach in the dark?* Okay, Mom. You're right, as usual.

"Let's get him out of there," I said, and grabbed a foot. Dak took the other and we slid him out, where he squinted up into Alicia's light.

"This salt water ain't doing your undercarriage any good, hon," he said.

"It's *my* undercarriage," Dak said.

"Whatever," the guy said, and belched. Then he sort of passed out.

I say "sort of" because he never went to sleep. He passed into an alcoholic fog where he wasn't really connecting with what was happening. He was docile as a baby, and in the morning he wouldn't remember a thing. Right now he'd blow a perfect ten on the lush-o-meter.

There's a good chance we saved his life. The tide could have easily taken him out to sea where he'd drown without ever waking up.

"What's your name, dude?" Dak was asking him.

"This dude is down for the count, my friend," I said. "We'd better get him out of here before the crabs eat him."

"Drag him back in the dunes?" Alicia suggested.

"Worse than crabs back in the dunes," Dak said. "Passed-out guy could get raped back there in the dunes."

"He'd never know it," Alicia said.

"Maybe a certain soreness in the morning . . ." Dak rubbed his ass, and we all laughed. Okay, so it wasn't so funny. I felt a little silly with relief. You think about it, you realize how your whole life can change in two seconds. We could have been gathered around a dead or dying man.

Kelly might almost have been reading my thoughts.

"We nearly killed him, don't you think we ought to try to take him home?"

"And have him blow chunks all over my upholstery? Let him fight off the fairies his own self."

"Gin doesn't come in chunks," Alicia said. She showed us an empty bottle of Tanqueray she had stumbled over.

"Yeah? Say he ate one of those World Famous Astroburgers an hour ago." Dak nodded toward the bar in the distance.

"Pretty good gin for a wino."

"He's not a wino. He hasn't been sleeping in back alleys. Look at his clothes."

It was true, the sneakers sold for well over a hundred dollars a pair, and they looked new. The shirt and pants were expensive labels, too.

"And he don't drink wine, either," Dak said. "So what's that make him? A *gin*-o? Whatever, it don't make his vomit any sweeter."

"So, we gonna take him home or not?"

"Where's home?" Kelly asked.

We all looked down at him again. He was still smiling, humming something I didn't recognize. A wavelet hit him and eddied around our feet, then sucked a little deeper hole under him as it ran back out. That must have been how his legs got buried. An hour from now he'd be under the sand, somebody else's problem. But none of us wanted that.

So I reached down and grabbed the side of his pants and pulled him up a bit, then fished his wallet out of his hip pocket.

It was hand-tooled leather and fairly thick. The first thing I saw was the corner of a hundred-dollar bill sticking out. I opened it and pulled out a wad of cash. I thrust it out to Dak, who looked startled and took it. He counted it.

"Eight hundred big ones," he said.

"So take out a taxi fee and let's get him home."

He handed the cash back to me. "What's eating you, anyway?"

I didn't really know. Part of it was that I sure could have used the money. Who would know? Certainly not this whacked-out jerk, lying there pissed out of his mind.

You'd know, Manuel, Mom said. She had this annoying habit of speaking just as loudly when she wasn't there as when she was.

"We'll just dump him in the back," I said. "I'll ride with him. He barfs, I'll clean it up." Dak waved it away, and I looked at the wallet again. Visa, MasterCard, American Express, all platinum, all made out to one Travis Broussard.

"Cajun," Kelly said, peering over my shoulder.

"Huh?"

"The name," she explained. "There's some Cajun families from the Florida panhandle, I think." I didn't know what difference that made, unless he lived in the panhandle. That would be too far to drive him. I found the driver's license, and as I pulled it from its pocket another card fell to the sand. Alicia picked it up. I pointed out the address on the license to Dak and Kelly.

"Is that far from here?"

"Forty-five minutes, maybe half an hour this time of night. Out in the boonies, though. Don't look at me that way. I'll take the dude. Won't even charge him for my gasoline."

Alicia whistled under her breath. "Look at this," she said. "The guy's an astronaut."

"Let me see that," Dak said, and grabbed the card. Then Alicia played keep-away with her flashlight for a moment until Dak and I over-powered her.

"This expired three years ago," Dak said. But before that it had been a gate pass to the Kennedy Space Center, and identified Broussard as a colonel and a chief pilot in the NASA VentureStar program.

3

THE QUICKEST WAY from the beach to Rancho Broussard involved twenty miles or so on the Florida Autopike. Dak eased *Blue Thunder* onto the ramp and allowed the Pike computer to interrogate his precious baby. There are several things about the Autopike that just rub Dak the wrong way. The most basic is simply that he hates to surrender control of his rig. "You go driving, you should have at least one hand on the wheel, like God intended."

I didn't argue with him on that one. There was still something profoundly creepy about cars that steered themselves, at least to folks like me and my mother. We could barely afford the thirty-year-old Mercury that Dak and I were always rescuing from a one-way trip to the junkyard. That Merk was not Pike-adaptable without spending about ten times what the old wreck was worth. Poor folks like us ride the Autopike about as often as we take the ballistic Orient Express to Tokyo.

The other thing Dak hates about the Pike is . . . well, let's face it, nobody likes to get passed, right? Nobody our age, anyway, and for sure nobody driving a rig as gaudy as *Blue Thunder*. But ol' Blue was built for power, not for speed. We were banished into the D lane, the outer one for vehicles that cruise at about eighty-five or ninety. What we call the "blue hair" lane, for all the old ladies in their well-preserved Caddies and Buicks. Now you can see them by the thousands in the D lane, going places they were too timid to drive to before the Pike opened. It's a drag to be tucked in among them while you watch the soccer moms in their minivans pass you in the fast lanes.

Dak pulled into one of the brightly lit authorization booths. Kelly and I scrambled out of the bed and set Colonel Broussard on his feet. He needed support, but he could stand. We shoved him into the narrow backseat as the Pike computer checked some eighty or ninety road-worthiness items every time you entered, from airbag sensors to tire pressure. We hopped in behind him.

"Is this my car?" Broussard asked.

"Just take it easy, sir," Kelly said. "We'll have you home soon."

"Okay."

"If he barfs in my car, man . . ."

"Please state your destination," the computer said. Dak told it the exit number, and the computer told him what the fare would be.

"Do not attempt to leave the vehicle while it is in motion." I heard the doors click as the computer locked them.

"Do not attempt to steer the vehicle until you are told it is safe." I could see Dak idly spinning the disconnected steering wheel.

"Do not unbuckle your safety belts at any time. The next rest wayside is thirty minutes away, so if you need to use the facilities, press the REST button on your Autopike Control Console now."

"I'll just piss in a Mason jar," Dak said.

"Don't miss," said the computer. "You're due for an oil change in five hundred miles. Your left front tire is showing some uneven wear. And all that salt and sand isn't doing your undercarriage any good."

"That's what I said!" Colonel Broussard shouted.

"Bon voyage, Blue," said the voice, which I now suspected was not the Pike computer. *Blue Thunder* pulled quickly away from the booth as Dak muttered something about "Big Brother." I looked over at the supervisor's tower and saw a guy waving at us.

The only time I was on the Pike the scariest part was the initial merge. The computer tucked us in between two semis with about three inches clearance fore and aft, and did it at eighty miles per hour. During rush hour they use every square inch of road available and the door handles and bumpers almost touch. Some people can't bear to use the Pike at all because of that. It's contrary to all your driving instincts.

No problem like that tonight. Traffic was light in all lanes. Over in the A lane there would be no traffic at all for a minute or two, then a dozen cars would zip by bumper to bumper to take advantage of drafting, like racing cars. They say in a few more years you'll be able to travel from Miami to Maine like this, but as of now the Florida part of the Pike only goes from Brevard to Jacksonville, by way of Orlando.

We'd hardly got up to Pike speed when it was time to get off again. The computer eased us to the required dead stop at the booths, and Dak engaged the manual controls. We rolled off the Pike and onto a main east-west highway.

We were on that for about fifteen minutes and then turned off on a smaller road. Then we took a shell road, deserted at this time of night. Dak watched the Global Positioning Satellite screen, where a red line was showing him the route over a maze of farm roads and hunting trails. This was about as far off the beaten track as you could get in this part of the world.

Off to our right we saw lights, the first ones in a while. When we got there we saw it was one of those little five-pew Baptist churches that dot the back roads from South Carolina to Texas. This one was a double-wide trailer sitting on concrete blocks. There was another double-wide sitting a bit back in the trees. It was probably the parsonage. You could tell which one was the church because somebody had built a big steeple over it and taped some colored cellophane over the windows. Somebody in there liked to paint. There were dozens of big plywood signs with biblical verses and end-of-the-world warnings lettered on them, and a lot of renderings of Bible stories done in flaking house paint. It was all lit up with floods and strung with colored Christmas lights. The whole place was surrounded by a high chain-link fence and the grounds were littered with the usual number of rusted-out cars and junked refrigerators and busted toilets you found this deep into redneck country.

Kelly was tugging at my sleeve. "Look at that one," she said, laughing. I figured she meant the one that read

YOU THINK GOD
IS JUST SOME BAGGY-ASS
OLD PECKERWOOD
IN A DIRTY SHEET?
THINK AGAIN, SINNER!

Dak took the next right and we rattled over a cattle guard and down a long potholed driveway that took a few gentle curves through the piney woods before it ended . . . in a basketball court.

There were lights on poles, but only one of them was working. There were cracks in the concrete with grass growing in them. Neither of the goals had a net.

"Let's shoot some hoops, friends!" Dak called out. I had to laugh. We all knew Dak's attitude about basketball. If you're black and you're tall, he once told me, you better not learn to play b-ball unless you're the next Michael Jordan. If they see you can shoot they'll never bother to educate you. Dak pretended to be the most fumble-fingered jerk since the game was invented, somewhere deep in Africa. "Don't believe those white boys who say it came from here. How many white boys you see playing NBA ball? I rest my case." Actually, the only time I got him to play a little one-on-one at a deserted playground he wasn't all that bad. My speed made up for his reach, so we were pretty evenly matched. But I didn't make the first team at school.

The rest of the place hid in the darkness. On one side of the clearing was a sprawling ranch-style house. It looked like the plantings around it had gone wild, and in Florida that can mean very wild indeed. Dak drove toward the house, but before we reached it we came to a big, empty swimming pool.

Dak drove close and cut the engine. We listened to the crickets for a while, then we all got out of the truck. Me and Kelly followed Alicia to the edge of the pool. She shined the light down into it, then jumped in surprise and gave a little squeak. Down there in the deep end, sitting on a lot of dead leaves and empty cans, was an eight-foot alligator. He turned his head, opened his mouth, and hissed at us.

"Whoever lives here, they're crazy," Kelly said. "Isn't it illegal, keeping an alligator like that?"

"Might be, but what's that?" Alicia said, and shined her light on a thick electrical cord that went from under the gator and up the side of the pool. "I think this is just one of those audio-whatsit things, like at Disney World."

"Go down and check it out, will you, babe?" Dak said. "We'll wait up here."

"And get electrocuted, right? I see some water down there."

She shined her light over the house and patio. I let my eyes follow the beam as it picked out a low diving board and groupings of lawn or pool furniture, including a big umbrella and table thing that had blown over.

The light traveled a little more, to one of those bolt-it-yourself sheet metal buildings you can buy at Sears and put up in a few days, if you have a concrete pad to set it on. There were four wide garage doors, closed, and each of them had a light fixture over it but only one was working. It was a large building, I'll bet you could put an ice hockey rink in it. Several rusting vehicles sat off to one side, some almost vanishing into the blackberry brambles. One of them was up on blocks, and it looked like a Rolls-Royce except the back half was gone and a pickup bed had been welded there.

"I don't think anybody's home," Kelly said. I didn't think so, either. We heard nothing suggesting a human was near. The mosquitoes had found us. We were all slapping at them, and I knew we couldn't just leave him in one of those pool chairs over there. He'd be one big skeeter bite in the morning.

"Where we gonna put the dude, then?" Dak asked.

Alicia reached in the open truck door and leaned on the horn, hard, for a good fifteen or twenty seconds.

Dak was about to honk again when a light came on above a door on the side of the aluminum barn. The door opened, and a short, tubby figure stepped out onto a small porch and stood there with his hands in his pockets.

"You know a Travis Broussard?" Alicia shouted at him.

His shoulders sagged. He ran a hand over a partly bald head.

"Y'all know where he be?" he hollered back.

"He be in my truck," Dak yelled. "He be *passed out* in my truck. He maybe be about to *barf* in my truck when he wakes up. You want him?"

"I want him, me. Y'all wait a minute."

He closed the door and then one of the garage doors rolled about halfway up. The guy came through it, pushing a wheelbarrow.

By the time he reached us, I think we were all grinning, at least a little.

He wasn't much over five feet tall and plump, a right jolly old elf. Trying to place him, I realized he looked a lot like a popular postcard we sell in the office, mostly in December. It shows Santa Claus stretched out poolside between two Hooters girls. He's wearing a loud aloha shirt and tacky cut-off jeans and huarches and holding a margarita and it says, "Deliver your *own* goddamn gifts this year!"

When he got to us he set the wheelbarrow down. His forearms were huge, like Popeye's. He was smiling, which made the creases in his face deeper. You could tell he smiled a lot. He made odd little bowing movements toward us, didn't see it when Dak started to offer his hand. He was twisting the hem of his tentlike shirt so hard I wondered why the hula-hula girls weren't screaming. From all the wrinkles I could see he twisted that shirt a lot.

He looked into the pickup. He stroked his snow-white beard for a bit, then reached in and grabbed Colonel Broussard's arm and was about to swing him up in a fireman's carry when Dak stepped up beside him.

"Here, man, we'll give you a hand," Dak said. The little guy looked confused, then did a few more bows in our direction. So Dak and I each grabbed a leg and we carried him. We arranged the limp carcass with his arms and legs hanging out of the wheelbarrow. He was still sleeping peacefully.

The elf stood there a moment, twisting the shirt again. I noticed he seldom looked into our eyes, but then his eyes hardly ever settled on anything.

"T'ank y'all," he said. "I owes y'all one, me."

Dak started some sort of aw-shucks routine, but it was wasted. The guy grabbed the handles of the barrow and almost trotted away from us. Broussard's arms and legs bumped up and down.

We all looked at each other, and Alicia had her fist at her mouth, biting hard on the knuckles. She held it as long as she could, till the guy was almost to the barn door, then she exploded in laughter.

"What a weird little man," Kelly said, and she started laughing, too. It didn't take long for me to join in. Dak looked at all of us and shook his head.

"Yeah, right. 'I owes y'all one, me.' Like we'll ever see him again."

"Did you notice there was no dirt or anything in the wheelbarrow? Like it never had anything in it."

"Colonel Broussard's personal rickshaw," Kelly said.

"Yeah, every Saturday night he gets a ride home in the barrow."

"Huh! More than every Saturday night," Alicia assured us. "The guy looked like a stone alcoholic to me." Alicia would know, I figured.

"Let's get the hell out of here," Kelly suggested.

So we all climbed back in *Blue Thunder* and bounced back to the highway, retracing our route except for the part on the Autopike. Dak didn't seem to be in a hurry to get home, and neither was I. There's an amazing number of things two people can do under a blanket in the back of a truck, and Kelly and I tried most of them. I didn't think of Broussard or his odd little friend all the way back home, and after a few days I'd almost forgotten about them.

IT WAS OUR interest in going into space that had brought me and Dak together. We went to different high schools but not long after getting our diplomas we came to the same realization. The Florida public schools had not prepared either of us for a career in science or engineering. It had not even prepared us to pass the entrance exam for a good college. We had a lot of catching up to do.

But a self-motivated student can earn anything up to and including a doctorate on the University of the Internet just by logging on and sitting in on virtual classes. No books, no tuition, no housing costs. Not that a dot-com doctorate was ever likely to rival a degree from Harvard, but you couldn't beat the price. I encountered Dak there, in a remedial math class. In a chat room after classes we found out we both had an obsession with finding a career in space, and we lived only a few miles apart. So we got together to study and soon were spending a lot of our spare time together.

I'm smart, but I'm not a genius. I found high school easy, it never challenged me much. I didn't work very hard. It came as a big shock that I didn't do well on the SATs.

So whose fault was it that I was now slopping out toilets and making beds, trying hard to catch up, instead of looking forward to my sophomore year at Florida, or State? What was to blame here?

Well, how about poverty?

Practically anybody can plead poverty these days when it comes to higher education. There are only three types of people who get into a school like Yale: the children of the wealthy, students on full scholarship, and those willing to accept student loans that can take the rest of your life to repay.

My family—Mom, my aunt Maria, and myself—owns property near the beach, and that is supposed to be a gold mine. But that property happens to be a battered, leaky, cracked and patched motel built in 1959, and every month we're less sure we can hang on to it for another year. After taxes and upkeep, the wages we pay ourselves put us *well* below the poverty line. So there's no doubt about it. We are poor. But that had nothing to do with my not studying hard enough.

So try again. How about The System? It's always safe to blame the system. It is politically fashionable, it makes you feel better about yourself, and it is (at least partly) true. Did it really speak well for the Department of Education that a guy like me who attended regularly, did the work, and even graduated from Gus Grissom High School in the top 5 percent . . . did it make sense that after twelve years I wasn't up to entry level in the state university system?

No, it didn't make sense. The system really sucked, no getting around it. But it sucked just as hard for some of my classmates who were now going to school at Cornell and Princeton.

If it ain't the institution, and it ain't the money, then it's got to be the color of your skin or the language you speak, right? It *has* to be racism.

I even mentioned it to my mother one day when I was feeling particularly put-upon and sour. *It must be because I'm Latino,* I griped. Well, half Cuban, anyway. When she had stopped laughing, she came close to getting angry.

"I hope I didn't raise a crybaby," she said. "Don't you ever blame your own shortcomings or anything else on racism . . . *not even if it's true.* When you see you are being discriminated against, you just make the best of it. You *deal* with it, or else you see racism every time you turn around and spend your life moaning about it. And besides, you're hardly any more brown-skinned than I am, and my Spanish is a heck of a lot better than yours."

Which was the simple truth. I got most of my looks from her side of the family, which was Italian. My hair is dark brown and curly. I wouldn't look out of place wearing a yarmulke. Only around the eyes, which are dark and deep-set and sometimes rather bruised looking, like Jimmy Smits, do I resemble the pictures of my dad. Sad to say, the rest of me doesn't look anything like Jimmy Smits, but I get by.

Like Jimmy Buffett said, it was my own damn fault.

In a mediocre system, the talented have no need to excel. I'm a fast reader, I have a good memory, and I'm quick with figures. With those qualifications, about the only way you could fail at Gus Grissom High was to never go to class.

After twelve years of that kind of schooling, both Dak and I thought we knew how to study. You go home, you read the material for tomorrow's classes. Thirty minutes, an hour, tops. Then you've got the rest of the evening and all weekends to do whatever you want.

In my case, doing whatever I wanted meant working about sixty hours a week in our family business, the Blast-Off Motel. That is, it was what I wanted if I also wanted to eat and have a roof over my head.

Dak and I got together to study in the hope of improving our self-motivational skills, which were sadly lacking. Sometimes it worked. If the weather outside wasn't just too damn gorgeous. If the surf and the wind weren't just so perfect it would be a sin to spend the day inside when you could be riding your windboard. If the college girls from up north weren't too plentiful and beautiful stretched out in scantily clad rows, trying to bake a Florida brown before spring break was over . . .

ME AND MY family had what you'd call a love-hate relationship with the Blast-Off Motel. Without it we'd all have been looking for jobs instead of working in the family business. I've pushed a vacuum cleaner the equivalent of twice around the Earth at the equator. I know fifty things that can go wrong with a toilet and I know how to fix most of them. I could pass the test for a Ph.D. in toilets.

Still, it's better than working for somebody else. I think.

Mom's grandparents built the motel and called it the Seabreeze. Cape Canaveral was just a missile testing base then. Locals had been enjoying the fireworks since the end of the Second World War, but nobody else knew it was there, except race fans coming for Daytona 500, and they ignored it.

Then Project Mercury brought a lot of attention to this sandy little corner of Florida. There was a housing shortage, and many of the workers and engineers who moved to the Merritt Island area were happy to find a room of any kind. And back then the Seabreeze was a pretty good place.

They renamed it the Blast-Off in honor of John Glenn's flight. Grandpa didn't realize that real Canaveral people always called it "lift-off," and by the time he did the big, expensive sign out front was already installed. The little red neon rocket on the sign has been taking off, practically nonstop, for over fifty years now.

When Mom's parents died in a car wreck she inherited a business already halfway to bankruptcy. For the last twenty years she and Aunt Maria, and me when I got old enough, have been trying to make a living at it. Now it was probably too late.

The Blast-Off had been built so that all the rooms had an ocean view. Technically they all still did. But we never had the gall to actually claim that. If you looked far to the north or far to the south from your Blast-Off balcony, you could see a bit of water and sand. But straight ahead was the Golden Manatee resort, twenty stories of New Florida opulence, directly across the four-lane highway from us.

Mom can hardly look at the Golden Manatee without spitting. Her father used to own the land the resort now sits on.

"He was dead set against 'building on sand,' " Mom would tell anyone who would listen. "He always felt *this* building was too close to the sea. He spent most of his life terrified a hurricane would wash it away. So he never built over there. He sold the land."

Now the Manatee wants to buy our land to use as a parking lot. But they don't need it bad enough to offer us a decent price. We'd get just about enough money to pay off our mortgage, and the next day we could start looking for work in the exciting tourist service industry. That is, as maids and waiters in somebody else's business.

"Well, they can just kiss my manatee," Mom said.

AFTER WE DELIVERED Travis Broussard to his odd little friend, Dak dropped me off, alone, a little after midnight in the quiet Blast-Off parking lot. Kelly had early appointments the next day, and spending the night with me would have added to her driving time, so Dak was taking her to her apartment. I wish she'd mentioned it before we got to my place. Maybe I wouldn't have fooled around so much under the blanket in the pickup bed. As it was, the first order of business was a cold shower.

I live in room 201 at the Blast-Off. The way we're set up, the owner's apartment is behind the office on the ground floor: living room and kitchen downstairs, two bedrooms upstairs. One of those used to be mine until Aunt Maria moved in to help. I moved into 201, which has the Toilet From Hell. I had worked on that damn thing a hundred times over the years and never could stop it from screwing up about once a week. Finally we decided we just wouldn't rent it anymore, as well as room 101, which had a collapsed ceiling from all the overflowing water above. It's not as if we ever had to turn guests away for the lack of those two rooms.

The sink and tub/shower still worked. When I needed the toilet I used the one in room 101. I took out the twin beds and put in a king-sized, brought in a big desk and a table and chairs and a sofa I got for a few dollars at the Salvation Army thrift store.

The arrangement suited me. That is, I knew I could do a lot worse. It took some of the sting out of still living with my family at age twenty. I had my own door and could play music and come and go as I pleased. If only I could take a leak without going outside and downstairs I'd be content.

* * *

ONCE OUT OF the shower I turned on my computer, a ten-year-old Dell laptop I'd picked up for twenty dollars. I went to the NASA public website, selected "Hall of Astronauts," and typed in a search for Travis Broussard.

"We're sorry, the search produced no results. Do you wish to try another search?"

"Damn right," I grumbled, and shut off the speech function.

I searched the whole site, and found numerous references to Colonel Broussard. His flight record was there, beginning fifteen years ago when he entered the astronaut corps as a rookie pilot trainee. He made six flights sitting in the right-hand seat before becoming a full-time senior pilot. Sounded pretty quick to me. I did an info scan and found it was the fastest anyone had ever made the transition. Twelve years ago Travis was NASA's fair-haired boy. I would have been eight years old then.

His name was blue-lined, as were all astronaut names at the site. Maybe this was a route to the bio. I clicked on the link, and got a screen saying, "This page currently under construction." I clicked on another name at random and was shown to an elaborate biography page, with eight screens of text and a hundred NASA pics and snapshots of the astronaut's professional and home life. I requested John Glenn's site, and it was gigantic, thousands of stories going all the way back to *Life* magazine, albums of pictures, hours and hours and hours of video and film clips, whole movies from *The Right Stuff* to the Glenn bio-pic aired only last year.

Okay, it seemed that Broussard was the only one of several thousand current and former and even dead spacers without a spot in the Hall of Astronauts. How come?

Back to his flight record. He was listed as chief pilot for seventy launches. There was a blue link after the date of his last mission, and once again, clicking it took me nowhere. More links, on Flights 67, 60, and 53, all leading nowhere. Another dead end on a link way back on

Flight 21. But there was mention of a commendation. I noted the date of his twenty-first flight and opened a window for the *Miami Herald.*

I had the newspaper search that day and came up with a six-paragraph story on page three, complete with a picture of a smiling Travis Broussard, quite a bit younger, shaking hands with . . . my, oh my, that was the President of the United States.

The story read, in part:

> WASHINGTON, D.C. (AP) In a brief ceremony in the west wing of the White House, President Ventura awarded Astronaut Chief Pilot Travis Broussard with the Alan Shepard Medal of Valor for his actions on the third of this month in guiding a crippled VStar Mark II to an emergency landing at a backup airfield in Africa, saving the lives of the crew of three and seven passengers.
>
> Broussard had been promoted to the rank of Astronaut Colonel the previous day at the Pentagon.

I was getting frustrated. A big hero like Travis, and at the NASA site he was the little astronaut who wasn't there. Absolutely nothing to be learned beyond the fact that yes, he had been an astronaut, had flown the VStar, and yes, he won a medal.

So I went to SpaceScuttlebutt.com, where a lot of spaceheads hang out, found a room with a few familiar handles in it, and posted:

Broussard, Travis . . . ?

Pretty soon this bounced back:

No such FUBAR. Un-person. Shame on you.

FUBAR meant Fouled Up Beyond All Repair. I sent:

Y no bio?

I could tell you, but then I'd have to kill you.

Funny guy. I was about to come back when he posted another line:

Spacemanny? Dat you?

Unfortunately, it was. I'd made that my web handle years ago, before it started sounding so dorky. Now it would be too much bother to change it.

Y.

A three-by-three window opened and I saw the head and shoulders of a very, very fat man about my mother's age. He had to weigh in at five hundred pounds. SpaceScuttlebutt.com was as close as he'd ever get to space and he knew it. He lived his spacegoing fantasies online, and his knowledge was encyclopedic. I had no idea where he lived or what his real name was, but his handle was Piginspace. A man with no illusions. I was lucky to have run into him.

"Broussard-san heap big bad medicine, Spacemanny," he said through the tiny built-in speaker on my antique laptop. "Bad juju. Say his name at Kennedy, you must leave the room, spin around twice, and spit."

He talked like that sometimes. He enjoyed having information someone else was looking for, and sometimes made you jump through hoops to get it. But not this time.

"I see he got a medal for an emergency landing. What do you know about that?"

"Everything, my lad, the Pig knows everything. Knows all, tells . . . well, whatever he feels young minds can safely handle. Short version . . . it was early days in the second generation of the VStar program. The Mark II had just received its spaceworthiness certificate from NASA. Some of the jockeys felt there were a few bugs still to be worked out, but the mandarins decreed it should be pressed into service most tickety-boo."

The VStar II *California* was less than an hour away from its de-orbit burn when there was an explosion followed by a fire. The cabin began to fill with smoke. Much of the cockpit electronics went down.

Travis, working from what NASA called "hard copies"—tech manuals and maps—and with only minimal help from his crashing computers, fired the de-orbit engines within three minutes of the explosion.

There were three airfields designated by NASA as "trans-Atlantic abort" sites, at Moron, Spain; Banjul, The Gambia; and Ben Guenir, Morocco. None of them had ever been used, and in fact there was nothing to recommend them other than a runway long enough for the old Shuttle's landing rollout. For that purpose, Cairo would have been a better choice, and Travis looked at it briefly, but it was too far north of his path.

Moron, Banjul, and Ben Guenir were already almost beneath him. Impossible to turn and glide back with the VStar's steep angle of descent.

Johannesburg was too far south. Nairobi was too far east.

He came out of the fireball hoping to make Entebbe in Uganda . . . but he couldn't see anything. The ship was filled with dense smoke. They all would have been unconscious or dead without the emergency oxygen masks. He had to find a way to clear the smoke from the cabin.

"He brought it down to about forty thousand and had another problem. How do you make a hole to the outside, when the whole vehicle is designed to prevent that? Can't open the door against the cabin pressure. Can't even use the emergency explosive hatch bolts without disarming a safety system, which was no longer disarmable because of all four computers going down.

"But he did punch a hole in a window, and the smoke got sucked out. So there he was, twenty thousand feet over the jungles of central Africa. Nothing but green, far as the eye could see. No hope of making it to Entebbe. Very little maneuverability in the VStar, even when things are going right. There were enough hydraulics surviving to steer the beast, a little, and that was about all he had going to him.

"So he rocked it to the left, looked out the window, and put the damn thing through a three-sixty roll, which no one had ever tested in a wind tunnel but anybody in his right mind would have said couldn't be done. While he was upside down he spotted a line of red earth through the trees, almost directly below him. Might be a runway, might not. He put the ship into a turn twice as tight as the manufacturer recommended, pulled about seventeen gees for a few seconds, blacked out along with everybody else . . . and when he came to, lined the ship up toward the red line.

"Turns out it was a runway, bulldozed out of the jungle and used by bush doctors, ivory smugglers, and such. And about half the length needed for a VStar rollout.

"Reconstructing it, later, the tire marks began just about ten feet from one end of the runway. There were branches and leaves stuck in the landing gear. The chutes and the brakes stopped the ship with its nose gear twenty feet past the other end of the runway. Hitting a water buffalo with the nose gear probably slowed it down a bit, too."

Travis had brought the *California* down at dusk. There were no lights at the field, so the first Americans didn't get there until the next morning. It was the ambassador to Congo and some of his staff, and a small contingent of U.S. Marine embassy guards. There had been no radio contact, so no one knew what to expect.

"The ambassador stepped out of his helicopter and into the remains of a fine African barbecue. The crew had raised enough money among them to pay for the water buffalo, and they had cooked it and danced and drank long into the night. The farmers and herdsmen from the area all had souvenirs of some kind. Space suits, crew seat cushions, packets of Tang, bits and pieces of the instrument panel . . .

"So they killed another water buffalo, and the embassy staff, the marines, the *California* crew and passengers feasted all day and toasted everything they could think of in buffalo blood mixed with vodka. And she sits there still."

"You're kidding."

"You doubt the Pig?"

"No. But I don't get it. NASA gave him a medal . . . but they made a much bigger deal out of other ships that almost crashed."

"Going all the way back to *Apollo 13,*" Pig confirmed. "Not much they can do if the mission *really* goes balls-up. Three astronauts burned to death on the pad in *Apollo One. Challenger* blew up on live television. No way to soft-pedal those.

"The *California* wasn't much of a news story for a lot of reasons. It was over before the media even heard of it. It was remote. Nothing to show but that big old whale sitting in the dirt. NASA found the image embarrassing. Everybody was okay, so what's the big deal? Give him a medal and move on. Nobody's career would be advanced by making a big deal, except Broussard's . . . and nobody quite knew what to do about him."

"Why not? He sounds like a hero to me."

"Oh, he was. Maybe the biggest hero NASA ever had. One hell of a bit of flying, and they still drink toasts to him in astronaut bars . . . quietly.

"You didn't ask me how he made the hole in the spacecraft. The one that sucked the smoke out and let him see. The hole that saved the *California* and crew."

"I was going to."

"It was hushed up. No one on the crew wanted to talk about it, and neither did anyone higher up in the bureaucracy. But these things leak. The Pig learned of it years ago, and because of his great respect for Colonel Broussard, seldom tells it. But I sense you mean Broussard no harm."

"Of course not. None of my business."

"Quite so. Broussard made the hole with a nonstandard piece of astronaut equipment known as a Colt .45 automatic."

We both just let that one hang there for a minute. A pistol? For what, protection from space aliens?

"He might have got away with it if he hadn't told the inquiry board himself. Not one of the passengers or crew said a word about it in their debriefing. They knew they were alive because of the gun and Broussard's piloting skills.

"I have it from one of the inquiry board members that Broussard told the debriefers he just 'felt naked' without a piece of some sort. So he'd carried the weapon on all his previous flights."

Travis became the sort of problem bureaucrats hate. There were those who wanted to kick his redneck ass out of the astronaut corps, a few who would like to send him a bill for the *California*. But he had saved a lot of lives, and those he saved promised a really ugly fight in the media if Broussard was punished in any way.

"So they did what the military customarily does when a man screws up so badly he ends up being a hero," Pig said. "They gave him a medal and a promotion, and swept the dirty details under the rug."

"Okay," I said. "But that doesn't really explain—"

"Why he's an un-person? No, of course not."

"So why is he?"

Pig grinned, and shook his head.

"I said I'd tell you about the medal, Spacemanny," he said. "Wild horses could not tear the rest of the story out of me. I have too much respect for Broussard, a real 'Right Stuff' dude if ever there was one." He waved, and was gone.

I guess that was enough to think about for one night, anyway.

IT WAS A week later, and it was the worst kind of day, for me. Low eighties, lots of sunshine. It was the start of spring break and every other car was a rental convertible full of college girls hurrying to get a Florida sunburn on their Minnesota skin in the few days they had. They were dressed minimally in bikinis and thongs. All of them on the lookout for handsome, suave beach bums like me and Dak.

Actually, the "bums" part was all we could manage so far. But there were wet T-shirt contests to attend, nightclubs to crash with our first-rate false ID, beers that needed chugging, gutters that needed to be puked in. Everything about the day cried out for me to be outside taking part.

Instead, Dak and I were holed up in room 201 with the drapes and the sliding glass patio doors closed and the air conditioner on in an attempt to block out all the distractions. It wasn't working that well. Every time we heard a horn honk or a girl's high-pitched laugh from just outside we both looked longingly at the curtains.

"We go out there," Dak said, "we doomed. We're just going to get 'faced and blow the whole day, and tomorrow with a hangover and maybe part of the next day."

"I know that," I said, irritated. "Hell, I remember last year. Do you?"

"Not much," he admitted.

Last year had not been anything to be proud of. Our friendship was new at the time, and both of us had been severely depressed at being turned down at half a dozen colleges. I knew a guy who produced Florida drivers' licenses as good as the real ones, so we invested some money meant for tuition, then went barhopping for three days and nights. No need to get into too many sordid details. A lot of it will be hazy forever, and just as well. I was sick for days.

"Girls up here at Daytona mostly a bunch of second-raters, anyway," Dak said.

"Right. All the pretty girls go to Lauderdale or Key West."

"You got that right."

Dak said a dirty word, then snapped his laptop computer shut.

"Look, no offense, but this place would depress that Crocodile Hunter guy."

"Yeah, but . . ."

"No, let's don't open the curtains, we'd never be able to resist it. I know a place we can go and study and not be distracted. Well, not by babes, anyway."

"Where's that?"

"Have I ever led you astray, amigo? Don't answer that. Come on, let's go."

What the hell. I closed my computer, too.

We left my room and the first thing we saw was my mother coming up the stairs at the other end, looking determined. She was carrying her long-barreled target pistol, checking the loads in the cylinder as she walked. She looked up and saw us, frowned, and looked even more determined.

"Jesus, Mom," I whispered as she tried to pass between us and the maid's cart Aunt Maria had left there on the walkway. I grabbed her arm and held on. "Didn't you say you would—"

"No time for that now, Manuel."

"It's drugs again, right?" It had to be drugs. If it was prostitution she wouldn't have bothered with the artillery, just told them to get out. Johns don't want any trouble.

But sometimes drug dealers just didn't care.

"Let us call the cops, Mrs. Garcia," Dak said. He already had his phone in his hand and had dialed 91. Mom pushed his hand away.

"I don't want cops, Dak honey. They get too many calls like that, next thing you know they're closing you down as a public nuisance. Don't worry, Manuel, I'm not going to shoot them unless they want an argument."

"Oh, great." I saw Aunt Maria hurrying toward us, holding Mom's fine old Mossburg gingerly. Maria doesn't like guns. Mom loves guns, as long as she's the one pointing and shooting them. I stepped around Mom and took the shotgun from Maria.

"Which room, Maria?" I asked.

"That one, 206. They've had six visitors in the last hour. I thought—"

"Yeah, it probably ain't a Mary Kay convention. Maria, you and Dak stay back. Dak, you hear shooting, you press that last 1, okay?"

"*Loud* shooting," Mom said, holding her pistol pointed at the sky. "This thing doesn't make much more noise than a cork gun."

She was downplaying it a little, but the revolver really wasn't very noisy. It was only a .22 but it looked strange, being a match weapon saved from the days when Mom liked to shoot competitively, and had the time for it.

How good was she? If you asked her to shoot a mosquito in the air, she'd ask if you wanted a head shot, or one through the kneecap.

She looked at me, took a deep breath, and nodded. We'd done this sort of takedown before. It was that kind of neighborhood. I moved the maid cart off to one side so it wouldn't get in our way. Mom rapped on the door with the gun barrel.

"This is the manager, Mr. Smeth. Open up, please." Later I got out the check-in slips and saw he really had signed in with that name: Homer Smeth. We get an amazing number of Smiths, but this was the first one who didn't know how to spell it.

"Buzz off. We're busy."

Mom knocked once more, got more or less the same answer, and nodded to me. She slipped her master key into the lock.

I reached up into the brickwork and pulled the little hidden toggle there. It was connected to a bolt that held the inside chain-lock plate to the wall. When the bolt was pulled, it looked like the door was chained securely, but it wasn't. I'd installed that little item on most of our rooms. Saves having to bust down the door. Lots cheaper.

I nodded at her, and she turned the handle. The door swung open and she stepped in, the gun held in front of her. I stepped around her and did my best to glower at them.

Homer Smeth was sitting at the desk, a baggie of white powder open in front of him. He had been busy measuring out doses with a razor blade and putting each dose into one of those tiny Ziplocs that, so far as I can tell, are not good for anything but dope.

Heroin? Probably coke. It made no difference. Neither were tolerated at the Blast-Off. Sitting on the bed partially dressed and watching television was Homer's sidekick, the guy he had checked in with a few hours ago. With him was a girl who looked about fourteen except in the eyes, which were a lot older.

"Now we told you when you checked in we didn't allow dealing in this place, Homer," Mom said. She waved the gun, indicating the door. "Y'all better pack your things and go."

Homer just stared at her with his mouth slightly open. It looked like he had about a pound of powder on the desk. He was mixing it with baby laxative. The couple on the bed didn't move, either.

At last Homer seemed to work it all out. He smiled, showing the two missing teeth I remembered from when I checked him and his scumbag friend in. He held up one of the little bags of dope.

"Don't get your panties in a twist, sister. How 'bout a couple snorts of this?"

Mom didn't hesitate. The gun came up and barked once, and the tiny plastic bag between his fingertips vanished. Fine white powder floated in the air like chalk dust. He stared at the empty space, once more too stoned to quite realize what had happened. All three of them were doing the stupidest thing a dope dealer can do, which is sample the product. At the Blast-Off, we didn't even get a very good grade of narcotics trafficker. And that's a good thing, because with *those* dudes we'd have been in a gunfight, and *those* dudes carried more firepower.

Still no motion from anybody. I racked a round and raised the muzzle so it pointed at Homer's chest. That sound, of the slide being worked on a shotgun, has the amazing ability to clear your mind. It sure helped with this bunch. All six hands reached for the sky. I moved away from the door and motioned to the two on the bed. They got up slowly, the girl reaching down to get some of her clothes from the floor.

"Uh-uh!" I shouted, scaring her badly. "Kick 'em over here." She did, and I could see there was no weapon in them. The guy did the same. I kicked the stuff back at them, and they started to dress.

In no more than thirty seconds they had their stuff together, which was just a little clothing, the pound of coke, and some free-basing equipment in a cardboard box. They slunk out the door, giving both of us a wide berth. We followed them out and watched them down to their car, an unbelievably rusty '60s model Oldsmobile station wagon almost full of bald tires and packrat junk. Aunt Maria came out of room 206 with a pair of sneakers wrapped in a dirty shirt. She threw it over the railing and it landed on the hood of the car. Homer glared up at us and gave us the finger, then backed out recklessly, put it in forward and tried to burn rubber on the way out. The car was too old for that, but it did put out an impressive cloud of white smoke.

"Now can I have the gun, Mom?"

"Where are you boys . . . sorry, where are you young men going?"

"Somewhere else to study," I told her.

"It better not be some bar full of snow bunnies."

"No way, Mrs. Garcia."

"I'm serious. You guys come home plastered and you can sleep it off in a pool chair, 'cause I ain't letting you in."

"We'll be good."

"Manny, you clean that desk and flush the paper towels before you go."

"I was just about to suggest that myself." She looked at me hard, trying to tell if I was kidding her again. Mom doesn't have the world's greatest sense of humor. At last she snorted, reached up and tousled my hair—and I wish she'd stop doing that—then took the Mossburg and headed back for the office and the gun safe.

"Hang on just a minute, Dak." I took a roll of paper towels from the nearby maid's cart and entered 206.

It still smelled of Homer and friends. I swear, there is a junkie smell, and if you'd smelled it as often as I have you'd never mistake it for anything else. It happens when they've been dusting or spiking for several years. I don't know if it's from lack of washing or something in their sweat. I'd smelled it on Homer, but if we turned away every person who might be using the room to fix in, we'd lose half our income. We have to pretty much overlook personal drug use, unless you get violent behind it. No selling, and no refining, that was our rule.

Twice we'd had to take down meth labs after they'd been running a few days. That's a total disaster to a motel operator. Both times we'd had to simply seal up the room and never use it again. After those chemicals soak into the walls for a bit, you need a permit from the Environmental Protection Agency to open the room again. It cost thousands of dollars in cleanup, which we just didn't have.

I went into the bathroom—every towel and washcloth filthy, and to look at them, you'd never have guessed they ever used a shower at all—where I soaked a handful of paper towels. Dak was looking down at the powder-covered desk.

"Don't even think about it," I said.

"I wasn't." He pretended to be offended. "That was some shooting."

"Don't tell her that, I have enough work keeping her out of trouble without you telling her what a great vigilante she is."

"No need to get snippy."

He was right. But I was feeling pretty awful, as I usually do when a thing like that is over. Mom doesn't seem to have any fear in her at all, but I sure do.

There was half a dozen baby Ziplocs scattered on the floor, what they called dime bags. All of them had a pinch of powder in them. I gathered them up and Dak helped me move the desk to be sure there wasn't anything illegal back there. I flushed the bags and the paper towels, waited to be sure it was all gone.

"You better make a note, you don't want no drug-sniffing dogs in this room."

"Not for at least a year," I agreed. "Now, do I have to frisk you, or can I trust that you didn't pick up any of those dimes when I wasn't looking?"

"Trust me."

"Okay." I turned and looked around, spotted the bullet hole about six feet up the wall. With the .22 there had been no chance of it passing through the wall into the next room. I stuck the desk pen in the hole, but the slug had fallen into the space between walls. I'd plaster and paint it that evening. No need to alarm guests with bullet holes in the walls. That could endanger our half-star Michelin rating.

"Let's get out of here," I said.

"Suits me. Let's go someplace we can do this free blow."

I threw the roll of paper towels at him but he was already out the door.

DAK'S FATHER OWNS a car repair business a mile down the road from us, four stalls with lifts. The big chains undercut him on lubes and oil changes and tune-ups, but his lot is always full because the people in the neighborhood know he can be persuaded to wait for full payment if you're in a bind. He sells a lot of recap tires. He is considered to be a magician by the people at Motor Vehicles, who send him the cars nobody believes will *ever* pass the Florida emissions standards. He usually can patch them up enough to qualify for another year.

Behind the main repair shop there is a two-car garage that used to hold stacks of used tires but now sports a sign: DAKTARI'S CUSTOM SPEED SHOP. This was where *Blue Thunder* was conceived and born.

Dak turned down the narrow shell alleyway that ran beside the main building and we roared through it and stopped on the cracked concrete next to Blue. We were on a screaming red and yellow Honda trail bike with me perched uneasily behind him. I don't know how girls can stand riding like that.

"See how you like that one," Dak said, pointing to a nearly identical bike, but with different colors. It looked okay to me. I got on, started it, revved the engine, grinned at Dak. I had an old Suzuki for a few months the previous summer until I sort of fell off and it wasn't worth fixing. Okay, I totaled it, and it was a good thing I landed in a ditch or I might have been hurt bad.

"You got a helmet for him?" I turned and saw Mr. Sinclair coming out the back door. He nodded to me, went to put his arm around his son's shoulders. Dak pretended to fight him off and they played that little game of grab-ass you see some fathers do with their sons. It made me jealous as hell, I'm ashamed to say. I'd never tell Dak.

As usual there were a couple bright but battered race cars parked there in the back. I'm not talking about Grand Prix or Indy cars. These were poor man's stock cars or sometimes the cheaper formulas. Racing people like to come to Daytona. They like to live here, Daytona is a magic zip code to put on your mail. Nobody who came to Dak's Custom Speed was going to be out there in the Fabulous 500 without paying a *lot* of dues first. Unless you're a third- or fourth-generation Petty or Earnhardt you're going to be working your way up through the Saturday night dirt track circuit. You'll be scrabbling to pay for enough good rubber to get through one more race, pounding out the dents with a hammer, and painting it all over with a Wal-Mart spray can. This was the kind of guy who came to see Dak.

Most nights after the garage closed, Mr. Sinclair was back here with him. Keeping beaters on the road was his bread and butter, but working on fast cars with his son was pure enjoyment.

Sometimes I wondered why Dak would *bother* with trying to get into space. I mean, if I was in his place, would I want to change it? His life seemed the next thing to paradise, to me.

Dak tossed me a helmet and I strapped it on.

"You boys aren't going too far on those things, are you?" Mr. Sinclair asked.

"We gotta check 'em out, Dad," Dak told him.

"Just remember they don't belong to you."

"We won't be out all night. So long." He waved at us as we sprayed some gravel around and zoomed out onto the highway.

I looked over at Dak and he was tapping one side of his helmet with one finger. I didn't get it. He did it again, and then pointed at my helmet and said something, but I couldn't hear him over the roar of the bike engines. I was about to shout that to him, when I felt the helmet where he was pointing. There was a knob there, which I turned.

"Can you hear me now?"

I turned the knob a little more.

"Cool," I told him, flipping out the little built-in mike.

"Only the best for the jerk owns these things. I may have fibbed a little when I told him I needed a couple more days to finish up. Can you dig it? Two radical rides like this, one for him and one for his girlfriend. And a radio so he can coo sweet nothings into her ears."

I glanced down at the tank of my bike, which was an electric pink. I guess that explained the Day-Glo peach color of my helmet. Well, at least it didn't have any adorable kittens or bluebirds or stuff like that painted on it.

WE GOT OUT of town fast, leaving the carloads of tempting, reddening Yankee-girl flesh and cold Florida beer behind us. We took smaller and smaller roads, pretty soon roaring down dirt trails. We spooked two possums, three deer, and a skunk. We missed the deer and the skunk missed us. It's getting so you can't go anywhere without running into deer, sometimes literally. They say there's about forty million deer in the country now. They're getting to be a real nuisance, and it seems every year there's fewer people into hunting them. Me, if I never taste another venison steak it'd be too soon. Mom freezes enough every hunting season to carry us for six months. "Free meat," she says, and who can argue with her?

It was a grand day to be alive.

I didn't really tip to where we were going until we went past the backwoods Baptists, or peckerwood Pentecostals, whichever they were, that I remembered from that night when we took the drunk astronaut home. There was a freshly painted sign out among the dozens of others:

THE LORD DON'T BLESS GOVERMENT MEN!
"INFERNAL" REVENOOERS NOT WELCOM!

"I guess spray cans of paint don't have spellcheckers," I told Dak. He laughed. "So what are we doing out here? Studying?"

"We could do that, yeah, we could."

I doubted it. But I followed him off the road and down the long driveway until we could see the house and outlying structures. What you'd call a compound, I guess, except it wasn't fenced or anything.

It looked a lot different in the daylight. With most of the outdoor pole lights burned out there had been a sinister aspect to it, everything in deep shadows and only a few stars visible overhead through the skinny pine trees. Now it looked unremarkable, much like a thousand other backwoods Florida ranches, maybe a little more prosperous than most.

One thing that hadn't been there when we arrived that night a week ago was Alicia, sitting in a canvas lounge chair in shorts, halter top, and big sunglasses, grinning at the surprised look on Dak's face.

"What you doing here, girl?" he wanted to know.

"What are you talking about? I go where I want to go, you know that."

"Yeah, but—"

"When I found out you were coming out here I figured I'd better see what kind of game you were running on this man, keep your fool ass out of trouble."

"Game? I ain't runnin' . . . how'd you know I was coming out here?"

"What, you were going to 'surprise' me?"

Dak looked a little sheepish, glanced at me, and I took the hint. Let them work it out, I didn't need to listen in on this. I casually strolled over in the direction of the swimming pool, but I couldn't help glancing back at them, and I couldn't help smiling. Dak runs to about six and a half feet. Alicia is about five-two, light brown with pale blue eyes, what an old slave owner would have called a mulatto and these days we call mixed-race. So why is it that when they argue, it's Alicia standing there with her head thrown back and her eyes flashing who is clearly in control and big gawky Dak who is trying to figure out how he lost it again?

* * *

HOW DO YOU spell neglect? I'd start with last year's 350ix Mercedes sports model parked near the back door of the house, looking like there was nothing wrong with it worse than a flat right front tire . . . but being slowly buried under a layer of pine needles. It would make you cry to see what the pine resin had already done to the paint job.

I don't know, does having a better grade of car sitting up on blocks and rusting out in your front yard qualify as being more prosperous? Whether it was a fairly new Beemer or a forty-year-old Pinto it still shouted redneck to me.

I wandered slowly around the house and grounds while Dak and Alicia worked it out. The place was both a little better and a little worse than it had looked in the dark.

The house itself was a few years overdue for a coat of paint. Let that go too long and the termites could take it right down to the foundation in a few years.

There was one of those 1980s-type satellite dishes, the ones about the size of a flying saucer that cost ten thousand dollars or more and didn't do half the job of the hubcap-sized dishes they *give* away now just to get your business. It was pointed about ten degrees *below* the horizon, maybe to pick up the ever-popular Earthworm Channel. It must have been impressive and futuristic in its day, but now it was draped with Spanish moss and caked with slimy-looking mildew. Mildew: the Florida state flower.

It was way too late to bring in a high-wheel brushcutter to deal with Colonel Broussard's lawn. You'd need a fair-sized tractor to cut most of it. Some places would need a bulldozer, just grade it flat and start all over.

A path led from the pool patio through some grapefruit and lemon trees to a lake with a pier jutting out. Tied to a pier was a small wooden rowboat. There was fishing gear in the rowboat.

There was an aluminum boathouse, prefab like the big barn back at the compound. I couldn't see what was inside it, but judging from the boat trailer sitting on a small concrete boat ramp, it was a fairly substantial craft.

Across the lake, maybe a couple miles away, I saw a few houses and other docks. Probably some good catfish in the lake. Maybe bass. I don't much see the point of bass when you can catch catfish.

Last year's crop of lemons were just dried rinds under the trees. It could be a heck of a nice place if somebody cared for it a little, I thought as I made my way back through the grove. But it would be a lot of work.

Off to my left as I went back toward the house was the prefab barn where the little chubby guy had been that night. The building sat on a low hill . . . well, call it a gentle rise. Florida is a vertically challenged state, and we natives tend to get way too enthusiastic about anything that raises you ten feet off the landscape.

That barn was by far the best-kept thing I could see.

I was about to head back to Dak and Alicia—I could see them sitting on the cushions of the lounge chair nuzzling each other, so I figured they'd managed to work it out—when my eye was caught by a glint of light on the ground in the direction of the barn. I'd probably never have seen it at all if it hadn't been rolling slowly down the hill.

No, not rolling. It was blowing, like a soap bubble in the air. It was hitting the blades of grass, but not bending them. In fact, for a while I thought it *was* a soap bubble, and I watched it, waiting for it to pop. It never did, so I leaned over and picked it up.

It was a little bigger than a Ping-Pong ball but it had a silvery, mirror surface like a Christmas tree ornament. It didn't seem to weigh anything at all. I held it up, between my thumb and two fingers . . . and almost lost it. It wanted to squirt right out of my grip.

I tried to toss it from one hand to the other, but it wouldn't do it. It was too light, it kept getting slowed down by the air.

I really liked the thing, right from the first, so I went to my borrowed bike and put the bubble in my helmet . . . and changed my life and a lot of other lives forever.

7

AS I REACHED the concrete patio Dak was shaking charcoal from a sack into a big kettle barbecue. One of the sliding screen doors to the house opened quickly, on a motorized track, and Colonel Travis Broussard came out, holding a platter of raw steaks in one hand and a cocktail in the other. He glanced at me, grinned, and put the platter on the big picnic table. I shook his hand.

"You must be Manny," he said. "Dak's told me about you. Why don't you go inside and grab something to drink out of the icebox? I got nineteen kinds of imported beer and I don't check ID."

"A little early for me, but thanks." I went to the patio door, which got out of my way as I was reaching to slide it open.

"Never too early for Trav," Alicia said as the door closed behind me. She was standing at a counter in the kitchen, looking out the window at Dak and Travis. "Man's a big drinker. Look there, three empties and they all still got dew on the outside." I saw the beer cans next to a big refrigerator. I mean, a *huge* refrigerator, the kind they use in convenience stores, with glass doors so you can pick out what you want before you open the doors. Beer and soda, Gatorade, fancy water, some bottles of white wine. Pretty much anything you'd like in the way of something cool. Beside it was a restaurant-sized ice maker and on shelves above that a real professional bartender's selection of hard stuff, racks of clear stemware hanging from the ceiling, other barware behind glass-doored cabinets. And on the other side of that, another refrigerator and a huge freezer.

"Look at this," Alicia said with disgust. She opened a refrigerator door and the big shelves were almost empty. A brown half head of lettuce, a couple fuzzy gray tomatoes, half a chicken and some bones drying out on a plate, a stick of oleo.

"And this." Inside the freezer were stacks and stacks of the same kind of thick sirloins he had carried outside and plastic bags of Ore-Ida frozen steak fries.

"Aren't you the nosy one?" I said. She frowned, then decided not to take offense. I got a can of 7-Up out of the fridge and popped the top.

"It's been a least a month since anybody's had any vegetables here other than French fries. There's cases of ketchup in one of those cupboards, I guess some folks call that a vegetable. I don't see any fruit at all. The only reason there's no dirty dishes in here is that nobody uses any dishes except forks and steak knives." She tossed a pair of plastic salad tongs into a matching plastic bowl and sighed. "I told 'em I was coming in here to make a salad to go with the steaks. I'll bet Mr. . . . sorry, I mean *Colonel* Broussard had a good laugh about that one."

I went over to a door I thought might be a pantry and pulled it open. Sure enough. The room was bigger than room 201 at the Blast-Off and there was enough food in it to feed a family of five for several years. On the floor were sealed metal barrels of dry pasta, rice, flour, sugar, stuff like that, safe from bugs and rats. On the shelves above them were cans of just about everything, tuna and Spam, peaches and pears, soups to nuts. All of it was covered with dust. I started tossing cans to Alicia.

"Pinto beans, wax beans, green beans, garbanzos, lima beans, kidney beans, black beans, aha! Even some pinquitos." She dropped the fourth can while trying to catch the fifth, then another, and another, and we were both laughing as I tossed her more cans. "Make him a three-bean salad, why don't you? Or maybe a seven-bean."

"I can make something out of this he'll *hate*."

I wandered into the living room. It was fairly neat, but dusty and stale smelling, with the occasional sweatshirt or pair of dirty socks tossed on the floor.

"Still early stages," Alicia said from the door. "No puke that ain't been mopped up. He still picks up stuff, when he trips over it."

"Maybe he's just sloppy."

She laughed. "Manny, this is a military guy. If he started out sloppy, you wouldn't be able to *bulldoze* through this place. He's gone downhill a *lot* since he was a spaceman. They don't let you clutter things up on a station. You know that."

She was right, I did.

"He probably doesn't even think he's an alcoholic," she said.

I turned back to the living room. There were a lot of framed photos on the walls, mostly of him with famous people, including the one of the President giving him his medal. I recognized some of the faces. One section showed two young girl children. Daughters? No wife anywhere I could see.

There were gaps on these walls, too, rectangles lighter than the wall. It didn't take Sherlock Holmes to figure out pictures had once hung there. Pictures of people the colonel didn't like anymore, was my guess.

The one bare wall turned out not to be a wall at all, but an eight-by-twelve-foot Sony Hi-Dee screen. The audio parts were hidden behind a mahogany panel, and a dozen speakers hung from the ceiling. Here was something very expensive that I could really appreciate. If he had termites in the walls, they'd be deaf by now.

I looked around once more, taking it all in. How the rich live. I'd never had much chance to get a close look at it.

I figured I wouldn't have all that much trouble swapping lifestyles with him.

ALICIA CAME OUT of the kitchen with her big bean salad in a bowl, Broussard trailing dubiously behind her. I followed them to the patio, where Dak was just flipping the steaks, wearing a grease-spattered apron. Broussard took over the grill.

"Dak tells me you run a hotel," he said.

"My family does. The Blast-Off down on—"

"Sure, I know it."

"Everybody knows the Blast-Off," Dak said. "It's a Florida institution. Can't come to the Canaveral area and not send a Blast-Off postcard back home."

"Sounds like a good business."

"The card business? It's okay." Yeah, I didn't say, and some weeks we make almost as much money on those damn cards, and the knickknacks Mom and Maria make, as we make renting out rooms. Disgusting, when you think about it.

"Well, you ever decide to get a new sign, let me bid on the old one. One of the first things I saw in Florida that I liked. You know, sometimes I could pick it out on the way up. Just look for the little orange rocket blasting off."

"No kidding? That's . . . that's great." I looked at Dak and saw the notion had tickled him, too. The crummy old Blast-Off, and an astronaut looking down on it . . . or even just driving down the avenue, passing it, feeling good for a moment.

"I'll keep that in mind, Colonel Broussard," I said.

"Just Travis, okay? You guys saw me falling-down, snot-slingin' drunk. I figure y'all have to swallow hard to call me Colonel."

Nobody had anything to say to that, but the awkward silence passed pretty quick. Travis went back into the kitchen to get the cardboard bucket of fries he'd popped into the microwave. He came back with forks and knives and paper plates.

He cut into one of the steaks, peered inside, and looked up.

"Who likes 'em so rare they're still chewin' their cud?"

Alicia and Travis did. Dak and I said medium rare would do. That left one on the grill, and Travis pushed a button on the outside wall before he sat at the table. Beyond the empty pool the barn door opened and the short, roly-poly guy came out. Travis heaped fries on all five plates.

"Jubal, these are friends of Dak. Alicia, and Manny. Y'all, this is my cousin Jubilation. Everybody calls him Jubal."

Jubal nodded awkwardly, bowed his head, then looked up again.

"Travis, would you offer a blessin' over dis here food?"

"Shouldn't we wait till your steak gets here, Jube?"

"You kin bless it from ovah here, you."

And by golly we all bowed our heads and Travis offered a short prayer. When it was over, Jubal tied a big cloth napkin around his neck and dug in to the plate of fries. When his steak arrived, mostly black on the outside, and not much better on the inside, he ate that in record time, then shuffled off to the barn again.

"Don't take offense," Travis told us. "Jubal never caught on to polite manners. He's just never seen the use of saying good-bye . . . saying a lot of things, actually. But I've got him pretty well used to 'please' and 'thank you.' "

I couldn't tell if he was pulling our legs or not.

"What's he do out there in that barn?" Dak asked.

"Invents stuff. Allows me to go on living in the style I don't deserve but have become accustomed to without having to go out and look for work."

This time all three of us waited for the punch line, but there wasn't one. Well, it was his house and his food. He could tell us as much or as little as he wanted.

I ATE MORE steak than I should have. I don't get top-quality sirloin that often, and I figured I'd make up a little for feasts I'd missed out on, growing up. In other words, I made a pig out of myself. But I wasn't the only one. We all sat around for a while, picking our teeth, trying to keep the belching down to a level that wouldn't frighten the swamp creatures.

Then Dak asked Travis to tell that story he'd told Dak the other day, you know the one, about what you did to that senator from Utah who finagled himself aboard the yearly "inspection" junket to International Peace and Cooperation Station . . . and Travis said that was no senator from Utah, that was a congressman from Oregon, and besides, he has recovered by now, though he walks with a slight limp and jumps at loud noises, and besides, it wasn't me, and if you ever say it was I'll have your ass in court for libel. We all laughed, and Travis said that called for another beer, and I decided I could safely have one, and he was off to the races.

Travis was a terrific storyteller. The great thing was, though they might not have been strictly, 100 percent *true*, they were all based on fact. And that was good enough for me, because they were stories of space, and of rocket piloting, of guys and girls actually getting out there and *doing* it. Kissing the sky.

When Travis got off a really good one, one of us would reach for the remote unit attached to the mechanical pool alligator by a cable, and start pressing the buttons. The phony reptile would rear up, thrash his tail, and let fly with a roar that sounded more like a grizzly bear to me—not that I know a grizzly bear from Yogi Bear, but I have heard pissed-off gators a time or two.

The rubber alligator was a story in itself. One of Travis's friends used to work as a mechanical animator at Disney World. Travis invested with the man when he left Disney and tried to start his own studio. The alligator was for a place called Gatorland. The day before it was about to open, some radical animal rights group, Free the Animals or something like that, broke in and let all the real gators go.

Gatorland wasn't exactly in the swamp, it was in a suburb of Tampa. In half an hour nine of the freed gators had been hit by cars when they tried to cross a freeway. Several people were injured in the crashes, and all the alligators were killed. Others had to be pulled from backyard swimming pools and rounded up on downtown streets, and some had to be shot. Later, a dozen neighborhood dogs and cats could not be found.

By the time all the lawsuits were settled Travis's friend was bankrupt and all that was left of their investment was the gator. So he and Travis took the *very* realistic critter to the home of the president of Free the Animals and . . . but Travis said the statute of limitations hasn't expired on that one yet, so he'd better be quiet about it.

"Not that the prick would likely press charges," Travis said. "They've all been keeping a much lower profile since the Gatorland fiasco."

I could have listened far into the night, but after a while Travis looked at his watch, drained and crushed his beer can, and told us to go get our computers.

You're kidding, I thought. But he was not.

So we set them up out there on the patio, plugged into his ground line, and signed on to the Infinite Classroom.

IT WAS ONE of the better ideas Dak ever had. Travis knew this stuff, he'd worked with numbers all his professional career. There were basic concepts in calculus that had been giving me hell, I'd started to wonder if I'd ever make the breakthrough, ever really make the grade. Maybe I ought to get a job selling shoes. It would be better than shining them, like my great-grandfather used to do in Havana.

"There's just things it's real hard to learn out of a book," Travis said at one point, not long after getting me to *finally* see a point I'd been struggling with for a whole month. "Math's one of them. I don't think I'd ever have got it if I didn't have a good teacher to help me over the rough spots.

"Don't get me wrong, I think this Internet U is a great thing . . . up to a point. But in pretty much any subject you get to a point where words and pictures on a screen aren't enough. You either have to get some hands-on experience, or get somebody to walk you through it, one on one."

"SO AM I going to hear how this all came about, or is that a secret?"

Dak looked over and grinned at me from under his helmet.

"Just dropped by a few days ago to see how the poor bastard was doing," he said. "Cousin Jubal had told him all about that night and Travis wanted to say thanks. I think he was pretty impressed we didn't take him for everything but the lint in his drawers. He's a man who has some experience in these matters."

"I'll bet," I laughed.

"Oh, yes," Alicia said. "Travis has been mugged before."

She was puttering along in her little 1965 VW Bug, ahead of us on the bikes. Dak had been helping her restore it. In fact, that little Bug was how they met in the first place. The outside was coated with primer except for the two front fenders, which were "screamin' yellow and hollerin' orange," according to my mom. Alicia hadn't yet decided what color to go with.

"We cracked a few brews, sat around shooting the breeze, making that rubber crocodile walk around on the bottom of the pool."

"And he offered to do our homework for us?"

"Not at first," Dak admitted. "He said, any little thing he could do for us, all we gotta do is ask. The dude may be a drunk, but he knows a lot of people, and I think a fair number of them still like him. These are the kind of people who can drop a hint, call in a favor from the right person at the right time, I figured. We got a long ways to go between here and the moon, Manny my man. We need to use every leg up we can get."

"No argument, pal," I said. "I just wish you'd let me in a little sooner. I felt like I was crashing somebody else's party."

"Sorry about that, man."

There was a momentary silence in our earphones.

"He was a hero, once," I said.

"No fooling?"

So I told them the story Pig had given me about saving the *California*'s crew and passengers. Dak loved it about as much as I had.

"Damn!" he said. "I'd pay to see that. Let's hop a plane to Africa, Alicia."

"Happy to, soon as you can pay for it."

"Yeah . . . how come I couldn't find any of that, Manny? I went to the NASA site, same as you. Didn't find diddly."

"For some reason, NASA wants to pretend Colonel Broussard never existed. They can't, but they sure did minimize him. I don't know why, Pig wouldn't say."

"Are we invited over again?"

"If you don't mind sirloin for breakfast."

"One more thing I'd like to know."

"Shoot."

"Alicia, how *did* you find out Dak had been coming out here?"

"Because I'm nosy," she laughed.

"You can say that again," Dak said. "Raiding the man's pantry."

"He ate three helpings of the salad."

"Salad? That what that was, salad?"

"It doesn't have to have lettuce, Dak."

"In my house it does. And tomatoes."

"Alicia, you never did answer my question," I said.

"Oh, that. You know Dak installed that inertial tracker—and I never knew why, since he already had the NavStar unit."

"Just another gadget he couldn't resist, I guess," I said.

"Hey, Manny, Alicia. I'm right here, don't forget."

"Well, Dak forgot that machine keeps a record of your location and your route. . . ."

"That's it, woman!" Dak exploded.

". . . it keeps that data for two weeks unless somebody remembers to erase it . . ."

"Who figured I *needed* to erase it? Damn, I'm surrounded by spies."

THE BIG NEWS at the NASA site that day was the departure of the American mission to Mars.

The crew had gone up the night we almost killed Travis. The ship had been finished when the final components were delivered two weeks before that. Captain Aquino had used the intervening weeks to conduct as many tests and drills as were possible in the limited time available to him before the very tight launch window closed.

I watched the countdown, and the totally unimpressive lighting of the plasma torch at the rear of the long, lumpy, completely unlovely congregate of landers, orbiters, propulsion modules, reactors, solar panels . . . and doghouses and kitchen sinks, for all I knew, and its departure for the Red Planet.

Its very *sloooooow* departure. Proving once again that, aside from the liftoff from Earth, space travel was not and probably never would be a feast for the eyes. Aside from the deathly quiet, everything I'd ever witnessed in space happened at a pace that would make a glacier look like an avalanche. No matter that everything I was seeing was hurtling around the planet at a speed of about sixteen thousand miles per hour. You couldn't see anything move. You never could.

The plasma engine was slow but steady. It was fifteen minutes before the mission could be seen to have moved at all.

It didn't bother me. It was beautiful.

8

I GOT MY housekeeping chores done, then sat at the computer working on my calculus lessons. I did three weeks' worth of reading and assignments in about three hours, now that so much more of it made sense to me. In fact, I found myself two days ahead of the recommended syllabus, for the first time since I'd enrolled. When I clicked the computer off, it was with a sense of satisfaction I hadn't felt since graduation.

Then I turned my attention to my little silver bubble.

It had been nagging at me all day and my curiosity was killing me.

I had put the bubble in one of my desk drawers, because it didn't want to stay in the same place. It drifted with the tiniest air current, like smoke. How could something so light be so tough?

Start by defining the problem. It's light, it's tough. How light? How tough?

The best scale I had access to was the postal scale in the office, and I knew without having to try that I wouldn't be able to weigh the bubble with that scale. I wouldn't even be able to get it to stay on the platform long enough to register any weight. By extension, I couldn't see how it would register anything on the analytical balance at school. But it couldn't be weightless, could it?

Now, hold on, was I getting weight confused with mass, like so many people did?

It stood to reason that if I could get the bubble moving, it would have some inertia, wouldn't it? If I could toss it against a scale, it would have to register something, right? Maybe. But I couldn't test that at home, because I didn't have any way of creating a vacuum to do the experiment in. Air density alone seemed to be enough to bring the bubble to a halt in midair as soon as it left my hand.

Okay, that got me nowhere, let's move on to the next question.

Is the bubble frictionless?

It sure felt like it. It was very odd to hold it in my hand. I could feel the presence of its shape, but I didn't actually *feel* anything. No texture, no unevenness, no pits. It was impossible to pick it up or hold it just between the tips of my index finger and thumb.

It was possible to secure the bubble using two fingers and my thumb. Not just the tips of those digits, though. Holding it with fingers curling around it established a multitude of contact points, so that if I held it that way, loosely, it would finally behave itself. More or less. If I squeezed it too hard the bubble would still squirt away, like when you squeeze too tight on a bar of soap.

So *now* where was I?

Results of first round of experiments:

It seems to be weightless.

It seems to be frictionless.

I didn't need to log on to my physics textbooks to know both of those things were impossible, in the real world. Weightlessness, frictionlessness, those ideas were useful in math, to define a pure condition the real world never attains.

Tentative conclusion: I'm probably missing something.

No weight, no friction. How tough?

I got a hammer and some nails. I cut a small hole in a piece of old linen sheet, not big enough for the bubble to go through. Then I used thumbtacks to pin the cloth to the desk with the bubble trapped inside, just a piece of it showing.

I held the tip of one nail to the surface of the bubble. I tapped the nail head lightly with the hammer. The tip slid off the bubble surface. I looked at the bubble through a magnifying glass. No dent or scratch I could see. I tapped it again, this time a little harder. Again the tip slipped off. No dent, no scratch.

I withdrew to seek counsel with myself.

I know a scientist is supposed to welcome a challenge, he's supposed to rejoice at results inexplicable and unexpected . . . but I'll bet a lot of them don't. I'll bet a lot of them try to shrug it off, especially if it doesn't fit their theory. If this thing was ever made public, I had a feeling a *lot* of theories would have to be rewritten.

The hell with it. I started whaling away at it with all my strength.

After seven or eight blows the piece of linen tore and the bubble floated up above my desk again, swirling in the eddies my swinging arm had made in the air. I caught it before it could float into a hiding place, and put it under a glass tumbler.

I put my face down close to the desk. There was a new, circular depression in the wood surface. And on the bubble . . . no dent, no scratch.

Answer: *very* tough.

I FOUND I couldn't sleep. I went out on my little balcony and watched the cars go by. Not as boring as it may sound, many of them were full of students shouting and laughing. People in convertibles would see me up on my balcony and wave, sometimes invite me down to join them.

Not too many people on the sidewalks. There used to be a few hookers who staked out corners within sight of the Blast-Off. Then the Golden Manatee moved in, and the cops ran them all off. Now, the preferred way to buy sex in this neighborhood is to get a room in the Manatee and call one of the escort services. I imagine you'll get a better class of hooker, but be sure to bring a lot of cash. You'll pay more tipping the bell captain to bring your escort in the back way than you would have paid for a whole night with one of the chased-away streetwalkers.

One girl seemed not to have got the message. She came strolling down the sidewalk, bold as brass, on three-inch cork platform shoes. She wore a silvery blouse tied up between her breasts and a hollerin' orange miniskirt. Lots of lipstick, lots of piled-up blonde hair, and big, dark, pink-rimmed sunglasses at one in the morning. She looked up at me and grinned.

"How about it, cowboy? Should I come up?"

Cowboy? I thought it over.

"Not sure I can afford it," I said.

"Sure you can, sweetie."

"Oh . . . well, all right."

"That's what I love. Enthusiasm. What's your room number?"

I told her, and in a minute I could hear the clunking sound of her huge cork soles. She knocked on the door and I turned off the lights and opened it.

"Twenty dollars gets you all night," she said.

"All night? Hell, it's already one-thirty."

"C'mon, stud." She put her hand in my groin. "I can tell you're glad to see me."

"That's a banana for my pet monkey. And all I have is ten dollars."

"That'll have to do, I guess." She came into the room and closed the door. I jumped her as she turned around. I pressed her back against the door.

"Lipstick! Watch the lipstick, you wild man!"

"Forget the lipstick," I said. Or tried to say, between kisses.

I was tearing at her skirt and she found my zipper. I wasn't surprised to see she was wearing no underwear. I took her right there against the door, then on the floor, and finally with her knees on the floor and her body bent over the bed. In about half an hour we both collapsed at the foot of the bed, leaning back against the sheets and blankets we'd torn up.

She still had on her silver lamé blouse and big clunky shoes. My pants were over by the door somewhere. I picked up the skirt and held it up to the blue light from the streetlight outside. It was even ghastlier that way.

"Where the hell did you get this?" I asked.

"Thrift shop," Kelly said.

"Which one? Whores 'Я' Us?"

"Yeah, I think that was the one." She pulled off the blonde fright wig and tossed it toward my garbage can.

"Did you have a permit to shoot that?" I asked.

She kissed my cheek, then bounced to her feet and headed for the bathroom. The high shoes made her bare bottom do things even more interesting than usual. She went in, flicked on the light, then the blouse came sailing out the door followed, one by one, by the shoes. In a minute I got up and joined her.

Kelly wears a green stone in her navel. It's big enough to fill the entire belly button and I'm pretty sure it's a real emerald, but I wasn't going to ask her, or take her to a jeweler to have her assayed. She was looking down, fiddling with the tiny gold rings that held it in. She looked up at me.

"Something wrong?"

"What could be wrong?" And really, what could? The emerald set off her greenish eyes nicely. Her skin was smooth and flawless, except for some tiny moles scattered around, what the upper classes used to call beauty spots and put on deliberately. She had lots of blond hair which she was unpinning. Everything else was where it ought to be, in ample amounts. Let's just say that picking out a bikini or a thong didn't give her anxiety attacks.

She was laying out mysterious female stuff from her crowded purse. I was far from through for the night, but first I had to answer a call of nature, and wasn't about to dress and go downstairs, so I used the sink. Kelly glanced at me.

"Boys," she said, disdainfully.

"Hey, it all goes down the same pipes."

"You rinse that out real good."

"You're telling me you aren't going to use it as soon as I'm through?" I reached for her arm, but she shook me off.

"Down, boy. Later. First, I need you to go down to my car and get the small suitcase in the trunk. I'm not going down there again as Sally Streetwalker." She tossed me her car keys.

"Did you have any trouble?"

"The doorman at the Manatee gave me a funny look. I parked in their lot, all the way over toward the beach."

"What's in the suitcase? Can you stay over?"

"Yes, if you bring me the decent clothes that are in the suitcase. I'm not walking out of here tomorrow and let your mother see that outfit."

"Don't worry about that. You're solid with my mother."

"Whatever."

"I guess I should bring the car over to our lot. Those bastards might tow it."

"Good idea."

"Are you sure you want me going out alone at this hour? I could get mugged."

"Hey, it was you called me up, remember?"

She was filling a plastic douche bottle so I pulled on my pants and left.

KELLY DRIVES A green Porsche 921, this year's model, that cost more than our income at the Blast-Off for two or three years. When your daddy is the biggest luxury car dealer in northeast Florida having a rad ride is something you just naturally expect.

Not that she lacked for anything else, either.

Kelly.

Every once in a while something drops into your life that makes you think that, in spite of all evidence you've seen so far, somebody up there really does like you. Meeting Kelly is the first time it's happened to me.

We went to different schools. She can't help being born rich any more than I can help being poor, at least until I get a better shot at carving out my own destiny instead of just settling into the level I'd been born into.

But I think we were both a little insecure about it. All sorts of awkward questions came up. Is he just after me for my money? Is she just trying to stick it to her asshole of a racist father by dating a half-Cuban? Does he secretly think I'm a dumb rich bitch? Is she enjoying slumming when she comes down here and dresses as a whore?

No, can't make that one stick on her. We both enjoyed sexual games, surprises, role playing, and she had gone to a lot of trouble for her little trick-or-treat tonight. Slumming? If volunteering two evenings a week at a battered women's shelter was slumming, then I think we need more slummers.

That's where Kelly met Alicia and since Dak and Alicia had been together for about a year, it was inevitable that Kelly and I would meet. It was also inevitable that I'd be greatly impressed by her. There's a lot of impressive things about Kelly, and her body is only one of them.

I couldn't see a thing she had to gain by being my girl other than the pleasure of my company and some damn good sex, so it must be love, right? She said it was, and Kelly always knows her own mind.

But did I love her? Jerk that I am, I was still trying to figure that out.

So far Kelly had never even hinted at matrimony . . . which made me even more nervous, because she was an incredible catch and I liked her boundlessly, I was pretty sure I loved her, if I could put aside the marriage anxiety. But . . . what if, by the time I was ready, she had found someone else? What if she didn't wait for me? I might be throwing away my only chance at happiness by not grabbing her *now,* when she seemed to like me so much.

It sure wouldn't be hard for her to find another lover more in keeping with her social position. Kelly worked as chief bookkeeper at her father's dealership. Guys her age were always coming in to trade up from last year's model, and plenty of them didn't need financing, they just wrote a check.

I don't know why it never occurred to me that a family and kids would get in the way of her goals just as much as it would screw up my college aspirations.

I found her car parked where she said it would be. I always worried a little when I saw it. It stood for all the things I couldn't give her for another decade, if ever.

I put the top down and slid in on the leather seat. The engine growled at me and I wheeled around the lot and out onto the road. It would get up to sixty in about four seconds, I knew because I'd tried it. No chance to unleash the beast in the spring break traffic, though. I crawled down the highway, getting some very interested looks from some of the snow bunnies, parked in our lot, put the top up, grabbed the indoor silent car alarm, and carried her small suitcase up the stairs and into my room.

LATER THAT NIGHT, just before we finally got to sleep, I took out the silver bubble and showed it to her. I put it through its paces, showed her its tricks. I'd been a little worried that her reaction would be, more or less, *So what?*

But it impressed her even faster than it had fascinated me.

"It's light as a soap bubble, and harder than a ball bearing," she summed it up. "I don't know of anything like that. You're the science student, do you?"

"Nothing even close," I told her.

She held it in her hand and frowned at it.

"Manny," she said at last, "you know I'm not the type to worry about nothing or get premonitions. But there's something frightening about this. Do you get a sense of great power from it?"

I had felt *exactly* that, but couldn't put my finger on it.

"I think it has a lot of power, and it might mean a lot of money."

"Really? Why?"

"Well, something new, something *really* new, it just turns the world upside down. Think of what the world was like before electricity. Or television, or cars."

"That big?"

"Maybe bigger."

9

I HAD PLANNED to get out to Rancho Broussard the next evening, but we were just too busy. Spring break is one of the few times of the year we actually do some pretty good business. We had already been sold out twice that week, for the first times that year.

Mom and Aunt Maria had been working all day, every day. I'd been helping with the chores even though both of them said *Let us handle this, you go study* every time I picked up a mop. So that night I worked the late shift on the desk, and the night after that as well. The night after *that* Kelly had something, I think it was some of her volunteer work, and the night after that wasn't good, either.

All in all it was a week before I got out there again.

This time it was in Kelly's car. She offered to let me drive but I waved it off. I'd taken the Porsche through its paces once, right up to 150 miles per hour, and then I hung up my racing gloves. To tell the truth, I was terrified of getting into a fender bender that would cost more to fix than the city budget.

This time I saw the Autopike from the supersonic lane, at the head of a drafting pack of twenty vehicles no more than two inches apart. Dak says that's no accident, that the software is set to always move the bitchin'est car available to the head of the draft. *Noblesse oblige,* he says, and Kelly agrees with him. Me, I don't have enough data, but it sure seems that way.

Not far from the gate of Travis's place we got behind a flatbed truck with a big farm tractor on the back. The thing was too wide and the road too rutted for us to risk passing, so we settled in at a stately twenty-five miles per hour, the Porsche's engine growling in frustration. We followed it for three miles, hoping for a turnoff. It did turn . . . right into the Rancho driveway.

We followed it in a cloud of dust until it reached the clearing, then it turned right toward the barn and the row of junked cars and we turned left toward the house.

Off to one side of us a dump truck had just spilled its load of crushed shell next to half a dozen other hills of shell. There was a guy using a weedeater to destroy the grass that had sprouted in the cracks of the tennis court concrete. He was wearing a blue coverall with a patch on the back that said HIAASEN LANDSCAPERS AND YARD WORK. So was another guy working in close among the plantings that surrounded the house. Already he'd rescued a few sick-looking rhododendrons and hibiscus from strangulation by morning glories and other vines.

"Are they tearing this place down, or building it up?" Kelly wanted to know.

"Don't ask me. This is all news to me."

We got out of the car and headed for the patio, where I could see Travis and Dak relaxing with tall drinks. The long hoses of an industrial carpet shampooer went from a van through the open patio doors and inside the house.

"Spring cleaning," Travis announced, as we reached the patio. He raised his glass in a toast. "You want a Virgin Mary?"

"Are you on the wagon, Col . . . I mean, Travis?" I asked.

"You bet he is," said Alicia, coming outside with another nonalcoholic cocktail in her hand. How do I know it was nonalcoholic? Because Alicia would have flung it as far as she could if it had any liquor in it. Alicia is death on alcohol.

I introduced Travis to Kelly, and he turned on his good smile and natural charm, leaning over to kiss her hand. Kelly smiled and let him.

Travis took the girls inside for a drink and a tour of the house, leaving me alone with Dak and two empty cans of Coke.

"So when did all this happen?"

"All this what?"

"The spring cleaning. You trying to take over the man's life?"

"Let me tell you, Manny. Dude's life can *use* some cleaning up."

Dak was silent for a moment, then made a sweeping gesture.

"All this, the spring cleaning and the Virgin Mary, this is all Alicia. I can hardly believe it, but she came out here and got to talking with him, and she says he sort of broke down. He found Jesus, and admitted to himself that he was wrecking his life."

"Alcoholics Anonymous," I said.

"Yeah, something like that. I don't mean he found Jesus literally—"

"That's a relief."

"Alicia convinced him what he's gotta do is clean up his act. Clean himself up, body, soul, mind, and surroundings. So we got half of northeast Florida out here doing they cleaning thing. Eat better, stop drinking, stop seeing your old friends—which is easy for Travis, since he ain't got no friends left, just a couple regulars at the Apollo he says hi to on his way to his next bender. So the next thing is 'Make new friends,' and here we are, the four of us, ready-made, the assorted-varieties family-sized package."

"Is that one of the twelve steps?"

"It's one of 'Leesha's steps. I don't know if AA has any truck with it."

We were quiet for a while, listening to Alicia, and then Travis and Kelly laughing loudly from the kitchen. I looked at Dak and saw he had a slight frown on his face.

"Are you okay with that?" I asked him.

"With what?"

"You know what."

He sighed. "It bugged me a little at first. Hell, at first I wondered if he wanted to get into *our* pants, you and me, but he didn't act much like a fag . . . I know, I know, I'm stereotyping an abused minority, like they used to say in the Tolerance Workshop 101. They have that class at your school?"

"They called it 'Struggling with Prejudice.' Sounds like the same thing."

"Right. Alicia says Travis ain't gay, and girls always know. But the important thing about Travis is, he's a drunk. Alicia would never allow herself to be interested in a drunk until he had five, ten years' sobriety under his belt."

"Besides, she loves you," I pointed out. He grinned.

"Yeah, there's that. Why date an astronaut when she can have me?"

When Travis and the girls came out of the kitchen there was even more startling evidence of the transformation in Travis. They were carrying bowls of sliced and peeled fresh fruit, yogurt, raw veggies and dip (crudités, Kelly called it), and a plate of assorted cheese slices and chunks. Alicia was carrying a battalion-sized blender.

We all sat around the table and dug into lunch, Travis looking a little desperate, I thought. We watched as Alicia began dumping things into the blender, including a raw egg, shell and all, bananas and chunks of other fruit, veggies . . . but I find it hard to go on. We all started laughing with every new ingredient, and Alicia did, too.

"So this is part of the recovery process?" Travis asked. "Eating rabbit food?"

"Rabbits don't eat cheese."

"Mouse food, then. Is this the thirteenth step?"

"Did you read the booklet I gave you?"

"Yeah. I figure seven steps out of twelve ain't too bad."

"You've done seven of them?" Kelly asked. "That sounds pretty good to me."

"He means he's willing to *try* seven of them," Alicia said. "Right, Travis?"

"And I'm sort of dubious about step five. Maybe I should only tackle six and a half steps. It's still a majority."

"What's step five?" I asked.

" 'I admit to God, to myself and to another human being . . .' " Alicia, Kelly, and Travis broke up as they realized all three were chanting in unison. Travis finished it:

" ' . . . the exact nature of my wrongs.' "

"That's very good, Travis," Alicia said. "Did you memorize them all?"

"I've got a good memory."

"Well, you're not the first one to stumble over the God business. Like I told you, just do the ones you can, for a start. That, and concentrate on taking your life one day at a time. Did you go to a meeting?"

"Part of one," Travis confessed. "I didn't speak. Except the part about 'Hi, my name is Travis.' "

The four of us shouted, *"Hello, Travis!"* It startled him, and for a moment I thought we'd done the wrong thing. Then he laughed, and really seemed to mean it. For the first time I began to get some idea of how lonely these years of being a drunken failure had been for him.

So Alicia proposed a toast: *"To our health!"* and we all drank or sipped from the tumblers of glop she had poured us. Travis chugalugged his, then fell off his chair and rolled around for a while clutching his stomach, moaning theatrically.

While most eyes were on Travis I used the opportunity to ditch the rest of my drink in a sickly looking potted palm under the kitchen window.

AFTER LUNCH DAK and I got out our computers and Travis took us through three more lessons. He gave us assignments that would probably keep us busy the rest of the afternoon. Then he and Kelly and Alicia went off down the newly trimmed path to the lake, fishing equipment in hand. They seemed to take an evil delight in looking back at us chained to the laptops until they were out of sight.

Ten minutes later we heard the deep roar of a big outboard. I gritted my teeth and kept my eyes on the screen. Soon the sound faded away.

"I never liked fishing much, myself," Dak muttered.

"What, when we can be out here improving our minds? Hell, no.

Big waste of time. Probably nothing out there but some big ol' bass, anyway."

"What you wanna bet all they get is a bad sunburn?"

"I hear you, Dak, I hear you."

"Maybe some catfish."

"Ugliest fish in the world, catfish."

We finally got settled in. We kept at it for two hours without a sign of Kelly and Alicia. I called for a break and Dak wasn't opposed.

"Let's go down to the dock," he suggested.

"You crazy? That's just what they want us to do. I wanted to talk to that guy, Travis's cousin, what was . . . ?"

"Jubal. Short for Jubilation. Gotta love the name."

About halfway to the barn Dak caught my arm, and he looked like he was having second thoughts.

"What's up?" I asked him. We continued walking, but at a slower pace.

"Jubal's odd, Manny."

"I heard that. What, is he dangerous?"

"Oh, hell no. He just takes some getting used to. He's got some kind of brain damage but he won't go to a doctor to get it checked out. He's scared of doctors. He's scared of a lot of stuff, including meeting new people."

"Is this a bad idea? We could wait till Travis gets back."

"Nah, I think we'll be all right. Just don't get insulted if he walks off in the middle of a conversation. Jubal is socially challenged."

We came to the door and there was a piece of cardboard stuck on it with strapping tape. Somebody had written on it with a grease pencil in block letters:

IS NO DORBEL & DO NOT KNOKC
IF LOKED DONT DISTRUB
IF UNLOKED YOUR WELCOM COM IN!

"Dyslexia," I guessed.

"He ain't illiterate, he just can't spell worth a damn." He tried the door handle, found it was not "loked." He gestured for me to go ahead, and pulled the door wide open. A full-grown bull alligator reared up and lunged at us, roaring like a grizzly bear.

"Very funny," I said. Dak was leaning against the doorjamb, in the middle of one of those soundless fits of laughter that can make it hard to get your breath. I glanced inside and saw Jubal himself just beyond the alligator. He was smiling broadly.

"Scared you a little, though, didn't it?" Dak wanted to know.

"A little. Till I saw the eyeball hanging by a wire."

"I t'ought I fix dat, me," Jubal said, and bent over his mechanical pet, stuffing the stray eyeball back in its socket. He was dressed like he was the first time I saw him, in khaki shorts, very loud aloha shirt, and flip-flops. A pudgy teddy-bear of a man, with his wild white beard and hairy arms and legs.

"Jubal, this is Manny, my best friend," Dak said.

"Meet him already," Jubal said, and turned and waddled off. Dak looked at me and shrugged. We decided to follow him.

Jubal's barn was full of dinosaurs. Most of them were torn into a lot of pieces with wires and tubes sticking out and metal bones and hydraulic muscles exposed.

"This is where old animatronics go to die," Dak explained. "When an attraction at some of the theme parks stops being popular, Travis and Jubal go buy it, cheap."

We moved out of the dino graveyard and in among a bunch of what looked like mad scientist equipment. There were things that made yellow and purple sparks, and racks of tubes and glassware with colored fluids moving through.

"Looks like Doctor Frankenstein's been here, right?" Dak said. "This is more props and stuff. They bought it off some of the movie studios. Like this Jacob's ladder, and this Tesla coil. And this Van de Graaf generator. Supposed to make your hair stand on end from static electricity." He put his hand on a brushed aluminum globe on the end of an aluminum pole. Nothing happened. "Well, it does for you white folks, anyway. Us AAs, our hair too kinky." He pointed at me and as his finger got close a spark jumped—and so did I.

"Hey, Jube," he called out, "how about we turn off some of the special effects? We can hardly hear each other talk in here."

In a moment all the sparking, spitting, popping, and hissing props got quiet. I followed Dak to the only open area we'd seen so far. Standing in the middle of it was Jubal, hands in his pants pockets, rocking back and forth on his heels, looking pleased with himself.

"Manny, how you like dis crazy place, you?"

"It's fantastic, Jubal."

"Every boy's dream clubhouse," Dak agreed, and Jubal roared with laughter, reminding me again of Santa Claus.

"Jus' junk, mostly," Jubal said. "Mos' dis stuff jus' git t'rowed away."

"What do you do with it?" I asked.

"Parts, mos'ly. Stuff in dere custom made, sometime I can twis' it around a little, make it do somethin' else."

"He's working on a robot," Dak said. "Come on, Jubal, show it to him."

He took us to the far side of the barn, where the equipment wasn't quite so eye-catching, but obviously a lot more useful. Tables and shelves were covered with tools and instruments and work in progress. I saw what I was pretty sure was an electron microscope, and a mass spectrometer. There were also more ordinary machines lined against a back wall, drill press, lathe, table saw, stuff like that.

But what my eye went to was a table with a metal skeleton on it. The table was waist high, a good level to work.

"Did you see that video, 'Frankenstein Meets Madonna'?" Dak asked. "This table was one of the props. Show him, Jubal."

Jubal spun a wheel at the side of the table and it slowly rotated until it was at a forty-five-degree angle. The thing on the table didn't have a head, but the torso, hips, arms and legs were all in the right spots.

Jubal picked up a robotic hand from his worktable. He pulled some levers at the base, and fingers twitched. Jubal seemed wildly pleased by each motion, like a kid with a toy. That's how Jubal seemed to approach all his inventions. Just a big, balding kid on Christmas morning.

"De han's, dey sto' bought, from . . . Sears and Roebuck."

Dak said, "Like, a catalog. Off the shelf, right, Jubal?"

"Off de shelf, yes! Dese from Universal Positronics. Dey figure out han's long time ago. Travis, he get 'em cheap, him."

"So he's got hands from the Sears, Robot catalog," I said.

Jubal looked puzzled for a moment, then his eyes widened.

"Sears Robot! From de Sears Robot!" And he laughed so hard he had to grab the table behind him to keep from falling over. And hey, I know it wasn't all *that* funny, but his laughing was the worst kind of infectious. You just could not watch Jubal laughing without laughing yourself.

Jubal finally calmed down, but the rest of the day he kept muttering "Sears Robot" to himself, and then laughing aloud.

"We figger, we make a robot can really walk, we make us a *fis'ful* a money," Jubal said.

"You bet, Jube, a fistful," Dak said.

"Here, watch dis, y'all." He cranked the table so it was perpendicular to the floor. He flipped some switches in the skeleton's belly. Jubal took the thing by one arm and pulled. It put out one foot, then the other. Now it was standing on its own.

"Gyros," Dak explained.

"Yessum, but dese don' hold him up like a . . . like a . . ."

"Steadicam?" Dak asked.

"Yeah, dat, what you say. Dese gyros tell him which way up be."

"Like an inertial tracker," I said.

"Yeah, what you say." He gave the thing a shove. Instead of falling backward it put a leg out and placed one foot behind itself, then straightened again. Jubal shoved it again, harder. It staggered, then it stabilized again.

"Pretty good," I said.

"Yeah, I know what you're thinking," Dak said. "You've seen it before. We've even seen something like this climbing stairs."

"I've never seen one run," I said.

"Dis one, neither," Jubal said, sadly. "Need some better sof'ware, me."

"Well, I think it's pretty damn fine already," Dak said, and I agreed.

"*Cher,* sell him for twenny t'ousand dollah, we make a *fis'ful* a money!"

"Twenty thousand . . ." Dak was grinning at me. "What does something like this usually cost?"

"Manny, no need to even walk into the showroom unless you can write a check for half a million. Jubal thinks he can make one for under ten grand."

"Maybe I kin," Jubal said, scratching his head. " 'Course, I done already spend fi'ty t'ousand on dis one!"

It was an awesome idea. A humanoid robot cheaper than a new car? I wondered if it could clean toilets.

"So what all do you figure it will do?" I asked Jubal. "Aside from walk around, I mean. Will it clean windows?"

"I t'ought long time on dat question, me. Dis t'ing, it could carry roun' a bag full a dem golfin' clubs, I t'ink." He put his fists on his hips and glared at me.

"Robo-Caddy," Dak said. "I think you got something there, Jube. And we could also walk dogs."

Jubal frowned at the floor again, and twisted his shirttails.

"Mebbe," he said. "Mebbe we could."

He turned away from us and went to a worktable across the room, where he started sorting stuff that had already looked fairly well sorted to me.

"He looks like I hurt his feelings," I whispered to Dak.

"Not your fault, man. I'd a done the same thing but Travis clued me in. Heck, it's my fault, I guess, I forgot to tell you."

"Tell me what?"

"It's more about . . . well, Manny, Jubal is some kind of genius, but he don't have a practical bone in his body. He makes these wonderful things and doesn't have any idea at all of what to do with them. Travis always figures that out. You and me, we think it over ten minutes, we'll come up with a dozen things to do with it. Jubal won't."

Jubal had taken the top off one of those big glass jars you see in convenience stores with spicy sausages floating around in them. It was half full of shiny silver Christmas tree ornaments.

I took my silver bubble out of my pocket and went over there.

"I found this in your yard the other day," I said. Jubal's eyes lit up and just like that, his sulk was over. He took the bubble from me, holding it with fingers loosely curled around it, just like I'd had to do to keep it from slipping away.

"I *t'ought* I was short a couple. It's hard to keep 'em all straight, dey jus' floats away. T'anks, Manny."

"Sure thing, Jubal."

He took the lid off the jar and popped my bubble in.

"Less'n you want it," he said. I looked at him. He seemed completely innocent of any idea that the thing was something special.

"Jubal, what I'd like to know is, what *is* it?"

He looked down at the big glass jar. He moved it around and the silver bubbles swirled. He let it go and the bubbles kept swirling for a minute, then settled down.

Jubal laughed. "That's jus' what I tryin' to figure, me. Ain't got no name for 'em." He looked back at the jar and shook it again. He seemed far away.

"One day my pa, he cut him down a li'l ol' spruce tree someplace and he brung it home. He set dat li'l tree right in de house. Not much taller dan me, no. An' when he had dat tree set up, he go out to his pirogue boat and he got him an ol' towsack. He say ol' Boudreaux didn' have no fi'ty dollah he done promised for a gator hide, he only had fo'ty-fi' dollah, him!" Jubal chuckled at this, and Dak and I smiled.

"So Boudreaux he tellin' my pa 'bout dis t'ing dey be doin' down de bayou, in Lafayette or maybe it was all de way to N'awlin, what dey call it Chris'mas.

"Now my pa he say, 'Boudreaux, you t'ink I'm a fool, me? I know all 'bout Chris'mas. Don't hol' wit' it, is all.'

"Now Boudreaux he say, 'I don' mean no such of a t'ing, Broussard. Ev'body on dis bayou know Broussard no fool, you. And dey know Broussard, he don't put up no lights nor set him up a tree, no. But lookee heah, Broussard.' An dat when Boudreaux, he show my pa de towsack wid all the Chris'mas pretties in it.

"My daddy, he say he had him a weak moment, Satan mus' a reach out to him, because he tooken dat towsack full a li'l pretties, him, 'stead of dat fi' dollah what Boudreaux still owe him."

Jubal had a good laugh about that, and I laughed with him, because I simply loved the way he told a story. Not laughing *at* his preposterous Cajun accent, but because of how it just made me *listen* harder to every word.

"My pa, he brung in dat towsack and open it up on de flo', an all dese Chris'mas pretties dey tumble out. Dey was lights on wires . . . and my pa laugh, him, and we all laugh, 'cause we don't have no 'lectric, no!

"Dere was little angels cut outta tin, an' my pa he give dem to my li'l sister Gloria and tol' her to tie 'em up to de tree anywhere she want. And dere was silver strings. And dere be fo' or fi' dozen roun' balls, all colors. I drop one an it break . . . yessum, it did.

"An' den my ma, she tie candles to dat Chris'mas tree, six or seven of 'em, and she say it was de pretties' t'ing she evah see."

He said nothing for a moment, tasting the memory I think.

"Bedtime, Ma, she put out de candle lights. *Ma père,* he go out jack-lightin' deer with Fontenot an' Hebert. *Junior* Hebert, not Alphonse.

"An' I got me outta bed and I light dem candle again so Santy Claus kin fin' de house, him. And what do y'know, dat tree it kotch fire and burn down de whole house. We sleepin' in leaky tents de res' a dat winter, we did, till de new house done got build." He chuckled again. This time I wasn't tempted to laugh along with him.

"Pa, he come home firs' light, see dat ol' shack jus' smokin' ashes and his family standin' dere in de only clothes dey own. He tole us, 'Dat's what Almighty God t'ink a Chris'mas trees, boys. And dere be y'all's Chris'mas. Yo firs' an yo las'!'

"And den he wallop me upside de head!"

He smiled again, and for the first time I could see, the way the light hit him, that there *was* a dent in the side of his head. I'd thought Dak was exaggerating. It was partly hidden by wispy white hair, but I could have laid three fingers in it.

I was at a loss what to say. Clearly, the story was over, but Jubal hadn't answered my question. I wasn't sure now I wanted it answered.

"So that's what those are?" Dak asked him, nodding toward the jar. "Some new kind of Christmas tree ornament?"

Jubal said nothing, just took the lid off the jar and handed a bubble to Dak.

. . . who immediately had it slip from his hand. He quickly reached down to catch it before it hit the floor, but it just hung there.

His eyes got wide, and he smiled. But the smile didn't last long. I shut up for the next ten minutes, letting Dak repeat the kind of experiments I'd done already. Finally he gave up and scowled at me. He probably felt like a fool. I know I'd felt that way.

"So what is it, and what's it for, Jubal?"

"Tol' you I got no name for it, me. You *could* hang 'em from de Chris'mas tree."

"Anything else?" I asked. I was trying to be careful, remembering what Dak had told me about Jubal and his limitations in practical matters.

He looked back and forth at us, then smiled like a little child with a secret.

"I got some ideers, me. Come look." He led us to another workbench across the room. There was a device there, I saw it was made from two video game controllers, one with a couple small thumbwheels, another with a pistol grip. It was held together with twisted copper wire and pieces of duct tape. Small plastic labels had been glued over the places where a particular button's function used to be.

The only label I could read was on one of the control wheels, and it said SQUOZE and DE-SQUOZE, with arrows pointing to the left for the one and the right for the other.

"Chris'mas, dat be de *reason* I build de Squeezer," he said. "Wondered if I could build me a silver ball dat don' break so easy, me. Done started readin' on optics, indexes of refraction an' reflection, stuff like dat . . ." He looked thoughtful, then scratched his head around the horrible dent and looked confused for a moment, as if he couldn't remember where he was. Then he smiled again.

"Den I had dis idea, me. An' you watch, it gonna make us a *fis'ful* a money!"

"So it's called the Squeezer?" Dak asked him.

"It is? Who said dat?"

"You did."

Jubal thought back, then laughed.

"I guess I did. How 'bout dat? De Squeezer. I guess dat's right. Now watch."

He took one of the bubbles out of the jar and placed it in the air. It just hung there, drifting in random air currents. But Jubal worked some controls on his device and suddenly it jerked to the left.

Jubal waved it back and forth, and the bubble stayed out there as if it were impaled on the tip of an invisible sword.

"Really neat, Jubal," I told him.

"Dat ain't nuttin'. Watch dis." He turned one of the wheels of the game controller and the bubble shrank down to the size of a marble, then a BB. "Don' wan' get her *too* small, no," Jubal said. "We lose her for sure."

Dak moved closer, and he looked at the bubble as if he found it offensive.

"That's why you call it a Squeezer?" Dak asked.

"Dat's why. Now, stan' back, *cher.*" Dak did. Jubal fired the trigger mechanism on the other game controller . . .

. . . and I must have jumped a foot. It sounded like a gunshot.

"Goodness gracious, as my grandma used to say," Dak breathed. "That was one powerful startlement."

Jubal laughed. Kids love to sneak up and go "Boo!", and so did Jubal.

"So where did it go?" I asked.

"Didn't have nowhere to go *to,*" Jubal said, "since it not here in de firs' place."

"Run that one by me again, Jube," Dak said.

"Wouldn't it leave a . . . a skin or something?" I asked. "Like a popped balloon?"

" 'Cep' it ain't no balloon!" Jubal crowed, enjoying himself.

"Well, it's *something,* isn't it?" Dak asked. Jubal folded his arms and smiled.

"Like I say, never was cain't go no place."

"Yeah, that's where it . . . *where* it isn't. But *what* isn't it?"

"Dat depend on what yo definition a *isn't* is, *cher*."

We finally got him to say the silver bubble was a field of some sort. Nothing could get into it.

"So, ma fren's, you buy one dese, somebody give you da chance?"

Dak and I looked at each other.

"What, one of the gizmos there, or one of the bubbles?"

Jubal pointed to the Squeezer, still grinning broadly.

"I sure would," I said. "If I could afford it."

"I don' t'ink it cos' too much, no."

"Whatever you say, Jube," Dak said. "If you can build a man-sized robot cheap, why can't you build a . . . dammit, Jubal, just what *is* it? What is it doing?"

But Jubal folded his arms and turned away from us.

"You bes' be goin' now, ma fren's."

It took me a moment to realize he was kicking us out. Dak had warned me, but it left me off balance. A thing like that ought to come after some argument, or name calling, or something. Dak and I were completely mystified.

"Jubal? Are you okay? Because I didn't—"

"Y'all jus' go 'way now, hear? I can't talk to y'all now."

"But Jubal . . ."

"Come back later. A few days, mebbe."

I took Dak's elbow and started pulling him away. He didn't resist, but kept looking over his shoulder all the way to the door.

"Was it something I said?"

"I think so," I told him. "Travis said something about cursing around Jubal."

"Sure, and I cleaned my act up. When he's around I haven't been saying . . . Wait a minute. You think we got kicked out because I said *'dammit?'* "

"That's my guess."

"Well gah-*da* . . ." He stopped himself. "How am I supposed to *talk* if I can't say . . . that word?"

"It'll be tough," I agreed. "But we can do it."

"Hel . . . *heck,* Manny, I know some dudes can't put a sentence together without saying motherf—"

"You know, that one offends me, too."

"—three times. It ain't my own favorite, tell the truth, but it plain old don't *mean* much anymore. If you *call* someone a moth . . . a MF, that's one thing, but mostly people just use it as an all-purpose modifier, 'MF this, MF that, MF the other thing.' "

"You don't have to sell me on it, Dak. I agree. But it looks like if we're going to spend any time around Jubal, we're going to have to *really* watch our mouths."

"Crazy, man. Plum crazy."

"What's crazy?"

I was startled, and looked up to see Travis, Kelly, and Alicia coming up the path from the lake. The girls had windblown hair, though I don't recall a lot of wind while we were studying. They must have been really moving along in whatever kind of boat Travis had, the one we'd heard roaring away a few hours ago. Their faces were shiny and flushed from sun, wind, and UV blocker.

Fishing? I doubted it. I was so jealous I could have spit.

Dak told Travis what he'd said, and Travis nodded as he set his rod and reel and tackle box on the big patio table.

"That was it, boys. Jubal won't hold with 'blasphemin', cursin', swearin', nor the utterin' of obscenities.' Learned that in the cradle, he did. Some of them he can just frown and pretty much ignore, but anything worse than 'damn' will send him into a silent depression that can last three or four days, sometimes."

"Jeez—" I started to say.

"Watch it," Travis warned. I slapped a hand over my mouth.

"You mean . . ." Dak had to pause as he contemplated the enormity of it. "You mean 'damn' ain't the bottom of the scale? It ain't the mildest . . . cussword there is?"

"Best not to take a chance, Dak," Travis said, taking a big rattan creel from Kelly, who had slung it over her shoulder. "Myself, I avoid heck and darn and gosh. Jubal feels . . . more accurately, Jubal's *father* felt those were just euphemisms for hell and damn and God. Not that a word like 'euphemism' ever had a chance to settle in Avery Broussard's head, ignorant, pious, brutal, hypocritical swamp rat that he is."

"So what *can* we say?" I wanted to know. "I guess we'd just better flush all those expletives we use in a normal day."

"Not a bad idea. But what I try to do is substitute some harmless word instead. And you know, everybody knows, there are times nothing but an expletive will do. Like, you hit your thumb with a hammer." He put his thumb on the table and mimed hitting it with a hammer.

" '*JEEZ!* . . . us loves me, this I know, for the Bible tells me so . . .' " Everybody laughed. Travis was not the world's best singer.

We made lists of words we could safely turn to when we wanted to say something we normally would express with a curse or an oath. Words like swell, and whillikers, and gloriosky, and rats, and glory be!

But that was later, because first Travis opened the creel and spilled six big catfish out onto the table, still gasping for air. Dak was trying not to gape, trying to be cool.

"No bass?" he asked.

"We tossed the bass back," Alicia said. "Decided to let 'em grow a little more."

"So . . . how do you cook those ugly things?"

"Thought we'd deep-fry 'em in cornmeal, sweetie," Alicia said, and Dak looked as if he might faint. I probably did, too, because I realized at that moment I was starving.

Alicia and Travis cleaned the fish . . . and did most everything else, none of the rest of us being very good cooks. When it was all done Travis set out six places. We heaped our plates with golden crisp catfish filets, mashed potatoes, okra, and hush puppies. I saw Kelly about to dig in so I patted her hand and shook my head when she looked up. I had a hunch. Travis saw me, and tapped his glass of white wine.

"This isn't for me, folks, but the fact is, Jubal won't eat any food that someone other than himself hasn't said a prayer over. I'll do that now, unless one of you has words you'd like to say."

I bowed my head, and was surprised to hear Alicia's quiet voice. It was so quiet, in fact, that I couldn't hear the words, but she sounded sincere. I did hear the last:

" ' . . . and the wisdom to tell the difference.' And bless this food. Amen."

"He won't come down to eat, Travis?" I asked.

" 'Fraid not, Manny. He'll hole up there the rest of the day."

I got up and picked up his plate. Travis grabbed my sleeve as I passed him, and said, close to my ear, "He won't take it, but don't leave it on the stoop. It brings the raccoons."

I went on, not sure now if I should have volunteered. But I knocked on Jubal's door anyway, and he answered on a speaker I hadn't noticed before.

"Suppertime, Jubal," I said.

"T'ank ya kinely, Manny. Did Travis bless it?"

"Alicia did."

"Den t'ank her kinely, too. Manny, I don' feel so good, me. T'ank whosomever cooked dem vittles, if you please."

"I'll do that, Jubal. And Jubal . . . we're sorry. We won't let it happen again."

"Not yo doin', not yo fault. I jus' a little crazy, me."

I put the food just inside the door and went back. Best catfish I ever had.

"If you know Jubal won't eat it," Dak said at one point, "why have Manny take the food up there?"

"Because it's important to make the offer, meathead," Alicia said.

"Same reason that I, an atheist, had a prayer said over it," Travis said, nodding at Alicia. "If Jubal *did* take it, he'd want it blessed. I try not to lie to Jubal. He's had enough lies for three lifetimes."

Nobody pursued that one. We cleaned the plates. Hell . . . I mean, *whillikers,* we cleared the whole table, and topped it all off with a berry cobbler Alicia made. I figured if I came out here much more I'd have to start watching my waistline.

10

★ ★ ★

MY PHONE RANG at three A.M. the next morning. I almost didn't answer it, but after eleven rings I figured whoever was on the other end wasn't going to give up easily.

"Hello?" I said, and yawned.

"Manny? Travis. I wonder if you could do me a big favor?"

I was sitting up now, fully awake. "I'll sure try, Travis. What is it?"

"I wonder if you could come on out here to the ranch."

"Come out . . . what, you mean now?"

"If you could. It's pretty important."

"Gee, Travis, I don't know . . ."

"It's about Jubal."

"Is he all right? Did something—"

"Please, Manny, just come on out. I can explain when you get here. Take a taxi if you have to. I'll pay."

"No, Travis, I mean, sure, I'll come, but—"

"Thanks a million, pal." And he hung up. Kelly rolled over and sat up.

"Travis?"

"Yeah, he wants me to go out there. Tonight. Right now."

"That's what happens when you have weird friends," she said, and bounced out of bed. "Let me wash my face and comb my hair, and we'll both go."

WE STOPPED FOR two giant Starbucks espressos and a dozen Krispy Kremes, then hit the road.

The place looked a lot better in the dark this time. It's amazing how much difference changing a few burned-out lightbulbs can make.

The tennis court, pool area, and paths to the barn and to the lake were now lit by lights on poles. Moths and June bugs battered themselves to death on them, and bug zappers hung all around the patio.

But the biggest difference was in the pool, all cleaned out and full of beautiful blue water, lit from below. I wished I'd brought my bathing suit.

Dak and Alicia arrived not far behind us. We went in through the patio screen door and found Travis sitting in the sunken conversation area, fully dressed. There was a bottle of Jim Beam on the table at his side, and a tumbler half full. Alicia made a face when she saw the bourbon, but she didn't say anything.

Sitting on the coffee table was Jubal's 7-Eleven jug of golf-ball-sized indestructible silver bubbles.

"So where's Jubal?" Dak asked at last.

"Jubal is out rowing on the lake. It's what Jubal always does when he's upset. You probably noticed the size of his arms. Jubal rows a *lot,* and it's usually my fault. It certainly is tonight.

"I'd like to know everything y'all know about these things." He looked from one of us to another, right down the line. "Unless you're going to tell me you don't know anything about them."

I told him everything I had done with the bubble since finding it in the tall grass not a hundred feet from where I was now sitting. It didn't take too long. I deferred to Kelly, who had very little to add, and then to Dak, who confirmed what Jubal had shown us of the nature of the bubbles, and some attempt to report what Jubal had said.

Alicia was one of those females, like Mom and Maria, who can't stand seeing people sitting around with nothing to eat or drink. She had been listening to us from the kitchen and came out now with a big pot of coffee and some cookies she had brought with her. There was oatmeal and brown sugar covering up the taste of the other health store stuff I'm sure was in there.

Travis took a deep drink of his bourbon, looked at the bottle, then at Alicia, and reached for a coffee cup. Alicia filled it, looking happy as a prohibitionist who's just set a barroom on fire.

"Okay, friends," Travis said. "Did I say friends? Well, Jubal likes you. If it was up to me, I might just chase all y'all's asses back to the beach where I found you—"

"You found *us?"* Alicia snorted.

"—where I found y'all, illegally rampaging up and down a public beach that innocent citizens were sitting on, minding their own business. But it happens I kind of like you, too, and I can't really figure how any of you did anything wrong . . . except I wish you'd a told me about this. I might have handled Jubal better."

"You really think so?" Kelly asked.

". . . Probably not. Anyway, things would be so much simpler if none of y'all had seen these things. But you have. And Jubal wants you to keep coming around. That's one area I've failed Jubal miserably, not bringing new folks around for him to visit with. Jubal's frightened of other people, often as not, but both of us know if he doesn't socialize now and then he's likely to grow a hide so tough he won't be able to talk to anybody else, ever. And I've pretty much used up all the old friends I used to have, which may be why I'm trying to be friends with as unlikely a group as y'all. Anyway . . .

"I reckon I'd better tell you a little more about Jubal. About me and Jubal. I've told this stuff to no one, nobody at all outside the family, and I wouldn't be telling y'all if Jubal hadn't said he didn't mind. So here goes.

"My friends, it ain't easy being Jubal . . ."

* * *

TRAVIS'S UNCLE AVERY Broussard was a few years older than Travis's father. When Avery was young he had been Travis's favorite of his six uncles. Of all the Broussard brothers and sisters, Avery lived closest to the land. He taught his sons and nephews to get along in the woods and swamps of Louisiana bayou country. It was Avery who always found the time to take the kids out in the middle of the night frog-gigging or jacklighting deer. Travis said he was nine before he realized jacklighting—shooting deer frozen in car headlights or powerful spotlights—was illegal. Avery just laughed at that, and said it was okay because they intended to eat the meat. It was just an easier way to put food on the table, and he wasn't surprised that the city boys and girls who never in their lives killed for the table would want country boys like him to hunt the hard way.

"Just think about it, *cher,*" Avery said. "Dem city boys, what dey be cryin' 'bout is it ain't fair to de deer. *Ain't fair!*" He had a good laugh at that one. "I tell you, I druther be shootin' at dem deer not movin' dan jus' run all over God's miraculous creation findin' a deer wasn't nothin' but just winged, and him hurtin' powerful all dat time. No, sir, Avery Broussard hasn't *never* missed no deer caught in de headlights. What is dat, if it ain't 'perventin' cruelty' to animals, hah?"

So they jacklighted and dodged the game wardens through the tangled bayou that Avery knew better than anyone else. And during the day, Avery would take them hunting for coon, possum, and squirrel. They raised their own rabbits. He would take them out on the water to run the trotlines and crawdad traps, fish for catfish and trout and alligator gar and just about anything else they could wrestle aboard a rickety pirogue, including alligators when the game warden wasn't in the parish. It was a Huck Finn life, and one that Travis and all his brothers liked a hell of a lot more than their own situation in town, in Lafayette, where their father, Emile Broussard, worked as a pipe-fitter.

They could all see the differences in the two families, but for many years it didn't seem to matter. Emile's family had enough money, a car, good clothes and food, a great house, all courtesy of wages and benefits negotiated for him by the Oil, Chemical, and Atomic Workers Union. Avery, on the other hand, had nothing. His children dressed in rags and hand-me-downs from his brothers' families, and were lucky to have one pair of shoes. But Avery didn't seem to mind, and neither did his kids, who hardly ever wore shoes, anyway. In fact, any jealousy went the other way. Even Emile admitted that sometimes he wished he'd opted for the independent life, living off the land. Most of the time the living was good out there in the bayous, and when it wasn't Avery had a large family that would pull him through the tight spots. Avery always repaid the help he got in fresh eggs, fish, rabbits, whatever the bounty of nature was producing at the time.

During those golden years, Jubal was Travis's best friend. Travis was three years older and it should have made a difference, except that Jubal was the smartest person Travis had ever known, child or adult. And Travis knew something about being smart, he was far and away the best of his class in every subject he took.

Travis knew from bitter experience what the other kids did if they learned you were intelligent. It could all be summed up, he felt, in Moe Howard, the mean Stooge, sneering at Curly and saying, "Oh, a wise guy, eh?" Then the fingers poked in the eyes. In the city schools a wise guy was the worst thing you could be, except for being a faggot, and Travis figured things wouldn't be any better out in the country.

They wouldn't have been, but none of the Avery branch of the Broussard family had to worry about that, because none of them were ever put in school. Though there may never have been worse candidates for home schooling than the Avery Broussard family, the school boards of Bayou Teche Parish were hard-pressed to educate even the children who came in willingly. They didn't have the heart to fight very hard about those whose parents would prefer their children to stay at home. Their high school graduates often had trouble passing seventh-grade-level tests. Could home schooling do much worse? They washed their hands of Avery Broussard and his brood, preferring not to notice that Avery's mildly retarded common-law wife, Evangeline, could neither read nor write.

It turned out in the Broussard case that home schooling could do *substantially* worse than the public schools.

Avery had been an extremely religious man most of his life. He had been raised Christian, of course, like everyone else in the parish, and Catholic, like many of his neighbors. But it was a wild, charismatic brand of Catholicism that just sort of naturally blended in with the hard-shell Baptists all around them until you could hardly tell the difference. Actually, the Broussard family church didn't have much contact with either the Catholic or the Baptist mainstream. The First Baptist Church in Lafayette, for instance, never released venomous snakes in their immaculate sanctuary, nor did the congregation of Our Lady of the Bayous drink poison. Avery's church did both of these things, and more. The church started small, and stayed small, new converts just about balancing out casualties.

In that part of Louisiana, it was common to be deeply religious yet far from saintly. A lot went out and raised some hell on Saturday night. Maybe that was the reason such extreme measures were thought necessary the following day, as if simple prayers and pleas would not be enough.

One night when he was twenty-two, dead drunk and coked to the eyeballs, Avery had gone out to the parking lot of the Gables, a local after-hours bucket of blood, to square off with Alphonse Hebert. Avery thought the matter should be settled with fists, and Avery was the best man with his fists for a good ten miles around. Hebert must have heard that, because he drew a revolver and fired all six shots at Avery from a distance of no more than six feet. Avery, suddenly cold sober but no more able to move than a jacklighted deer, stood there and pissed himself, then felt all over his body for bullet holes, then fell to his knees and began to pray as three of his brothers worked Hebert over with pool cues and boots, and the rest of the patrons of the Gables stood around and watched, the general feeling being that Hebert was getting no more than he deserved.

Now, while it was agreed that Hebert was easily plotzed enough to miss at that range, he was unlikely to miss with all six. And examining the bullet holes later, it surely did appear that most of that lead ought to have been slowed down appreciably by various parts of Avery before hitting the clapboard wall behind him, which would have been good news for old Charlie Wilson, who soaked up two of the bullets after they came through the wall, one with his chest and the other with his head, and as a result gave up drinking and never quite walked right for the rest of his life.

"It weren't no burnin' bush, no," Avery later told anyone who would listen. "But I knows de hand a God when I sees it, oh yes." He swore off liquor, fornication, and fighting, which left quite a gap in his social life, as aside from sleeping, eating, and working as a roughneck on an offshore drilling rig when he needed money, drinking, fighting, and screwing other men's wives was about all he did.

He filled the gaps with marriage and praying and preaching. He became even less employable than he had been before the miracle, as he could seldom go through an entire day without getting into a heated argument with his boss or a customer or fellow worker about religion. He never hesitated to point out sin, which did not make him popular. He moved deeper into the swamp and started in on a family.

Evangeline had been picked for the fertility of her lineage more than beauty or brains, as she had little of either, but she was fertile and prolific, and able to work like a horse even when eight and a half months gone. And that was good, because she spent the next fifteen years pregnant, giving birth usually in March or April, usually on a Sunday, and three times on Easter Sunday itself. Avery and Evangeline had seven sons: Veneration, Jubilation, Celebration, Sanctification, Exaltation, Consecration, and Hallelujah. They had five daughters, all named Gloria: Gloria Patri, Gloria Filly, Gloria Spiritusanctu, Gloria Inexcelsis, and Gloria Monday. They lost three, a boy and two girls, stillborn.

Most people in town knew the legend of how their youngest, Hallelujah, got his name. There had been complications in his birth and, against his better judgment, Avery had taken Evangeline into town, where Hallelujah had been delivered by C-section. When the doctor told her she would not be able to have any more children, Evangeline had shouted out the infant's name on the spot.

Jubilation, known to everyone but his father as Jubal, was six the first time Avery saw Jesus. From that moment the lives of the Avery Broussard clan became a race to see if any would grow large enough to fend off their father before his increasing insanity killed them all.

Avery was called to the pastorship of the Holy Bible Church of the Redeemed when the previous preacher succumbed to multiple spider bites from a brown recluse he was attempting to swallow. He had become allergic to the spider's venom, and expired on the altar from anaphylactic shock.

Being called to lead the flock of the Redeemed didn't require a certificate from any seminary. It was mostly a matter of stepping forward and taking the microphone from the cooling hand of the previous shepherd and starting to preach. Avery bellowed for two hours that night, without notes, quoting long passages from the Bible, and when the last hymn of the night had been sung it was clear there would be no challenge to his leadership.

From the first Avery was never shy about his meetings with Jesus. A small number of his parishioners left the church, feeling his descriptions of the Son of God to be blasphemous, but about twice their number heard of Avery's wonderful stories about what it was like to literally walk with Jesus, and joined up. So in the early years, Avery's church thrived.

And the stories were wonderful. Avery didn't just walk with Jesus, he fished with him and hunted with him, too. He declared Jesus to be the best shot he'd ever seen with a .22, and he'd hunted with hundreds of men, in pretty near every parish in southern Louisiana. If Jesus saw a squirrel a hundred yards away, that squirrel was *doomed*. And Jesus didn't look much like that sad sack fairy-boy all y'all seen nailed to a cross or praying in Gethsemane looking like he needed a good dose of Ex-lax, either, Avery told his congregation, nor did he wear hippie robes and beatnik sandals. Jesus walked the bayous in good, sturdy work boots. He wore J. C. Penney overhauls and made-in-America red-and-black-checked flannel shirts or T-shirts with a pack of cigarettes rolled up in the sleeve. Jesus chewed Red Man, Avery said, and smoked Luckies.

Avery's idea of education was fairly simple. He believed in the three R's, but not too much of any of them.

He figured a person had to know how to read the Bible or he would be at a severe disadvantage in life. To that end he laboriously taught his three eldest children their ABC's and had them play an old "Hooked on Phonics" tape over and over again on a thrift-store Walkman. It was all he could do. His own reading skills were not the best, though his memory was phenomenal.

He knew how to sign his name, so his children learned, too. Any efforts beyond that, he felt, were strictly advanced classes for special credit.

He felt a person had to be able to count money, to not get short-changed and to render unto Caesar all that you can't hide from Caesar. So his children played counting games with real coins and Monopoly money.

Teaching them to read brought up a special problem, though, to Avery's way of thinking. Like many of his neighbors, he did not allow his children to go to the picture shows or watch the television set. Avery, as he so often did, took things a little further. The only thing in the world worth reading, and therefore the only book his children would read, was the Holy Bible.

Jubal taught himself to read at the age of three by watching over his father's shoulder as he took them through their daily Bible lesson. His father was delighted at first. He began letting Jubal do most of the reading.

But when he heard his son had started to hang around with his cousin Travis, Avery became suspicious. Everybody knew Travis was too smart for his own britches, and in Avery's experience, that smart-ass attitude could be catching.

Once Jubal realized that his ability to read the Bible carried over to hundreds of other books and magazines and newspapers, he was lost. He set out to read every book in Louisiana.

Travis got him off to a good start by loaning Jubal his textbooks, which the boy read in a night, and by checking books out of the junior high school library. Jubal had to stash them in a secret hideout he built, and read them by the light of a kerosene lamp in the middle of the night. Sometimes Travis joined him. It was the best time of Jubal's life.

One message Jesus kept repeating to Avery was "Spare the rod and spoil the child." Avery's punishments of his children for the slightest infractions of his rules and the Lord's grew increasingly harsh.

He began chastising them with an ordinary oar, cut down to a useful size, an implement virtually all of his neighbors approved of, and used on their own children's behinds. "Time-outs" and withholding of favors as ways to discipline a child had never made much headway in Avery's neck of the woods. There were frowns, though, when he began hitting them on other parts of the body. But people didn't see Avery's brood for weeks, even months at a time. Who was to know, when one of them was sighted with black eyes, bruises, or a broken arm, that their story of having had an accident was a lie? The kids all stuck by their daddy, as they'd been taught.

Avery graduated to a chopped-off pool cue, which he carried with him everywhere.

Not long after that, fifteen-year-old Veneration "Vinnie" Broussard fell fifty feet from a live oak he had climbed to get a dead possum his father had shot, which had become lodged in a branch. Or so Avery said. He explained the bruises on the boy's body as having been caused by hitting branches on the way down.

The parish coroner said that was hogwash. He counted forty-eight bruises about eight inches long, and two straight, deep depressions in his skull. The sheriff looked at the tree Veneration had allegedly fallen from and concluded there was no possible way to fall through it and receive forty-eight bruises unless those limbs were batting him back and forth, up and down, like the ball in a pinball machine.

Vinnie had lived for three days in a coma, according to Avery's testimony. Avery had sworn off hospitals since the day that "abortion doctor" ruined his Evangeline's womb before the two of them had truly started to be fruitful and multiply.

The parish prosecutor brought him to trial on a charge of second-degree murder and lesser offenses.

One of Avery's congregation was a pretty good backwoods lawyer. He concentrated on the religious freedom aspect of the case, tried to get the jury to look away from the pool cue and stand up for the right of a man not to seek conventional healing but to pray to the Almighty. It worked fairly well. Avery was sentenced to one year for manslaughter.

Jesus Christ shared his cell. From then on, Jesus was his constant companion. When Avery was brought to trial the next time, for almost killing his son Jubilation, Avery's defense lawyer sat to his left and Jesus sat on his right. Christ must have had some awfully funny stories to tell, from the way Avery would incline his head as if listening, then roar with laughter.

11

★ ★ ★

"IT IMPRESSED THE jury enough that they bought the 'not guilty by reason of insanity' defense," said Travis. "It was the first one anybody can recall in that part of the bayou. But nobody could look at Avery talking and listening to Jesus for more than about a day before they gave up on the theory that he was acting. Nobody figured Avery was *smart* enough to act that well."

Travis finished the dregs of his third coffee of the night, looked longingly at the bottle of bourbon, then held out his cup to Alicia for a refill.

"He's been in the state hospital ever since, and he won't ever get out, because all the doctors there know they will be held personally responsible by the rest of the Broussards if Avery is ever judged sane and released. And also because Avery doesn't really want out. He's perfectly happy to sit and visit with Jesus all day, every day, and that's just what he's been doing all this time."

He sat back in his seat, looking at a spot slightly over our heads. I shifted around, trying to get comfortable. Travis had talked for a long time, and I don't think I so much as twitched during most of it. I told myself that the next time I was feeling sorry for myself for being poor and fatherless, I'd think about Jubal's youth.

"How bad was Jubal hurt?" Alicia asked.

Travis focused on us again.

"Very bad. It started with Jesus whispering in Avery's ear again. It turns out Jesus was a snitch, and a liar. While Avery was serving his six months with six off for good behavior, Jesus told Avery me and Jubal were 'sodomites, buggers, and nancyboys,' and it was reading sinful stuff made us go bad.

"Avery found Jubal's stash and spent a whole afternoon leafing through it. There was a biology textbook that discussed evolution, other sinful things, too. Avery lay in wait, and when we showed up that afternoon he lit into Jubal. He didn't have his pool cue. He had found a two-by-four and driven some nails into it.

"He hit me once with it, backhand. I don't know whether I was just lucky or he didn't intend to strike me with the nail side. I've still got a scar, right here . . ." He fingered a spot near his hairline where I'd noticed a faint scar before.

"Then he started in on Jubal. I don't know how many times he hit him, all I could do was sit there in a daze. The doctors found four punctures that went through his skull and into his brain. Both his arms and most of his ribs were broken.

"I ran away while he was still beating Jubal. I . . . I still have nightmares about it, and I will probably always blame myself."

"Not fair," Kelly said. "You were too small to stop him."

"I should have thought of something. I've thought of plenty things since. Get on his blind side, hit him with a stick, stand off and chuck rocks at him . . . hurt him or distract him. But I didn't think of any of those things, so I ran for the nearest house, which was about a mile away. Two very large men, the Charles brothers, came back with me. Avery had built an altar. Jesus had told Avery to offer Jubal up to God, like Abraham with Isaac. God was bluffing, but Avery wasn't. They got Jubal off the altar, put out the fire, and got Jubal to a hospital. On the way the Charles brothers didn't quite kill Avery, but they bloodied him up something awful.

"Jubal had so much brain damage the doctors didn't think he'd ever walk or talk again. He might not even be able to feed himself. That didn't matter, because I intended to take care of him for the rest of his life.

"His brothers and sisters wouldn't allow that, though. They told me to go on and get my college education, and they'd take care of Jubal. And they did. He never lacked for any material thing from the day his daddy almost killed him to the day I moved him here to be with me, seven years ago. His memories before the beating are almost nonexistent."

"He told us about his only Christmas," I said. I was going to say more, but suddenly felt I might start to cry if I did. My only memory of my own father is a very hazy one from Christmas day. He is rolling a Tonka truck toward me, making sputtering sounds, and I am laughing. I think I was four.

Kelly took my hand and squeezed it.

"That Christmas story gives you just a glimpse of what Avery was like. Jubal remembers a few things about reading with me in our hideout. He remembers the day I sneaked him into the picture show. It was *Deliverance.* You know what part Jubal liked? The rushing water. The mountains and cliffs they went through. Jubal had never been more than twenty miles from home, mountain streams were new to him.

"Anyway, he's shown he's able to relearn things, and frankly, many of his memories of living with his family are better lost, anyway.

"Jubal is still as smart as he ever was, and you can believe it or not, up to you, but I'm talking Einstein, Hawking, Edison, Dyson. A few years after the assault I showed him Einstein's equation, *E* equals *mc* squared. Jubal said, 'What dat big *E* fo'?' I told him, and he asked about the *m*. 'An de *c*?' I told him it was the speed of light. He looked at it for a second or two, and grinned, and said, "Dis gonna upset all dat Newton stuff you showed me. Gonna make a big bang, too.' In the next hour I fed him more data and a few equations, and he pretty much deduced the General Theory of Relativity.

"That mind still works, but not always according to the laws of logic you and I know. But amazing things can come out of that mind."

He looked down at the silver bubble he had been playing with.

"Like that," he said. "That . . . that violates just about every law of physics I was ever taught. And something that different, something that violates so many rules . . . well, friends and neighbors, that scares me."

"Jubal was making them for some sort of target-shooting game," I told him. "Or to put on Christmas trees."

"Yeah, that's pure Jubal," Travis said.

We were all silent again for a time. Jubal wanted to use the silver bubbles as children's toys, but it was pretty obvious they meant a lot more than that. Just *what* they meant was still an open question.

Which Travis meant to solve. He got up from his seat and stretched. Then he looked at all of us again, in turn.

"I told you, I'd be a lot happier if it was just Jubal and me aware of this."

"We won't steal anything from you," Dak said.

"I trust you guys more than anybody I know."

"Because we didn't rob you on the beach?" Alicia laughed. "I'll fess up, I told Dak he ought to take a hundred for the taxi service."

"You had a right to," Travis said.

"And you said yourself you've used up all your friends but us. Who else *is* there for you to trust, except Jubal?"

"Do you ever pull any punches, lady?"

"Not that I ever saw," Dak said, standing and stretching, too. "So what do you want from us, man? Swear us to secrecy?"

"Until we've had a chance to learn more about it from Jubal."

"I'm okay behind that. What about the rest of you, musketeers? All for one . . ."

"And one for all . . ."

IT WAS JUST starting to get a little light in the east when Travis, Kelly, and I found Jubal out on the lake. When Jubal was rowing at night, he hung an old kerosene lamp from a davit in the bow, just as his father had done in the Louisiana bayous when out hunting at night. We could see it from some distance, flickering like an orange firefly.

Travis's boat was about what you'd expect from a guy who had been letting a Mercedes cook in the Florida sunshine. It was low, fast, and plush, with a tiny cabin and head up front and room to seat six or seven in the open in back. But it was showing distress from the indifferent care it had been getting since drinking became a full-time occupation for Travis. Some of the seat material was cracking and there were patches where green slime was growing on the Fiberglas.

The big Mercury outboard seemed healthy, though. It started at once, and then burbled with quiet authority as we pulled away from the dock.

We eased up from behind. He didn't acknowledge us in any way. I was amazed at the speed he was making in the old craft. It was easy to see how he got the big arms.

"I'm sorry, Jubal," Travis said. "I shouldn't have snapped at you like that."

"Don't matter none, no," Jubal said. And kept rowing. Travis kept us off to Jubal's right and just behind the sweep of his oars.

"We'd all like to see those target bubbles again, Jube, see what they can do."

"Dey don' do much," he said. "Jus' go *pop!*" He giggled.

"Maybe you could show us how," Travis suggested.

"What I be out here fo'," Jubal admitted, and now his brow furrowed. "Tryin' to 'member how dey works."

"You mean you can't make any more?"

"No, *cher,* no, I can make plenty wit' de squeezy t'ing I show you. I tryin' to member how I make de *Squeezer.*"

"It'll come to you, *mon ami,*" Travis said.

"Mebbe yeah, mebbe no."

"Come on, Jube, let me tow you in, we'll have us some *petty dejournez.*"

Kelly leaned over the side of the boat with an open cardboard box. "We got Krispy Kremes, Jubal," she said.

Jubal's steady rowing pace faltered. Kelly angled the box so he could see inside it.

"Only one lef', *cher,*" he said. "I don' take you las' Krispy, no."

"More coming, *cher,*" Kelly said. "Can you smell 'em?" It was clear he could. Finally he grinned and tossed a rope to Travis, who tied it to a cleat at the stern of his boat. Kelly and I helped Jubal aboard, and we turned around and headed back home through the early morning light. There was a mist on the water, and a small V of ducks arrived, quacking loudly, and settled gently on the lake. I put my arm around Kelly. It showed signs of becoming a good day.

SWAMP BIRDS AND other critters were greeting the day when Travis, Jubal, Kelly, and I walked the path back from the lake, with its crunching covering of new white shell. Dak and Alicia were pulling up in *Blue Thunder.*

It seemed that Krispy Kremes were Jubal's biggest weakness. They were Travis's last resort. If he really *had* to get Jubal's undivided attention, he offered him donuts.

"Gotta be careful, though," Travis had said. "Jubal would live on nothing but Krispys if he could drive a car to go get them."

"Like driving a spike straight into his own heart," Alicia told us.

"Would you believe Jubal was a skinny little thing when he lived on the bayou? Not much sugar in his diet out there, lots of rice and fish, collards and mustard greens and poke salads. He's got a sweet tooth you wouldn't believe."

Dak had wanted to get three dozen, but Alicia held him down to two. They also brought back supersized paper mugs of Mississippi Mud espresso. We all gathered around the patio table and the food. All of us were yawning.

We dug in like wild javelinas, Alicia watching in horror and volunteering to make some oatmeal if anybody wanted it. But it wasn't an oatmeal morning, and eventually even she admitted it and ate two donuts. I don't even want to know how many sit-ups she did that day to make up for it.

At last we all sat back, and I watched Jubal cleaning up the donut boxes like a kid licking the cake icing out of a bowl. He saw me looking at him, and we grinned.

Travis had brought the Squeezer out and set it on the table. Jubal eyed it unhappily, but finally settled back and laced his fingers over his big belly.

"Jube," Travis said, "I'd like to ask you some questions about this thing, what it does, how it does it . . . and so forth. I'm *not* angry, *mon cher,* and I'm not going to get angry later. We're just trying to find out, okay?"

"Fire away, Travis," Jubal said. "Mebbe you get lucky, you." And he laughed.

"So, what's in the bubbles, Jubal?"

"In dese bubbles? Jus' air. Nuttin' but air."

"So you . . . you make this silvery stuff . . ."

"A force field," Jubal said. "Like in de comics books."

"A force field. You've lost me already."

"Los' me, too, mos'ly. It don' really ack like nuthin' else I know from de books."

"From your physics textbooks."

"From *any* my books." He frowned, then looked surprised. "It don' take no power, no. No power to make de bubbles, no power to move 'em roun'."

"You've lost me," Dak said. Travis nodded.

"No power. Lookee here." He popped open the battery chamber of the Squeezer. The two AA batteries that would normally be there were missing. Wires had been soldered to the two little springs that normally would have touched the bottom part of the battery cylinders. The wires went through two holes that seemed to have been burned with a soldering iron.

"Dis gizmo here, dis be de part initiate de bubbles. Dis part, it take de . . . de . . . it take de framework an it *twis'* it, ninety degrees from ever'thin' else, so it ain't really here in dis . . . dis . . . space-time condominimum." When he mangled that last word, Jubal's almost impenetrable Cajun accent was nearly gone. I could tell that talking about science was hard for him. His basic vocabulary was limited to the words he learned growing up, and everything he had learned since then was the result of incredibly hard work. Clearly, the idea of a space-time continuum was not one that got a lot of discussion down on the Broussard bayou.

"No power," Jubal repeated. He took a huge Swiss Army knife from the pocket of his khaki Dockers, pulled out a thin blade. He peeled back a corner of duct tape, then popped that remote open.

You didn't need a degree in electronics to tell the inside of the remote hadn't looked that way when it came off the Sony assembly line. There was something in there that had started life as a printed circuit board, but pieces of it had been roughly sawed off—maybe with the saw blade of Jubal's Swiss Army knife. There was a rubber band holding two parts together, and what might have been a big glob of Elmer's glue. And other things. Right in the middle were two pieces of bright metal that I had to stare at for a moment before realizing they were the snipped-off barbs of fishhooks.

"Dis where de continimum get twisted," Jubal said, pointing with a finger callused from rowing. "Dis where de six-D-space get cut down to fo', which has to cover itself up." Jubal laughed. "Oderwise, it be a nekkid sinfularity."

I translated: six-dimensional space, naked singularity.

"Jubal . . . maybe you just ought to show us what it can do," Travis said. "And explain what's happening, if you can. Can you do that?"

"I can do dat." He picked up the Squeezer, closed it back up. "To make a bubble," he said, "all you got do is punch de little button here. De one used to say 'Play.' I done scrotched de word 'squeeze' here under it, see?" He showed it around. He frowned at it. "I ain't perzackly sure I done spell 'er right. I don't spell so good, me. Is dis right?" He showed it to Dak.

"Jube," Dak said, "the things this gizmo can do, I think you'll have everybody spelling it your way."

"A whole new verb," Kelly agreed.

Jubal didn't look convinced, but shrugged and pointed the Squeezer into the air. He pressed the button with his thumb, and a silver bubble the size of a baseball appeared out of thin air.

"De space done *twis'* itself, see?" He looked at us, slowly realized none of us had any idea what he was talking about. "Dis button here, dis lock it. Hold dat rascal in place." He waved the Squeezer around, and the silver bubble stayed exactly three feet from the business end of the device, no matter how quickly Jubal cut it back and forth.

"She work jus' on de ball," Jubal explained. "Now, dis button turn de bubble back t'ru ninety degree, all on a sudden." He pressed the button marked STOP, and the bubble was gone.

"Now I make me anudder . . ." He pressed the SQUOZE button again, and an exact duplicate of the first bubble appeared. "Shoulda call her de TWIS' button, me, but I done dis befo' I done realyize what goin' on.

"Okay. Now, I twis' dis dial rat cheer, and de bubble, she squeeze down some." The bubble shrank until it was BB sized. Jubal thumbed the control several times, turning the dial after each bubble was formed, until we had half a dozen silver BBs floating in the air above the picnic table.

"Now de fun part," Jubal said with a big grin. He pointed at one of the BBs and fired. Kelly jumped a little as the BB vanished with a bang, about as loud as a firecracker.

Jubal grinned wider as he aimed and shot at the rest of the BBs.

"De air, it be compress, see? Den when de bubble go away . . . *Boom!*" He was happy as a kid with his first air rifle, only Jubal's BBs exploded.

"Let me see it, Jube," Travis said. Jubal handed it over. Travis studied it, then hit the SQUOZE button to create a bubble. He looked happy, too. He slowly turned the dial, and the bubble shrunk.

"So you can make them larger, too, right?"

"Dat right, Travis. Jus' click dat little clicker dere de odder way, to de lef' . . ."

Travis held the Squeezer in front of him, squinting, and he turned the wheel . . .

He didn't turn it much, maybe about an inch. If an inch in the one direction had made a golf ball squeeze down to a BB, it seemed logical that an inch in the other direction would expand a golf ball to . . . oh, maybe a softball. None of us but Jubal knew the scale was not linear, and Travis had inadvertently moved the switch two clicks to the left instead of one. . . .

The Richter scale, for earthquakes, is logarithmic, which means an 8 is *ten times* the force of a 7. . . .

Jubal's device was not logarithmic, it was *exponential*. Which meant the expand/contract wheel on the Squeezer was now *one hundred times* more sensitive . . .

The weird thing is that nobody saw it for a couple of seconds. The bubble, floating three feet above the business end of the Squeezer, suddenly seemed to warp in a weird way. I felt a breeze strong enough to muss up my hair, and saw Kelly's hair blown around, then I finally looked up.

And saw myself, looking down.

It took another second for my mind to adjust to what I was seeing. Somebody had hung a perfect mirror, three feet above us. Looking up, I saw five people with their mouths hanging open, sitting in chairs around an upside-down picnic table.

When Travis saw it, he gave an involuntary twitch . . . which probably saved us all from "a world a hurtin'," as Jubal said later, because his thumb twitched on the PUSH/PULL button, and the bubble immediately rose to about fifty feet over our heads, just as I had been reaching up to touch it. The bubble had been *that* close.

"Jesus," Travis whispered, still staring up.

And I saw his finger going to the OFF button . . . and I lunged toward the Squeezer in his hand as Jubal shouted, *"Travis, no!"* . . . and Travis pushed the button.

I've ridden out two hurricanes . . . from a safe distance inland, Mom maintaining the Blast-Off wasn't worth dying for. Neither of them were square hits, but I know what a seventy-mile-per-hour wind feels like.

This was worse.

With no warning at all, like a flash of lightning, we were swept up in a howling gale. There was a clap of thunder, too. I was lifted along with my aluminum chair. Kelly was blown into the air with me, and we managed to hold on to each other's hands. For a second or two we were swirling around in the funnel of a tornado, like Dorothy Gale, only she had a house all around her when she took off for Oz. Something bumped me in the side, hard. It was the picnic table. Leaves and dirt sprayed over us. I realized we were both in the air, maybe ten feet off the ground.

Then, almost as quickly as it began, the storm let up. I felt myself falling, still holding on to Kelly's hand.

I fell headfirst into the swimming pool.

I could hardly tell up from down, there was so much trash swirling around. I had lost my grip on Kelly's hand, and that worried me. But I finally got myself oriented and kicked for the surface.

I came up looking right at Kelly, who spit out some water, brushed her wet hair out of her eyes . . . then pointed behind me and shrieked. I turned around and probably shouted, too, because a giant alligator was no more than five feet from me, and it seemed to be headed my way. . . .

Goddam rubber alligator. I'd disliked it from the first time I saw it.

"Is anybody hurt? Is everybody okay?" It was Travis shouting, I could see him running along the edge of the pool. I looked around and saw Jubal and Dak, chins out of the water. The pool surface was almost solid with dry leaves and grass and sticks and even some fairly large branches. I saw the picnic table, floating with just an inch of the tabletop above the water. I saw an empty cardboard box that used to hold Krispy Kremes.

What I didn't see was Alicia.

We all started calling her name. Travis was looking frantically around him, in case she hadn't been thrown into the pool. Dak immediately began diving, and I tried to, but the water was so thick with dirt and leaves she could have been two feet away and I wouldn't have seen her.

I came to the surface about the same time Kelly did. She shook her head, looking scared, and I probably did, too. It had only been fifteen or twenty seconds, but it felt like an hour. I saw Dak surface . . . and then Alicia came out from under the floating picnic table. I relaxed slightly. What a relief.

"She's bleeding! She's bleeding!" Dak shouted, and swam to her as best he could with all the debris in his way. Travis was running around the

pool to where Alicia was, and he got to her before Dak and pulled her from the water.

"Call a doctor! Call nine-one-one!" Dak was shouting. Travis had her in his arms and was examining her face.

"It's okay, Dak," Alicia called out. "I'm not hurt bad."

Dak pulled himself out and ran to her, and hugged her.

"Just a bloody nose," Travis said. "I don't think it's broken." Then he turned away from the two and looked bleakly at the ground. It was easy to see he was kicking himself for the dumb stunt he just pulled. Well, he ought to, I thought. But we got lucky, like I said. If that bubble, which must have been five hundred feet across, had been only three feet above us when it vanished, and the air all around us had instantly rushed in to fill the vacuum . . .

That's what it was, of course. That's what Jubal and I had seen just at the moment it became too late to do anything about it. If squeezing a bubble compressed the air that was trapped inside, then expanding one with only a golf ball's worth of air inside to the size of the Goodyear blimp was going to make one hell of a good vacuum.

Travis had been thrown against the brick barbecue and managed to hang on until the wind died. Just about everything else in the backyard lighter than Jubal or the picnic table had been swept into the air, most of it coming down in the pool. All five of us landed in the pool . . . another stroke of luck, I realized, that the pool had been filled the day before. I had come down headfirst, from at least twenty feet in the air. . . .

TRAVIS'S HOUSE HAD three full bathrooms, all of them with big showers. Kelly and I took one. It wasn't until I got there that I began to feel any pain. Excitement desensitizes you, I think, pumps some good chemicals in your blood so you can keep functioning, injured, until you're away from danger.

Then the chemicals go away, and you start to hurt.

I had my pants unzipped and was starting to pull them down when I felt a sharp stab in my side.

"I think I may have cracked a rib," I said. My shirt was torn on my left side, and there was some blood. Kelly carefully lifted the shirt and we looked at a rough scrape there at the bottom of my rib cage. The flesh around it was already a big purplish-yellow bruise. Kelly pressed gently above the bruise.

"Does it hurt when I do this?"

"It would if you pressed any harder." She moved her hand below the bruise.

"How about this?"

"Yes." I looked at her face, soaking wet, hair tangled with some dried leaves stuck in it, looking intently at my bruised side. Her shirt was open and her nipples crinkled from the water and the air conditioning, which Travis liked to keep set around the North Pole. She looked up and smiled. She reached down into my pants.

"How about this? Hurt?" she asked.

"Hurt me," I said. Then we were kissing, and trying to wriggle out of our wet clothes at the same time. Wet jeans are the worst, and Kelly's were pretty tight even when they were dry. It didn't help that pretty soon we were laughing, then I'd gasp from a pain in my side and we'd try to be careful, and start laughing again. She was shivering, too, wet and cold. Finally we made it into the shower stall and turned on the hot water and made love there, she being careful not to touch my side, me not really caring.

We managed to get each other all soapy before one thing led to another again, and by the time *that* wave had crested we'd used up all Travis's hot water.

"What are we going to wear?" she asked as we got out.

"Towels, I guess," I said. "I'll go see if Travis has anything."

I wrapped a big towel around me. When I opened the door there was a pile of clean clothing there on the floor. I brought it in and held things up, one at a time. Two pairs of Bermuda shorts in Travis's size, and two of Jubal's tentlike Hawaiian shirts.

"Who gets the hula girls, and who gets the surfer dudes?" I asked her.

"Surfer dudes for me, dude," she said, and I tossed the shirt to her.

The shorts were a few inches too wide for me. The other pair were a tad tight in the hips and loose in the waist for Kelly. Both of us were almost swallowed by the shirts.

I heard a clothes dryer, found it at the end of the hall, and tossed our clothes in with Dak's and Alicia's, then found our way to the living room.

Alicia had a Band-Aid on her nose where it had been cut slightly, but it wasn't broken. If any of us had been hit much harder than I had been by the picnic table we surely would have had some broken bones, but Alicia had hurt herself coming up beneath the table, not while we swirled through the air. Jubal and Kelly and Travis and Dak hadn't been hurt at all.

"We got lucky," Travis said. "I'm very sorry, ladies and gents, I didn't know what sort of tiger's tail I was twisting. My apologies."

"It's okay, Trav," Dak said.

"No, it's not okay. It's not okay at all. I'm going to have to ask you all to just go home today. I don't want anybody else around while me and Jubal sit down and figure out just what we've got here."

"We aren't afraid, Travis," Kelly said, surprising me. She looked at the rest of us. "Well, we aren't, are we?"

"Not me," Dak said.

"I *am* afraid," Travis said. "Not of blowing up my own old ass, but of hurting one of you children. I couldn't live with that."

"You couldn't if we were children, which we are not," Alicia said. "It's Jubal's gizmo. What do you think, Jubal?"

Everybody looked at him, and Jubal seemed to shrink.

"Oh, *cher* . . . I don' know, me . . . I mean . . ." Alicia realized a decision like that was far beyond the man's capabilities. She put her arm around his shoulder and whispered something in his ear, which seemed to cheer him up. He grinned at her.

"Jubal will go with his family, like always," Travis said, not unkindly. "You can all come back tomorrow, and I'll fill you in on what we've found out."

"That's cool," Dak said. "Come on, folks, let's hit the road before the morning rush hour starts."

"Not for another thirty minutes or so," Alicia said, looking at her watch, which seemed to have survived the dunking.

"What, you like traffic, babe?" Dak asked her.

"No, I like my own dry clothes. I'm not going to be seen in public in Jubal's shirt and Travis's pants. I got my reputation to consider."

12

★ ★ ★

I'D BEEN FALLING behind on my work at the Blast-Off, so I tore through piled-up chores that morning as well as I could with a bruised rib. I had the noon-to-six shift that day. I really should have taken Mom's six-to-midnight, too, as she had covered for me twice that week . . . but I couldn't. I fell asleep twice in the desk chair behind the reservation computer as it was.

At six, Kelly pulled into the lot at the wheel of a sexy little red Corvette. In addition to having the bitchin'est new cars in town, Strickland Mercedes gets the best trade-ins. Sometimes Kelly decides to test drive them for a day or two. What a hard life she has.

She hurried into the office. I could see she was as excited as me to get back to Rancho Broussard and see what Travis had found out. But Mom was there, too, so time had to be made for a hug and a kiss and a short chat. Mom approves of Kelly. Aside from being beautiful and rich, Kelly has been known to help us with some chores she has probably *never* had to do at her own house. How could a mother possibly object? So she pecked Kelly on the cheek and watched us climb into the red death machine, and waved as we pulled out of the lot.

* * *

WE SPOTTED *BLUE* *Thunder* a quarter mile ahead of us soon after we got off the Pike. Kelly pressed the accelerator and we caught up with Dak without taxing the engine much. With a short toot on the horn, Kelly pulled past and then let the Corvette have its head for a bit. *Blue Thunder* was just a blue dot in the mirror when Kelly hit 90 mph.

We passed the jackleg backwoods church with all the signs again. There was a guy up on a ladder painting one of them. He was a little guy, in his seventies, dressed in paint-spattered overalls with no shirt. His bare arms looked incredibly scrawny, but I'll bet he could have arm-wrestled me to death. I know this type of peckerwood, they work hard all their lives and why we don't have guys like that lifting weights at the Olympics I'll never know. There were a couple dozen open cans of what looked like interior latex sitting on the ground, all bright colors.

He was actually getting pretty good results. I'd sure seen worse roadside art, anyway. Nobody was ever likely to hang his stuff in a museum, but I liked it a lot better than that dude who slung paint at canvases and then sold his crap for thousands of dollars, and his stuff *is* hanging in museums.

He'd erected a few more four-by-eight slabs of grade-Z plywood, riddled with knotholes, and was creating new signs on them. He'd already altered some of his old ones.

"Looks like he's had a new revelation," Kelly said.

"Born again, again," I suggested.

I saw Jesus several times on the signs, with a face as mournful as a basset hound. Blood was flowing from his thorny crown. He was on the cross in one picture, preaching on a mountaintop in another. And in a new one, he seemed to be coming down a ramp from a flying saucer. It looked like the one in *The Day the Earth Stood Still.* He probably saw that movie when he was twenty. A new sign read:

JESUS IS HERE
IN HIS FLYING SAWSER

DO YOU HAVE YOUR
HEAVENLY BORDING PASS?

The sign he was working on read:

EZEKIEL SAW THE WHEE

He stopped his work and glared at us as we passed.

We turned the corner onto the Broussards' private road . . . and Kelly slammed on the brakes. There was a heavy chain suspended between two posts, with a NO TRESPASSING sign hanging from it. We sat there looking at it for a while, then heard *Blue Thunder* sliding to a stop behind us. Kelly and I got out of the car. Alicia and Dak joined us at the chain.

"Looks like we've been stood up," I said.

"And me with my brand new party dress," Dak said. "Damn."

Nobody said anything for a while. Dak kicked at the loose shell a few times, then once more, *hard,* for luck.

"Should we walk in?" Alicia wondered. "He did say he'd see us today."

"You think so?" Dak said. "I think the chain is pretty clear." He showed us the shiny new—and very heavy-duty—padlock. "They're avoiding us. We get to the house, nobody's gonna answer the door."

"I think he's right," I said.

WHEN WE GOT back to the Blast-Off the parking lot was almost full of the kind of twenty-year-old vehicles normal for the early evening, with a smattering of even older rattletraps that would be classics if they weren't so rusted out. And parked close to the office in the yellow-striped "Manager" spot was a low, wide, brawny civilian version of the military HumVee, or Hummer. It was black and red, and looked as if it had just been driven off the showroom floor.

"Gotta be Travis," Kelly said.

Dak and I paused for a moment to admire the thing, so we were a few steps behind Alicia and Kelly as they ducked around the front desk and into the apartment behind. There was a great smell coming from back there, and laughter.

Jubal, Travis, and my mom were sitting around the worktable in the living room. Aunt Maria was just coming through the kitchen door with a steaming tray full of fried plantains and conch fritters. She set it on the table and scooped up a big bowl with tortilla chips at the bottom and another bowl that had held some of her famous homemade salsa, and headed back into the kitchen.

"Smells mighty good, Maria." Travis ate a plantain from the tray.

"Real good, ma'am," Jubal said, munching one. There was a salsa stain in his beard and another on his shirt.

The worktable is just an ordinary ten-foot folding cafeteria table. It's usually covered with junk, knickknacks in various stages of assembly.

Aunt Maria is artistic. She had tried her hand at hundreds of kinds of handmade souvenirs until she found the best money-maker, which was shell sculpture. She made little tableaux of shell people, mostly with clam shells but with small cone and spiral shells and bits of coral and other stuff, stuck together with glue and clear silicone. She made shell families standing before shell houses, shell golfers swinging bobby-pin irons, shell surfers on oyster-shell boards hanging ten on shell waves, shell dogs peeing on shell fire hydrants. Some of her larger scenes were based on abalone shells, or conch shells sawed open. No two creations were alike, and we sold a lot of them.

My mother is not so artistic. While Aunt Maria glues her shells together, Mom paints four-inch plastic replicas of the Blast-Off Motel sign, mounts them on bases, and puts them in clear globes with water and plastic snow or glitter. *Snowing in Florida?* is usually the first thing the tourists say, but then a surprising number buy one.

Over the years we've made and sold dozens of different kinds of kitschy items like the snow globe and the shell people. I put out a plywood sandwich board every morning advertising SOUVENIRS, LOWEST PRICES IN TOWN. It made the difference between staying open and filing for bankruptcy, sometimes.

Jubal was sitting on a folding chair at one end of the table, bent over a "tree" of six plastic Blast-Off signs, all connected like the parts of a polystyrene airplane model kit before you break them off. He would frown intently at the sign, laboriously trace one of the letters with a fine paintbrush, then sit back to regard his work. He saw me looking at him and held up another tree he had finished.

"You ever made none of dese, Manuel?" he asked. *About ten thousand,* I thought.

"A few, Jubal. I've made a few."

"I'm makin' a dozen, me. You mama, she—"

"Betty," Mom said, smiling at Jubal.

"You Betty, she give me dis one here." He picked up a finished globe and shook it up, hard, then held it up and watched the snow swirl. "I never see no snow, me," he said.

"One day, Jubal, one day," Travis said. He was sitting between Mom and Aunt Maria's empty chair, working on some unidentifiable shell sculpture. There was glue on his fingers and a small patch of his hair was standing straight up with silicone sealer in it. He seemed to be enjoying himself.

I suddenly felt feverish and a little sick to my stomach. I needed some fresh air. The closest way was through the kitchen.

Aunt Maria was in there, cooking up a huge pot of her famous picadillo. Nothing makes Maria happier than new mouths to feed, and I could tell from the empty jars on the stove that she was pulling out all the stops. Picadillo is basically just beef hash, but then you add olives and raisins and *huevos estilo cubano* and three or four kinds of peppers, pickled or fresh, all of them hot. We had it fairly often, but without all the trimmings and with cheaper cuts of meat than Maria was using today. I could smell her wonderful coconut bread baking in the oven.

No friend of mine could possibly enter Mom's and Aunt Maria's house without being offered food and invited to stay for dinner. Anything else was unthinkable. But the snack would be nachos and salsa and the dinner would usually be macaroni and cheese until they knew you better. The plantains and fritters and picadillo told me that Travis and Jubal had charmed them pretty quickly.

I hurried out the back of the kitchen, which led to the busy street outside. I couldn't seem to get a good breath, so I walked up and down the sidewalk for a bit, and finally started feeling better.

I watched from the street corner as our back door opened again and Travis stepped out. He was dressed a lot like Jubal today, with sandals and a Hawaiian shirt. He cupped his hands and lit one of the short, thin cigars he smoked every once in a while, then stood there with his hands in the pockets of his shorts, looking up at the Golden Manatee. For a moment, in profile, I could see the family resemblance with Jubal.

He caught sight of me, and ambled down the sidewalk.

"Bummer about the hotel," he said, pointing at the Manatee.

"Lot of bummers around here," I said.

"Shouldn't let it get you down, though. Maria sent me out to get a few things. She said there was a good bodega around here somewhere. . . ." He looked up and down the street.

"A few blocks inland," I said. "I'll take you."

WE DIDN'T SAY anything for the first block. I could tell he was watching me.

"I like your family," he said after a while.

"What there is of it," I said.

"What's that mean?"

"Means my father is dead. My mother's parents won't speak to her because she married a spic. My dad and Maria's family won't speak to my mom because she's a gringa and they blame her that my dad's dead."

"Yeah? Well, you're better off not knowing assholes like that."

"My dad's family, the Garcias, could help us put the motel on a good financial footing, maybe help us sell it. Mom won't hear of it, of course."

"Goes without saying, Manny. That's one of the reasons she's good people. She won't kiss anyone's ass."

"Instead, we turn our living room into a third-world sweatshop."

Travis puffed a few times on his cigar, which had almost gone out.

"You got nothing to be ashamed of. It's honest work."

"I just wish you had . . . maybe given me some warning. . . ."

"So you could fold up the table and vacuum and dust? That's what Betty said when I knocked on the door. Ninety-nine out of a hundred women would have said the same thing, whether they lived in a pigsty or a place as clean as yours. I'll say it once more: Don't be ashamed of them, or of your work, or of yourself.

"Happens to most of us, Manny," Travis went on. "Rich or poor, we get ashamed of Mom and Dad and what they do, or how they talk, or how they don't have any money or how they have too *much* money, the dirty capitalist pigs.

"The year I started school, my dad was out on strike. Money was very tight. You want humiliation, try showing up for the first day of first grade in a pair of Kmart sneakers with holes in the sides and have half the school calling you a barefoot coon-ass. I ran all the way home and cussed my daddy with every step."

I mulled that over while we shopped, mostly for fresh fruits and vegetables. I could see Tia Maria was going to set out a Cubano feast we might all be a week recovering from. Travis paid with a hundred-dollar bill, which Mr. Ortega, the greengrocer, held up to the light and examined suspiciously before making change. We packed most of the greens in a plastic bag, and the heavier stuff in Aunt Maria's souvenir mesh shopping bag from the Bahamas, which Travis produced from his pocket.

We stopped on the sidewalk outside, and Travis got out his wallet again. He counted out thirty hundreds, folded them once, and held the money out to me. I made a move toward it, pure reflex, then backed off a step.

"What's happening here, Manny, is I'm going to have to go off for a while. I haven't learned much yet about the silver bubbles, but I know some people in various places who will give me an hour or two with some very large and expensive machines, and they won't ask to see what I'm doing and they won't blab about it later. I'll be going to Huntsville, Houston, and Cal Tech, and maybe all the way up to Boston. I'll be gone at least a week, maybe two weeks.

"Now, Jubal ain't a dog, and he ain't a child, but I can't leave him alone at the ranch for that long. Just can't do it.

"So I arranged with your mother to get a room for Jubal at the Blast-Off. He'll do fine there, so long as he knows Maria and Betty are around somewhere. He's okay with walking down to the Burger King by himself. I'm paying for his grub in advance. If y'all would take him to the movies a time or two, I'd really appreciate it."

I wanted to grab him and shake him and shout out *Take me with you!* But I knew he wouldn't, and I really couldn't get away, either, with the extra burden of work Jubal's presence was likely to bring about. So I took a deep breath and nodded, and Travis stuffed the money in my shirt pocket before I could stop him.

"Betty wouldn't take the money in advance, so this is how we'll do it. You give her the bread after I've eased on down the road. Okay?"

"O . . . okay," I said.

"Good enough," he said, slapping me on the shoulder. I didn't say anything.

Two weeks of baby-sitting—in spite of what Travis said—a 230-pound semiautistic genius second-grader with attention deficit disorder, or something very much like it.

Oh, boy. I could hardly wait.

IT WAS WELL past dark when we all finally managed to refuse another slice of pie and push away from the table. Travis wouldn't hear of leaving the apartment until the dishes were washed and dried and put away, with his help. Mom and Maria wouldn't hear of letting him help. I thought they might get into a very polite fistfight until Kelly and Alicia took him by the arms and hustled him out of the kitchen, which was crowded with only two people trying to work. So then Mom and Maria had to chase Kelly and Alicia out, too, and finally things could be cleaned.

Travis decided he would help me at the front desk then, and watched over my shoulder as I checked in the late-night trade. We don't rent to women we know are prostitutes, but we don't know all of them. As for the other couples who check in at ten and are gone by eleven, what are you gonna do? None of our business.

A few minutes before midnight, when I was about to turn off the VACANCY sign, I got called to one of the rooms with fresh towels, and when I got back Travis was checking in the last couple of the night. He was frowning at the computer screen, then slowly shook his head.

"I'm sorry, sir," he said, "but we already have a 'Tom Smith' checked in. We don't want to cause any confusion. But you could be Bob Smith, or Bill Smith."

The guy looked confused and I thought he might get angry, but his girlfriend or bar pickup got it, and laughed.

"Bob will be fine, won't it, Bob?"

Bob put his cash down on the counter and Travis gave him a key and waved them out the door. Dak was there, and twisted the key in the lock, then sat down on the floor, unable to hold in his laughter anymore. Kelly came in and looked at him.

"What's his problem?"

"Come on," I said, "let's get Travis out of here before he puts us out of business."

I'VE GOT TO admit, Travis really knew how to sweeten the pot.

There was an old Triumph motorcycle in the back of the Hummer. We wrestled it out and set it on the ground, then pulled out an old sidecar. Travis showed me how to attach the sidecar to the bike.

"All it really needs is some paint," he said. "Runs like a top. Jubal is the world's worst driver, don't ask me why. Anyway, he loves to go for rides in this thing. He likes to go real fast. I trust you'll keep it below about Mach one, not cause any sonic booms."

He showed me where to put the key, how to start it. He was right, the thing purred like a kitten. At that moment there probably wasn't a happier man in Florida than me.

Dak and Alicia, and Mom and Maria came out to see him off. Mom knew there was something going on we hadn't told her about, but she kept quiet about it. Travis was paying his way and seemed to be good people, so that was enough . . . for now. Mom shook his hand and Maria actually gave him a hug. Then Travis hugged Kelly and Alicia, climbed into his outrageous suburban assault vehicle, and pulled out on the almost deserted streets of Daytona.

I looked up and saw Jubal standing at the second-floor railing in front of his room, watching Travis's Hummer out of sight. He turned and went back inside.

13

★ ★ ★

I SETTLED JUBAL into the room next to mine with a set of our best big towels, not the little scratchy ones nobody bothers to steal from the regular rooms. The television was one of our best ones, too. I showed him how to use the remote . . . feeling pretty silly halfway through the demonstration when I remembered this was the guy who turned remotes into magic wands with no batteries.

He had brought a very old suitcase made out of thick cardboard, stuffed with Hawaiian shirts and Bermuda shorts and lots of clean underwear with—I swear—JUBAL written on the elastic band in black felt tip. I wondered just how big a deal was this for Jubal, being away from Travis? Part of him was perpetually twelve, I kept reminding myself.

I helped him stow his stuff away and headed back to my room, fifteen feet away. It had been a long and eventful night. I was dead on my feet.

AN HOUR LATER I still hadn't managed to get to sleep. I was thinking about too many things.

Jubal, and the responsibility I had assumed for him.

Travis and his mysterious mission.

The Squeezer, and all it might mean.

Kelly, and why she had decided to drive home instead of spend the night.

The Triumph, what it would be like to ride it tomorrow, where to go, whether or not Travis would sell, and if he'd take payments or if I should just offer to cut off my right arm and give him that.

There was a knock on my door and I jumped out of bed. Kelly? But before I got to the door I knew who I'd find there. Sure enough.

Jubal was dressed in baggy yellow pajamas. His pillow was tucked under one arm, and he was dragging the bedspread behind him. All he needed was a teddy bear to look like one of those Norman Rockwell framed prints we used to sell in the store. He was looking down at the floor.

"Cain't sleep, me," he mumbled.

"Come on in, *cher,"* I said. Now he had me doing it.

"I'm not usual a'scared," he said. "Not by country noises, no. But I heered people's voices goin' by outside, and *po*-lices and *fahr* engines and *am*malances and what-not. . . ."

I hadn't heard a thing. It was a city boy, country boy thing, I guess. I'd never spent much time sleeping in the swamp. A bullfrog croaked, I'd probably wet my pants.

"Yeah, it can be a hel— . . . a horrible racket, can't it? We'll get you squared away, I've got a king-size in here, it won't be a problem."

"I kin sleep on da couch."

"Wouldn't hear of it. I'll shut that street-side glass door and turn the air on low, unless you think that'd be too—"

"Nah, I be fine." He looked at me for the first time. "Usually I sleep t'ru anyt'ing. I could fall asleep 'hind de altar, me, while de congregation be moanin' an wailin' an feelin' de spirit. Wake up, fine a little ol' rattlesnake curl up wit' me." He laughed, but sobered quickly. "Jus' fo' tonight, Manny. Jus' fo' tonight."

Then he knelt beside the bed and steepled his fingers and closed his eyes and began to pray very softly.

When he was done he lay down and pulled the bedspread over him.

He was sound asleep in less than a minute. He didn't snore, belch, whimper, or fart in his sleep as long as I was awake, unlike a few girls I could mention.

The sun was coming up before I finally drifted off.

THE SUN WAS high when I woke up. Too high. *Way* too high.

I hadn't slept until eleven in a long time for a simple reason. At seven Mom or Maria was always pounding on my door.

I jumped up, remembered Jubal had come to my room in the night. But he wasn't here now. He wouldn't just wander off in a strange neighborhood, would he? I got a little angry thinking about it. He wasn't a dog, damn it, that you had to leash or watch every minute. If he was that helpless . . . well, I hadn't signed on for that. But I'd better go look.

I found Jubal high on a ladder, leaning through the service hatch of our sign. Mom and Betty were down below, holding the ladder and looking nervous. When I joined them I heard a funny sound coming from inside the sign. It took me a moment to realize it was Jubal, humming and singing. The melody had a definite bayou flavor to it, and the words sounded like Cajun French.

He eased himself out of the hole and held up a frayed length of thick electrical cable like a dead snake. He looked very happy.

"Dis be de rascal, right here!" he boomed. "I'm real lucky dat you found me, yeah. Dis critter 'bout ready to cotch fire, you bet. Burn down de whole place, mebbe. Betty, you flick dat switch yonder, please ma'am." He glanced over at me and smiled again. "*Bonjour, monsieur* sleepyhead! Sleep till de noontime, I declare!"

"Did not," I said. "It's only elevenish."

Mom threw the master switch and the sign came to life better than it had been in a few years. Most everything was working except for a few burned-out bulbs that I could replace in five minutes. One of the little neon rockets was cracked.

"We get her recharge, seal her up again. Cheap. Betty, she say dere's a place on de way over to Dak's."

I looked at Mom, and she nodded, maybe a bit reluctantly, meaning I was excused from working my butt off to make up for all the morning work I hadn't done. I kissed her forehead, and then me and Jubal dragged the Triumph and sidecar out of the small room where we keep janitorial supplies, my tools, a small workbench, and cases of generic soda pop for the drink machine, which we own, and boxes of stuff for the snack machine, which we don't. Jubal had spread some tools from his own toolbox on the worktable. He'd been busy all morning, it looked like.

We got the 'sickle out of the workroom and spent about twenty minutes bolting the sidecar to the frame. Jubal had a mental checklist for that operation, and he went through it methodically, testing each bolt to be sure it was tight enough. A runaway sidecar might be a funny thing in the movies, but not in real life. Jubal was a careful man.

The great black and chrome beast rattled to life immediately when I hit the starter. It trembled beneath me, ready to go. Jubal squeezed himself down into the sidecar and put on his plain black helmet. I put my own helmet on.

"Want me one like dat, yes sir," Jubal said. My motorcycle helmet is one of the finest things I own. Ironic for a guy who doesn't even own a car, much less a cycle, I guess. It was painted by Henry "2Loose" La Beck, king of the Daytona taggers.

It only took me a few blocks to get the hang of handling it. With a sidecar, you have to lean differently. Jubal gave me a few pointers without making me nervous or being a side-seat driver.

I pulled into Dak's dad's parking lot the king of all I surveyed. Mr. Sinclair looked at the Triumph with lust in his eyes. He had been a member of a club when he was a young man. He rode a Harley back then, but he had told me how much he liked the Triumph. Most of what I knew about cycles I had learned from him.

He greeted Jubal warmly and helped pull him out of his seat. We went over the bike thoroughly and spent a few hours with toothbrushes and soapy water and wax. That spruced it up quite a bit. The frame and tank would need repainting sometime soon, but we'd have to take it apart to do that, and I didn't have the time, if I was going to get any use out of it before Travis came back.

"Think about this for the tank," Mr. Sinclair said. "Deep, midnight blue, with a little flake in it so's it sparkles. Five or six coats ought to do it. Come on in here, let me show you what I'm talking about." He showed us several books in his office. It was plain that he'd love to do the work just for the cost of the paint.

IT TOOK TRAVIS the full two weeks he had mentioned as an outside estimate, and a few days beyond that. It was one of the best two and a half weeks I'd ever spent.

Jubal had the energy of ten men, and the know-how of a couple dozen. He could fix anything he could reach and take apart. Things around the Blast-Off that hadn't worked since John Glenn was in orbit just magically started working again. I'd ask Jubal about it, and he'd say he just saw it wasn't working and took a few minutes to fix it. He found it hard to walk past something that wasn't working, or sometimes even something that wasn't working as well as it should.

Dak's dad had a name for it, sort of. He watched Jubal work on a few car engines at the garage and pronounced Jubal a "natural born grease monkey."

"Some people got perfect pitch," he said. "Some folks never get lost. Some got what they call a 'green thumb.' And some just understand engines."

But being a grease monkey doesn't begin to describe Jubal's skills. He fixed three annoying glitches in my old computer that I'd been working around for months, and did it in fifteen minutes. He fixed plumbing and wiring. He fixed small appliances, and three televisions sitting in a storage room because I'd been too lazy to throw them out. He even fixed the toilet in room 201.

I watched him working on the televisions, and I can't say how he did it. It was eerie, like watching a faith healer. Jubal would take it apart, stare at it, trace pathways in the air with his fingers, all the time humming music that I later figured out were hymns. He touched his tester wires here and there, and next thing I knew he was snipping a transistor off a circuit board. Then he whipped out his pocket computer—the absolute most up-to-the-minute model, thousands of times bigger and smarter than mine—and pretty soon he'd located a place in Kansas or Oregon or South Africa where you could get that transistor for a few pennies plus postage. A few days later it would arrive, and he would solder it in place . . . and the television worked.

TRAVIS HAD EMPHASIZED Jubal's social anxieties, and it was true, when Jubal was around people he didn't know he muttered, hung back, never made eye contact, and just generally seemed to want to be somewhere else. But after he'd had a little time to take your measure he could loosen up quite a bit, and when he regarded you as "family," which could take as little as a microsecond with Alicia to a couple of days with me and Dak . . . then all bets were off. With his family Jubal liked to laugh, and sing and dance and generally have what he called a "fais do-do," which is Cajun for party, I think.

He changed my family a lot in two weeks.

For the first few days we kept the television on during dinner. But everyone was laughing and talking so much that by the third day we just forgot about watching or listening to it. Kelly, Dak, and Alicia started eating the evening meal with us as often as not, and we even got Sam Sinclair, Dak's Dad, to join us a couple of times.

After, there was no telling what we might do. I took Jubal to Rancho Broussard to pick up his record collection, which was about fifty vinyl 33 ⅓, and his old turntable. All of it was Cajun dance tunes, music from *way* back in the bayou. Jubal loved to dance to this music, and to sing along. He was a good singer and an enthusiastic dancer, alternating between his "four young ladies," or just dancing by himself.

Or sometimes we got the Monopoly board out. Jubal had never played but he told us how he'd learned to do his "numberin' " using that kind of money. He picked it up easily enough, and he loved it. He was ruthless, and won more often than not. He took the little racing car from the very first, and I never told him that was traditionally my piece. And Mom says I've got a lot of maturing to do. I wanted the little racing car, that car was *mine,* but I let our guest have it. Is that mature, or what?

I remember at the first game, when Kelly was putting a hotel on Pacific Avenue, he asked, "Why the Blas'-Off Hotel ain't on dis board, hah?" He suggested we rename Park Place or Boardwalk.

"Park Place is more like the Golden Manatee across the street, *cher,*" Mom said. "The Blast-Off, when they built it, might have been on one of the red properties, Illinois Avenue maybe, or New York at the worst. Now we're a lot closer to 'Go.' "

Then we started arguing about what space the Blast-Off should be on.

"Oriental," I said. "One step above the roach motel on Baltic."

"Hel— . . . uh, pooh!" Dak said. "Baltic, that's a SRO, a 'single room occupancy' joint, bathroom down the hall. Oriental, that's where the desk clerk sits in a booth behind bulletproof glass. The ol' B-O Motel, I figure we're on Saint Charles Avenue. Which, incidentally, give me two houses on Saint Charles. Next time around, Manny, those houses gonna wipe you *out!*"

Probably. I didn't tell Dak that we'd seriously considered installing one of those Plexiglas booths. After the second time you're held up by some wild-eyed angel duster I think anyone would. We'd been robbed four times since I've been old enough to remember. Mom shot the first one, right in the gun hand, just like in an old cowboy movie. After that, the police and me persuaded her to just hand over the money. It wasn't enough to die for, or even to kill for. Nobody ever ran out of our office rich.

One amazing thing was that, with Jubal around, we all had more free time. It got to where there sometimes wasn't anything really urgent to do by the afternoon, so Jubal and I would go for a ride. Mostly we went up and down the beach, because Jubal loved the ocean. We got to be a regular sight. Many a tourist snapped our picture as we roared by, Jubal in his loud shirts and dark sunglasses and white beard and sunburned nose smiling and waving to everyone we passed.

Other afternoons, with Jubal around to help out, Mom and Maria got to go out together for some fun. Mom said she'd pretty much forgotten how.

Mom hit the roof when I gave her the money Travis had pressed on me.

"I told him his credit was good with us, but he gave me his plastic anyway," she hissed at me after I gave her the roll of hundreds. Mom doesn't like shouting, but she can make a hiss carry a city block. "You know Jubal's room won't come to anything like this much. He could stay four months on this."

"Travis said it was for food, too."

She drew herself up and glared at me.

"We don't run a restaurant here, Manuel. Jubal is a friend. He's welcome at our table at any time. You don't charge your friends for food."

I knew that. I could only shrug.

"It's just crazy," she muttered. "The way that man works. We should be paying *him*. In fact, I offered to, but he wouldn't take it. Unlike my spineless son."

I wasn't going to sit still for that, but she relented and apologized to me. Then she went away muttering about how she'd stuff it up . . . well, she'd be sure he took it. I decided to make myself scarce for that little scene.

I'm not so sure about the food business, it just seems like common courtesy to pay for your suppers if you're staying a while. But Mom's biggest fear was to be thought of as common. She had that prickly pride some chronically poor folks get . . . actually, far too few of them, in my experience, but some. She was quick to take offense at any suggestion she couldn't get by on her own, or pull her own weight, and never, never ask for a handout, nor accept charity.

Jubal just started cleaning out our little kidney-shaped pool one day. What are you going to do, just stand there and watch him? Dak and I joined in—after our regular studies, Jubal would not allow us to shirk that—and soon the bottom had been caulked and painted, the pump and filter refurbished, and the pool was filled with water for the first time in three years. We held a pool party to celebrate and I saw my mother and aunt in bathing suits for the first time I could remember. Owners of neighboring businesses came and ate Aunt Maria's fabulous cupcakes and cookies and sipped Alicia's tofu punch before tossing it to the potted palms and grabbing a beer. They complimented us on how great the old joint looked and spoke of their own plans to renovate, refurbish, and upgrade, often glancing up nervously at the looming concrete of the Golden Manatee. They knew they were in trouble and were looking for a way out. Half our neighbors had already sold to the Manatee's parent corporation, Pillock and Burke. More would sell soon, you could lay money on it.

We sent an invitation to the Manatee, as a joke. To everyone's surprise the manager showed up. His name was Bruce Carter. He was courteous to Mom and Maria and spoke briefly to most of the business owners there. He even talked to me for a bit. He told me how much he admired the Triumph. He'd seen me and Jubal going by. He said he'd owned one, once, so we talked motorcycles for a while. Then he went back to work, leaving me depressed. I think it's easier if your enemy is a genuine prick. This guy didn't seem to enjoy what was happening to us. He never gloated. But he knew as well as we did that the days of the Blast-Off were numbered. If Pillock and Burke didn't drive us out, somebody else would.

ON THE TENTH, maybe the eleventh night of his stay with us we were deep in a Monopoly game and I was about to be driven to the poorhouse, as usual. It was my night on desk duty, so I was listening for the doorbell with one ear.

Suddenly Jubal stood up and shouted, "Holly!" We all looked at him and he was pointing at the television screen. I looked, and it was one of those group portraits NASA is so fond of, with the seven Mars astronauts hovering chipmunk-cheeked and bushy-haired in their weightless wardroom. One of the women, Holly Oakley, was holding the mike and answering a question.

"It's Holly," Jubal said, a bit more calmly.

"That's right," I said. "Do you know her?" Not too tough to believe, what with his cousin Travis having been an astronaut.

"Where she at? She at de station?"

"No, like it says there at the bottom, she's aboard the *Ares Seven.*"

"What dis *Ares Seven*?"

"The Mars ship, Jubal," I said. "I'm surprised you haven't heard of it."

"Don' watch TV, me," he said, with a frown. Jubal didn't follow current events at all, if he could help it. He turned up the volume.

"—and we'd like to thank all of you for giving us so much of your valuable time. Captain Bernardo Aquino, First Officer Katisha Smith, Brin Marston, M.D., and mission specialists Doctors Holly Oakley, Cliff Raddison, Lee Welles, and Dmitri Vasarov. America's *Ares Seven* astronauts. Good luck, and Godspeed, all of you!"

There was a pause of fifteen full seconds as the astronauts hung there stupidly, smiles frozen on their faces, while the radio signal went out to the *Ares Seven* and came back at the speed of light. Television stations had taken to adding a countdown clock in a corner window so people didn't become too impatient, but it didn't help much. This was going to be the last live interview. From then on reporters would ask their questions all at once and the astronauts would answer them the same way, and it would be turned into a standard Q&A by tape editing.

. . . 0.03 . . . 0.02 . . . 0.01 . . . "It was our pleasure, and thank you," Captain Aquino answered, and the seven of them waved for a few seconds before we were returned to the show, which was *60 Minutes,* I think.

"So, you know that woman, Jubal?" Aunt Maria asked him.

"Oh, my, used to know her real good, me. She de mother a Travis's two sweet daughters. She Travis's ex-wife, she is."

THAT WAS THE end of Monopoly for that night.

I think we were all amazed and delighted to have a connection to the Mars mission, however tenuous. We wanted to know more about her, but we didn't get much. It was too painful for Jubal, for he was endlessly loyal to Travis and yet liked Holly and the children enormously.

Jubal wanted to know everything there was to know about the Mars mission. That mostly fell to Dak and me, as our girlfriends and parents were not nearly so interested or informed on the subject as we were.

But where to begin? It was as much a political story as a scientific one, just like Apollo, and Project Mercury before that. Back then it was the Russians.

"Today it's the Chinese we wanted to beat," I said.

"Good luck," Dak snorted.

THE CHINESE HAD been developing a space exploration program for the last decade. Russia's once grand space program had been reduced from lack of money to a few station components here and there, and those arrived late and underfunded, often as not. In addition to the U.S. and Russia, a few other nations were in the lucrative satellite-launching business, including Japan, France, Brazil, and Indonesia. Analysts assumed China would find its place in that group.

They had developed a type of vehicle known in the space business as a Big Dumb Booster, something NASA critics had been advocating for forty years or more. The Russians had had a BDB practically from the start, the *Energia*. The idea behind the BDB was easy to state: Make it big, and make it simple. It was much cheaper to put heavy payloads into orbit with a BDB than with a manned space vehicle like the old Shuttle or the VStar. Manned vehicles had to devote a huge amount of mass to life support facilities. The level of safety required for a manned launch was an order of magnitude higher than for an unmanned one, and all that was costly.

The Chinese BDB did put big satellites in orbit. Then, in a surprise that did not quite rival the launch of *Sputnik One* in the 1950s, the Chinese lofted a small space station and a crew of three.

Not too long after that, they sent out three Mars probes. Two of them landed safely on Mars. They were "pathfinder" ships, carrying the supplies needed for a long stay on Mars. Then came the *Heavenly Harmony*, a manned ship taking the minimum-fuel Hohmann orbit path to Mars, and once more Americans went nuts.

THERE ARE A thousand paths to Mars, but they all must take into account some inconvenient facts.

First, all ways to Mars start off in the same direction. Before you even fire up your rocket, you are already traveling at 66,700 miles per hour, Earth's orbital speed. To go in the other direction you would first have to kill that speed. So rule number one is: You go with the flow.

You must always bear in mind that Mars and Earth move at different speeds in their orbits, and Mars is farther away from the sun. You must accelerate out of Earth's orbit, and then bear in mind that every second of the way the sun's gravity will be slowing you down.

The third thing to remember is that you can't aim at Mars when you fire your rockets. You have to aim at where Mars *will* be when you get there. It's like a hunter leading a bird when he pulls the trigger.

Then there comes the toughest of all the tough things about going to Mars. You can't just set down on the Red Planet, scoop up some rocks, snap a few pictures, and then take off and head for home the next day. Because of fuel limitations and the movements of the two planets, all proposed trips to Mars involve a waiting period while the planets move back into a position where a flight between them is economically possible. With the Hohmann orbit the Chinese supply ships had used, the wait was over a year.

A human needs three pounds of food, seven pounds of water, and two pounds of oxygen every day. All round trips to Mars that we can currently envision take well over a year. A crew of seven would consume thirty thousand pounds of food, water, and oxygen in a year, and that doesn't include water for bathing and brushing your teeth. All that weight must be put into Earth orbit, and then accelerated to a speed sufficient to reach the orbit of Mars. It takes a lot of fuel.

On your way to Mars, you had better be prepared to fix any broken thing with what you've got, because Triple-A won't be along any time soon to give you a jump start.

Out there, you're on your own.

* * *

"THE CHINESE TOOK what most folks believe is the most sensible route to Mars," Dak said. "You send unmanned ships first, by the slow but cheap path. Takes a year to get there. You send your astronauts along with just enough food, water, and air to get there. Then they use the stuff that went ahead of them. They figure to make their own fuel from the carbon dioxide in the Martian air. The Chinese are well on their way now. How long is it, Manny? Six months?"

"About that."

"But what 'bout de Americans?" Jubal asked. "Dey be gonna get dere fust?"

Dak snorted.

"No way. People think if our guys just step on the gas pedal a little harder we could pass the commie ba— . . . bad guys, but it don't work that way. The Chinese will hit Mars in six months, and either make a real big crater or come down soft. Our guys and gals will get there about two weeks later. End of story. The first foot on Mars will be a Chinese foot, dead or alive. Dammit."

Dak looked like he wanted to bite his tongue, but Jubal took no notice of the swearing. He was staring off into space, his mind occupied with calculations I doubted I'd ever be able to follow. Then he focused again.

"De Americans, dey swingin' by Venus, no?"

"Yes," I said. Wondering how he deduced that. "They swing by Venus and get a free boost from the gravity well there. They get to Mars, and then they only have to wait about a month before they can launch and return the ship to Earth. Our guys will be back before the Chinese."

Jubal brooded again, then looked at me.

" 'Merican ship, it don' use reg'lar rockets, hah? Somethin' else, I figger."

"It's called VASIMR," I said. "Variable Specific Impulse Magnetoplasma Rocket. It's a plasma drive, very high specific impulse, very low acceleration. But you can keep thrusting through the whole mission. It adds up."

"I'm afraid you lost me," Kelly said.

"Those astronauts a while ago," I said. "They looked like they were weightless, but they weren't, not quite. Their engine is firing, but it's only putting out a fraction of one gee. Not enough to hold you in your seat. The VASIMR is slow, but it's steady."

"The tortoise and the hare," Alicia suggested.

". . . Sort of," Dak said. "But this time, the bunny wins."

Jubal was still pondering. At last he looked at me.

"Manuel, *mon cher,* I need to know all I kin fine out 'bout this VASIMR."

"Sure, Jubal," I said. "I can show you some websites that will get you started."

"Good 'nuff," he said, and slapped his knees and headed for the door. I heard him mutter as he walked ahead of me to my room.

"Fus' people on Mars got to be Americans," he said.

If anybody could make it so, I would have bet on Jubal.

14

★ ★ ★

THE SUN HAD gone down, and the pool party was almost over.

The Golden Manatee manager had returned to his glittering tourist trap.

Aunt Maria had just brought out her sixth and last pan full of muffins and they were disappearing about as fast as the others had, even though everyone said they'd already had too many.

Mom was sitting in a plastic lawn chair, talking guns and shooting with Ralph Shabazz, who owned the pawn shop a few blocks away.

Dak was in the pool with a few of my old classmates from Gus Grissom High, using an old volleyball to play some variation of water polo with no goal cage.

Alicia was tidying up the snack table, wondering if she should make another bowl of tofu punch for people to throw in the potted plants.

Kelly was sharing a lounge chair with me. Since the chair had been designed for one, it took some squirming and a great degree of closeness to share it, but that was okay with me. She had had one drink over her usual limit and was making hickeys on my neck when she wasn't running her tongue all around my ear.

There were half a dozen guests still present, milling around as guests do when they're not sure if they should go home or stick around for one more free beer.

That's when the red and black Hummer pulled in. The windshield was spattered with bugs. There was a brief toot of the Hummer's horn and Travis got out, waving and smiling at us.

THE SIX OF us, the Rancho Broussard crowd, were gathered in Jubal's room half an hour later. Alicia sipped at a 7-Up and the rest of us opted for bottles of beer.

For a while nobody talked about what we all wanted to hear. He told us a few unlikely stories about adventures on the road not connected with his search for answers about the bubbles, and we filled him in on events at the Blast-Off. It all seemed interesting at the time, but looking at it later, what really went on? Jubal won a lot of Monopoly games, people checked in, people checked out, we repaired and filled the pool. Story of my life, so far. Listening to it, I vowed even more strongly to be *out* of here come this time next year, even if it meant finding a job desk-clerking in California . . . or Maine, or Alaska, or Timbuktu. *Anywhere.*

At last Travis settled back against the headboard of Jubal's bed, where he was sprawled, looking like he'd been driving a long time. Most of the day, he told us later.

"Well, friends," he said, "I know a lot about what the bubbles are *not.*"

Dak groaned.

"Yeah, it is discouraging. Most of what I know now, we knew before I left, only now I know it even *more* so, out to the limits of currently available testing.

"It's hard. Diamonds make no mark.

"It's tough. A *big* hydraulic press ruptured itself trying to crack it. Everything I fired at it bounced off, from a high-velocity bullet to high-energy protons in an atom smasher, to coherent laser light powerful enough to knock a plane out of the sky.

"It's reflective. *Perfectly* reflective. One hundred percent of visible light that hits it comes right back. Same with gamma radiation, radio waves . . . probably neutrinos, if I could figure out how to measure neutrino reflectivity.

"I declare to you now, friends, this thing is the most significant discovery of the twenty-first century, sure-fire Nobel Prize material . . . and it scares me silly."

"What for, Travis?" Alicia asked. "Jubal *deserves* a Nobel Prize."

"You bet he does, hon. But I don't think he wants one, do you, Jube?"

Jubal, who had been studying the new Reebok sneakers on his feet, looked up, shivered and shook his head, and looked down again.

"Jubal wouldn't enjoy it, Alicia. Big fuss like that, reporters all over the place, buying a tuxedo and going to Stockholm to meet the king . . ."

Jubal shivered some more, and I thought he was about to bolt out of the room, looking for his pirogue boat to row around the lake. But Travis steadied him with a squeeze on his shoulder, and Jubal settled back on the floor.

"There's a side to this thing you may not have thought of. Lots of power wrapped up in these." He took a silver bubble from his pocket and held it carefully up to the light. "Free energy. Don't look for *that* in any physics book. Energy is paid for, *always*. Only not here. Jubal's Squeezer works without using any energy I can detect. You saw how much power was unleashed when I . . . stupidly . . . turned one of them off."

"But that wasn't power," Kelly said. "That was just a vacuum. Wasn't it?"

"It takes power to *make* a vacuum," I told her.

"That's pretty much it," Travis agreed. "Reverse it, Kelly. You *know* it takes power to compress air into one of the bubbles, because you hear the explosion when the bubble goes away. Same with the vacuum, only in reverse."

"I don't *know* anything much at *all* about this," Kelly said, with a smile. "I think I follow you, though."

"Me, too," Alicia confirmed.

"So . . ." Travis said, and scowled. "I suppose there are things we could make to take advantage of the bubbles' perfect reflectivity. I can think of a few. And as for its durability, everlasting ball bearings would be just the beginning.

"But it just stands to reason that the application most people will be most interested in is the ability to make a big bang. A *real* big bang."

"A really, *really* big bang," Dak said, and I knew he'd been thinking pretty much like I had, though we'd never talked about it.

"Lots of money in big, big bangs," Travis said. "And I'm not talking about fireworks, sorry, Jubal."

"No problem, Travis," Jubal said, still studying his shoes.

"The people who like big bangs the most are the generals, of course. Put a small one of these in a cartridge, turn off the bubble, you got a free bullet. Put one in a steel pineapple, you got a free grenade. Make a real big one full of vacuum, you could probably implode a building. Jubal, how big can these things get?"

He looked up again, briefly, and shrugged.

"Don' know, me. Maybe not too much bigger than you seen."

"That would be a relief," Travis said. "But I'm not going to put it in the bank just yet. Thing is, you and me all know that some of the people who like big bangs are not very nice people at all. Think about a terrorist who gets his hand on a Squeezer. Free bombs, an unlimited supply.

"There are people who would do anything to get this thing. Anything. Our own government is only one of them. Word of this gets out, we'd be lucky if all that happened was they took it away from us."

Everyone was silent, thinking that one over.

"For now, can I get your word you won't talk about this?"

He looked at us one by one, and we all nodded. Kelly squeezed my hand. I'd never seen her looking so serious.

Travis looked relieved . . . a little. I could pretty much read his mind: *How far can I trust these flaky kids?* Well, short of torture, he could trust me all the way, and I was pretty sure of the others, too.

Travis scowled.

"I hate this thing. I really hate it. If only there was a way to release its energy slowly. Control the release. We could be solving the world's energy problem."

"I can do dat t'ing," Jubal said. For a moment Travis looked like he was about to go on with what he was saying, then he did a double-take right out of Laurel and Hardy.

"Say again, Jubal?"

"I can maybe fix dat t'ing, do what you say. Dribble it out, maybe."

"Maybe? You haven't actually tried to . . ."

"No, *mon cher*. Travis, why don' you tell me 'bout de folks goin' to Mars, huh?"

Travis got a bad case of conversational whiplash over that one. *Mars?*

"You never asked, Jubal. And I didn't know you'd be interested."

"I'm innersted, me. Travis, de fus' folks on Mars, dey should be Americans."

"Yeah, I wish it was going to be Americans, too. But it's too late."

"Not too late. No, suh! Not too late at all. I'm goin' to Mars, yes, I am, and I beat de Chinese, too. Even if I hafta make my own spaceship, me."

Travis stared at his cousin, then drained his long-neck bottle of Dixie beer.

PART TWO

15

★ ★ ★

THE BUILDING KELLY wanted to show us was over on Turnbull Bay, across from the New Smyrna Beach airport, one of a dozen similar structures built in marshy ground as part of an industrial park that never quite panned out. Only three or four of the buildings were currently occupied.

It was made of corrugated metal lapped over a steel framework. There were streaks of rust all over the sides and tall weeds growing in cracked concrete and along a railroad siding that was one of the chief reasons we were looking at the building. A sign along the roof ridge read: THE R. W. WHITE COMPANY.

Kelly parked in front of a loading dock with three truck bays, all closed and locked. Dak and Alicia pulled up in *Blue Thunder* as we were getting out.

We all stood there for a while, taking it in. It was noon on a hot, muggy day, five months away from M-day, the day the Chinese were going to land on Mars.

"Railroad siding goes right into the building, that's good," Dak said.

Kelly took a big ring of keys out of her purse and led us to a small door scaled for people, not boxcars. The third key she tried turned out to be the right one.

It was cooler inside, which surprised me. The concrete floor was part of it, but I saw that overhead there were big fans that kept the air moving.

"I left the fans on after I saw the place yesterday," Kelly said. "It was like an oven in here without them." She turned to an electrical panel and flipped six rows of switches, one row at a time. Big overhead lights came on in sequence and we could see the extent of the space inside.

"We don't need no more than a third of this space," Dak said.

"Dak, if you think there's another place within fifty miles of—"

"Shush, babe, I ain't complaining. Better too much than not enough."

"It was a hell of a list you gave me." She began ticking off points on her fingers. "Railroad spur. High ceiling—but you never said *how* high. On the water. Heavy lifting capability—and again, you didn't say how heavy. That traveling crane up there is rated for five hundred tons."

"More than enough, more than enough, Kelly," Dak said.

Kelly got out her laser range finder—a real good thing to take along if you're hunting for an empty factory, lots better than climbing to the ceiling and dropping a string. She pointed it at the roof, then glanced at the readout.

"One hundred twenty feet," she said. "Is that enough?"

"It'll have to be," I told her. "We'll build it with that in mind."

Our voices echoed in the big empty space.

The building consisted of two distinct areas. The part where we were was 120 feet high, as Kelly had just determined, maybe a hundred feet wide, and two hundred feet deep. Running on heavy rails overhead was a big traveling crane that could cover that entire area.

The rest of the building was only about twenty feet high. It accounted for two-thirds of the floor space. In a far corner of this lower area was standing water. Above it were rust streaks. Kelly saw where I was looking.

"That leak would be easy to patch," she said.

"I don't think we'll really need to," I said.

We followed her to the big doors. She slapped an outsized button and the big doors began to slide back, making warning beeps like a bus backing up. The sun streamed in and we all squinted but Kelly, who was wearing her sunglasses.

Outside was a wooden wharf. An old guy sat on the pier and dangled a line down around the pilings. He looked at us, then went back to fishing. I could smell creosote, and warm brackish water, and fish.

"The rails for the crane run right out to the end of the wharf," Kelly pointed out. "You said something about a barge. You can get a barge right up under the crane here."

"That'll make loading it a lot easier," Dak said.

Kelly pointed to the east, then north.

"Turnbull Bay here connects with Strickland Bay. Then under the bridge on U.S. 1 and you're in the Ponce de Leon Cut, turn left, and a mile later you're in the open ocean."

"Right there by the Coast Guard station?" I asked.

"That's it."

"Port," Dak said.

"What's that?"

"You don't make a left turn in a boat. You steer to port."

"Oh, the great admiral speaks," Kelly muttered. She was not in a great mood.

"How high is the highway bridge?" I asked.

"I don't know."

"We'll measure it later."

"Wait a minute," Alicia said. "Strickland Bay? As in Strickland Mercedes? As in . . . Kelly Strickland?"

"My family has lived in the area a long time," Kelly said. Myself, I hadn't even known that wide stretch of shallow water *had* a name.

"Mine, too," Dak said. "Only we been fixin' the cars your daddy been selling."

"Has somebody got a problem with this?" Kelly asked, angrily. She looked at each of us. Nobody said anything. She sighed and shook her head.

"We got lucky here, people," she said. "I looked at seventeen places that were *almost* right, but then one thing or another didn't work. No heavy lifting, no rail spur, crowded neighborhood, or *way* too expensive."

"How much for this?" Alicia asked. Kelly named a figure that made me a little short of breath.

"So, doing the math," I said, "we're looking at six months at that rate, which—"

"Did I say month? That figure was per week."

I needed a place to sit down. Talking about that much money makes me queasy.

"I can find you a dozen places much cheaper . . . but without the crane. Here's the deal, folks. This place is in a legal limbo at the moment. The original developer went broke. There are lawsuits working their way through the courts. They can only rent month to month, which suits us down to the ground. There's a group of investors who want to tear all this sh— . . . this stuff down and build a golf course."

"Just what Florida needs," Dak said. "Another golf course."

"How'd you find it?" Alicia asked. Kelly gave us a small smile.

"In my father's files. He's the man behind the investors. He may or may not own this building, depending on how a judge rules on whether it was all done legally."

"I thought your daddy sold cars," Dak said.

"He's thinking of getting involved more in land speculation."

"Just what Florida needs," I said. "Another land developer." Kelly punched my arm, playfully, but with an edge to it this time. She really was feeling bad.

"So what do you say? Should I put down a deposit?"

"We'll run it by Travis this evening," I said.

"Travis. Right," she said, bitterly.

No love currently lost between Kelly and Travis. And to think, no more than a week ago we were just like one big happy family. . . .

16

★ ★ ★

NOTHING FURTHER WAS said the night of Travis's return about Jubal's plan to build him his own spaceship, him. Travis helped him bundle up his belongings, which now included a nice selection of original shell people by Aunt Maria. We stood together and waved good-bye as Travis drove out of the parking lot.

"I'm going to miss that Jubal," Mom said.

Little did she know how soon she would change her mind about that.

A FEW DAYS went by. After all the togetherness while Jubal was staying with us, we four who were in on the big secret stayed apart, maybe taking a breather from each other. I only spoke to Kelly twice in that time, over the phone.

On the fourth day Travis called me.

"Jubal wants to talk to you," he said. "He hates talking on the telephone, won't do it unless it's an emergency. Could you come over sometime this afternoon?"

"Sure," I said. "Things are running more smoothly here since he fixed things up. I can be there in two, three hours."

"Good enough. Thanks, Manny."

I hurried through the rest of my chores and hopped on the Triumph. I figured it would be my last ride on the grand old masterpiece, so I opened it up a little, as much as I dared with the damned empty sidecar cramping my style.

TRAVIS WAS WAITING for me by the pool. He had a big pitcher of iced tea, and he poured me a glass without asking if I wanted one. I took a big drink, then sat down.

"Thanks for coming, Manny," he said.

"Sure. What's the problem?"

"Jubal and his pipe dreams is the problem."

"He said an American should be the first man on Mars."

"He meant just what he said. And if those Ares Seven clowns aren't up to the task, he'll just go there himself."

"Sounds nuts."

He rubbed his unshaven chin with one hand.

"No, the nutty thing is, it might actually be possible. Outrageous, goofy beyond belief . . . but I can't actually say it's impossible. In fact, we're going out tomorrow to the 'Glades to do a little testing on the Broussard drive, see just how possible it is."

"Broussard drive?"

He grinned. "Got to call it something. But there's things I need to know, now that Jubal says he can release the energy slowly. Like, just what comes out after you've squeezed a cubic acre of seawater to the size of a tennis ball? Protons? Atomic nuclei? Gamma rays? I haven't tried to do the math on it because it makes my head hurt."

"Has Jubal done the math?"

"I don't know. Jubal and me . . . well, we're hardly speaking, Manny."

I didn't like the sound of that at all.

"Manny . . . I know this isn't fair. I know it's a lot to ask. But . . . could you take a shot at talking Jubal out of this?"

"Travis, I . . ."

"He says you're his best friend, Manny. He'll listen to you. I don't know if you realize just how much of an impression you and your family made in his life. All he talks about, except about building a spaceship and flying it to Mars, is you and your friends. *His* friends. All I ask is you take a shot. Will you do that for me, Manny?"

I FOUND JUBAL where Travis had said he would be, deep in the darkness of his laboratory in the prefab barn. He had made a big, primitive desk with sawhorses and a four-by-eight sheet of plywood. He was surrounded by stacks of downloaded books, printed out, two-hole punched, and bound together with string. It made me think of a child's fortress, made of bricks of compacted snow, though I'd never had a chance to build such a thing. His high-speed printer was spitting out another book at about ten pages per second.

I saw his face before he saw me, and the expression there was one I'd never seen before. Jubal was mighty worried. Then he looked up, and the frown wrinkles vanished as he recognized me. He used a number two pencil with the eraser chewed off to mark his place in one of the Big Chief elementary school pads he used to take notes.

"Manuel Garcia, my fren'! I am so glad dat you see me! *Entrez, entrez,* come on in, chile, you wanna Popsicle?" He hurried to a small freezer in the shadows and came back with a grape Popsicle, which he knew was my favorite.

The next little while was taken up with the social pleasantries Jubal would no more think of dispensing with than he would eat a meal without saying a prayer. I told him we were all doing fine, that the business was running better than it ever had, thanks largely to him. He asked about several people in the neighborhood, many of whom I'd never met until he brought his infectious enthusiasm into our lives. People like Mr. Ortega the grocer, who I had dealt with since I was old enough to cross the street by myself, but who I had never really *talked* to until Jubal and I bought a bag of fresh oranges from him and spent the next twenty minutes learning about fruit.

"Still got dat rifle I tell Ralph Shabazz I fix," Jubal admitted. "You tell him Jubal been mighty busy dis week, hah?"

"I'll do dat t'ing." He laughed like he always did when I spoke a little Jubalese. He knew I wasn't mocking him. He knew his accent was sometimes almost impossible for strangers to understand. He said he'd tried to shake it, speak like the people on the television, "Spit de crawdads outta my mouth an comb de swamp moss outta my hair," as he put it. No luck.

"Travis is worried about you, Jubal."

"I know dat, me. He t'ink I'm crazy." He touched the depression in his head, the awful wound given him by his father.

"I don't think you're crazy."

"T'anks, *mon cher*. T'ank you fo' dat. But he worried, Travis. He plenty worried."

"About what?"

He sprang to his feet and hurried to the plywood desk. He swept papers aside until he came to the notebook he wanted. I could see him writing his home-school lessons in a book just like that one.

Looking over his shoulder, there was very little I saw that I could relate to. I knew it was math, but it was Greek to me. Actually, a lot of it *was* Greek. I recognized the letter *pi,* and *theta*. I didn't think it meant he was pledging fraternities. I saw a few equals signs. A square root radical. That was about it. Nothing else was familiar.

"What is this?" I asked, without much hope.

"Dis de Vaseline drive." *Vaseline? Oh, right. VASIMR.* The ion drive the Ares Seven were currently using to get to Mars.

"Slow, but steady, right?" I asked.

"Should be, oughta be. But is it slow *enough,* hah?"

"What do you mean?"

"Dey in a big hurry, yes dey are. Dey aimin' to get dere, get back to home fus', steal some glory, oh yes."

He looked into my eyes with an intensity I'd never seen before. This was Jubal the genius. This was Jubal zipping, flashing, flying through regions I knew I'd never even crawl through. This was a Jubal to stand in awe of, and believe me, I did, from that moment on.

"Look, rah *cheer,*" he said, and pointed at his notebook, talking so fast that even if he spoke fluent Floridian I'd probably never have understood. That notebook led to another. Stacks of printouts toppled as he bored through them, hunting for the diagrams he wanted. I tried signaling him that I was in *way* over my head, but he was off in his own world. So I stood there and tried to soak up at least an idea of why he felt the American *Ares Seven* was doomed.

IT TOOK HIM half an hour to make his presentation to what was, for all practical purposes, an absent audience. Absent, as in the space between my poor ears. I mean, I wasn't even fit to pound the erasers in Jubal's classroom.

"You see, Manny? You see why it so *important*?"

Anyone but Jubal, I'd be wondering if he was just rubbing it in. Because I *didn't* see, might never see . . . and my appraisal of my own prospects for an education in science had never been lower.

On the other hand, how many people get tutoring from Albert Einstein's smarter brother, and how many could keep up?

"I see that you think there's something to worry about, Jubal," I said.

He nodded, absently chewing on the end of another pencil. The eraser broke off and he took it out of his mouth and frowned at it, as if wondering how it got there.

"Travis, he t'ink dis idea of us all buildin' us a spaceship an goin' to Mars, he t'ink dat a stupid idea."

Us? First I'd heard of it. *All of us?*

"I dunno. Travis, he know a *fis'ful* more 'bout de 'impractical amplications' of t'ings dan I can do, oh yes." He tapped his head, shrugged fatalistically. "Maybe getting' dere fust, maybe dat ain't important. But dem Ares Seven folks, dey gonna be in a *heap* a trouble. An dat means de mother a his two sweet little girls, yes. We gotta go out dere, Manny. We be de onliest one's what can be dere to help out, de time comes."

"I'm convinced, Jubal." *All of us? When do we start?*

"But not *Travis!* Manny, I . . ." he trailed off, muttering to himself.

"Go ahead, Jubal. Say it. We're friends, you can ask me anything."

He studied me. Jubal had never completely trusted anyone but Travis, which was why he was finding it so hard to go against him.

"Travis, he ain't talkin' to me, Manny."

I thought it was Jubal who wasn't talking to . . . Well, I knew the same story often looked entirely different to two different people.

And I knew that was exactly the sort of problem you didn't want to get in the middle of. Never in a million years. No way, José! Include me out.

"Would you go talk to Travis, Manny?"

"Sure, Jubal. Sure I will."

SURE I WILL, Jubal. Sure.

I got as far as the tennis court and stopped. I looked back. I looked forward. I was about halfway between Travis's house and Jubal's barn and I had no idea where to go from here.

I'd parked the Triumph on the tennis court. I got the cell phone out of the sidecar and dialed Kelly's work number.

"Strickland Mercedes-Porsche-Ferrari. How may I direct your call?" At least it wasn't a mechanized phone menu. But it was supposed to be Kelly's direct line.

"I'll take two Boxsters and a Testarossa, to go."

"You want fries with that?"

"Put me through to Kelly, please, Lisa."

"Manny, I was told—"

"Lisa, you know how pissed she's going to be if you don't put me through. And you know we won't tell on you."

There was a silence. I didn't envy her, stuck between the boss and the boss's daughter, neither of them being the type of person you wanted to mess with. She sighed, and I heard Kelly's phone ring.

"Jubal?" she answered, sounding worried.

"Me, Kelly. My call didn't go through."

She sighed.

"Oh, don't worry about it. Just my dad being an asshole again."

"Yeah, but your caller ID thought this was Jubal calling. It's his phone. The one in the sidecar that he never uses. So he's blocking calls from Jubal, too." Not that Jubal would ever call, but Mr. Strickland probably didn't know that.

I could almost hear her simmer.

"Yeah, when I get home I'm gonna rip him a new . . . Can you believe that? He must have his spies working again, and now he's messing with the computers. *My* computers. Oh, Manny, he's going to be one sorry, racist mother—"

"I'm out at the ranch," I said. Don't want to let Kelly get started on her father, she could damage the phone.

"Some problem?"

"Yeah . . . you could say I've got a problem. I don't know what to do."

"Start at the beginning."

I did, and I didn't get very far before she cut me off.

"Don't do anything. I'll be right over."

I FIGURED NOT doing anything didn't apply to fishing. If you're seriously doing something when you're fishing, you're missing the whole point.

I walked down the dock. The boathouse door wasn't locked. I found a rod and reel in there, and borrowed a trowel. At a likely looking spot of ground, I turned over a few scoops of soil and immediately had half a dozen red wigglers.

That's where I was an hour later when I heard footsteps. I turned and saw Kelly, dressed in a smart blue suit and blouse that looked uncomfortable out here in the blinding sunshine. She kicked off her medium-heeled shiny black shoes, then hiked up her skirt and quickly peeled down her pink panties and taupe pantyhose. It was over almost before I knew she was doing it. She stuffed the frillies in her purse and sat beside me on the end of the pier and dangled her feet in the cool water, just like I was doing.

"Catching anything, Huck?"

"Could I have an instant slo-mo replay of that? I think I missed some of the finer points." I lifted the stringer almost out of the water. Two big bass flopped on the end of it. I grabbed the other end of the string and unthreaded it from their gills. They floated there a moment, not quite sure they were free, then swam off. I never would have kept them at all except that, the one time me and Kelly went fishing together, I couldn't even land a scrawny little perch. I had to show her I *could* catch fish. Manny, the mighty hunter, bringing the mammoth meat home to the cave.

"So, start at the beginning, okay?" she said.

"Well, Travis called me and . . . and he . . . you have *no* idea how distracting it is, you sitting there and me knowing you're not wearing any panties."

She looked at me dubiously, and snorted.

"Boys. Can't educate 'em, can't understand 'em, can't do without 'em. Or so I've been told. I can't dangle my feet in the water wearing pantyhose, Huckleberry. It wasn't about you at all." But I could tell by the glint in her eyes that it had been, at least partly. And I knew she was filing the fact that it turned me on, and one day soon I'd be treated to some little scenario she had worked out involving not wearing any underwear.

Life is so tough sometimes, ain't it?

AS IT TURNED out, I didn't tell my story then. Kelly had called Alicia, who had called Dak, and they were due out at the ranch soon. They arrived a few minutes later, and both kicked off their shoes and rolled up their pants legs and sat beside us. Not nearly as interesting to watch as Kelly.

When I finished telling them what I'd heard in the last couple hours they were all quiet for a while. Then Dak turned to me with a dubious but hopeful expression.

"It's that 'all of us' interests me the most," he said. "You're sure that's what he said? *All* of us? You and me? Not America, not NASA?"

"*All* of us." Kelly pressed down *hard* on the first word. "As in me, you, Manny, Alicia, Jubal, and Travis. Okay?"

"What would you want to go to Mars for, Kelly?" Dak looked honestly puzzled. I was, too, but I knew better than to show it. "Sell BMWs to the Martians?"

"I'd want to go because it's an adventure," Kelly responded quietly, not taking offense. "You don't get a shot like this twice in one lifetime. Plus, I have to watch over Manny." She smiled at me, making me feel great, and a bit worried at the same time.

"Me, too," Alicia chimed in. "Hell . . . heck, I rode every ride at Disney World, Universal, *and* Florida Adventure. This couldn't be any scarier than that."

Dak looked us over one at a time, then nodded. "This is what I was looking for from Travis from day one, only I was thinking more along the lines of a foot in the door at a good school."

"It's going to take some careful pushing and shoving," Kelly said. I could already see the gears turning in the fabulous head. This was the sort of thing Kelly thrived on. "If it works out right, he won't know what hit him, just one day he'll wake up and realize he's agreed to fly us all to Mars."

"Don't worry, hon," Alicia said with a sniff. "The day I can't push a coon-ass peckerwood in the direction I want him to go . . . that'll be a cold day in heck!"

"I don't think Jubal—" I began.

"Not Jubal, Huckleberry," Alicia said. Did I really look like that much of a hayseed with my pants cuffs rolled up? "I'm talking about Travis, the Big Coon-Ass Peckerwood himself. Pardon my pejorative."

"No problem, hon," Dak said. "Ain't nobody here but us darkies, the spic, and the white chick."

"White chick? White *chick?*" Kelly said. "Yo momma."

" '*My* mamma?' Gal, yo momma so dumb she tripped over a cordless phone."

"Oh, yeah? Well, yo momma so ugly she stuck her head out a car window and got arrested for mooning."

"Oh, yeah? Sister, yo momma so—"

"—so fat she looks like she's smuggling a Volkswagen," Alicia said. "Now you guys cut it out."

Fine with me, too. The way Dak felt about his absent mother, you'd think "yo momma" jokes would really bother him. But he and Kelly had discovered they were very good at the game, they could carry on for ten minutes and never repeat themselves.

"It's just creative dissing, Manny," Dak had once told me. "It ain't about yo momma or my momma, it's about the words. It's street poetry, like rap."

Which was clear as mud, because Dak had almost as little use for rap as his father, who called it antimusic, though Sam Sinclair admitted he'd stopped listening to new music about the time Marvin Gaye died.

A little Racism 101 footnote: "Coon-ass" doesn't mean a black person, as many Yankees assume when they hear it. That would be "coon." A coon-ass is a Cajun, and probably just as insulting as coon, but Cajuns usually don't make a big deal of it.

"Dak, Manny," Kelly said, "we love you guys, but try to let me and Alicia do most of the talking. Whatever you do, do not ask if you can help Jubal build a spaceship and take you all to Mars. We've got to ease him into that frame of mind."

I was more than happy to leave it to her. Who's going to out-talk a car dealer? I figured it was in her genes, from when the Stricklands landed on the bay they named after themselves, and started selling buckboard wagons.

THE GIRLS WENT on ahead, whispering to each other, as Dak and I stowed the fishing gear back where I'd found it. When we reached the tennis court Kelly was nowhere to be seen, and Alicia came out the barn side door, Jubal following reluctantly behind. In fact, I was sure that if Alicia hadn't been pulling on his hand he wouldn't have been moving at all. But he did come, looking like a Macy's Thanksgiving Day Parade balloon beside tiny Alicia.

We went into the house and found Kelly and Travis standing there. The colonel had his hands in his pockets and was looking at the floor. The big baby.

"Now, you boys are going to kiss and make up," Alicia said. "Then we're all going to sit down outside around the grill and eat the soy burgers I'm going to make, and talk about this thing that has come between you. Okay? Travis? Jubal?"

Kelly gave Travis a shove, and the two slowly came together. They embraced, and Travis did kiss his cousin, and pounded him on the back.

"I'm sorry, Jubal." He was a little hoarse. "This thing has got me behaving even worse than my normal shi— . . . lousy standard. Forgive me."

"Nothin' to fo'give, *mon cher*. I actin' stupid, me."

I was pretty sure I saw a tear in Travis's eye. But Kelly grabbed them both, still hugging, and got them moving through the sliding doors out on to the patio.

IT TURNED OUT Alicia did have a sense of humor. She knew how popular soy burgers would be with this crowd so she didn't even try. I started a fire in the kettle and she and Dak sliced huge beefsteak tomatoes and purple onions and Kelly formed half-pound burgers with her hands and Travis and Jubal set the picnic table and put out the deli mustard and pickles and a big jar of sliced jalapeños. I cooked the burgers from "almost raw" for Travis to "black and crispy on the edges" for Dak and Jubal. We didn't have any lettuce, so Alicia volunteered to pick some dandelion greens and show us how good they were on burgers. We all declined, with varying degrees of panic.

It had been Alicia's idea to do the lunch, let emotions get back under control before we all locked horns with Travis. Sitting there, working my way through a sheer masterpiece of a hamburger, I figured it had been a good idea.

I wouldn't have wanted to be Travis just then.

IT TOOK A while to bring Travis up to speed on Jubal's new calculations. From his reactions, I could see he hadn't understood that Jubal had gone beyond being simply worried about the chances of the Ares Seven, to feeling sure they were headed for a catastrophe. He followed Jubal's presentation, Jubal pointing wildly at this or that part of the hundred or so diagrams he had brought with him.

The four of us non-mathematical-genius types watched, at first trying to follow it all but by the end just sitting there in Travis's comfortable patio chairs. I don't think sulking would be the right word, but we were all a bit chastened to see just how peripheral we really were to Jubal's project. What the hell had we been thinking? There had to be many thousands of people who could understand all the stuff Jubal was explaining, who would now be nodding grimly as the flaws of the Vaseline drive came to light. Thousands of people, I could now see, much more qualified to ship out to space with Jubal and Travis than we were.

As it turned out, more qualified than Travis, too. He sat back in his chair and rubbed his eyes. Jubal got him a bottle of aspirin without having to be asked. Travis swallowed four of them.

"I don't understand a lot of what Jubal just said," Travis said.

"Oh, wonderful," Alicia breathed. "I was feeling so *dumb!*"

"Join the club," Dak said. "Jubal, can I have one of those aspirins?"

"So what's it going to do, Jubal?" I asked. "Will it blow up?"

"Might could," Jubal said, gnawing at a piece of his beard. "Dey didn' do 'nuff long-term testin', I figure. More likely, de engine she jus' shut off and dat de end a dat. Won't start no mo', no."

Alicia frowned at him.

"Well, what's the big deal, then?" she asked. "I thought it was gonna blow up. Didn't you say it was gonna blow up, Manny?"

"All I know for sure was that Jubal said they were in trouble," I said. "But Alicia, if their main engine won't fire . . . they'll get to Mars still going . . . what, Jubal?"

"Real fas'," he said, shaking his head. "Too dad-gum fas'."

We were all momentarily stunned by Jubal's use of what was, to him, a swearword. We'd never heard it before.

"Like he said, too fast," I told Alicia. "They'll go right on past Mars and nobody can do a thing about it. They can't slow down, nobody's got the juice to catch up with them. They'll head on out to the stars and get there in about ten thousand years."

"Nobody kin stop 'em but us'n," Jubal said. "We got de juice to git us dere." He looked at Travis. "Now we gotta git de *ship* to git us dere."

Travis had his face in his hands. Now he looked up. Not a happy man.

"History repeats itself," he said. "This country has never really had a 'space program.' What we've had is a series of races. *Sputnik One* went up in 1957 and scared the be— . . . the dickens out of us. Up to then the biggest part of our space program was something called Project Vanguard. Run by the Navy, of all things. In the '30s the Navy ran the airship program, too. I don't know why."

"To keep it out of the hands of the fly-boys, that's why," Dak said.

"See there?" He pointed at Dak. "Your dad was a swabbo, wasn't he?"

"Watch yo mouf', white boy. My dad was a chief petty officer. Probably still would be, but he got kicked out during a force reduction. And I'll give you Army and thirteen points right here and now." Dak slapped a twenty on the table.

"You're faded," Travis said. "And the Navy wrecked every airship they had, the *Akron*, the *Macon*, the *Shenandoah* . . ."

"Prob'ly had Army pilots. Naval carrier aviation is the best—"

"Boys," Kelly said. "Can we get back to the subject?"

"There was a subject?" Alicia wondered.

"Yeah," Travis said. "Going off too soon, half-cocked. The Navy never *did* get a Vanguard off the ground. So *Sputnik One* goes up and goes, 'beep, beep, beep,' and every citizen of America sees the Russkis own outer space, and they are asking their leaders what they're going to do about it.

"What they did was hand it to Werner von Braun, the top Nazi Kraut we captured at the end of the war. He takes a Jupiter rocket, modifies it a little, and ninety days later there's an American satellite in orbit.

"And we were off to the races. President Kennedy said we were going to the moon by 1969. Everybody knew it was not enough time, there was no way to get there that fast . . . safely. That's the key word.

"There's two ways we could have got to the moon. The way everybody assumed it would be done in the '40s and '50s was the piece-by-piece approach. Develop a ship something like the VentureStar, an SSTO, single-stage-to-orbit vehicle. Start putting hardware and people into orbit. Build a space station. It could be *huge* by now if we'd started in 1958. Then build your moonship in orbit. Make it a ship like the Lunar Excursion Module, in that it will never land on Earth, but *not* like the Lunar Excursion Module in that you don't throw it away after you've used it once. It returns to Earth's orbit, refuels, and goes right back to the moon with more people. *More* people, because right there, right from the *very first flight*, we would have been on the moon to *stay*. Put up some shelters on the first landing, stay there a week or so. Your moonships start regular trips back and forth. In a couple years you've got a decent colony, a few hundred people. By about 1990 you're sending people to Mars, by 2000 you've got ships on the way to Jupiter's and Saturn's moons.

"That's the way everybody figured it in engineering circles in 1958."

Travis was up and pacing now, and he paused, getting his second wind. Obviously he had been angry about this for a long time.

"But there was another way to get to the moon. You've heard of 'fast, cheap, and dirty?' Call this the von Braun plan, fast, *very* expensive, and very dirty. But it was the only way to get there by December thirty-first, 1969.

"Say Columbus took the Apollo route to the New World. He starts off with three ships. Along about the Canary Islands he sinks the first ship, just throws it away, deliberately. And it's his biggest ship. Come to the Bahamas, he throws away the second ship. He reaches the New World . . . but his third ship can't land there. He lowers a lifeboat, sinks his third ship, and rows ashore. He picks up a few rocks on the beach and rows right back out to sea, across the Atlantic . . . and at the Strait of Gibraltar he sinks the lifeboat and swims back to Spain with an inner tube around his shoulders.

"If that's what it took to cross the Atlantic, this part of the world would still belong to the Seminoles."

"Would that be so bad?" Dak asked.

"Not for the Seminoles," Kelly said.

"The Apollo program was possibly the stupidest way of getting somewhere the human mind has yet achieved . . . but it was the only way to win the 'race.'

"And the race took a toll beyond the money it squandered. It cost three astronauts their lives. They burned to death in a pure oxygen environment that was *loaded* with combustible material. Strapped in, the hatch bolted, those guys burned to death because there hadn't been time to do the slow, methodical testing that should have been at the heart of the Apollo program.

"Don't get me wrong. I am in awe of the pioneers who flew in those things, and the people who built them. Nobody will ever see a Saturn 5 launch again, but believe me, it was an incredible sight.

"The whole thing, from Sputnik to Neil Armstrong, was done using methods we usually only see in wartime. It wasn't so much a race as a war. Look at the Manhattan Project. Time is critical, money is no object. We need the bomb *now*. So, if there's six different ways to refine uranium 235 out of ore, which way do we try first? Answer: Try all six, all at once.

"It worked. We got the bomb.

"The Apollo managers got all the money they needed because we were at war with Russia. Never got to shooting at each other, luckily, but it was war.

"Then, suddenly, we've made it to the moon . . . and what do we do for Act Two? Why . . . nothing. Nothing much, anyway. The public found the whole show boring. The funding dried up. We launched five more . . . and those guys were incredibly lucky, because the LEM functioned perfectly every time, something we had no right to expect. Even so, we almost lost Apollo 13.

"So when we were building a space plane, the next logical step, what happens? There's not enough money to build the ship we *should* have built, a very big, *piloted*, first stage that flies back to the Cape after the launch, mated to something that would have looked a lot like the original Shuttle. Instead, we give the Shuttle a pair of solid fuel boosters that fall in the ocean. It's madness to put a solid fuel booster on a manned craft. Once you light a solid booster you can't turn it off if something goes wrong.

"So something went wrong—with the *booster*, notice—seventy seconds into *Challenger*'s last flight, and seven more people die.

"Hurry-up is death, when you're dealing with rockets. So is underfunding."

"An' now," Jubal said, "now it happening all over 'gain."

Travis threw himself down into his seat, puffed out his cheeks.

"It appears so. The powers that be decided we needed to go to Mars, if the Chinese were going. And soon. Hang the cost. Hang the engineering quibbles." He looked dubiously at his cousin.

"Tell me this, Jubal. You say we can build us a spaceship, we can go out there and get them home if they get into trouble. And we can do it all in five months. Isn't this another space race? Aren't we likely to build something that will blow up in our faces?"

"Not my Squeezer machine," Jubal said. "It won't blow up, I guar-on-*tee*!"

"Okay, I believe you. But what about all the other things we'd have to do? You really think we have time?"

"Don' know. Maybe not."

"This race is a little different, Travis," Kelly said. "This time there's no choice as to whether we take it slow and careful. Lives are at stake if we *don't* build the rocket."

"We can try it a step at a time," I said, and Kelly looked sharply at me. "We can go test the rocket tomorrow, like you said. If it blows up, well, that's that. But we tried." Kelly gave me a short, relieved nod.

"Makes sense," Dak said. Alicia grabbed his hand.

"We do that t'ing tomorrow, Travis," Jubal said. "Jus' de test."

Travis looked at each of us in turn, and sighed.

"Just the test," he agreed. "Come on, I want to start in an hour."

IT TOOK AN hour and a half, but we got rolling by that afternoon. I called home and told them I'd be out all night. Mom said things were going smoothly, not to worry.

By nightfall we were passing through Miami.

17

★ ★ ★

WE TURNED EAST on the Tamiami Trail and drove on into the night. We were in three vehicles: Travis's Hummer, *Blue Thunder,* and a Ferrari demonstrator Kelly had chosen because it would piss off her dad to find it gone all night and the next day. The thing would go like a bomb, but what with the traffic we picked up around Palm Beach we never got a chance to open her up. The long, low, infernal machine seemed to be pouting most of the way.

It was one in the morning when we pulled into Everglades City, which was an exaggeration if there ever was one. Most of the few hundred inhabitants were snug in bed as we bounced over mud and shell roads until we stopped in front of an old Airstream trailer set up on cinder blocks. The porch light was on. Flowering plants hung from the awning and from poles.

As Travis pulled the Hummer in beside the rusting hulk of a pickup truck, a dog I later learned was a black-and-tan coonhound lifted his head and bounded down the steps. Half a dozen more came out from under the deck. The dogs didn't bark, but circled the vehicles nervously. Travis held his hand out and the dominant male sniffed it, then started running in circles, wagging his tail. On the other side of the Hummer

Jubal was getting out, laughing and tussling with two other dogs, who were so happy to see him I thought they might have a little urinary accident, but they didn't.

"I figure we stay in the car until we're introduced," Kelly said.

"Good plan."

The screen door flew open and a huge man came out, followed by a woman almost as big. Not fat, either of them, just built large and powerful. I could see immediately that the man was related to Jubal. They had the same eyes and the same mouth. One of his many brothers?

He shouted something at the dogs and they all came to him and sat, quivering.

"Y'all can come out now," Travis called to us. "Let the dogs sniff your hands and you'll be okay. They're hunting dogs, not guard dogs. Cousin Caleb breeds the best black-and-tans in the state of Florida."

"Georgia and Mississip', too," the big guy bellowed. Then he had his arms around Jubal and was pounding him on the back hard enough to kill a normal man. Travis embraced the woman, then they switched and did it all over again.

Introductions were made all around. Caleb was officially Celebration Broussard, but like all but one of his brothers, he had simplified his name "when Pappy went away." His wife was Grace. Behind the two of them a boy—young man, really, about fourteen or fifteen—had come out of the trailer and was introduced as Billy, their son.

"Lord have mercy!" Caleb shouted when all that was out of the way. "If that ain't the finest rig I ever *did* see. You do all that work yourself, Dak?" Dak allowed as how he had, and the two of them talked pickup trucks while Billy's eyes went straight to the red Ferrari . . . and the gorgeous woman who had been driving it. The pimply-faced little jerk. He blushed when Kelly shook his hand. Out here in Everglades City, he probably never saw a pretty female except on television.

"Y'all been driving a long time," Grace said. "You must be real hungry."

"We had some ham sandwiches at a 7-Eleven," Travis said. "Don't put yourself out, we're fine."

Well, *I* wasn't all that fine, I was famished. But I was far too polite to say so.

It didn't matter. Grace would have stuffed food into our mouths with a funnel, if that's what it took. Pretty soon we were sitting around a big table groaning with fiery, rich, fattening Cajun food, and there's no finer food in the world.

Jubal was on my right, and he jabbed me with an elbow. He had a twinkle in his eye and was practically wriggling with suppressed joy.

"Watch dis, Manny," he said, then bowed his head, but looked up under his brow.

"Would somebody say grace?" Jubal asked.

"Grace," Travis said.

"Yes?" Grace said.

Jubal giggled, and soon we were all laughing. Not much of a joke, I guess you had to be there. Jubal could be so childlike and innocent, and when he laughed it was almost impossible not to laugh with him.

". . . and tell my peckerwood little brother not to let another five years go by 'fore he visits us again," Caleb finished.

"Amen," Jubal said, with feeling. Travis nodded, looking a bit guilty. Well, he should have been, if the brothers hadn't seen each other in that long.

Then we all dug in.

I'd already demolished a plateful before I realized the big table was actually *too* big. Too big for the trailer, anyway. I saw then that Caleb and Grace had added on to the rig, tearing out one side, welding a second trailer to the one out front and then adding a structure on behind that. No telling what all was back there. Welding was one of Caleb's many professions, along with carpentry and plumbing and "anything needs doing around here." It looked like very good work to me, not the sort of redneck chaos I'd expected when we pulled up in front.

When we had each turned down a third invitation to eat more, Grace got up and called me and Kelly and Dak and Alicia to the doorway leading further into the trailer-building. We found ourselves in a narrow hallway with doors on each side.

"We'd all love to sit around and chat with y'all all night," she said, "but Travis says he wants to get an early start, so I figure y'all better catch a little rest. When Travis says early, he means *early*."

It turned out all the doors were bedrooms. Grace opened a door and beckoned. On the other side was a room clearly belonging to a girl. From the rock star posters on the wall my guess was she would be twelve or thirteen. The room was immaculate, and smelled slightly of a floral air freshener. There were towels and washcloths neatly folded on the double bed.

"This is Dottie's room," Grace said. "She's my eleven-year-old. The bathroom's down at the end of the hall."

"Oh, Grace," Kelly said, "we don't want to put your daughter out of her room. We'll be all right just to—"

"Don't you worry about Dottie, honey. She's stayin' over, slumber partyin' with friends, and I'm sure they're havin' a ball. Probably all still awake. Y'all get some rest now, hear?"

She closed the door, and Kelly leaned close to my ear and spoke softly.

"I should have known nobody in the Broussard family would have only one child," she said. We tried to laugh quietly since the walls were thin. It turned out there were eight bedrooms in the rear extension, one for each child, with Caleb and Grace's bedroom in the original trailer. "Just added a room on every time a new one was born," Travis told us later.

We sat on the bed and fooled around a little, then admitted to each other that we were worn out from the long drive. We got into bed, and I was asleep instantly.

BREAKFAST WAS RUSHED. Travis kept us all moving. Me and Dak and Kelly were bleary-eyed, Dak muttering that if he never saw another crawfish it'd be too soon as he carefully sipped at a glass of milk. Alicia was one of those hateful people who woke up with a spring in her step and a song in her heart. She hummed as she made one of her horrible concoctions in Grace's blender, adding who-knows-what that she'd brought along herself to whatever fruit Grace had handy, then even got Grace to taste it. Grace was either an accomplished liar or she actually dug the stuff.

Travis and Jubal had been up all night and didn't look the worse for wear. They each downed cups of strong coffee while I nibbled on the buttered toast Grace had made when she couldn't persuade me to let her get out her skillet. We all drank lots of coffee.

I got in *Blue Thunder* and Kelly sat in the back of the Hummer with Jubal. That was Kelly's idea. We'd decided we didn't want to leave the two of them alone unnecessarily or they might cut us out of the spaceship project. I didn't know what Kelly could do to prevent that, but if someone could, she was the one.

When Caleb started his pickup it shuddered hard enough to rain flakes of rust down on the dirt. He put it in gear and started out . . . and the whole tailpipe and muffler and cat converter assembly fell off. Caleb sprang out of the truck, grabbed the pipe, and tossed it on the side of the road.

"Dak, that is the sorriest truck I ever saw that could actually move," I said.

"He done used it hard, all right," Dak said. "Especially when you consider it's only four years old."

I looked again, and saw he was right.

"Running through salt water, carrying heavy loads down roads ain't much more than deer tracks . . . it takes it out of a vehicle. But don't be fooled. That engine is excellent, he's got good struts and good rubber, heavy-duty power train. Caleb just don't give much of a . . . flip what the thing looks like."

We got under way as the sun was just breaking over the eastern horizon. I hoped we weren't trying to sneak up on anybody, since Caleb's truck with no muffler was now about as loud as an armored invasion.

We had left the Ferrari at the Broussards' and I could soon see why. That Italian terminator would have high-centered out within the first quarter mile as we bounced over a deeply rutted road into the swamp.

Actually, *further* into the swamp, as daylight had made it clear that Caleb and Grace's place was already well into it.

"Don't worry about your car none, Kelly," Caleb had told her as he climbed into the cab of the pickup. "Anybody looks at that whiz-banger crooked, Billy'll wrap a gun barrel round his fool head. Slept out here on the porch last night with a shotgun 'crost his lap. Lucky thing a dog didn't bark or he'd of blowed off a toe."

Much of the vastness of the Florida Everglades is roadless, trackless, "where the hand of man has never set foot," as the saying goes. The Jeep tracks that lead into it, like the one we'd used to reach the Broussard abode, tended to peter out in a few miles. Then, here and there, the passage of a few four-wheel-drive vehicles a week has made some informal routes along what little ground isn't four feet deep in quicksand or gumbo mud. Some of them are indicated on maps, others aren't. But we didn't need any maps with Caleb leading the way. He knew them all, or claimed to.

This was not the Florida I knew. I could identify some of the plants from seeing tamer versions in people's yards or in city parks. They grew differently out here. But I'm a city boy, don't know much about plants even in town.

Don't know much about birds, either, but this was the place to come if you wanted to learn. I never saw so many birds. They'd explode from the reeds and moss-hung trees when they heard us coming. Big birds, little birds, great big flocks of black birds, thousands of egrets or cranes or something like that who just stood there and watched us go by.

Me and Alicia both craned our necks the first time Dak pointed out a big old alligator sunning himself beside a ditch. We watched him glide powerfully into the water and vanish up to his eye sockets. Wow!

Two miles later it was here a gator, there a gator, everywhere an alligator. Ho-hum. We actually had to wait for one to get out of the road in front of us. The gator probably thought of it as a gator track . . . and he'd be right. He was here first, he'd watched the dinosaurs come and go, and maybe he'd be here still once this critter calling itself "humanity" killed itself off.

They say the Everglades are in trouble, what with the water being siphoned off up north, Miami advancing from the east, pesticides, global warming, I don't know what all. And I believe them. But just driving through for the first time, I was in awe at the sheer numbers of the wildlife we saw.

Unfortunately, among that wildlife you had to count the mosquitoes.

Billions of mosquitoes.

Now we knew why Caleb had tossed a big plastic bottle of Off! on the front seat of *Blue Thunder*. We coated ourselves with the stuff, Alicia slathering it on Dak as he drove. *Blue Thunder* didn't have an air conditioner—one of the few vehicles in Florida without one—but it wouldn't have mattered, because we all knew we'd be out in the open soon enough, whenever Caleb got where he was taking us.

The repellent helped, but about one in a hundred of those critters seemed to think Off! was just there to oil up their bloodsucker, make it easier to slide it into the skin. It appears we're breeding a better, stronger skeeter out there in the swamps, and when their kids grow up, look out!

OUR DESTINATION TURNED out to be the rotting remains of a dock, smack in the middle of nowhere. I know, because somebody had put up a sign: MIDDLE OF NOWHERE. Redneck humor, I guess. The sign was about to fall over.

A flat-bottom Cajun pirogue could have made it through the shallow channels we saw winding around the hammocks and cypress knees and mangroves, but you'd have to pole it. An outboard propeller would have stuck in the mud.

Caleb and Travis pulled a big canvas tarp off a big lumpy thing sitting next to the dock and I wasn't too surprised to see it was an airboat. Where the four-wheel tracks end, that's where the airboat trails begin.

It was a wide, flat-bottom aluminum hull, extremely shallow draft, designed to skim over the water rather than cut through it. At the back was an aircraft engine mounted high in a safety cage. In front of it, almost as high, was a sort of crow's nest seat for the pilot to sit in, way up where he could more easily pick out his route. An airboat didn't need much water under the hull. An inch was plenty. If you had a good head of steam and kept going, it would glide right over mud, too. Even dry land, for a while. "Don't need no more water'n a skeeter can spit," Caleb said as we boarded.

This one had once been a tourist boat. There were four rows of comfortable bench seats, with pads faded and cracked open by the relentless sun over the years, yellow foam stuffing showing here and there.

We all piled out of the vehicles, the mosquitoes swarming again now that we'd stopped. We put on more repellent, but nothing was going to make them go away completely, so we worked quickly, hoping to get moving again soon.

Travis and Jubal lifted a big cardboard box out of the back of *Blue Thunder*. It didn't appear too heavy. They opened it and for the first time we saw the experimental test vehicle Jubal had cobbled together.

I can't really say that it looked too impressive.

It was a five-foot tube of heavy-duty six-inch gray PVC pipe, the kind you'd buy for an ordinary plumbing project. A tapered nose cone had been fitted on the top of it. Below were three metal fins that also acted as legs for it to stand on. Under the tube was a spherical metal cage, the only part of the contraption that looked as if a fair amount of work had gone into it. Without knowing about Jubal's Squeezer dingus, I'd never have known what it was for. It was intended to hold a silver bubble about the size of a softball.

I'd seen better rockets at the school science fair.

They put it on its side on the front bench of the airboat and tied it down with bungee cords. Two aluminum suitcases were set on the floor in front, and we were ready to go. Caleb climbed up into the pilot's seat and started the engine.

Soon we were flying along on the smooth water.

THE WIND IN our faces whipped away even the steroid-pumped Everglades mosquitoes. The day had not yet begun to get hot. The water below us was the color of weak tea and the sky above blue and cloudless. We barreled along through a primeval world where I could easily imagine duck-billed dinosaurs browsing in the trees. Kelly squeezed my hand and smiled at me.

I'd had worse days.

ON A MAP you can see hundreds of what they call hammocks scattered through the Everglades. There are also islands, streams, creeks, sloughs. The hammocks on the maps could be miles long, but even the smallest-scale maps didn't indicate the ones that were only an acre or two, because they weren't very permanent features.

Caleb finally beached the airboat on a bare knuckle of cracked mud that might have had enough room to park a dozen cars . . . if you didn't mind seeing them sink like mammoths in the La Brea Tar Pits. We had to step carefully when we got out. My first step cracked through the skin of dried mud and I almost lost a shoe. The footing was a bit firmer in the center of the little island.

Looking around, I wasn't sure why Caleb had selected this place, an hour's ride from where we'd left the vehicles. Most every mile of swamp we passed through seemed just as isolated as any other mile, though I knew this wasn't strictly true. We saw other airboats passing in the distance, and once came close enough to wave at the driver.

We quickly saw that we were basically just along for the ride, and because Jubal wanted us there. Travis and Jubal set the rocket on its end near the center of the hammock, then started placing other devices around it. Neither of them had anything to say, they just worked steadily stringing wires, plugging things into other things, sweat dripping off their foreheads. The rest of us stood around, slapping at mosquitoes.

It occurred to me that, if this thing worked, we might be about to witness something as historic as the Wright brothers' first flight. But to tell the truth, all I wanted to do was get it done and get out of there. I was getting eaten alive!

I mentioned the Wright brothers analogy to Kelly, and she slapped her forehead and dug around in her purse. In a moment she found a pink throwaway PrettyPixel camera and started snapping pictures as fast as she could click the shutter. Travis frowned, and told her those pics would have to be considered classified information for the time being.

"Yes, sir, Colonel Broussard," she said, and kept snapping away. "And stupid me, I left my vidcam home sitting on my desk."

Which is why there is no video of the maiden—and final—flight of the good ship *Everglades Express,* and why Kelly appears in only one picture taken that day, when Caleb insisted the six of us pose in front of the completed rocket setup, a bug-bitten family looking like they'd rather be anywhere else but this hellhole.

They had it all ready in no more than half an hour. Jubal stood looking at it, his fists on his hips, nodding in satisfaction. He put his hand on the conical nose cone. There was a round piece of glass set into it.

"Dis eye," Jubal said, "dis eye find de sun, yes she does. Lock on to de sun, den keep herself in dat attitude fo' all de flight. Dat way she go straight up."

We all piled back in the boat and Caleb eased us off the mud flat and back through the shallow water as Travis paid out a cable from a Radio Shack reel.

At two hundred feet Travis looked at Jubal.

"Far enough, Jube?"

I didn't like the frown I saw on Jubal's brow. He muttered, then looked around, and smiled when he found what he was looking for.

"Ovah dere," he said. He was pointing at another hammock, this one a bit bigger than Rocket Hammock. Caleb moved the boat over there, and we could see on the other side there was a small eroded bank, maybe three feet high, with a fallen tree trunk lying on top of it. Now we could crouch down behind the bank and the tree and be protected if the rocket should blow up.

Travis and Jubal took another five minutes plugging the ends of the wires into an old laptop computer and then they were ready. Travis handed out safety glasses and hard hats from the boat, and we all put them on.

"I think we should all get down behind the bank," Dak said.

"Can't we peek over the top?" Kelly asked. "I want to get pictures."

We all looked at Jubal, who was again looking nervous.

"Go ahead on," he said. "Peek. But be careful, *cher.*"

Travis had the remote control in his hands. I put my arm around Kelly. Then I looked at Jubal. He grinned, and shrugged.

"T'ree, two, one, an—"

He flicked the launch switch as he said "zero," and the world exploded.

There was a shock wave that blew my helmet off, an explosion that sounded like a bomb going off. And directly ahead I saw a wall of mud rushing toward me.

"Oh, me oh my," Jubal said, and the wall hit us.

It was actually a wall of water, a big wave maybe four feet high, but it was thicker than water had any right to be. It was full of mud, decaying leaves, twigs. We all tried to fall back in front of it, but there was nothing but more water behind us. I staggered a few steps before sitting down in the glop, and the wave crested over the bank we'd been sheltering behind, then over us.

For a few seconds everything was dark, then my head broke through and I was gasping . . . and that's when the water and mud that had been blown into the air started to rain down on us. I don't think the planet has often seen a filthier rain. A bullfrog landed on me and sat in my lap for a moment, stunned.

Travis was shouting something I couldn't hear clearly, something about covering our heads. My hardhat had been swept away. I found Kelly and we huddled together, hunched over, hoping the explosion hadn't been powerful enough to throw any sizable rocks or tree trunks into the air.

It was over in a few seconds, though it seemed a lot longer. The water settled down, the mud stopped falling from the sky.

"Did it blow up, Jubal?" Alicia shouted.

"No 'splosion, *cher,*" he said, then pointed into the air. *"Look!"*

We did, and saw a straight white line rising from the launch site, already twisted a little as the air currents caught it. Far, far away the line was still growing as the tiny rocket reached the upper levels of the atmosphere. Kelly and I stood up unsteadily and watched the line dwindle and lengthen . . . and suddenly it stopped.

"What happened?" I asked Jubal. "Run out of fuel?"

"No, Manny." Jubal entered some numbers on the mud-covered computer. "Outta de atmosphere. She up 'bout eight mile now."

Caleb was standing in the boat, bailing with a galvanized metal bucket. He looked up and tossed me a plastic bait bucket.

"Bail, son," he said. "We gotta get outta here. This tub don't fly too good with two ton of mud in her, and she got no scuppers."

I didn't know a scupper from a yardarm, but I could see what he meant. I got to work, and was soon joined by all the others using their hard hats, except Travis, who was reeling in cable as fast as he could wind it. We worked like a road gang in hell.

One good thing about the mud. The mosquitoes couldn't bite through it.

We had the boat about as dry as it was going to get when Travis pointed into the sky and shouted. Squinting into the glare, I saw four contrails way, way up there. They were flying close, then they moved apart and circled around the remains of the rocket's vapor trail like bloodhounds casting for a scent.

"Fighter group," Travis said. "Probably from the base at Boca Chica Key."

"Navy jets," Dak said.

"You think they're looking for us?" Alicia asked.

"They ain't counting alligators, hon. What else is there out here they might want to see? I never thought the sucker would go up so *fast!*"

"I t'ink I mighta dropped a—"

"Later, Jube. We got to get outta here. Try to look like tourists!"

We scrambled in and Caleb got us moving. Look like tourists? How were we going to do that, covered in mud?

Kelly started scooping handfuls of water and splashing it over her hair and her face. The rest of us did, too. I dipped a plastic bucket into the water . . . and promptly lost it, snatched right out of my hand when I let it go too deep. I held on to the next one better, and dumped it over Dak's head. He sputtered and grabbed the bucket from me.

"I don't need cleaning up!" he shouted. "I don't show the dirt like you whiteys do!" And he dumped a bucketful on me. Pretty soon we were mostly free of mud, though we were ankle deep in chocolate-colored water. Even though the air was humid, I figured the rushing wind would dry us pretty soon.

"Over there!" Travis yelled in my ear, and I looked where he was pointing. Far away three elongated specks were moving through the air at treetop level. Travis reached up and tapped Caleb's leg. Caleb nodded. Travis pointed to a thicket of mangroves, and Caleb arrowed straight for it. He turned off the engine and the silence surrounded us. After a moment we could hear the sound of the distant helicopters.

"Hueys," Travis said, quietly.

"Did we do something wrong?" Kelly whispered.

"Why are we all whispering?" Alicia whispered. Dak laughed.

"We probably broke some federal laws about fireworks in a nature preserve, something like that," Travis said. We knew he wouldn't be behaving like this if that was all that was the matter. "I don't want to get noticed by the military. Or even the Everglades rangers, for that matter. This has all got to stay secret."

Before long the Hueys were too far away to see or hear. Caleb backed us out of the briar patch and headed us back home. But soon he was slowing again. He waved, and I stood up and could see another airboat piloted by a grizzled old conch who must have been seventy. There was a tangle of weeds and vines between us, keeping us about twenty yards apart. A tourist couple was sweltering in pants and long-sleeved shirts, wearing safari hats with netting veils. They waved happily to us and we waved back, smiling. Kelly snapped their picture, and the woman snapped right back at her.

"Broussard!" the old man shouted over the idling engines. "Did you hear an explosion, ol' hoss?"

"Heard something, McGee," Caleb allowed. "Back yonder, I think." He pointed at an angle at least ninety degrees away from where the launch had actually happened.

"Saw something takin' off like a rocket, too."

"Probably just some kids. You know how they are."

"Yeah . . . in my day it was cherry bombs."

"These days, it's likely to be an H-bomb," Caleb laughed.

McGee leaned over and spit in the water, which didn't make his female passenger too happy. "Y'all take care, now, y'hear?"

IT WAS FUNNY how, on the way out, I figured we were probably the only human beings for twenty miles in any direction. Coming back, I thought somebody needed to install a traffic light.

I'm exaggerating. But we saw maybe a dozen other airboats. There were pickups and SUVs and ATVs on the dirt roads, and small planes overhead. None of them gave us any reason to believe they were looking for us.

We made it back to the Middle of Nowhere in about an hour, then to Caleb's trailer-home in fifteen minutes. Travis was in a big hurry. We took hasty showers, said our good-byes, thanked Grace for the food—and accepted a picnic basket crammed with more of it—then piled back into our vehicles and hit the road.

When Kelly saw that Nephew Billy had washed all the road grime and bugs off the Ferrari she kissed him on the cheek. I shook his hand anyway.

IN WHAT I thought was an excess of paranoia, Travis insisted the three vehicles not drive together, but maintain a five-minute separation. We were taking Alligator Alley back to Fort Lauderdale, so it wasn't hard.

"I've been asleep at the wheel as far as security goes," he told us during a cellular conference call. "From now on, we're going to be more careful than we've been. You gotta remember—"

"Travis," I interrupted. "If we're going to be careful . . . do you think we should be discussing these things on cell phones?"

There was silence for a moment. Kelly looked over and gave me a thumbs-up.

"Manny, you're a genius and I'm a jerk-off idiot. Everybody hang up and meet me at Bahia Mar in Lauderdale. We'll have lunch."

* * *

BAHIA MAR IS one of your nicer marinas. About a zillion dollars' worth of rich folks' playtoys were tied up at the finger piers, motor and sail, blinding white and those deep blue tarps they wrap sails in. We found each other easily enough, and Travis led the way to a pretty city park and we all unloaded Grace's lunch onto a picnic table. There was a bucket of fried chicken and a big Tupperware box of potato salad and scratch buttermilk biscuits and a watermelon for dessert. There was also a red-and-white checkered tablecloth to put it all on, heavy plastic plates and spoons, and a big thermos of grape Kool-Aid.

"I have screwed up just about everything I've tried so far," Travis said after the food had been distributed. "You notice my crazy neighbor lately? He's ready to take off on a flying saucer with Jesus. Which is what he saw the day I landed you all in the pool by fiddling with something I didn't understand.

"As for today's fiasco . . . what was I thinking?"

"I'm sorry, Trav—"

"Not your fault, Jubal."

"It was a decimal point, jus' a little—"

"I know, Jube, I know. But I can't afford to drop any more decimal points. Friends, Jubal did a search while I was driving . . . show 'em, Jube."

Jubal went to http://liftoff.msfc.nasa.gov/RealTime/JTrack/3D/JTrack3D.html on his computer. I knew the site. It kept track of all satellites in orbit. We saw a display of the Earth surrounded by thousands of dots, many of them in a ring at the geosynchronous distance of 22,500 miles. Jubal zoomed in on Florida, then the southern tip of Florida, and entered the time of the launch. We saw a handful of satellites and lines representing their orbits. Jubal moved the cursor over one.

"Dat be Friendship Station. She were 'bout two hunnerd miles away when de rocket go shootin' by."

"Jes . . . You mean we could have hit it?" Alicia asked.

"It would have been a trillion-to-one shot to hit it," Travis said. "That doesn't worry me. No, the thing that worries me is that our bird would have showed up on their radar. Also this satellite, and this one. Not to mention ground radars. Now some people in our government know there's something out there that can outperform any rocket in their arsenal. I mean, our bird was accelerating at *twenty gees,* and it would have kept it up until it was out of radar range. When they lost it, it was traveling faster than any man-made object has ever traveled. *Ever,* in the history of the world."

We all digested that for a while. Suddenly I didn't feel so hungry.

"Now our government knows there's somebody out there with a powerful new technology. I'm sure they're going to want it. And what I worry about is our alphabet soup of intelligence agencies. FBI, CIA, NSA, DIA."

"What about SMERSH?" I asked, joking. Travis didn't laugh.

"I've often asked myself that question," he said. "Is there a super, *super* secret agency in the government, accountable to no one, licensed to kill, like in a James Bond movie? I hope not, but there's no way for us to know. By its nature nobody would ever have heard of it."

" 'If I told you, I'd have to kill you,' " Dak said.

"Exactly. So it's a waste of time to worry about something like that. I'm worried enough about the ones we *do* know about.

"By triangulating the radar signatures they know where we did it. I can't think they would learn much from the launch site. It's hard digging in the 'Glades. That hole in the ground filled up with muddy water before we even left.

"What worries me most is that I stupidly let us drive into a small, isolated town in three of the most memorable vehicles in Florida."

I looked at our little automotive fleet. It was so obvious once he'd said it, but it hadn't occurred to me. Even now, there were half a dozen neighborhood kids standing around the vehicles, gawking.

"They've got satellites that can read a license plate from orbit, and it was a clear day, but I strongly doubt they took any pictures. Why would they?"

"But people will talk," Kelly murmured.

"You said it. Old man McGee saw us, and so did those tourists. As for McGee, he wouldn't be apt to have much to say to a federal agent, on account of the five years of federal time he did behind a marijuana smuggling conviction back in the '70s. Not to mention that he'd assume they were revenuers out to find his still.

"We drove straight through town. Those folks aren't inclined to gab, but it will come out, and it may be linked to Caleb."

That was the worst news I'd heard so far. How far would those snoops go, if they suspected Caleb and his family had something to do with the launch?

"What's done is done," Travis said. "We can't take it back. But we can lie as low as we are able for a while, and we can be more careful in the future. Deal?"

We all agreed . . . and pretty soon Dak wished he hadn't.

"Kelly," Travis went on, "I guess you'll be putting that Roman firebomb back in your father's lot. Not much we can do about it, I guess. I'm hoping that anyone comes snooping around won't figure a Ferrari demonstrator was likely to be the one showed up in Everglades City today."

Kelly looked thoughtful for a moment.

"I can probably do better than that. Let me think on it."

"Good enough. Dak . . ." I could see Dak hadn't gotten it yet. "Dak, could you . . . could you garage that blue beast for a while?"

Dak's eyes widened with surprise, then he gave a deep sigh.

"Sure, Trav. For a while. You got a bicycle I could borrow?"

"No, but I've got another bike somewhere. You could use that." Dak looked a lot happier. "Manny, you keep the Triumph for a while."

"Oh, gosh, do I have to?"

"Such a sacrifice," Alicia laughed, and slapped my back.

Kelly held out the chicken wishbone, hooked around her greasy pinkie finger. I took the other end and pulled.

Oh, please, let us build this thing.

Short end.

"Don't worry, sweetheart," she said. "Maybe we wished for the same thing."

18

★ ★ ★

"JUBAL THINKS AMERICANS ought to be the first people to set foot on Mars," Travis said. "I agree with him, but before a few weeks ago it was impossible. Now it is possible, with something Jubal has made, and I'm going to tell you how it can be done."

Travis, who had been pretty much on the wagon for several weeks, had told us he had to have a shot or two . . . or three, before facing an audience scarier than any he had ever faced in his life: Mom, Aunt Maria, and Dak's father. Alicia had doled the whiskey out to him, and he had walked into the lion's den.

The three of them sat in Mom's living room on the old sprung couch and easy chair that qualified as a "family heirloom" in my poor family. It was after midnight, the VACANCY sign had been turned off and the office door locked. It was now just the six of us and the three of them. Travis was going to explain how he and Jubal proposed to build a spaceship and take their precious sons to Mars.

You couldn't find stonier faces on Mount Rushmore.

Sitting on the coffee table along with a couple open two-liter bottles of generic cola and some Dixie cups was a pitiful torn bag of stick pretzels and a small plastic container of cold supermarket guacamole dip. I swear, if Fidel Castro himself climbed out of his grave and came to visit, Aunt Maria would have at least heated up a little refried beans and salsa.

Travis sighed deeply and started in on his spiel. I squeezed Kelly's hand and said a silent prayer to Ares, the God of War.

THE NIGHT AFTER we launched the test rocket we all pulled into the lot behind Strickland Mercedes and parked. Travis and Jubal got out of the Hummer and squeezed into the backseat of *Blue Thunder*. Dak beeped the horn once as he pulled out, and Kelly and I went to the back door. One of her keys opened it, and she hurried over to the security control on the wall and punched in a five-digit code.

Kelly's dad was the kind who liked to keep a close eye on his employees, even when he was busy with other things. Therefore, he'd had his office located above and slightly behind the salespeople's cubicles. He could look down through a glass wall onto the tops of their desks, and beyond them to the showroom floor.

"Master of all he surveys," Kelly said as we climbed the broad spiral staircase. Another key got her into his office, and another five-digit number entered into another keypad got us secure access.

I couldn't help feeling like a burglar, and like a goldfish in a bowl. I knew I hadn't done anything illegal, Kelly had a perfect right to invite me in, but I also knew I was emphatically not welcome by her father. And what Kelly was going to do *was* illegal. I hated it that I could see right outside to the new cars parked out in front, and the road, and the I-95 freeway just beyond it. Traffic was light at three A.M.

She booted the computer and I pulled up a chair to watch an artist at work.

"Enter Daddy Dear's security code, right out of the book . . . done," she muttered. "Password . . . oh, my, now whatever could his password be?" She looked at me, and I shrugged.

"Let's try something . . ." She typed, her fingers moving too fast for me to get any of it. In the password box ************ appeared, then the security page disappeared and a menu came up.

"Pretty good," I said. She smirked at me, and pulled out a flat wood panel above the side drawers on the big executive desk. She turned it over. Taped to the bottom was a piece of paper with the word *ferraristud* in ballpoint, and several numbers.

"PIN numbers," she said.

"Dumb."

" 'Ferrari-stud' is his online handle, too. He uses that when he goes to an escort service website and has one of the girls drop by here when he's working late. I have quite a file on him. I read all his mail. I know all his secrets, and believe me, some of them could get him ten to twenty in Raiford."

She called up an internal database and easily changed the color of her borrowed Ferrari from "red" to "black." She did something involving dealer plates and registrations that I didn't really understand. Then she went to the DMV.

"Every car dealer in America has some kind of fiddle going with somebody at the DMV, if they can afford it," she said. "The guy I'm leaving an e-mail with makes good money on the side by doing little chores for us, when the need arises."

A patrol car was passing along the street out there. His turn indicator was on, and he was about to enter the lot. I tapped Kelly on the shoulder and pointed.

She stood and waved. The officer riding shotgun spotted her and waved, said something to his partner, and they sped off.

"Safer up here," she pointed out. "The cops are used to me working late."

When she shut the computer down we went to her office, where a printer was chattering. She pulled the paper out. It was a dealer's window sticker listing equipment and options and price. She pointed to where it now listed the color as black. She said it was listed that way in all the documentation at the dealership, and in the morning it would be listed that way at the DMV, too.

"They'd have to go all the way back to Italy to hear any different," she said. "We don't have any red Ferraris in inventory. They'll have to look elsewhere."

"The one problem I see with that," I pointed out, "the car actually *is* still red."

"Not for long."

Out back, a guy was sitting in the car scraping the old dealer sticker off the window with a razor blade. Another, younger man was standing by the car. The older guy smiled at Kelly.

"Midnight black, right?" he asked.

"As soon as possible." She held up two key rings.

"Let my boy drive the Hummer. This is my son, Josh." Kelly tossed him the Hummer keys. "What color you want it?"

"Whatever's most ordinary."

"That would be Desert Storm beige. Most of the right-wing militia generals in Florida drive around in Desert Storm camouflage Hummers."

They drove off, and Kelly told me that by this time tomorrow Travis's flamboyant red-and-black super-jeep would look like a Gulf War veteran.

"Sounds expensive," I said.

"Bob owes us some favors. He almost got himself in trouble a few years back, some pesky business about changing engine block numbers and paint on some cars whose ownership was . . . not quite crystal clear, let's say."

"Stolen."

"We car dealers don't like that term much. Misplaced." She grinned at me, and I realized Kelly was more of a pirate than I'd ever suspected.

I didn't have a problem with that.

THAT MORNING I caught up on some chores, got a few minutes' sleep in the afternoon, and then spent the evening and night in Kelly's little apartment on the beach south of town. We swam, lay on the beach and talked until it was dark, bought a pizza and took it to her place.

Kelly talked a lot about making a final break with her father but she hadn't done it yet. The fact was, she still kept a lot of her stuff in the huge, gated, fake-Greek pile of stone where her father lived with his second wife. She spent some nights there, some with her mother in Ormond Beach, some with me, and some at her own place. She didn't really *live* anywhere, in the way that most of us do.

The fact is, she didn't make enough money to afford the payments on her Porsche if she'd had to buy it herself.

She had money. I didn't know how much, but I figured it was substantial. It was in a trust her father had set up so she couldn't use any of it until she was twenty-five. Until then, she had to get by on the wages her father paid her—which even she and I, who loathed him, had to admit were fair for the work she did. He knew her value, and intended to keep her under his thumb as long as he could.

"I could quit and find another job pretty easy," she said. "I would probably take a small cut in pay, but it might be worth it not to have to deal with him every day. But I'd be just as bored as I am now. What I know is the *car* business. And I *hate* the car business. But what I do like is *business,* and I think I'd be good at it."

So she vacillated, and we talked. She never laughed at my plans to find a career in space, and she helped me with my studies. And we never talked about getting married.

THE NEXT DAY Travis and Jubal picked us up, very early, in a five-year-old Ford van with enough seats for the six of us. Before getting in Kelly looked it over quickly and asked Travis what he'd paid for it. When he told her she winced.

"You should have talked to me, Trav," she said.

"Just get in, Ms. Strickland Mercedes, okay?"

We picked up Dak and Alicia and hit the road, destination unknown. Boxes of Krispy Kremes and cups of strong coffee were passed around.

We took the A1A exit and crossed Merritt Island and entered the Kennedy Space Center grounds through an entrance I'd never used before. Travis showed a special pass to the gate guard, so I guess he still had a little pull around there.

We got there in time to witness something I'd never seen before: the raising of the world's largest garage doors to reveal the retired Shuttle

Atlantis and the old *Saturn 5,* newly restored after many years of sitting in the Florida sunshine and rain, now standing proudly and awesomely erect in one of the bays of the old Vehicle Assembly Building. All done to music, of course . . . *Also Sprach Zarathustra,* which was probably always going to be the anthem of space exploration, thanks to Stanley Kubrick.

"I want y'all to just look at that *Saturn 5* for a moment, kiddies," Travis said. "I want you to look at it, and I want you to consider the concept of *hubris.*"

"And dat be . . . what?" Jubal asked.

"That's what the ancient Greeks said when somebody was getting too big for his britches . . . or whatever Greeks wore under their togas. Excessive pride. Arrogance. I want you to look at that rocket and ask yourself . . . 'Are we biting off more than we can chew?' The builders of that thing are gods, in my book. And the Greeks warned mortals not to try to act like gods."

"It's not the same, Travis," I protested.

"No. We've got a few advantages over the guys who built and launched these things. Chiefly, unlimited fuel. Ninety-nine percent of that rocket was fuel, liquid oxygen and liquid hydrogen, which are very tricky to handle, very dangerous in themselves, even if you don't burn them in those huge engines. We don't have to worry about that.

"But we have to worry about just about everything else. Do you know how many million parts were in that thing, fully loaded, on its way to the moon?"

"No, how many?" Alicia asked.

"Well . . . I don't know, but it's a bunch. Somebody here can tell us. My point, though, is one faulty transistor could bring this behemoth down in flames. One screwup in space, and we'd be dead. Can we build that well?"

"Sure," Dak said, but it was impossible to stand in the shadow of that thing and say "sure" with any confidence. So I backed him up, and so did Alicia and Kelly. That left Jubal, and we all turned to him, the only guy whose vote really counted.

"I t'ink we can, ma fren's. But I promise you dis. De firs' minute I t'ink we *cain't* do it, I tell you right off."

It didn't bring a smile to Travis's face, but eventually he nodded his head.

"Let's go see the museum," he said.

KELLY AND ALICIA had never seen it. Isn't that always the way? I think our visit to Kennedy that morning fascinated them, gave them a glimpse of the fire that burned in Dak's and my guts. And if you were even vaguely considering something as screwy as going to Mars in a home-built spaceship . . . well, you couldn't help wanting to know more about the ones who had gone before you and the hazards they faced. The hazards *you* might soon be facing.

We ate our picnic lunch at a table in the shade near the rocket park, where many of the early missiles launched from Cape Canaveral made a metal forest of white trunks. It was hot, there weren't many tourists around. I had a funny thought. If we do this, and get famous, when they made a movie about us the director would want to shoot right here, where it all was decided.

"Have you given any thought to how much all this will cost?" Travis asked.

We all looked at each other. I'd certainly thought about it, but I didn't have a clue. The one thing I could say with absolute certainty was that it would take far, far more money than I had. Another thing I was pretty sure of was that if Travis didn't have enough money to do it, then it just wouldn't get done.

"One million dollah," Jubal said.

We all looked at him. Travis was frowning.

"Where did you get that number, beloved cousin of mine?"

"I pick it outta de air," Jubal admitted, and we all laughed. "But it oughta be plenty enough, I t'ink."

"I t'ink so, too," Kelly said, and Jubal patted her on the back.

"Okay, where did *you* get that figure?" Travis wanted to know.

"It's what I have in the bank, more or less," she said quietly.

Stunned silence.

"But I thought—" I started, then felt the daggers she was staring at me. Well, of course. The night before last I had watched her turn a red car into a black one. She had the computers, she had the security codes, the passwords, the bank account numbers, the PIN numbers. She could probably steal her old man blind, if she wanted to.

But that wasn't something we had to share with everyone.

"I know, it's awful," she said. "One person having so much, others having not anything. I can't help it. It's not easy, having money when your three best friends don't, and they won't let you give them some help here and there, when it's needed. It hurts me to see Manny's family struggling so hard . . . but none of them have ever asked me for a thing, and they haven't held my money against me.

"So, yeah, I've got money. About a million dollars. And I've been drifting since high school. I've been looking for something to do with my life. I've tried a lot of things. I met Alicia while I was volunteering at the battered women's shelter."

"She did more than that," Alicia said. "She put her money where her mouth was a couple times, saved the place from closing down once."

"It didn't take much," Kelly said. "And that kind of work is not for me, I found out. I'd get too depressed at the hopelessness of it all if I tried to make it my life's work.

"Today I learned about people who wanted to go to the moon, and they did it. It hasn't been my dream, and it may never be, but it's a place to start." She looked at Travis. "So how about it, Mr. Ex-Astronaut? Do you want to go to Mars, or will you let the chance pass you by? I'll bet you a million dollars we can do it."

Travis shook his head and smiled, slowly.

"I won't take that bet. Because if we do this thing, I'll jump in with both feet. So I'd be betting against myself."

"You faded, Kelly," Jubal said.

"What's that?" Travis asked.

"I say, I bet her one million dollah we cain't build us no ship and get to Mars. Dat way, I win, I kin give her back de money she waste jus' on account a believin' in me. *She* win, we go to Mars and she get my one million dollah."

"Jubal, I hate to remind you of this—"

"I know. You my loco parent. I always figgered dat one loco parent was plenty enough, yes." He smiled, and I tried to smile back, but it was tough, thinking of Avery Broussard and what he'd done to his brilliant son.

"In loco parentis," Travis said, wearily. "It means I'm your legal guardian."

News to me, but not surprising. Somebody like Jubal would have to have someone to look after his affairs.

Travis had mentioned once, before this whole scheme got started, that he and Jubal were living on the earnings from Jubal's patents. Jubal was the creative one, he had the crazy visions and built the marvelous things. Travis was the financial side. Though he didn't claim to be a whiz at handling money, he did it a thousand times better than Jubal ever could, and in fact, without Travis or someone like him to figure out the practical applications of Jubal's inventions and discoveries, Jubal would have nothing at all. "We do well," Travis had said. "Jubal's never going to lack for anything."

Oh, no? Well, now little Jubal wants a toy, Travis.

And now Jubal was frowning.

"You done said it was jus' to proteck me," he said. "From dose bad folks, take our money away, we ain't careful."

Travis was looking uncomfortable. I looked at Kelly, who was following with intense interest. She raised one eyebrow at me, and shook her head. *Don't interrupt.*

" 'Bout all I ever spent it on is de Krispy Kremes," Jubal said. Alicia laughed, and patted Jubal's hand.

"Is it my money, Travis? Is it my money?"

"It's your money, Jubal. Well, half of it is, anyway."

"And I gots de million dollah?"

"Yeah, you gots it. More than that. I'll show you the books, you don't believe me." He looked around at all of us, and got angry. "I'll show all of you the goddamn books if you want. I've never cheated Jubal out of a dime. Excuse the language, Jubal."

"Nobody ever thought you did, Travis," Kelly said. "But have you maybe . . . sheltered him too much? I'm not criticizing, it's none of my business, but Grace told me they'd like to see Jubal more. I think Jubal would like that, too."

Travis hung his head, then nodded, still not looking at us.

"I'm a drunk, okay? I've spent a lot of the last five years pissed out of my mind, as bad off as I was the night you almost killed me. I went out there on the beach to watch my ex-wife take off on her way to Mars . . . *because I was supposed to be on that ship!*

"I've *always* known, since I was a child, that I was going to be the first man on Mars. I planned for it, I worked hard. I made myself into the best pilot in the space program, so they *had* to choose me, there would be no one else.

"And then I drank it all away."

We were all quiet for a time. I watched a seagull that seemed to be building a nest in the top of one of the old rockets surrounding us.

"I knew I wasn't doing right by Jubal, but mostly I was too drunk to care. Since I met you guys I've been sober—mostly—and I want to thank you for that."

"It's all up to you, Travis," Alicia said.

"I know that."

"I be doin' okay, *cher,*" Jubal said. "I been worryin' 'bout *you,* oh yes, but you done good by me, you has."

Travis looked up and spread his hands in surrender.

"Okay. We'll build the ship."

None of us said anything. You could feel the excitement in the air, but there was no celebration.

Just as well.

"As soon as we get permission from your parents."

TRAVIS WAS GOOD. I think even Mom and Aunt Maria would have agreed, though nothing in their faces and their postures would admit to it. Sam Sinclair just sat, neutral, not accepting and not rejecting Travis's words. Sam Sinclair was a cautious man.

I knew a terrible surmise was growing in my mother's mind. Why was Travis telling them all this? There was really only one way to go with it, wasn't there? But she was afraid to let herself acknowledge it, because then she'd have an impossible problem. *How do I tell Manny he can't go . . . when I can't tell him he can't go?*

Travis outlined the present situation in space, with the Chinese due to arrive on Mars first, and the Americans taking a new, radical, and untested technology on a different path, which could not beat the Chinese . . . and might get them killed.

The spiel faltered only when he tried to get Jubal to help him explain the problems Jubal had found with the "Vaseline" drive. Jubal just wasn't up to it. His best effort so far had been calling his bubble-generating device a "Squeezer," and even then his mangled syntax had rendered it as "Squozer."

"Get on with it, Travis," my mom said, eventually. "If Jubal says it's going to blow up, I'll believe it's gonna blow up."

"That's enough for me, too," Sam said.

So Travis moved on to Part Two. That was good. Part Two was the real crowd pleaser. In Part Two he got to put the Squeezer through its paces.

Sam Sinclair sat up alertly from the very first time Travis made a silver bubble appear in the air. Mom and Aunt Maria looked puzzled. Clearly they understood this was something out of the ordinary, but they weren't sure why. Travis made the bubbles pop loudly both from vacuum and from compressed air. Then he fitted one into a small device Jubal had made. With Jubal operating his controller, they made compressed air leak out of a minute pinhole, what Jubal called a "dis-continual-uity," and particle physicists would more likely call a "discontinuity." He let them feel the air coming out, and experience the pressure the little thing exerted on their hands.

"That's thrust. It's the same thing that happens when all the smoke and flames come out the bottom of a VStar. You can fire all your thrust in a few minutes and get up to a very high speed and coast all the way to Mars. Or you can fire continually, like the *Ares Seven*. You'll speed up slowly, but eventually you could end up going faster than the Chinese ship."

"This don't make too much sense to me," Aunt Maria admitted.

"I know, I know," Travis said. "Nobody gets this stuff easily," he went on, "not without studying physics for years. Because it goes against everything you know. Cars don't work like that, do they?"

Mom tried a question. "But with this thing Jubal has made . . ." I think I was the only one who knew how much this was costing her, to ask a question that might sound like a *dumb* question. Mom was mortified by her lack of education, and she didn't deal with mortification well. "With this Squeezer thing, you can fire it all the way to Mars and never run out of gas?"

"Exactly. We get the best of both worlds with the Squeezer. We can fire a powerful rocket, the equal of any rocket that's ever been built in terms of thrust . . . and we can fire it *all the way there!*"

Short pause for everyone to think about that, me included. I still found it almost impossible to believe. *Free energy.* The world had never seen anything like it. And every time I thought about it, it scared me more.

Sam Sinclair, too.

"I don't like what I'm hearing here," he said.

"How's that, Sam?"

"Like you said. It's a lot of power. In my experience, power is dangerous, if you don't handle it right."

"I couldn't agree with you more."

"How big can Jubal make these things?"

Travis paused, then looked at his cousin. I think he might have prayed a little, too.

"How about it, Jubal? How big?"

Jubal had been dying inside for almost an hour now. He hated it that Mom and Maria and Sam, his friends, were acting so hostile, and he hated it even more that he was the cause of it. Or the thing he had created, which was about the same thing.

"I don' know, me. Plenty big, oh yeah."

"How about a ballpark figure?" Sam asked.

Travis fielded it, and Jubal relaxed some.

"We can make enough power to blast at one gee all the way to Mars and back," he said. "That's all we need to know to build the ship."

"Yeah. But there's power, and then there's *power.* You know what I'm saying?"

"I think I do."

"Why you? Why should you and Jubal control all that power? Shouldn't it go to . . . I don't know. The people in charge?"

Dak was looking at his father with admiration in his eyes . . . and panic everywhere else. Proud of the old man for seeing to the core of the issue, the part we'd hardly discussed, worried that the cat was coming out of the bag.

"Do you trust your government that far, Sam?"

"I'm an American."

"So am I, and God bless her, forever. But that's not what I asked you."

Sam said nothing, but nodded slightly, allowing Travis the point.

"Why me?" Travis said. "Better ask *why us*? Because it's on *us* now. Not just me and Jubal, and not just your sons and Kelly and Alicia. You, too, the three of you. We nine people are now the only people on the planet who know about this . . . and if there had been any way to keep your children out of it, I would have. But for better or worse, Jubal discovered it, and he didn't know what he had . . . sorry, Jubal . . ."

"It's okay, *cher.* I ain't got no practicals about me, no."

"He means he never sees the practical side of something he makes. That's my job. Anyway, Manny found out about it, and that makes all of us responsible for it."

He sighed and shook his head.

"I started out here asking you all to keep this matter private, to never tell anyone about it. I see now I can't hold you to your promises about that. It's too much. Sam, Maria, Betty, if any of you think the thing to do here is to turn it over to the government, say the word, and I'm on the phone to Washington."

I hope I concealed my horror a little better than Dak did. He looked like he'd been stuck with a hot poker. Alicia looked worried, too, but patted his knee. Kelly was imperturbable. Don't let anybody know your business, she had once told me, and in this case it meant not showing your feelings openly.

"I'll reserve that decision for now," Sam said.

Mom and Maria looked at each other, then at Travis.

"Go on," Mom said.

"Thank you. I promise you this. If we give this thing to anybody, it will be the United States."

"If? What's the alternative?" Mom asked. She was leaning forward now, a lot more interested in practical questions than blue-sky engineering. "I presume you mean sell it, not give it away. Or do you mean you might just hold on to it?"

"Forever? That might be an option if only me and Jubal knew about it. I'm not dissing anybody here, but secrets *always* leak, if more than one person knows the secret. I assume there are people who are looking for us. Some of them might resort to some pretty strenuous methods to get the secret. But I don't think I'd try to hold on to it even if I was the only one who knew. Because someday someone else will discover this and . . . well, I can think of a lot of possibilities, none of them very good."

"What do you think we should do, then?" Sam asked.

"For now . . . just hold on to it." He sat back in his seat, let his breath out slowly. "I haven't discussed this part yet with anyone. Not the kids, not Jubal.

"This is a powerful technology, and a lot of good can come from it. No more energy crisis, energy is now free. Tear down all the dams, shut down all the nukes, stop mining coal, oil, and gas. Think of the environmental benefits of that alone. We can even solve the garbage problem. No more landfills, no more burning, just squeeze it all down to the density of a neutron star, and let the energy out a little at a time."

He saw he had lost them with the neutron star business, and leaned forward again.

"But it can also be worse than the hydrogen bomb. The only *good* thing I know about atomic bombs is that they are hard to make, and expensive. What if everybody could make something just as powerful? What if that crazy kid shot up his junior high school last month got his hands on a Squeezer?"

"Sounds like the best thing to do is just shoot you and Jubal," Alicia said.

Travis didn't smile.

"Don't think that wouldn't occur to some people," he said. "Only they wouldn't stop with us. I hate this like hell, Sam, Betty, but your children know too much for their own good."

I couldn't hold back anymore.

"It's my fault," I choked out. "I never should have picked the damn thing up." To my horror, I felt tears running down my cheeks.

Mom looked stricken, and started to get up. I waved her away. What more to make my humiliation complete but to have Mommy come rushing? I guess she figured that out, because she sat back down, reluctantly. Kelly put her arm around me.

"Not you, Manny," Jubal said. "Me. Me and dis . . . dis t'ing I gots, cain't leave nothin' alone where it oughta be, no."

"Not either of you, Manny," Travis said, quietly. "You can blame me. If I'd been paying attention I'd have been with Jubal when he learned how to do this."

"There's no point trying to point a finger," Sam said. "What's done is done."

"I don't mind pointing a finger," Mom said, through clenched teeth.

"Let's hear what he wants to do, Betty," Sam suggested.

"Thanks, Sam. I thought about just handing it over. We can still do that, at any time, unless they find us and take it from us first. The alternative is to go to Mars."

"That's stupid," Mom said.

"No, Betty, stupid would be going to Mars to get there before the Chinese. I know that's what started us down this crazy road, but even Jubal agrees it's not enough reason to go. A better reason is to be there to help if what Jubal says is likely to happen, happens. To save lives. But it's not enough, and Jubal can't say it's a certainty.

"I need a platform. Something to stand on while I shout the news to the world. Right now, what am I? A disgraced astronaut, and a drunk. What is Jubal? A tinkerer, and a man with a communication problem that people are going to interpret as retardation. Nobody's going to listen to kids, and nobody's going to listen to any of you.

"But the first people on Mars . . . *them* they'll listen to."

He paused to take a drink of his soda pop. Aunt Maria got up and went into the kitchen and I could see her gathering tortillas and beans and pulled pork from the fridge for making *carnitas*. Maria, at least, had decided this gringo was worth listening to, thus worthy of being fed. But before starting she poured some of the cheap sangria she enjoyed one glass of most nights, and carried it to Travis.

"Go on, everybody, I can listen from in here," she said. Travis sipped the wine and smiled like it was the finest French vintage.

"One glass," Alicia said, primly. Travis saluted her.

"The only hope I can see for this thing," Travis resumed, "is to get it out in the open. The *fact* that it exists, and its dangers and its possibilities—*that* we have to make public, in a big, gaudy way so the news media will cover it and people will listen. I don't think one country, or more likely, a small group of powerful people in one country, should control it, because they will classify this Ultra Top Secret. I don't think one country should control it."

He sat back, drained the rest of his wine, and folded his arms.

"God damn you to hell, Travis Broussard," my mother said, quietly.

"Yes, ma'am."

"How stupid do you think I am? You come here, you talk about needing my son's help to build this crazy machine. You talk about how *you* need to go to Mars . . . to Mars, for heaven's sake! It's *you* this and *you* that, and did you think I'm just some redneck bimbo runs a worthless *mo*-tel and I'd be easy to fool?

"Don't you think we know you plan on taking these children with you?"

"Is that true, Travis?" Sam asked.

"All I'm here to do tonight is tell you they want to help build the ship, which has to be done quietly."

"Don't you lie to me," Mom said. "Did you tell them they can go with you?"

"Only with their parents' permission," Travis said, quietly.

"God damn you to hell."

"I wish I was there now," Travis admitted.

19

★ ★ ★

TRAVIS WASN'T THE only one to go through hell that day. As soon as he told us about asking our parents' permission, earlier that day at the Cape visitors' center, Alicia got up from the table and walked away. Not a word, she just left. Kelly leaned close to Dak.

"What is it with Alicia and her parents, Dak?"

"I don't know. Every time it's come up she just clams. Not a word. I don't know if they're alive or dead, even."

"Me, too," Kelly said. "Maybe I'd better—"

"No, I'll do it," Dak said, and he got up and ran after her. We watched them for a while, too far away to hear. Dak had an arm around her, talking. She was just shaking her head, not even looking at him.

"I don't know what *her* problem is," Kelly said, "but I'll tell you, this isn't fair."

"Didn't say it was," Travis said. "All I'm saying is, I'm not getting into a thing like this without talking it over with your parents. I just couldn't do that."

"Travis, be reasonable! We're not old enough to drink legally, but we're old enough to vote, and serve in the military. And we're old enough not to need our parents' permission on anything anymore. Not a one of us comes from a sitcom family. Manny's father is dead, Dak's mother pretty much abandoned him. My parents are divorced and my father is remarried. You want to talk this over with my stepmom, too?"

"Just your mom and dad would be okay."

"Then why not just buy a big ad in the *Herald*? 'Ex-Astronaut Going to Mars!' It wouldn't spread the news any quicker than telling my dad. And I guarantee you, the people he'd be telling it to would be the police and the media and his lawyer. Correction, his *lawyers.* He'd tie you up so bad you wouldn't be able to walk to the bathroom without getting a writ, much less go to Mars."

They glared at each other and I thought it might have come to blows, but over the cawing of the seagulls we heard Dak shout something. We all looked, and Dak pulled Alicia into a hug. She fought him for a moment, then relented.

"Should we do something?" Travis asked.

"Leave them alone," Kelly said. "We'll know about it soon enough."

They came back to the table, Dak holding her protectively, Alicia walking stiffly and not looking at any of us.

"Alicia has something she wants to tell you," Dak said.

"Not that it's any of y'all's business," Alicia said with a harsh laugh. "You want to talk to my papa, Travis, you'll have to drive a while. He's in Raiford, doing twenty-five to life for killing my mother."

"Oh, God," Kelly moaned, and squeezed my arm. Then she was up, rushing to Alicia, and Jubal was, too. Travis and I were left to stare at each other.

HER EARLIEST MEMORY was seeing her father hit her mother.

"Daddy was a taxi driver until he lost his license for one too many traffic scrapes. Then he became a full-time drinker. Mom was a table dancer, she made pretty good money without actually whoring. She was very pretty, lots prettier than I am. She was black, did I tell you that? Almost as light as me, though. Dad is white.

"I was fifteen. It got three paragraphs in the paper. There was nothing really different about the fighting that night. I'd heard him a thousand times, 'One of these days I'm gonna get my gun and blow you away, sugah!' The only difference was he *did* get his gun that night, and he did blow her away.

"I was sitting on the porch. I came in the house, and he pointed the gun at me and pulled the trigger. The bullet went right through here." She pulled the waistband of her denim shorts down a few inches over her left hip. There was a round scar there. "I hardly felt it, I was kind of fat then; it was just a pawnshop .25, I'm surprised it fired at all. Kind of fat? Hah! I was a pig, I weighed two hundred pounds.

"He fired at me three more times. I remember the hate in his eyes. It wasn't just for me, he hated the whole world. He figured he'd just destroy his piece of it.

"The gun didn't have any more bullets in it.

"He looked down at my mother, lying there, and he started to cry and he put the gun to his head, like this, and he fired it three or four more times. Forgot it was empty, I guess. Then he sat down and cradled Mom's head in his lap.

" 'Better go call nine-one-one, sugah,' " he said. "That was the last words I ever heard him say.

"I didn't go to the trial. I've never visited him in jail, five years now. He writes me letters, and I throw them away. The only thing in the world that scares me, much, is the idea that he might live through twenty-five years at Raiford. And that, friends, is the last time I will talk about him to any of you. Travis, do you want to take me up to Raiford to get his permission?"

"No, no, of course not," Travis said, mortified. "He's clearly lost any parental right he might have had."

"Thank you."

Travis looked down at the table, but not quick enough to miss the glare Kelly gave him. Kelly knew this wasn't the time, she would never bring up her problems in the face of Alicia's shattering story . . . but her eyes told Travis this wasn't over.

* * *

MOM WENT TO the door with Travis and Jubal; there are certain things you do, a certain politeness to be observed even with an enemy. But she didn't offer to shake hands, and she most emphatically did not open herself to a hug. Aunt Maria was in the kitchen cleaning up, removing herself from the scene of anger so thick you could cut it with a knife. And Jubal looked more in need of a hug than anyone I'd ever seen. So I got up and hugged him. Then they left.

"I've got to get up in a few hours," Sam said. "I'm not going to say any more until I've had some time to think it over. The food was wonderful, Maria."

Maria bustled out of the kitchen with a Tupperware box.

"How would you know? You hardly ate any of it. Here, to take home."

Sam laughed, and took it.

"I'll go with you, Dad," Dak said. He showed me his crossed fingers as he followed his old man out the door.

"I'm going to see my mother," Kelly said to me.

Kelly's real mom was a delightful woman, by now over the shock and shame of being kicked out of the house to make room for her husband's girlfriend, who was once Miss Tennessee. She lived in a nice apartment, cashed her nice alimony checks, and was studying to be a real estate agent. Kelly spent more nights there than with her father, and possibly even more than with me. I never added it up.

"You want me to come?"

"Not tonight, Manny. I need to talk some things over with her. And don't worry, I'll keep all our secrets. Alicia, would you like to go with me? I'd like it if you did."

Alicia had been looking at least as gloomy as Travis. Now she brightened a bit.

"I'd like that. Thanks."

Then it was only the three of us, and Maria quickly made herself scarce.

"I can't talk about any of this tonight, Manuel," Mom said.

"That's fine by me, Mom," I said, and kissed her cheek and skedaddled.

It felt mighty good to get out of that pressure cooker and back in my room.

NATURALLY, I COULDN'T sleep.

I wasn't the only one. After about an hour there was a knock on my door.

"Door's open," I called out, and sat up in the bed. Mom came in and sat beside me. We didn't say anything for a long time.

"Is there any way I can talk you out of this thing?" she asked.

I knew what her problem was. Sam Sinclair had said it, just before leaving. "The way I'm seeing it, it's this, or something else. I like to died when Dak got into racing dirt bikes, I got a thousand gray hairs every time he fell off one. But I knew he could do it then, and respect me, or wait till I couldn't do anything about it, and detest me."

"Do you believe what Travis said?" Mom asked me now.

"Do you?"

"I want to, because if he's right, you're not going to Mars or anywhere else."

BY THE END Travis knew he wasn't going to be winning any popularity contests, so he simply laid out the facts. "Here's how I see it," Travis had said. "One, we can start out to build a spaceship . . . and fail completely. I think this is pretty likely. I'm not sure thirty engineers could do it.

"Two, we build a ship . . . and we're too late. The Chinese land, then the Americans, and I have to start thinking of another way to attract enough attention so no one government gets this thing.

"Three, we build a ship . . . and it ain't safe. I will swear to you right here and now, by everything I hold holy, that I will never lift that ship one inch off the ground unless I believe it can get us there and back safely. Believe me, I'm not anxious to subject my worthless old hide to danger any more than I'd risk your precious children. I promise you right here that I would never agree to pilot that ship unless I was willing to take my own daughters along with me. One is six, the other is eight. Maybe you'll meet them someday." He glanced at his watch. "In fact, I'll be leaving and you won't see me for a few days, because my monthly visitation starts tomorrow and I'll be in New Jersey, where they're staying with their grandparents while Mommy goes to Mars.

"Then there's possibility number four. We build a ship. It's a good ship. We go to Mars, we come back, we're heroes, we're rich and famous. I've got no way of calculating what the likelihood of that is, but my guess is it's one chance in a thousand that we ever even *get* to possibility number four.

"And that, Sam and Betty, is as honest as I can be."

I waited for it . . . but nobody brought up possibility five, and six, and seven, and eight through eight thousand, which were all ways we could get killed along the way. Nobody needed to. It was right out there, unsaid, bigger than all of us.

"I DON'T KNOW if I've ever told you how much I've always wished you'd outgrow this astronaut business," Mom said, in the wee hours, the two of us alone in my room.

"You didn't have to. I could see that."

"When I was young, boys always wanted to be policemen, or firemen, or cowboys. Jet pilots. They usually gave it up later."

"I'm not going to give it up."

"I know that." She shivered. "I hate those things, those VStar things. I'm always afraid they'll blow up. I have nightmares about them falling down on us."

"They're pretty safe, Mom."

"Don't you start lying to me tonight, boy. Travis didn't lie, or I don't think he did, so don't you start. I know they're not as dangerous as I fear they are . . . but you can't tell me something like that is safe as a hobbyhorse, either."

"Okay."

"After your father died, you were all I had to live for. I could hardly bear to watch you cross the street. When you flew off on that airplane, I just knew it was going to fall out of the sky."

She was talking about my one trip out of Florida, to spend a month with my mother's parents in Minnesota. Mom had thought they might be holding out an olive branch, but it turned out they still couldn't stand their little spic grandson. It was a total disaster, and I was never so glad to get any place as I was to get back home.

"Well," she finally sighed, "I'm still going to talk more to Sam Sinclair about this . . . but what he said sure seems to sum it up. If it wasn't this, it'd be something else, wouldn't it?"

"Probably so," I admitted. She put an arm around me and hugged tight.

"I love you, Mom."

"I love you, my only son. Stay alive for me, please."

"I'll try."

I couldn't remember ever seeing my mother cry, and she didn't cry then, either. But she had to hurry to the door.

When she opened it Maria was standing there, not even pretending she hadn't been listening. We both heard Mom's quick steps on the stairs going down, then Maria leaned in the door and spoke softly.

"When I was eight and your father six," she said, "we and seven other family members came over on a raft no bigger than my kitchen. Seven days we floated, with no food, the last two days without water. Your family is tough, Manuelito, we're survivors. Mars will be a piece of cake, eh?" She winked at me.

"I am so proud of you. Your father would be proud of you. And your mother will be proud of you, too. Now go to sleep."

" 'Night, *Tía María*."

20

★ ★ ★

SO WE HAD the go-ahead to build us a spaceship.

Hooray!

So we buckled down to work . . .

And nothing happened.

Nothing seemed to happen, for a while, anyway. Our biggest accomplishment during that early period was Kelly's searching for and finding the ideal industrial facility where we could put the thing together and not be bothered too much.

But the first step of a project like this was planning. We didn't know quite where to begin. In fact, for the first three days or so, Dak and I felt the whole load of this insane idea fall squarely on our backs, and we were terrified. Because Travis said that, at the beginning, this was our ship to design, and he'd consult, he'd help, he'd move mountains if he could . . . but getting started was up to us.

Actually there was what you might call a *pre*-preliminary stage. There were legal and financial questions to settle.

Legal? Are you seriously suggesting we bring *lawyers* into this, Travis? Dak and Alicia and I were appalled. Jubal just stayed out of it, content to let Travis, his loco parent, handle his affairs. Only Kelly saw the wisdom in it. Count on the rich girl to understand.

"Believe me, sweetness," she told me one night, "the best way to turn dear friends into deadly enemies is to have a handshake deal on an enterprise as complicated and potentially profitable as this one is. We don't need to spell out every penny, but we need to outline the shape of the thing, the broad strokes."

I certainly wasn't going to argue. It was her fifty million pennies, and fifty million from Jubal, that made the thing possible in the first place. Myself, I'd have been happy to work for union wages and let the two of them split all the profits, if any.

In the end, Dak and Alicia and I had to lobby hard against her first proposal, which was a simple division of any profits into six equal shares.

"Not fair, not fair at all," Dak said, and Alicia and I backed him up. "No way you two dudes put up all the money and don't get back but a sixth."

Eventually, after some dickering, Travis came up with a compromise. Kelly would get twenty-five percent, Jubal twenty-five, and the other fifty percent would be split three ways between me, Dak, and Alicia.

"What about you?" I asked him.

"My share is in Jubal's, as always."

Before we even got to the money part we had formed a corporation so things could be settled by voting. That was complicated enough in and of itself, even with Travis's lawyer helping smooth the way. We were officially the Red Thunder Corporation.

I started to think that, after this, the engineering part would seem simple.

SHORTLY AFTER TRAVIS returned from visiting his daughters he and Jubal left for two weeks of testing the Squeezer.

"This time we'll talk it over first," he had said. "If I'd had us put our heads together before I dragged you all out into the swamp we might not be looking over our shoulders for secret agents now. And by the way, if any of you see me running off like that again, I want you to bring it up, okay?"

What he proposed was to go on the road with Jubal and test more toy rockets.

"They saw something take off from the Everglades. I know a place we can do static testing quietly. But since it's no longer possible to retain total secrecy, my thinking is that it would do us a lot of good if we kept them looking . . . in the wrong places. What if they detect another launch, but from North Dakota? Then another in Texas, and then one in Nevada. My feeling is, if they have to look all over the country, it will spread them too thin to do much good. Comments?"

"More launches will make them more interested," Alicia had said. "Maybe if we just leave it alone, they'll think the Everglades test was . . . I don't know, a faulty radar or something."

"Good point. But this bogey would have appeared on multiple screens. I think they'll be looking hard, and they'll keep on looking, whether it's one launch or a dozen."

"I think Travis is right," Kelly said.

"Sorry," Alicia said.

"Hell, no, Alicia. It was a very good observation. Keep 'em coming."

The consensus was that Travis should fire off the red herrings, five or six of them, widely scattered, with no pattern.

Travis and Jubal took off in the van for points unknown. They carried Jubal's tools and, of course, the Squeezer, of which there was still only one. They would buy the instruments and the materials they needed along the way.

So Dak and I could have waited for their return in two weeks. But two weeks wasted put us a lot closer to the deadline, and there was no way we were going to greet Travis without at least some proposal of where to get started.

That's when I had my brainstorm about the railroad tank cars.

KELLY EXPLORED THE world of tank cars for us. Like so many things, it was a lot more complicated than you'd think.

"Your 'average' tank car is forty feet long by ten feet across," she told us. "I've found half a dozen companies that make them. They're all made of solid, thick steel, they're very strong."

"That's what we need, strong ones," I said.

"You can order a standard model, or name your own specs. You don't carry milk in the same kind of car you'd carry gasoline in. Some are lined, some are refrigerated or insulated to carry liquid gases. You can have just about anything you want . . . and the price for a new one is one hundred thousand dollars and up."

"Just your standard car," I said, once more intimidated by the price tag.

"I presume you don't mind a used one?"

"Please, yes, *please,* a used one."

"Run you from ten to twenty thousand each. We're in luck, there's a glut right now. I can probably shave some off even that ten-thousand-dollar figure."

Dak wondered if we should put a deposit down until Travis got back, but Kelly said there'd be no trouble getting as many as we needed.

We needed seven.

We tried for most of one day to figure out how to fit everything we were going to need into just one, but it was impossible. Next step up was three, bundled together, but that didn't look good, either.

"Remember, weight is no object," Dak said. "We can brace this sucker any way we think is necessary, inside and out."

With a few mouse clicks he created a bundle of seven cylinders. Looked at from the end, it resembled a honeycomb, one circle in the middle surrounded by six others.

"Put the bridge in the center one," Dak said. "It's a longer one than the others, about ten feet or so. Put some windows in that. On the deck below the bridge we have flight stations for the rest of us."

"So one deck below that," I said, moving the mouse, "we have sleeping quarters. Still got a lot of space below."

"Remember our cardinal rule. If you think you might need it, *bring* it. Right?"

"Roger. And if you really have to have it, bring *three*."

So it began to take rough shape.

"A HUMAN BEING needs about six pounds of water every day," Dak told Kelly and Alicia the day we showed them Design A, about halfway through Travis and Jubal's road trip. "That's just for drinking. We want to stay clean, we'll need more."

"I'll vote for clean," Kelly said.

"It's not a problem. A gallon of water weighs about eight pounds. Say we all drink one gallon a day. That's forty-eight pounds a day. Trivial. Add another ten gallons for washing, brushing teeth, cooking, water balloon fights . . . we're looking at five hundred pounds of water per day."

"So how many days will we be gone?" Alicia asked.

"We're expecting about two weeks," I said. "That's three and a half tons of water. But we intend to carry enough for twice that, as a safety margin. Say seven or eight tons. Two thousand gallons."

"Seven *tons?*" Kelly asked.

"Two *weeks?*" Alicia looked surprised. "I thought we'd be gone, I don't know, months and months."

"Don't have to with Jubal's gadget, hon," Dak said. "We can get there in about three and a half days. I don't think you even want to know how fast we'll be going when we get to the halfway point and turn around to slow down."

I wasn't sure I did, either. Three and a half *million* miles per hour. That's almost a thousand miles per second, a long way from light speed of 186,000 miles per second . . . but we'd have to reset our clocks forward a few seconds when we got back. One day I'd have to do that calculation, too . . . when I figured I was emotionally ready for it.

"We figure the water can come in handy for radiation shielding, too," Dak said, and I could have kicked him. In fact, I figured I *would* kick him, first chance I got.

"Radiation . . . ?" Dak might as well have suggested we eat cyanide.

Alicia would not eat genetically engineered vegetables or fruit, but her special dislike was irradiated food. I liked Alicia, but she usually fell for the line of the Health Food Mafia.

"Yeah, hon, there's radiation in space. Mostly it won't be a problem, it isn't strong enough to penetrate our steel hull. Astronauts get exposed to it every day."

"So what's the problem?" Kelly asked. She was looking dubious, too.

"The sun," I said. "Every once in a while there's a storm on the sun, a flare, and the radiation gets stronger. We'll be cutting in toward the orbit of Venus, so we'll be closer to the sun than anybody's been yet."

"Yeah," Dak said, "but it varies on an eleven-year cycle, and we're not at the peak."

We're only a few years before it. But I didn't say that.

"We figured we'd make the thousand-gallon water tanks wide and tall and thin, spread it out to cover as much area as possible. Then, if a storm comes, we orient the ship so those tanks are between us and the sun."

"We'll probably fly in that attitude anyway," I said. "Might as well be safe. But we'll have detectors, too, all around the ship, to let us know if the level's rising."

"What good does that do?"

"The water soaks up the radiation, babe."

"And then we drink the water?"

"The water doesn't get radioactive. Don't worry about it. This ship will have steel walls that'll stop ninety-nine percent of it. We won't have any trouble keeping within safe limits." But Dak and I could both tell Alicia was going to want to see figures, and that "safe" limits were endlessly arguable. And there was no way to pretend we weren't going to get any more radiation than if we stayed home.

In the end, it would be up to her. I was betting she'd go.

"So, that's the water situation," Dak said, changing the subject as quickly as possible. "Then there's oxygen. We need about two pounds per day, per person. We figure on taking regular compressed air. A pure oxygen atmosphere is touchy, a fire can get completely out of hand in half a second, just ask Gus Grissom's ghost if you don't believe me. So for every pound of oxygen we bring we'll also be bringing four pounds of nitrogen. Can't be helped, but again, it's not a problem. We'll have air scrubbers that take out the carbon dioxide. My feeling is we'll need an 'air officer,' or something like that, who worries full-time about the air quality."

"How about 'environment control officer' ?" I suggested. I figured Alicia would be a natural for that.

"Okay, that's air and water taken care of," Kelly said. "How about food?"

"I thought we'd go buy a freezer at Sears or something," I told her. "Fill it up with frozen pizzas and TV dinners. Bring a hotplate and a microwave oven."

Kelly laughed, thought I was joking at first . . . then laughed again when she saw it was *not* a joke.

"Except for 'Leesha," Dak said. "For you, we figured we'd buy a big brick of tofu and a sack of rabbit pellets. Keep your dish full, you can graze whenever you like."

"I'm getting a little tired of health food jokes, gang," she said, and shoved Dak hard enough he fell off his kitchen chair, pretending to be injured.

We were having this discussion in Kelly's office, that is, the office of the project manager. When we were deciding which of us would be the best at keeping all the details straight, all the bills paid, raw materials arriving in a timely fashion, all the jobs to be done, big and small . . . Kelly had won unanimously.

The space was in one corner of our warehouse, up one flight of steps over an area that had been used for storage but was now empty. There was a row of windows looking down on the warehouse floor, and I couldn't help thinking of her father's office. I wondered if she'd made the connection.

"That's one thing we decided early on," I told them. "When we can buy something off the shelf, that's one more thing we don't have to make. I know it sounds nuts, but a Sears freezer is just the sort of shortcut we will take any time we can. Now, maybe it's best just to bring dry rice and pasta and canned stuff, maybe the hot plate is all we need, really . . . but if we want to take frozen food, we can."

"It's amazing how much stuff we'll be able to buy, when the time comes," Dak said. "Like, the best way to get electrical power in a ship is with fuel cells. And it so happens you can buy them in any electrical supply house, just like the ones that go up in the VStar, and they're not even that expensive. A space program spin-off."

"And we'll bring batteries as backup," I said. "Plain old nickel-cadmium car batteries, about the size of a lunch box."

"Well, I'll provide a better menu than frozen pizzas," Alicia sniffed, and before she knew it she'd been elected ship's cook. Oh, boy. I could hardly wait.

"So. Water, oxygen, food . . . what are the other necessities of life?"

"Music," Alicia said.

"Damn right. Bring your whole collection, we'll be equipped to play everything but eight-tracks and Edison cylinders."

"Food, water, and air are three of the big five," I said. "Then there's clothing and shelter. Shelter in Florida means a place to get out of the rain. In Minnesota it means protection from the cold. Where we're going, pressure is the big deal, and heat or cold right after that. The ship will be our shelter."

"So we need a big space heater, or something?" Alicia asked. "Outer space is freezing cold, didn't I hear that?"

"You probably did," Dak said, "but it ain't strictly true. Space is a vacuum, it's not hot or cold, either one. If you're in the sunshine it can get real hot, real quick. We gotta be ready to cool the air, *or* heat it, since if you're in a shadow you lose heat, and you get real *cold,* real quick."

"Not to mention the weather on Mars," I said.

"Now *that's* cold," Dak agreed. "Nighttime, figure on it getting down around a hundred and fifty below, most nights."

"You're kidding." Alicia looked alarmed.

"No joke, kiddo. Hottest it's ever been—the last million years or so, anyway—is about sixty Fahrenheit, high noon, equator, perihelion."

"And perihelion is . . . what?"

"Closest point to the sun. Mars's orbit is a lot more eccentric . . . that means it's not circular, it's elliptical, from one hundred thirty million to one hundred fifty-five million miles from the sun. On Earth the seasons are determined by the tilt of the axis, which part gets the most heat, northern or southern hemisphere, which is why Christmas is in the middle of the summer in Australia. On Mars it's the shape of the orbit that determines the seasons, such as they are."

"Sixty degrees doesn't sound so bad," Kelly said.

"I wouldn't bother to pack any sunscreen," I told her. "For one thing, it's not Martian summer right now."

"For another thing," Dak said, enjoying this, "the air pressure is about one hundredth what it is on Earth, and ain't none of it oxygen. That's *way* below the pressure on top of Mount Everest. Ninety-five percent of the air is carbon dioxide, which, when you freeze it, is what we call 'dry ice.' And it does freeze on Mars, the carbon dioxide, most every night. So in addition to some real good thermal underwear, we're gonna need us some space suits if we plan to leave the ship."

" 'If we plan to?' If we *plan* to?" Alicia looked scandalized. "We couldn't go there and never set foot on it, could we?"

Dak shrugged, but the truth was, we were worried about that. You couldn't just run down to the Goodwill store and pick up a few used space suits. I wasn't sure you could buy them anywhere at all, new or used . . . or if we could afford them if we *did* find some. A custom-tailored NASA suit ran right around one million dollars, and that was a great savings over what they'd have run you ten years ago. Since our whole budget was one million dollars, I figured we had a problem.

Because, when you got right down to it . . . would landing on Mars *count* if you didn't get out of the ship?

It sounds crazy, but what were Neil Armstrong's first words while standing on the moon? "That's one small step for (a) man, one giant leap for mankind," right? Anybody who knows anything about space history or any history at all knows that.

Actually, in the only way that makes sense to me, his first words were, "Houston, Tranquillity Base here. The *Eagle* has landed."

Think about it. If I'm standing in the pickup bed of *Blue Thunder,* I'm standing on Planet Earth, aren't I? If not, then I spend very little time on the planet. Most of the time I'm standing on concrete, or asphalt, or wood, or carpet or I'm on the second floor of a building or I'm sitting in a vehicle.

Yet it is universally agreed that Armstrong was not "on" the moon until his foot was planted on lunar rock. His *thickly booted* foot, remember, or else his foot would have suffered a severe burn, not to mention the harsh effects of vacuum.

I had a sneaking feeling that, unless we were photographed actually standing on the Martian surface, our achievement of getting there first simply wouldn't count. Or it would have an asterisk beside it, like Roger Maris's sixty-one home runs. "They *went* there, but they didn't *go* there." They didn't *stand* there.

It was a real problem. Because the difficulties of building a spaceship began to seem small beside the problem of making a space suit. A *safe* space suit. What could we buy and then adapt, perhaps a diving suit?

"So what about the rest of our clothing?" Kelly said, bringing me back to Earth again. Dak frowned at her.

"Blue jeans and T-shirts, right?"

"Well, I don't plan on wearing any evening gowns," she said, "but if we're going to be on television, if we're going to be famous, we shouldn't look like slobs."

"Maybe some kind of uniform," I suggested. Kelly looked dubious. "Not dorky stuff like Captain Picard and his crew. Something cool."

"I got a friend, she's good at clothes," Alicia said. "I'll see if she has any ideas."

"But don't tell her, 'Make me some uniforms for people going to Mars.' "

Nobody said anything. We couldn't avoid being noticed, and we had to be able to tell people *something* when they asked what we were doing. We needed a cover story.

Alicia came up with the best idea the next day.

"Say we're making a movie. Sort of a *Tom Swift Goes to Mars* thing."

Dak looked stunned, then slapped his palm on the table.

"That's exactly right, baby. That way, we can make a spaceship, but we're not making a *spaceship*. Just look at the damn thing. Is anybody going to look at that and think, 'These kids going to Mars, by golly!' Hell no! Even if the spy spooks come by and take a look, in two seconds they'd walk right out. The thing don't have an *engine!*"

He was right. We were all looking at the first rough mock-up of the ship, made from HO-gauge model railroad cars. It looked mighty silly. My confidence in the design, which went up and down, had reached a low ebb when we put it together. You looked at it, you had to figure whoever thought this up was nuts.

We did adopt the cover story of being prop makers for a movie in development. We went so far as to register the title *Red Thunder* with the Writers' Guild, to announce we were in preproduction, and to set an imaginary start date almost a year away. The only downside to the idea was getting phone calls from agents and hopeful actors almost every day asking when we were casting. We always told them the script was in rewrites, and we'll call you back.

"But the movie isn't Tom Swift," Kelly pointed out. "It's *The Little Rascals Go to Mars,* right?"

"Perfect," I said. My generation loved those old "Our Gang" black-and-white comedy shorts just like Mom's generation had, and the generation before that. The only difference was, we had watched them on DVD.

"I'm Stymie," Dak announced. "You figure Manny for Spanky?"

"No," Kelly said. "Manny is Alfalfa."

"*Alfalfa?* That cross-eyed freckle-face dork? No *way* I'm Alfalfa."

"I always liked Alfalfa," Alicia said. "It's true he wasn't as handsome as Manny . . . but Dak is much handsomer than Stymie, too." Dak kissed her.

"Alfalfa was the romantic one," Kelly said. "He had the most heart." I realized she was right. So that settled it. I was Alfalfa.

"Who gets to be Darla?" Neither of the girls leaped at it. The Little Rascals were mostly boys, now that I thought of it.

"Kelly's gotta be Darla," Dak said. "Darla wasn't half bad, you know. She could be kinda sweet. And Alfalfa was in love with her."

"No way out of it, Kelly," I said. "You're Darla."

"And that means Alicia is Buckwheat," Dak said, with a grin.

"Buckwheat? *Buckwheat?* Was Buckwheat a girl?"

"What the hell *was* Buckwheat?" None of us were sure.

"So who's Spanky?" she asked.

"Who do you figure?" I said. "Little fat kid, smartest of the bunch . . ." We looked at each other and said it simultaneously.

"Jubal!"

WE WERE STUMPED for a while about what to call Travis. In the end it was so obvious we wondered how we'd missed it. Travis was Hal Roach.

It took our minds off our other problems for a while, but eventually we had to buckle down to the planning again.

Never in my life had there been so many things I had to buy. Kelly set us all up with Platinum MasterCards and sent us out shopping every morning for a week. We had to rent a U-Haul truck just to cart it all back to the warehouse.

We saved money where we could. Heavy equipment we mostly rented. We got the very best welding equipment because our lives would depend on every weld in the ship. We needed pumps, to create vacuum for testing the durability of components, and to create pressure for testing the tank cars. I thought we should wait on pumps until Travis got back and either approved or shot down the entire idea of using secondhand railroad rolling stock to get to Mars. Kelly said no, we'd need the pumps one way or another, and time was passing.

We bought a standard cargo container like you see on railcars, the kind that can be loaded and off-loaded from freighters and then travel by either rail or truck. We welded it airtight, built a small air lock in its side, and started pumping the air out of it. It was going to be our vacuum testing chamber.

The pressure gauge was nowhere near the point we needed when I heard a squealing noise like a rusty hinge . . . and the container collapsed on itself with an earsplitting *clang!* as if we'd dropped it from the overhead crane.

"Jesus squeezus," Dak breathed. Alicia and Kelly came running down the stairs from the office, and we all stood together and stared at what had once been a rectangular container, like a huge box of Velveeta. Stomping on an empty aluminum Coke can, you could hardly have smashed it as flat as that container.

I felt every ounce of confidence drain right out of me. Were we nuts?

"Well," Alicia laughed, "like you said, we need to make all our mistakes right here on the ground, because we can't afford any mistakes out in space."

I didn't point out that there were plenty of mistakes we could make right here on the ground that could *kill* us.

"We gotta get that thing out of here," I said. "If my mother sees that, she'll have a heart attack."

We rented a flatbed and hauled the twisted hulk away, sold it for scrap metal, which was good, because Kelly had paid not much more than scrap metal prices in the first place. That same day we went ahead and bought our first tank car. I got goose bumps watching the switch engine pushing the car over our siding and into the warehouse.

This was actually going to happen!

We cut away the wheel carriages then lifted it with the overhead crane and lowered it onto a cradle we'd slapped together out of used two-by-fours and plywood—Kelly being frugal again. I was beginning to see just how her family had got rich and stayed that way. She never spent an unnecessary penny. But she never scrimped when only the best and newest would ensure safety.

The weight of the empty car was stenciled right there on its side: LT WT 72,500 LBS. Thirty-six tons, and a bit. Also the capacity weight: 190,500 LBS., or about ninety-five tons. Over two and a half times the empty weight. That was very strong, I thought.

We hauled the wheel assemblies to a public scale and weighed them, subtracted that number from thirty-six tons, for a tank weight of twenty tons. Seven tanks would weigh 140 tons. To that we would add the weight of the cradle we would build that would connect the thrusting engines to the main body of the craft, plus the landing legs, plus everything we added inside, including the Sears Kenmore freezer and six people. We guessed we could bring it in under two hundred tons.

No worries about keeping weight down, no fuel weight to consider, virtually unlimited thrust for a virtually unlimited time. If only Werner von Braun could see us, I thought, lifting far more weight than his *Saturn 5*s could, using little silver basketballs. He'd be flabbergasted!

We fitted the tank car cap with an extra-heavy-duty round hatch door, lined it with aircraft-grade silicone seals, dogged the door shut, and turned on the vacuum pump. None of us got close as the air was sucked out. It took a while, and the entire time my ear was listening for that first, awful rusty-hinge squeal.

It never came. The car held up under fifteen pounds per square inch pressure differential applied from outside. I had no doubt it would easily contain one internal atmosphere against the vacuum of space.

"We're in business," Dak said, as I turned the relief valve and air screeched into the tank. "You talk to Hal and Spanky today?"

"Mom did. He says to look out for them about noon tomorrow." Travis had been calling in every day, and the calls had originated from places as distant as northern Maine and the Mojave Desert.

"Might as well hang it up for tonight, then," he said. "We got a big day tomorrow, trying to sell this thing to him."

"We'll sell it," I told him.

21

★ ★ ★

TRAVIS GRABBED MY face with both hands and kissed me on the forehead. While I was still too stunned to speak, he turned to everyone else, his arm around my shoulder.

"If they had a Nobel Prize for engineering, these guys would get it," he announced. He let me go and moved toward Dak, who backed away cautiously.

"It was Manny thought it up," he said. "I don't need no kissing."

"Genius. A stroke of sheer genius," Travis said.

We were in a room we had been using for meetings, which had become a nightly ritual where we could all be brought up to speed on what everyone else had been doing, and figure out what most urgently needed doing the next day. It was down a short hallway from the office Kelly and Alicia shared, one of half a dozen rooms on the upper level of the warehouse, most of which were empty. This one had a big conference table and a few desks and tables against the back wall, all rented. There was a big brass espresso machine sitting on one of the tables, a gift from Kelly's mom from when she dropped by one day to see how the "movie prop" business was coming. Now I was afraid I might be spoiled forever. It would be hard to go back to cheap coffee after getting used to a couple lattes every morning before getting to work.

Boxes of Krispy Kremes had been set out in anticipation of Jubal's return. At the rate he'd been going through them I thought we might look into getting a franchise ourselves, in case this whole Mars business didn't pan out.

We had gone to the Blast-Off to meet them when they arrived, but Kelly and I had both overslept and didn't wake up until Aunt Maria pounded on the door and shouted, "They're here, Manuelito!" We dressed quickly and went down to be embraced by Jubal and Travis. My guts were churning, because that afternoon we had to present our ideas to Travis and the whole project would either continue, or crash and burn, depending on his reaction. I didn't even want to admit how much it had all come to mean to me.

Before long we all piled into our various vehicles and were on our way to the warehouse, except Maria, who had to work the front desk while Eve, the temp girl we'd hired with money we really couldn't spare, cleaned up the rooms.

Travis had done a complete walk-around of the warehouse when we got there. The four of us kept up a constant nervous patter, handing it off from one to the next as we went, trying to anticipate any questions he might have.

For the life of me, I couldn't tell if he was giving us an honest chance. We had all realized during the two weeks of his absence that, let's face it, all he had to do at any time was to say, "It's not safe," and the whole project would be over. Was he already determined to shoot it down? Was he just humoring us—and more important, misleading and humoring his brilliant but dependent cousin—never having intended to give his okay? Were we going to get a fair shake? And would we even know if we weren't?

THEIR VAN WAS good for some laughs. They had taken it into some places that would have been a lot easier in Travis's Hummer. There was a dent in the left side where they'd slipped on a muddy dirt road in the

Oregon Cascades and banged into a tree. There were scratches from where they'd squeezed through thick brush. And there was dirt. Lots of dirt, with only the windows wiped clean.

"We were in a hurry," Travis had explained. "No time for car washes."

The inside was revealing, too. The front seats and floor were neat and orderly, but from there on back it could have provided some students with an interesting two-week archaeological dig. Travis's military training apparently wouldn't allow him to tolerate trash in his immediate vicinity, but once it was tossed over his shoulder into the backseat it was gone, as far as he was concerned. There were fast-food wrappers and boxes from all the major companies.

"Krispy Kremes hard to find, up Yankeeland way." Jubal sounded scandalized.

There were plenty of soft drink cans and paper cups, too. I saw Alicia's eyes scanning the litter, eyes that could spot a can of Bud in a mountain of empties a hundred yards away. She didn't find a beer can. Which was a big relief to me, because the one time Mom and I had talked about this whole thing while they were gone, it was because Mom brought up Travis's drinking.

"That man takes one drink," she had said, "that man takes one *drop* of liquor, Manuel, and I withdraw my consent. Then you can go or stay, which you'll do anyway, but it will be without my permission."

"Mom, that man takes one drink, you won't have to withdraw your consent," I had said. "I won't go if he drinks." And ever since, I'd wondered if that was true.

NOW OUR HO-gauge model spaceship was sitting in the middle of the conference table, considerably spruced up since we first glued it together.

Inside what would be the bridge we had put a light to glow through the windows. We had mounted radio antennas and a big dish receiver on it. We'd built a cradle of plastic girders to set the whole thing on, made from bits scavenged from model plane and car boxes, just like they used to do it in Hollywood. The three landing legs and pads came from, of all things, a model of the old Apollo Lunar Excursion Module. The big springs we'd need had come from a radio-controlled Hummer model. Tiny red and green flashing clearance lights gave it a more animated appearance.

Down beneath were three globular cages built to hold five-foot-diameter Squeezer bubbles, now represented by silver Christmas tree ornaments. We didn't know what that part would actually look like. That would be entirely up to Jubal.

Then we'd sent it out and had it painted high-gloss candy-apple red. There was an American flag embossed on one side, and the bold words *RED THUNDER* on the other.

In fact, we'd spent more money on this whole presentation deal than I had thought necessary, and I had questioned Kelly about it.

"Never skimp on the gloss and glitz," she told me. "I would never try to sell a dirty car. We've got guys, soon as a rain shower passes over, their job is to go out in the lot and swab all the cars down with a chamois, so they don't dry with streaks on them."

"I agree," Alicia had said. "Guys, if Travis intends to give us a fair hearing, we need to give the impression that we do thorough work. For that, appearance counts."

So we made sure the plan, the ship model, and all the backup materials were as professional as possible, and hang the expense.

We rented a huge flat-wall SuperHiDef screen and spent a few hours learning to use the Telestrator system in our shipbuilding program so we could point and click with an electronic wand to expand, slice and dice, rotate, swoop and swirl, pan, zoom, and dolly in or out with ease as we explained the various features. Pretty soon we were creating graphics as good as any television sports broadcast, in real time.

Hanging on the walls around the Telestrator screen were three-by-four-foot color prints of some old magazine covers and Walt Disney posters from the 1950s, for no better reason than that they looked good . . . and showed some spaceships that actually looked like *Red Thunder*.

We had found them during computer searches. An artist named

Chesley Bonestell had painted covers of spaceships for science fiction magazines, the result of the best scientific thinking of the time, some of them in space, others sitting on the Martian surface. And the Disney organization had made some short subjects around that time, speculating about how we might conquer space. One of the Disney ships bore a startling resemblance to *Red Thunder*: a central cylinder surrounded by cylindrical fuel tanks, though the tanks were not as large as *Red Thunder*'s tank cars. Printing and hanging them had been my idea, I admit it. I thought that, surrounded by these lovely old renderings, my crazy idea for a Martian ship didn't look quite so crazy. I'd downloaded them and had them printed professionally, photo-quality.

So what was the first thing that happened when Travis walked into the conference room with us and saw the model, sitting there in the middle of the conference table under a baby spotlight?

He stopped and frowned for a moment, then he burst out laughing.

My face felt like it was on fire. I actually felt dizzy for a moment. It's not an experience I'd like to repeat. It was undiluted humiliation.

Luckily, Travis realized it in a second, and the next thing I knew he was hugging me, kissing me, calling me a genius.

FROM THERE, THE sailing was pretty smooth.

We each took our turns at the Telestrator, as we had rehearsed it. Travis would watch, and nod or occasionally frown. When he frowned we waited to see if he had a question. We felt . . . we *hoped* we had an answer to all but a few of his possible objections, and thought we ought to get them taken care of as quickly as possible. But he always told us to go ahead.

And he did seem to enjoy it. He kept looking back to the model, turning it slowly, squinting at it, so we'd stop and wait for his attention to return.

We had divided the presentation into four parts. I got to go first because I'd been named chief design officer. Sure, I thought, until Travis gets back, and I pray for that day. I was terrified that, once he saw the details, he'd be laughing again.

But he didn't laugh again. Most of the time he was nodding, some of the time he was even smiling. I got my part over in about twenty minutes, giving the broad general outlines of our thinking, showing everything we had on the screen. Then I handed the control wand to Dak and sat down, wishing I had a towel for the sweat that was drenching me in spite of the powerful air conditioning.

Dak was wearing two hats on the project. First, he was systems engineer. He had been hard at work learning what communications we needed to keep in contact with planet Earth. He was also struggling to design the ship's internal power systems, and it was becoming a problem. He didn't exactly gloss over it but he didn't spend a lot of time on it, either. I knew a mental note had been taken.

The second hat was surface transportation, and Dak hadn't been around the warehouse much in the last few days as he and Sam got started on that.

Then it was Alicia's turn, and the rest of us crossed our fingers. We had named her environmental control officer. Yes, we were all officers. Why not?

Alicia labored under a triple inferiority complex. The first part was math and science anxiety, which most girls I've known have. It seems to come with the territory. Second, she had never finished high school. Given her life story, I thought it was a miracle she had attended school at all, and learned anything at all. But Alicia felt outclassed by her three honor student friends.

Third, she felt that Dak was much, much smarter than she was, and she was afraid she would never be able to keep him because of that.

Some of that was obvious to anybody who was watching, and some of it I learned lying on my pillow with my arm around Kelly, who was doing everything she could—as Dak and I were, too—to convince Alicia she was wrong to worry about all three points. Which was the simple truth. Alicia might not know how to extract a cube root, but she had tons of smarts, in areas that really mattered. Come to think of it, I can't extract a cube root, either, without a calculator.

But, my lord, how that girl had been working.

Her desk in the other office was piled high with printouts. Dak had gotten her started, showing her which sites to go to for the information she needed. Most of them were government sites, many of those part of the NASAWEB. It's amazing how much stuff you can get free from the government if you know where to look.

She spoke for about twenty minutes, using the clicker to highlight the air tanks and fans and ventilation ducts we'd designed. As she went on, her confidence grew. She talked knowledgeably about carbon dioxide scrubbers, carbon monoxide and smoke detectors, about the heating and cooling systems, and our biggest bugaboo, radiation.

She had learned more about it than Dak and I had known.

"Astronauts working on the space stations and flying in VStars have a radiation protection we're not going to have," she said. "The Earth's magnetic field captures a lot of the radiation from the sun and twists it and turns it down at the poles, where you can see the results in auroras. The level of that radiation varies with activity on the sun's surface. Solar flares and prominences produce high-energy protons that can be harmful if you aren't protected from them." With a click, she brought up a series of pictures of solar flares, beautiful and potentially deadly. "That radiation can even reach down to the Earth's surface. In 1989 a flare shorted out the power supply in Quebec. Six million people didn't have any electricity for a while.

"But we can have a little warning about the solar radiation. We'll have a piece of optical equipment aboard that will watch the sun and if it spots a flare, it will sound an alarm." She brought up a graphic on the Telestrator. "The light from a flare will go faster than the dangerous protons. We would have a minute or so to get into what they call a 'storm cellar.' Basically, we'll surround one room in the center of the center module with polyethylene, which will stop the protons. They use this stuff on atomic submarines to shield the crew from the reactor."

One more point Dak and I hadn't known, discovered through Alicia's diligence. I glanced at Travis and saw him nodding.

"The other radiation is scarier, to me."

"Me, too," Travis put in, quietly.

"They call it 'cosmic radiation.' It comes from far out in space, from stars that blow up in a supernova. This stuff travels at almost the speed of light and it's very powerful. Even the Earth's atmosphere doesn't stop all of it, but exposures are higher in outer space. There's no practical way to shield from it."

She paused, and it didn't seem like a good place for a pause, to me. *Skim over this part,* I wanted to shout. But in the end I guess it's better to be straight and honest.

"To tell you the truth, I wouldn't want to be on that *Ares Seven* ship, or the Chinese one, either. The best way to deal with cosmic radiation is to limit your exposure to it. We'll get to Mars in somewhere between three and four days. That's a chance we all agreed we're willing to take."

I thought I heard a grumble from my mother, but when I looked at her she was just glaring at the flares on the Telestrator screen, looking as if she'd like to put a lot of bullet holes in it. Somehow I had just known that the idea of radiation passing through her son's body was not going to exactly thrill her.

It was only toward the end Alicia faltered a bit.

"I haven't had time to work on waste management," she admitted. "I guess we'll need some plumbing. Toilets, some way to heat water . . ."

"When you go to Sears to get that freezer," Travis said, "pick up a water heater, too. And a toilet seat." Alicia smiled uncertainly. "I'm not kidding. Don't worry about it, Alicia. It won't be a problem."

"Well, I guess that's about it. . . ."

Kelly was already up. She embraced Alicia and invited her to sit down. Then she began her own presentation, clean, crisp, well ordered, and comprehensive without being long-winded, just as I'd expected from her. She covered the financial situation and the procurement status, all the business side of the project.

When she sat down there was silence for almost a full minute. Who would fire the first shot? Mom, or Travis?

Travis. And of course it wasn't a shot at all.

"Well, I've seen worse briefings before a liftoff. Many worse, in fact. Practically all of them." He turned to Mom. "Betty, I'll tell you the bad news first."

"Travis, the only news I want from you is that you can build a safe ship. These kids are going to Mars if there's even a one in a hundred chance of getting back, I know that. I figure Manny'd go if he had to pedal a bicycle and hold his breath. They'd lie to me if that's what it takes; I would have, when I was their age. But from you, I expect the truth, or I'll find a way to make you pay."

"Then the bad news is actually good news," Travis said, not seeming to mind the threat. I did, though. I was getting a little bit pissed off at her.

"We've got a terrific start here. They've laid out the basics of a ship that can get there and back."

"Then you'd let your daughters fly in it, is that what you're saying?"

"No way. There's a hundred things wrong with it, and until I satisfy myself that they're all fixable, and then that *we* can fix them, I'm nowhere near ready to sign off on it. The thing is, I expected there'd be a *thousand* problems. We're much farther along than I'd dared hope." He turned to Sam Sinclair. "What's your feeling, Sam?"

"I have to admit, it looks sound," Sam said. He smiled wryly. "Given that the basic idea is flat-out nuts."

"I couldn't agree with you more. We've got a lot of work to do before it stops being nuts. Here's where it stands, Sam, Betty . . . and the rest of you, too.

"The biggest hurdle facing this project is that we're not going to be able to test the ship before we set out for Mars. If I had my way, I'd take her into orbit first, alone. Then the moon. I'd only go to Mars after that. But you know why we can't test that way.

"So Jubal and I have been testing it every possible way *but* a full-scale liftoff. We spent about half our time experimenting to measure the thrust levels we can achieve. We know now how much reaction mass we'll need for the trip. The bubbles seem to squeeze out just about the maximum power, total mass-energy conversion. So one bubble could produce thrust for years and years. Hell, for centuries.

"The rest of the time we tried to make the system fail.

"And we *did* have failures on the ground. Nothing to get alarmed about, every research project has failures along the way, and it's best to have them early on, on the ground, than to have them sneak up on you at the worst possible time, which is what usually happens.

"I'd confidently raise ship and put her in orbit tomorrow, for a short orbital flight, if we had a full-scale ship ready and didn't have to worry about who would see the launch and return. Jubal has engineered a system of containment and release of the ship's thrust that is as foolproof as anything made by imperfect humans can be.

"We told you about my fiasco in the 'Glades. That wasn't any flaw in the bubble technology, it was caused by us not knowing how much energy would be released, and how fast, by Jubal's . . . by what we're calling the Phase Field Interrupter. The PFI. We got it calibrated now, I can release energy accurately down to one percent.

"I told you the PFI makes a pinhole in the bubbles. That's not strictly accurate. Jubal showed me the math but it was beyond me. What it does, it puts a twist in space so the matter trapped and squeezed inside the bubble makes a little trip through another dimension—and I'm not even sure if it's the fifth or the sixth dimension—"

"Fift'," Jubal said. I was surprised, I'd almost forgotten he was there.

"If you say so. The energy twists through some sort of wormhole and travels a distance much shorter than the diameter of a proton, and ends up in our universe, and when it gets here it produces thrust. I know this is hard stuff, I can go back . . ."

"Go on," Sam said, and my mother nodded.

"That's just about it. We couldn't get the bubbles to blow up, or release any energy at all, except with Jubal's PFIs . . . and they're the only ones on Earth, so far as we know. If someone else has one, they're being as careful as we are, because there is absolutely no sign that anyone but Jubal is aware of this new branch of physics.

"What I'm saying . . . in a long-winded way, sorry . . . I consider the engine part of this rocket to be as safe as any source of power can ever be. Foolproof. Lots safer than a VStar, which is pretty safe.

"But when we light one of these off, we'll get thrust that will be applied to . . . well, to a ship I'm *far* from confident about.

"This will be our problem. Very simply, the quicker we get there and get back, the happier I'll be. Space is an incredibly hostile environment, and the longer we're out there the better chance of something going wrong. Assuming we go at all, of course."

Again, a silence. Travis had his arms on his knees and was staring at the floor. Jubal was nodding quietly. Then Sam spoke.

"A shorter trip is better, right? Safer?"

"Shorter in time, yes. Up to a point. We could boost harder, but that would stress the ship more, and it wouldn't be any fun for us, either."

"How long you figure on staying?"

"One week in space, and about a week on the ground."

"Three weeks total, then?"

"Oh, no, that's one week total travel time, there and back."

Sam frowned and shook his head.

"Don't seem possible. Mars is so far away."

"We'll be doing three million miles an hour, Sam."

"How can you go that fast?" Mom wanted to know. "I'd expect it'd kill you."

"We won't even feel it. We won't even be able to tell we're moving."

Mom shook her head again, and stood up.

"I'll never understand it." She grimaced, then tried to smile. "I'm sorry I'm acting like such a bitch, Manny, and all y'all. It just scares me. But . . . I'm really impressed at what y'all have got done. I almost felt convinced there, for a minute."

"You will be convinced, Betty," Travis said solemnly.

"Not likely. Anyways, I'd best be getting home. 'Night, folks."

Sam joined her, and Travis and Kelly and the others took them out the door. I could hear them talking on the way down the stairs. Myself, I didn't want to face her just then, I might say something I'd regret.

So I sat there for a while, looking at the model ship. It was weird, but it had its own beauty. I imagined her lifting off on a pillar of flame. . . .

NEXT THING I knew, Travis was shaking my shoulder. I'd fallen asleep in my chair.

"Nobody here now but us chickens," Travis said. "Fill your coffee cups and join me at the table in five minutes. We've got some talking to do, but it won't take long."

I made a very strong cup of espresso and fumbled my way back to the table.

"Manny, you're looking like a raccoon," Travis said.

"It's just my Jimmy Smits eyes, Travis," I said.

"Jimmy Smits after a three-day bender, maybe. How much sleep are you getting?"

"Travis, I haven't got more than six hours of sleep a night since I was ten."

"Four hours? Three?"

Two, the previous night. Never more than four the last two weeks.

I knew it was a problem, but I didn't know what to do about it. Even with Eve helping out, Mom and Maria couldn't get everything done every day without my help. We were in the middle of another financial emergency. Business was just enough to make too much work without being enough to keep us out of the red. But I didn't see any reason to bother Travis with all that.

"Never mind," he said. "I know how to fix it." The others found their way to the table and sat down.

"Good news first," he began. "First-rate presentation. If I was an investor, I might actually put some money into this venture. Not a *lot* of money, you understand. Because I did notice some weak spots, and some spots you got through maybe a little quicker than you should have. But all in all, great.

"Now the bad news. You're not going to be able to do it. Not as things stand. We can shut it down now . . . or we can make some changes."

We all looked at each other. I honestly hadn't expected that. I thought we were going to get the green light.

"What kind of changes?" Dak asked suspiciously.

"Bring in some help. Help from the family."

"The Broussard family?"

"Exactly . . ." He stopped, and lowered his head, then looked up again.

"Sorry. There was one item of business I meant to cover first. Back up a minute. We've got to figure out who's in charge here."

"Who's in . . ." Alicia looked around at us. "It's you, isn't it?"

"So far, I figure we're a limited democracy. Limited, because I told you I have to make the final go, no-go decision . . . aided by Jubal, who has the only vote that counts about that. And I did set that one condition, that your parents had to be aware of what we're doing. Sorry, Kelly."

Kelly shrugged. She wasn't likely to ever join Travis's fan club, but over the last weeks she seemed to have resigned herself to not going. She seemed to be putting herself into the work wholeheartedly. At least, if this was how hard she worked when she was *half*hearted, then wholehearted would be a wonder to see.

"I nominate myself to be captain of this boat. That means, I make the final decisions on how the ship is made and I'm in charge of the mission from Earth liftoff to Earth landing, with the powers of a ship's captain as established in space law."

"Second the nomination," Alicia said.

"All in favor . . ." I said, and everybody said, "Aye."

"Thank you," Travis said. "It probably sounds silly to you, but it's like the contract we signed. It *has* to be written down. Some situations we could get into, I'd need to expect . . . to *count* on . . . total, unquestioning obedience, just like a Navy ship of the line. Get your dad to tell you how that works, Dak, and fill the others in."

"Will do, Captain Broussard."

This time Travis didn't correct us, as he had done when we called him Colonel. I realized he was dead serious, and I figured he was probably right.

"Here on the ground I'm not a dictator, okay? You can question orders, refuse orders, even jump ship entirely, fold up your tent and go home if you don't like the way I'm doing things. But after launch, if I issue orders I will expect them to be obeyed."

Nobody objected.

"Fine. Next, I nominate Kelly to be project manager."

"Thanks, Travis," Kelly said, with a look that could melt through steel.

"She will be in control of building the ship. She will coordinate everything, she'll have to be familiar with all the hundreds of tasks this project entails."

"I second the nomination," I said. There was a chorus of ayes again.

"Which is pretty much what I've been doing"—she held up her hand to silence Travis—"and yes, I agree it needed to be formalized. So I accept. And I have a suggestion to make." She turned to Alicia.

"You've done a great job on the environment systems. But now I'd like you to turn your work over to Manny and Dak. I want you to go full-time on the medical stuff we discussed a few days ago. By launch time, I want you to be qualified as an EMT. You'll be the medical officer."

"Great idea," Travis said.

"Well . . . okay," Alicia said. She seemed a little conflicted, worried that Kelly was pushing her out of work she wasn't qualified for, but relieved at the same time to be back at work she could understand. She already had some training as a nurse, and she was a natural for it.

"Anything else?" Kelly asked, and I realized she had taken over the meeting. Which was exactly what Travis had wanted and expected.

"Yeah," Dak said. "I got a question for Trav . . . sorry, for the captain."

"Don't worry about the captain stuff till we're aboard," Travis said.

"Whatever. I hope this isn't out of line, you don't have to answer it if you don't want to . . . anyway, you say you're worried the *Ares Seven* will blow up . . . and your ex-wife is aboard. I figure I'd be pushing this thing a little harder, maybe be willing to take some chances . . . you know what I'm saying?" Dak looked embarrassed to have brought it up. But it had bothered all of us.

"No problem, Dak, you've got every right to ask about that." He took a deep breath. "It was a messy divorce, friends. I don't love her anymore, don't even like her very much. We'd probably have broken up anyway, even without the drinking . . . but it was the drinking did it.

That's why I barely have any visitation rights with the girls. And the judge was right. I was the party at fault, even though she *is* a bitch.

"And she is still the mother of my daughters, and I want her to stay alive if for no other reason than that. Her death would hurt them. For that matter, I want them *all* to stay alive and healthy . . . but we can't do it by blasting off in a home-built spaceship and then die freezing when it falls apart.

"The morals of rescuing people are hard to define precisely. You hear about it, three or four people drowning, trying to save one guy who may already be dead. Helicopters crashing trying to pull people off the roofs of burning buildings. If I'm going down a cliff face to rescue a stranded mountain climber, I have the right, even the *obligation,* to see that my rope is sound. Do you see what I'm saying?" Dak nodded, looking embarrassed.

"The odds of rescuing the *Ares Seven* if a disaster *does* happen . . . the odds are terrible." I think we were all surprised, though I had wondered about it. "Most accidents I can envision would kill them all, instantly. But say there are survivors and they're just drifting, helplessly, with no rocket to power them . . . just *finding* them is highly problematic. You can't really imagine how vast space is, even here in the cozy little solar system. Friends, what we'd all better do is cross our fingers and hope Jubal is wrong, because our chances of rescuing them are small."

We all thought that one over. None of us liked the sound of it.

"So this idea of being there to get them out of a jam . . ." I said, and didn't know how to finished the sentence. Travis did it for me.

". . . is the only reason I'm still in this at *all,* and the only reason I will push as hard as any of you, maybe *twice* as hard, to get this thing built and on its way. I want them to live, so badly that I'm buying into what is probably the most cockamamie idea since Queen Isabella hocked the crown jewels."

"Sorry, Travis," Dak said.

"Don't be sorry. When in doubt, ask. Any more questions?"

"I've got one," I said. "Dak and I are stumped when it comes to space suits." I told him my notion that unless we stood on the Martian surface, our trip would be suspect. He grinned slowly, and then slapped me on the shoulder.

"You're a worrier, Manny, aren't you? Well, the funny thing is, I think you may have a point there. But I got an order for you. Stop worrying. About the suits anyway. I'm putting myself in charge of suits from this moment, and you are not to think of it again until you see them. Okay?"

"Okay." Worrier? Well, I guess so. My life thus far had certainly prepared me to be a world-class worrier.

"All right, boys and girls, class dismissed. Go home, get some sleep, I'll see you back here tomorrow morning.

"And you know what? Maybe we've got a chance of going to Mars!"

22

I HAD THOUGHT we were operating in high gear the two weeks Travis was gone. Turns out I didn't even know what high gear was.

Early the next day Travis sent me and Kelly out to the airport to meet a plane full of Broussards. We went to the general aviation terminal, got there just as a Gulfstream private jet was landing. First out was Caleb Broussard, followed by Grace and Billy. Then we were introduced to Exaltation "Salty" Broussard. He was a small, quiet man, almost completely bald, and didn't look anything like Jubal and Caleb.

Last out of the plane was Gloria Patri "Patty" Broussard-Wilson, an attractive blonde in her late thirties who could have been Caleb's fraternal twin. She was the pilot of the plane. It belonged to her employer and she had borrowed it for a few days, to pick up Caleb and Grace in Fort Myers and Salty in Huntsville, Alabama, so they could all drop in and visit brother Jubal and cousin Travis. She let me and Kelly go aboard and look around while the baggage was being unloaded. There was a bar, a full-service media center, and all the way in back, a bedroom. This is the way to travel, I decided.

Kelly . . . well, Kelly had been riding in a plane much like this for as long as she could remember. Her father and a few other businessmen leased one together, the price tag for one of these babies being a bit steep even for a Mercedes dealer.

I HAD NEEDED a rest, or at least some kind of break, and the trip back to the Blast-Off, while you couldn't say it was restful, was certainly refreshing. These people talked a lot, loudly, and laughed a lot, just as loudly. They hadn't seen each other in a year in one case, and three years in the other. There was a certain amount of catching up to do, though they talked and e-mailed frequently. Patty's stories of bush piloting in Alaska and Africa had me anxious to hear more, and I was sorry to hear she wouldn't be staying on beyond the next day.

I felt enveloped and warmed by a feeling of family I'd longed for all my life. An *extended* family, something the racism of all my grandparents had deprived me of. By the time we arrived I was ready to change my name to Broussard . . . but eventually realized I didn't have to, as I'd already been adopted into this big, messy, ornery clan.

FOR THE FIRST few minutes things were a little chilly when we arrived at the Blast-Off. Caleb, Salty, Grace, and Patty immediately picked up on the hostility between Mom and Travis. You would have had to be in a coma to miss it. But between Aunt Maria's determined efforts and the magic of the Broussards, it was soon put away. Grace insinuated herself into Maria's kitchen without making Maria feel crowded, quite an achievement, and soon it was clear we were about to be treated to a Battle of the Brunches, Cajun versus Cubano. The only sure winner in a contest like that was our pepper-blasted taste buds, and the only sure loser was our waistlines.

We pulled all the outdoor tables together around the pool, and when that whole bunch sat down around them it was a toss-up, for me, as to whether I'd rather go to Mars or just stay right there, soaking up the love.

"Will somebody say grace?" Jubal asked.

"Grace," I said.

"What?" Grace asked, and first the Broussards, then the rest of us, broke up. Then Jubal offered up the prayer—"Please bless dis *fam'ly,* O Lord!"—and we dug in.

Soon it became clear to me that the new arrivals were aware of the nature of the Red Thunder project. I wasn't worried about that. It was clear to me that "family" meant as much to these people as it did in the Mafia. Being closemouthed was deep in their genes, they would never reveal anything important to any outsider.

Without ever asking a question, I learned a lot about them from the constant happy chatter. I learned, for instance, that Salty was an electrician. And I learned that, among many other skills, Caleb was a welder, that he plied that trade on offshore oil rigs when his family's myriad other enterprises weren't bringing in enough cash.

Somehow, I doubted this was a coincidence.

"So," I said to Caleb at one point, "did Travis hire you to do welding on . . . the project?" He laughed, finished a mouthful of boudin sausage.

"Travis couldn't 'ford me, Manny. I get union scale, and triple time on Sundays." I must have looked confused. "But that's when I hire out. I got me my own company, too, and I can charge as much or as little as I like, since I'm the boss."

Kelly had been listening.

"Caleb, Travis didn't tell me he'd offered—"

"He's not buttin' into your department, Kelly. We done our own deal, I'll get my money outta Travis and Jubal's share. Keep it off the books, that way, help keep the expenses down under one mill."

Kelly didn't look entirely convinced, but she let it go. It turned out Salty had the same arrangement. By bringing in a professional electrician, I thought maybe Travis was horning in on *my* department. I told Dak about it, and we drew ourselves up in righteous indignation . . . for two seconds, purely for form's sake. I was never so delighted to see someone in my life, and Dak felt the same way. We were in *way* over our heads, trying to design a system to meet all the electrical needs of *Red Thunder.*

The brunch meeting went well. I saw Caleb talking shop with Sam

Sinclair, and Salty sought out me and Dak and questioned us about the work we'd done so far, mapping out the electrical system. I gradually realized he was a lot more than an electrician, he was an electrical engineer, with a degree from LSU. And Dak and I were about to become apprentice electricians, in a *big* hurry.

The only worry was when I saw Travis take my mother to the other end of the parking lot. They talked for a long time, mostly with my mother shaking her head in that dogged way she can do better than anyone else. *You don't have a chance, Travis,* I thought. No matter what you're trying to sell her.

It turned out he was selling her some free help . . . and he *sold* it, which was a first in my memory. Not long after that she pulled me aside.

"Grace and Billy are moving in for the duration," she said, not making eye contact with me. What was she worrying about, that I'd think less of her for accepting help? "It was either that, or pack it in. Shut the doors and let the sheriff put all the furniture out on the street. I almost wish I'd done that, too."

"I'll support you either way, I hope you know that."

She put an arm around me as we walked, and she hugged me close.

"I do. The only reason I've kept at it so long is . . . it was your father's dream. And it wasn't even really a dream, I guess, I think it was more of an obsession."

"You don't need to let it be your obsession, too."

"But I did. You're right. Your father was determined to make it work, he wanted to show his parents . . . and even more, my parents, the white folks who never said a racist word to him but always managed to let him know he was their social inferior, right up to the day we married.

"He wanted to make it work so bad . . . that he got a little stupid. Just once. He did something he'd never have done if he hadn't wanted this so bad, for you, and for me."

And what was the stupid thing? What would be the worst possible way for him to die to perfectly satisfy my mom's parents' expectations? Why, a drug deal, of course.

Just this once, it was going to be. He lived long enough to tell Mom that, as he lay dying in the hospital. I remember Mom was crying, not much else.

It wasn't even a very big drug deal, certainly not by Florida standards. Just two Cubans and three Colombians and half a kilo of cocaine. But one of the Colombians was flying high, and he got mad, pulled out his gun, started shooting. None of the others could even recall what the fight was about. None of the others were hurt; the Colombian was too stoned to shoot very well, except for that first shot at point-blank range.

They left my father there, all four of them, to bleed almost to death in a deserted parking lot and die of septic infection the next day. All of them are out of prison now except the one who was killed inside. I know their names. Maybe one day I'll do something about that. Or maybe it's better to just bury that kind of hatred.

"Travis made a lot of sense, Manny," Mom went on. "He asked why I hang on here. Why work so hard to keep this goddam place running when I know, when *everybody* knows, that one day it's all going to come together at the same time, all the bad things, no customers, a big lawsuit, a hurricane, and the only thing different than if we'd gone belly up ten years ago would be ten years less of heartbreak.

"When I think of selling it, it just hurts that after all our hard work it's come to nothing. I think about getting another loan, someplace, do some renovation, make it nice, like your father wanted it. But this place is Old Florida, and it always will be, until some New Florida outfit comes along and puts up a shopping mall.

"Well, I'm tired of being Old Florida. So I'm going to accept Grace and Billy's help while you're working on this thing you're working on. Travis is right, you're going to work yourself to death trying to do both things at once, you're too good a son to let me and Maria handle it by ourselves, even though I've already told you to. You're your father's son, that way . . . and I'm proud of you.

"But I'm telling you right now, Manuel. Whether you go or not, whether you come back or not . . . I'm through here."

"I'm glad, Mom."

"When you . . . when you get back, we're getting out of this life." She shook her head and looked up at me. "You're already out of it, Manuel, and I can't tell you how glad that makes me. And, yes, I thank Travis for that . . . even though I'll kill him if he harms one—"

"I'm coming back, Mom. And we'll be rich and famous."

She squinted at me, looking too old and too tired in the merciless sunshine.

"Is that what you want, Manuel?"

"Famous? Not really. But we probably will be. I only want to be rich enough not to have to worry about every dime, all the time. Have enough money to pay for college, maybe have a few nice things. Not have to . . . to worry all the time that I can't get Kelly the things she's used to."

"Well, you know I like her. Even though she's rich." We both laughed at that. "And if you don't want to be famous, you'd better have a talk with her. She's figuring on cashing in on this thing right from the git-go. She's been talking to Maria and me about it. The lady has big plans."

"What do you mean?"

"Talk to her. And you go with Travis, and you come back." She kissed me on the cheek, hugged me very tight, and we rejoined the people around the picnic tables.

Big plans, huh? First I'd heard of it.

SIXTY DAYS.

That's how much time we had if we were going to beat the Chinese to Mars. We put up a big calendar on a wall of the warehouse and Kelly marked off each day at midnight, when we were supposed to have been in bed for an hour, per Travis's instructions. We were supposed to get up at six and run, having theoretically gotten seven hours of sleep. Instead, we were always up at four or five, unable to sleep.

But . . . run?

Mom got a big laugh at that, when she heard. And nobody could have been more surprised than me. I know I *should* exercise, get into the habit of it since I didn't plan to be a lumberjack or a rodeo rider, or anything else strenuous. Astronaut? In truth it's a very sedentary occupation, especially in the free-falling space stations. They have to put in one or two hours' exercise every day just to keep themselves from losing too much muscle mass and bone density.

But running around and around a track always struck me as a stupifyingly boring waste of time. Running on the street was only slightly better.

"That's gotta change," Travis told us, early on. "I want all of you to be in tip-top shape when we leave, not shriveled up from staring at a computer screen twenty hours a day. A strong mind in a strong body, that's what I want."

I was going to ask Travis how much running he'd gotten in during the last four or five years of steady alcoholism . . . but then I saw how much one hour of jogging was costing him, the first time we all went out together, with the sun just coming up and dew sparkling on the leaves. But he was out there again the next morning. Neither Dak nor I could let an old ex-alky outrun us, of course, so we really pushed ourselves.

And the girls? It was easy for them. They'd both been doing it since high school.

"You think this gorgeous body comes for free?" Kelly had chided me, puttering along at half her normal speed as I huffed and puffed beside her.

"Hell, no. I paid ten dollars for that body."

"Which you still owe me, come to think of it."

It took a week of torture, and a considerable amount of denial, for me to admit that after the morning runs I felt more rested and alert than at any other time of the day. After that I relaxed to the inevitable. After two weeks even Travis was getting back into shape. Jubal . . . well, Jubal was exempt, because nobody made Jubal do anything. Most of the time he was too engrossed in his calculations to drag himself away from the computer. But then one morning he did run with us, and he held his own. I'd forgotten about the midnight rowing trips on the lake.

We moved spare beds and dressers from the motel into some of the empty offices in the warehouse, and set up a prefab shower inside the rest room. Most nights Kelly and I slept over, and so did Dak and Alicia. Pretty soon the delivery boys from the local pizza and Chinese places could find their way to the Red Thunder Corporation blindfolded.

THE SHIP WAS to be in two parts, the cradle and the life modules. Dak and I were ready to start construction on the top part quickly, but it couldn't be built until it had something to sit on, which was frustrating. We devoted the time to materials testing. We also had weekly meetings at Rancho Broussard.

"It's a good thing we didn't start building the cradle a week ago," Travis said at our second meeting. "We thought we were ready, but Jubal did some more tests, and what he found out changed the parameters pretty radically.

"You'll recall I set out radiation sensors at that first test in the swamp. Didn't find any. But now Jubal has found there's two types of . . . maybe we should say 'quantum states' inside the Squeezer bubbles. Most of the ones we've tested, they've been what we're calling Phase-1 bubbles. I'll come back to them.

"But there's a second type of bubble."

"Let me guess," Dak said. "Phase-2?"

"I'm surrounded by geniuses. The stuff inside a Phase-2 is compressed so hard, so tight . . . we're really not sure just what the matter inside them is like, but it may be like a neutron star, all the electrons stripped away and nothing but neutrons packed together like Japanese on a Tokyo subway car.

"Whatever. What comes out is *very* hot, *very* fast, and releases radiation. If you were close to the exhaust, the neutrons would boil you like an egg.

"But early on, I did a test I didn't tell y'all about. I got to wondering what if we put a bubble over a city, like a big Bucky Fuller geodesic dome? Could it protect that city from a nuclear bomb?"

I glanced at Dak. We'd had the same idea, a while back. But it didn't have anything to do with the trip to Mars, so we filed it away to ask Jubal about later. We had our hands full with just the work we had to do, without wasting time on hypotheticals.

"So . . . we tried it on a rat."

Jubal came back in, carrying a battered old U-Haul box, which he set on the coffee table in front of us. He reached in and came up with a white rat, the kind you can buy in any pet store to feed your pet pythons and boa constrictors. With his other hand he took out a three-legged lab ring stand, the kind you set up over a Bunsen burner. A piece of plywood was glued to the top. He put the stand down and put the rat on the platform. It sniffed around, exploring all the edges.

"Travis," Alicia said, "is this going to be gross?"

"Not unless you love rats."

"Well . . . I don't like animal research . . ."

"Bunny rabbits and dogs and monkeys and stuff," Dak explained.

". . . but for rats I make an exception. I killed a lot of rats, growing up."

"No sympathy for rats," Dak agreed.

"No lyin', *cher,*" Jubal said, "it won't do de rat no good, no. But no blood."

"Go ahead, then." She moved closer to Dak.

Jubal reached into the box again, pulled out his new, improved Squeezer. It was all housed in a unit the size of a shoebox. He fiddled with it, and a basketball-sized Squeezer bubble appeared where the rat had been. The three ring-stand legs clattered on the table, sliced off neatly by the formation of the bubble. The bubble hung there. I didn't think I'd ever get used to that.

"Now, what happens in there seems to happen instantaneously. There's going to be a little bang, okay? But no explosion. Jubal?"

Jubal hit a button and the bubble vanished. There was a *pop,* and a very fine gray powder swirled in the air. What looked like a handful of iron filings fell to the table. The gray powder was so fine it took a few moments to settle into a small heap. Travis put his finger in the stuff and showed it to us.

"Your basic powdered rat," he said.

* * *

WE ALL FELT that called for a drink. Travis took a long swallow of the raspberry-flavored Snapple he favored these days.

"The powder is carbon, calcium, little traces of this and that, everything that was in the rat but water. The water turned into monatomic hydrogen and oxygen. That's what made the sound."

Dak got some on his finger, pondered it. "Powdered rat, huh? Hey, maybe what we got here is *instant* rat. Scrape it up, put it in a package, like Kool-Aid, then you just add water, stir it up . . ." Alicia shoved him. Jubal thought it was hilarious. All day long he was muttering "instant rat, instant rat," and laughing all over again. When Jubal found a joke he liked, like saying Grace, he stuck with it.

"You figure out how to put the rat back together again, Dak, that'd be something," Travis said. "Anyway, it's the same with the iron from the stand. It's chopped up so fine it basically oxidizes in midair, rusts before it hits the table.

"But the deal here, ladies and gents, is that chemical bonds are broken. We don't know why. Maybe it suppresses the charge on the electrons."

"It turn off dem little hookin' t'ings," Jubal said.

"What he means is, it does something to the valence electrons, which is what allows chemical bonds to happen."

"But if we squozes on jus' water . . ." Jubal said.

"He means, with just the right amount of water, and just the right amount of squeezing . . . show 'em, Jubal."

Two more things came out of Jubal's box of mischief. First was a small construction of metal mesh. It was welded to a heavy metal base. Arching around the cage were the three brass or bronze prongs, sharp pointed, that caused the discontinuity, that let the power inside come out in a controlled stream.

Sure enough, Jubal took a small container from his box, opened it, and took out a marble-sized bubble. He put it in the cage, and expanded it until it fit snugly.

"This is a Phase-1 bubble," Travis said. "There's just water inside it, squeezed just enough to . . . well, show them, cousin."

Jubal manipulated his control box, and we heard a high whistling sound. The powdered remains of the rat stirred in a faint breeze.

"Coming out of the top of the bubble is hydrogen and oxygen," Travis said. "We've adjusted the load inside so it doesn't fully collapse, like a neutron star. No radiation is produced. Now look." He struck a match and moved it over the bubble.

With a whoosh, it ignited in a fine, hard, bright yellow flame that went two or three feet into the air. It continued to burn while we all watched. After a full minute it was still firing, and Travis signaled Jubal to turn off the gas. The flame died.

"Clean power," Travis told us with a satisfied smile. "Hydrogen plus oxygen plus ignition, equals power, and water. Just like the VStar, only they burn liquid oxygen and liquid hydrogen. Not an environmentalist in the world could complain."

"There's enough to get us to Mars and back?" I asked.

"No. Well, not in any reasonable time. Lots of power, but not *that* much power. We'll use these to get up above the atmosphere." He unrolled a printout and pointed to the schematic drawing of the power cradle we were about to start building.

"Phase-1 bubbles here, here, and here, under tanks one, three, and five. Phase-2, what I'm calling *Super*Squeezer bubbles, under two, four, and six. These bubbles will have enough power to get us to Alpha-Centauri and back, if we were foolish enough to try that. Plenty of power for Mars and return. And when we come back, we use the Phase-1 bubbles again to land."

The doorbell rang. Travis frowned—he didn't get a lot of visitors out at the ranch—and he excused himself to go answer it.

Dak was bent over the plans so he didn't see what I saw . . . which was Travis glancing at the video screen just outside the dark vestibule. He stopped, stared, and then pivoted and hurried back to us. He spoke in a loud whisper.

"*Cops!* I want y'all to stay quiet. *Very quiet!*" And he hurried over to a big bookcase beside the television screen. He shoved some books aside and reached behind them. He came up with a flat pint of Jack Daniels.

I was stunned. *Travis, no!* But he twisted off the metal cap, raised the bottle to his lips, took a drink . . .

. . . and gargled with it.

He sprayed the mouthful of whiskey into the air, breathed deeply a few times, pulled out one side of his shirttail, kicked off his shoes, and mussed his hair. All of us tiptoed to the television screen, out of sight around the corner. I heard him open the door and we saw the two men in suits standing on the porch. The air *reeked* of Black Jack.

"Hey, hey!" Travis bellowed. "Watch-y'all want? I can't eat Girl Scout cookies on account of bein' on a diet."

One of the men took a step back. The whiskey stench coming off Travis was pretty powerful. The other said something, and all I could make out was ". . . Federal Bureau . . ." I figured I could fill in the blanks easily enough.

"Well, shit fire and save the matches," Travis said. "What'd I do this time?"

Travis stepped out onto the porch and pulled the door almost shut behind him, and the FBI agents' voices didn't carry very far. But Travis's did.

"Say, are either of you ol' boys from Texas? Friend of mine, he says nine out of ten FBI agents are from Texas." A pause, something mumbled by one of the agents. "Oh, yeah? Where in Texas?"

Mumble mumble ". . . Dallas."

"No fooling? My wife's got folks in Dallas. Ex-wife, that is. And you're from Lubbock? I don't know anybody from Lubbock. Thank God."

Travis listened a moment, then laughed himself into a coughing fit.

"Oh, that's great. That's great. We got guv'mint men checking out the likes of him? You figure he's gonna be another Waco or something? Let me tell you gents, I don't know what that ol' boy saw that brought y'all out here, but he don't do nothing but paint, paint, paint road signs and hold all-day prayer meetin's on Sunday where they shout *hallelujah* all the goddamn day long. I swear, you look in the dictionary under 'eyesore,' you're gonna find a picture of ol' Roscoe's place. Unless you look under 'damn fool religious nut,' 'cause he's there, too."

He went on like that for a good long time. We could see easily enough from their body language that the agents just wanted to get out of there, as soon as possible. Which they finally did, thanking Travis, giving him bland FBI smiles.

We all hurried to the curtained front window and eased the drapes back. Travis joined us, and we all watched the car back out of the shell driveway and onto the road, and spray crushed shells all over as the wheels spun.

We dropped the drapes back and looked at each other, not knowing what to say. Then Alicia came up with something. "Travis . . . ," she said, and that's all it took.

"I know, I know. It shouldn't be in the house. There's one more bottle, way back in the pantry under a sack of flour. You can get that one and pour it down the drain, too."

"Did you drink any?"

"No, I haven't, not even just now, and I can prove it." He reached into a pocket and pulled out a prescription drug bottle and tossed it to Alicia. "I've been taking this Antabuse stuff. And you know what? Looks like even the taste of booze is enough . . . You'll have to excuse me a minute . . ." He was looking green, and he hurried down the hall and into the bathroom. We could all hear him vomiting.

Alicia smiled at the sound. Whatever gets you off, I guess.

"I FIGURE THEY must be getting pretty desperate to start checking out old UFO reports, don't you?" Dak asked us all.

"Of course, there's the other possibility," I said. "That they're on to us, and closing in for the . . . kill? Arrest?"

"Always the bright side, huh, Manny?" Travis laughed. He still looked rough. It had taken quite a while to get his system back under control and he was sipping his raspberry iced tea very carefully. "Nothing we can do about it either way. Might as well operate as if they're following a cold, cold trail, looking for a revolutionary new technology in the backyard of a Jesus nut or a pathetic drunk. Checking out leads like that, they *got* to be desperate. Right?"

We decided to leave it at that, but none of us got much sleep that night.

NORMAL SPACECRAFT DON'T have anything you could really call a keel. Our spacecraft did, in a way. Right from the initial acceptance design we'd known the upper part and the lower part would be joined at a structural member that had to be a certain size and shape to hold the seven upended tank cars above it. It was to be a circular girder; circumference of that circle was twenty times pi, sixty-two feet and almost ten inches.

This is a pretty big circle, and it had to be very strong. It had to bear the considerable tonnage of the rest of the ship sitting on it, and also the high temperatures associated with firing the engines. As such, it was to be built from the highest-quality aircraft-grade titanium alloy.

Two days before FBI Sunday we got permission from Travis to begin work on the supporting structure and the thrust ring itself. We made the supports from ordinary scaffolding. Then we laid out the diameter of the ring and began learning how to build things out of the super-high-grade steel. Parts were welded, parts were drilled and bolted.

The welding on *Red Thunder*'s cradle was particularly fussy because of the exotic material we were using. Caleb couldn't trust anyone but himself for most of the work, so Travis and Jubal and Dak and I were sometimes welder's helpers, and sometimes just in the way. More often we were relegated to the job of preparing the structural members to Caleb's exacting specs before he did the final assembly. I lost count of how many tons of steel we had to throw away and begin again. Every weld was critical. Every weld could become the source of a potentially fatal air leak or structural collapse.

Just because we were little or no help on the critical cradle construction didn't mean Dak and I didn't get plenty of welding done. We had enough to occupy us preparing the tanks for the final assembly. We cut the tops off all of them and welded hefty flanges in place top and bottom. When they were all standing upright on the cradle, we'd lower materials in from the top, building decks and ladders and installing the larger, heavier components from the bottom up. Five of the outside tanks would connect with the central tank at about the midpoint, where the tank caps had been. Each connector had to be fitted with a round airtight hatch, so if we lost pressure in one of the outer tanks we could close and dog that hatch and still be in business. Three feet was big enough to let any of us pass through, even Jubal, but we intended to spend most of our waking hours in the central tank with all hatches sealed.

Naturally Caleb had to pass on all our work, adding to his already impossible workload, but it never seemed to bother him. He seemed tireless. "Working offshore rigs is a bunch worse than this," he'd laugh, when we asked him. I'm proud to say that only twice did he have to make us do a job over. We were learning fast.

There were a thousand things needing to be done, ten thousand pieces all needing to come together in the correct sequence . . . well, I'd rather have tried to *walk* to Mars than handle Kelly's job.

She had endless lists, endless schedules. Before we could tighten a nut or grind a pipe fitting we had to check with her to see if we were out of sequence. Any time of the day we might look up to find her standing there with her electronic clipboard, asking us to clarify this or that system, what do we have to do *first,* what do we have to do *second,* and third, and fourth, and nine-hundred-and-fifty-ninth. The next day a new set of printouts would be added to the growing folders of work assignments we all were carrying around, meticulously ticking off each item as it was done, then handing the completed forms to Kelly so she could mark them DONE in her computer files.

This in addition to compiling and writing the "owner's manual" for *Red Thunder*, the specs of every piece of equipment in her, the proper way to troubleshoot a fan or a water pump or a Sears Kenmore freezer, the preflight checklists for each crew member.

This in addition to keeping the books straight and paying all the bills.

This in addition to helping Alicia with her homework every night. *And* in addition to massaging my shoulders at the end of a day of welding and heavy lifting, before we both fell into bed too exhausted to make love. Some nights, anyway. I began to think seriously about asking her to marry me. If I came back alive, anyway . . .

MORNINGS, DAK WORKED with me in the warehouse. In the afternoons he left to join his father at the garage, where they were working on our Mars surface transportation vehicle. They were being very tight-lipped about it, not showing the plans to anyone, not allowing anyone to have a look at the work in progress. Not even billing the Red Thunder Corporation for parts, much less labor.

"It'll be my contribution to the effort," Sam had said. "It works, or it doesn't work. We'll know in a month." Travis hadn't objected, glad to have one less piece of the puzzle to worry about. We didn't have to have a surface transport at all, but it would be kind of a downer to get there and then be limited to trips within a mile of the ship. So we had set aside one tank to carry it, and Dak had showed us what needed to be done to the tank to accommodate the vehicle. It would be the only tank not accessible from the interior of the ship, which meant one less hatch seal to potentially go bad.

Alicia spent all day in her EMT classes. In the evenings she joined Dak and Sam and came with them to the warehouse, where Dak and Kelly, sometimes both, helped her with her homework. Dak reported she was tops in her class, something that made Alicia fairly glow with pride. She had found her life's work, no question.

I was in charge of product testing. I did that in my vast amounts of spare time, five minutes here, ten minutes there. Even Mom and Aunt Maria and Grace got into the act on product testing, coming over one at a time to help me be sure that every seal, every bolt, every thingamajig and doodad in the whole huge stockpile of building materials and store-bought assemblies was up to the task for which it was intended.

Back in the 1950s a test on living in an enclosed environment had ended early because the floor covering, some sort of linoleum, turned out to be outgassing some really toxic stuff and everybody in the experiment got sick. We would have scrubbers to remove both carbon dioxide and most contaminants that might show up in our air, and detectors for carbon monoxide and a wide range of other poisons. But it was best if we eliminated all those potential problems on the ground.

Luckily for us, NASA had already tested a vast number of substances to assess their suitability for use in launch vehicles and space stations. So 99 percent of the stuff we used was precertified. Again, as in so many things, if that work hadn't already been done there was no way we could have met our deadline.

But there were a few items here and there that had never been scrutinized, and if we absolutely had to have them, we tested them ourselves in a small sealed chamber.

That was one kind of testing. We spent far more time and effort seeing if this or that could stand up to heat, cold, and vacuum.

Take automobile tires.

"Tires?" I asked Dak, thinking he was kidding.

"Yeah, tires, man. Just your ordinary synthetic rubber steel-belted radials. I want to see how they stand up to cold, and vacuum."

I knew Dak wouldn't waste my time, and I knew he probably wouldn't answer too many questions, so the next day we had a top-of-the-line Goodyear tire delivered.

Our vacuum-testing chamber now had a tank of liquid nitrogen, three hundred and some degrees below zero, and a pump to move the supercold stuff through a grid of pipes inside the tank. We had powerful radiant heaters for testing the other extreme.

We put the tire in the chamber and cooled it down to 150 below. Through the little Plexiglas window it looked okay.

"Take her down to one eighty, one ninety or so," Dak said, so I did. We left it that way for twelve hours, then pumped out all the air for another twelve, and turned on the heater to about 150 Fahrenheit.

When we opened the chamber Dak picked the tire up in a padded glove . . . and chunks of hard rubber just peeled away from the tire. Dak didn't say anything, just carried the tire to the trash Dumpster and tossed it in.

He frowned for two days after that. I began to think that expression would imprint permanently on his face. A couple times he shouted at me for nothing much, which was not like Dak at all. Then on the third day he came in with a big smile on his face.

"Something?" I asked him.

"You'll see, a few more weeks," he said, so I left it at that.

The next day sixteen king-sized pink Wal-Mart electric blankets were delivered to the warehouse. The next morning they were gone. Dak had taken them to the garage.

Problem solved, I figured, and turned to other things.

AND ON THE seventh day we rested . . . long enough to hold the weekly meeting, and for Kelly to tell us we were five days behind schedule. "The cradle is proving to be a lot more difficult to build than we'd planned," Kelly said.

"Sorry, Kelly," Caleb said. "If I'd been around for the early planning I'd of told you it was gonna take a bit longer than that."

"How many more days you figure you'll need?"

"Another week."

Kelly began tapping on the screen of her clipboard.

"There are a few items here and there that I can move up. But in about four days there's not going to be much for the rest of us to do until we get the upper stage in place."

"There's still the matter of the space suits," Travis said.

"I've trusted you on that one," Kelly said. "If you tell me it's going to take two weeks to make them, we might as well all relax, because the race to Mars is over."

"I'll need three, four days, tops," Travis said. "I have to take a trip. Now might be the best time to take it, if Dak and Manny can handle the metal fabrication work alone, under Caleb's orders, of course."

"I can help, too," Kelly pointed out.

"Sure," Caleb said. "If I can pull Dak off the rover project four or five days, have him working full-time out here, then with Kelly . . . then I don't figure we'd get 'er done any faster with or without you, Trav."

"I can do that," Dak said, but he didn't look happy.

"What if I helped out?" Alicia said.

"No," Kelly and Travis said at once. Kelly gestured for Travis to go on.

"You getting an EMT rating is one of the necessary factors made me agree to get involved at all. We've got to have somebody aboard who can handle a bigger medical problem than a hangnail, which is about all I'm qualified to do."

"You make me nervous, Travis," Alicia said. "If you figure I'll be able to do a heart transplant when I'm done, you're wrong. Why not take a doctor along?"

"I considered it," Travis admitted. "I expect you to be able to treat most types of trauma, from a skinned knee to third-degree burns to sawing off a leg. What we're going to have to deal with, if we have anything at all, is physical injury, pretty much like a bad car wreck. If there's any hip bones that need to be rebuilt, or plastic surgery, or skin transplants, the patient will have to wait till we get back to Earth. I just want you to have a good shot at keeping trauma victims alive for a three-day ambulance ride."

"I guess I can handle that," Alicia sighed.

"You still making that list of stuff?" Dak asked her. Alicia dug in the pocket of her jeans and came up with a rumpled piece of paper which she passed over to Kelly.

"I've bought a lot of stuff already," Kelly said, "We're going to have a well-equipped infirmary for diagnosis and treatment. We've already got just about all the instruments, from a sphygmomanometer to a little rubber hammer."

"A spigomo . . ." Jubal looked delighted. A new long word!

"Measures your blood pressure," Alicia told him.

"I won't buy plasma and whole blood until we're ready to leave," Kelly said. "I've got a list of drugs, and only about half can be bought over the counter."

"I can probably handle that," Salty said. We all looked at him. Salty was a man of few words, he seldom had anything to say at the Sunday meetings. "I know somebody in Mexico. He can buy most of them over the counter down there, and anything he can't buy legally, well . . ."

The obvious question hung in the air, but nobody asked it. His business, I figured.

Salty shrugged, and answered it anyway.

"He's my connection. I'm not a user, what I buy from him is marijuana, sometimes codeine and morphine. My wife's got rheumatoid arthritis, and the weed is the best thing she's found for the day-to-day pain. On her worst days she takes the pills."

It was clear that Caleb and Grace had known this, but Travis and Jubal looked shocked. Jubal looked ready to cry.

"It's fairly well under control, don't worry," Salty said. "The doctors kept undermedicating her, so we took things into our own hands."

"Naturally."

"Sure thing."

"Sorry to hear it, Salty."

We all offered sympathy and Salty looked uncomfortable, so Alicia brought us back to the subject.

"Morphine's on my list," she said.

"I'll get it for you."

There were a few more items of business, dealt with in about half an hour. Then, I was ready to head back to the warehouse, but Travis insisted we go out on the lake and fish for a while. "And there will be no talking the project," he declared.

It was hard to do that for the first hour. But then I landed a big bass, and took the fishing seriously for the next several hours.

Travis was right, I think. You have to take a break every now and then. But when we got back we all went to work with even more determination.

That night Kelly told me where Travis was going.

"I just booked him Daytona, Atlanta, Moscow, Star City, and back," she said.

"Star City? *Star City?"* I have to admit, the Russians' name for their main space base beat the heck out of our old Cape Canaveral. I sure would have loved to go see for myself. "Maybe I could go along, help him carry his bags."

"Want me to book you?"

"First class, or tourist?"

"First class, naturally. But he's paying for the ticket himself. 'This is a below-the-line cost,' is what he said. It's what they say in Hollywood for items not on the regular budget. Like the star's thirty-million-dollar salary."

"What do you figure he's gonna do in Russia?"

"Well, I've had a few hours to think it over. Unless he's selling us out to the dirty Tsarist Russkis, he knows where he can get a deal on some used space suits."

"Huh!" I was remembering my earlier thought, that there was no thrift store where you could pick up half a dozen used space suits. But there was, of course. Ever since the collapse of Communism, Russia had been one big thrift store, selling out to the bare walls. *Crazy Boris Says, "Everything Must Go!"* Spacesuits ought to be easy enough to find over there, with Travis's connections.

WHEN KELLY WAS notified about Travis's return flight, we flipped coins and I got to be the one who drove the U-Haul to Atlanta to pick him up. It rained all the way there and back, but I didn't mind. It was nice to get out on the highway for a day.

Travis was waiting at a freight terminal with ten wooden crates covered with stenciled Russian instructions and warnings. Five of them were four-foot cubes, but the other five were pretty much the size and shape of coffins. I asked him how the trip was. He seemed tired, but too wired to relax much.

"Mostly flying," he said. "I don't know if I'd a made it back in tourist class. I'm not as young as I was. I won't lie to you, Manny, without the Antabuse I don't know if I'd a made it. Free drinks all the way there and back. And everywhere you go, it's 'Let's drink to this!' and 'Let's drink to that!' " But then he grinned at me. "But I did it, boy-o. Clean and sober, there and back."

"Congratulations. We're all proud of you."

I figured he had more to talk about than the drinking, but he wasn't through yet.

"Over there, I'm still something of a hero, Manny. Not like here, where I'm washed up and most of my old friends have left. But the Russians . . . there was a Russian aboard that flight I had to set down in Africa, and they've never forgotten. That I was drunk doesn't matter. In fact, there's something in the Russian soul that makes them respect me *more* because I was drunk when I did it.

"Anyway, I got friends over there, friends I never got a chance to alienate. All it takes is a little cash to grease the wheels, then a little more for whatever it is you're buying . . . and pretty soon you've got what you want, at a tenth of the cost."

"So those are suits in the boxes?"

"You bet."

"Why ten boxes?"

"Space suits ain't like T-shirts. You need a few specialized tools. The helmets and backpacks are in the other boxes, too." He looked out the window and shivered.

"Georgia, Georgia, on my mind. Can't get me out of Georgia soon enough."

"What's the matter with Georgia?"

"I hate coming to Georgia. I wish Kelly had booked me through Dulles, or even Miami. But you know Kelly. She saved me about five hundred dollars finding that fare."

After ten minutes with his eyes closed he sat up and shook his head. He cracked the window to let the wet breeze blow in his face.

"It was raining like this the day I set the *Montana* down at the Atlanta airport."

"Yeah?"

"Yeah. Didn't I tell you about that?"

"I don't think so." I was pretty sure he knew he hadn't told me. Why he'd decided to tell me now I had no idea, but I decided to just let him go. Which he did.

"There were warning lights from the diagnostic tests during my preflight. They'd come on, then they'd go out. I wanted to postpone the reentry, do an EVA, get out there and bang a few things around with a hammer, see if I could get the lights to stay on or stay off, one way or the other. But they sent me a 'fix,' they swore if I ran their program everything would be fine. That's how it worked on the ground, anyway.

"I told 'em to go stuff their fix, I wasn't pulling away from the station till I'd eyeballed the thing. And they told me to remember Senator So-and-so was aboard—as if I'd forget it—and he had to be back to make an important vote on the Senate floor, and my head would roll if he was late."

"Senator So-and-so?"

"Yeah, I forget which one he was, now. God knows I took enough of 'em up back then. Ever since Garn and Glenn went up, back in the '90s, a U.S. senator figures he ain't no great shakes unless he's been up. The ultimate boondoggle junket. Hell, some guys paid twenty million dollars to go up! Senators get to go for free.

"Sure enough, halfway down one of the speed brakes deployed at about Mach six. We flipped right over. Five times we rolled, me cussing and fighting all the way. I stopped the roll and looked out the window for the landing strip, and there she was. Happiest I'd been since I found that little grass strip in Africa. I brought her in, very hard and very fast . . . and about a hundred feet off the deck I spotted a 787 crossing the runway in front of me. Must of given the captain of that 787 something to remember, because we missed by maybe ten feet.

"And when we stopped, that's when I knew I had landed in Atlanta."

He stopped for a while, sipped at the coffee he'd bought from a machine at the freight terminal. Then he shook his head.

"I'd a found and fixed that hydraulic leak if they'd a let me go EVA. But since nobody at Hartsfield knew I was coming until I showed up on their radar dropping like a stone and because Senator So-and-so got a whiff of my breath, and since I was still blowing a one-point-eight an hour later . . .

"We compromised, NASA and me. When the inquiry happened I wouldn't mention the warnings they'd told me to ignore, also that the reason for ignoring them was the senator's goddamn fault . . . and I'd hand in my wings and never fly again."

There was another long silence. I listened to the hiss of the tires on pavement and the sound of the wipers moving the red Georgia mud around my windshield.

"Sometimes I wish I'd a just gone for it, Manny. Tell the whole story, give the senator and those NASA turkeys what they had coming. But I *was* drunk. I was *stinking* drunk. The breath test was probably unconstitutional . . . but hell, lots of people knew I was a drunk, a drunk who'd been pretty lucky for a long, long time, and a bunch were ready to testify to that.

"Still, I might have . . . Then somebody mentioned Jubal. Didn't make a threat, nothing like that. Didn't have to. They'd looked into my private life enough to know about him. They could drop a hint here, a few bucks there, and the judge takes Jubal from me and puts him in an institution for retarded adults. . . ."

We didn't speak for the next twenty miles. I couldn't think of anything to say. *I'm sorry?* Didn't quite cover it, did it? Then I did think of something.

"Don't tell that story to my mom, Travis, okay?"

"Deal."

Pretty soon he was asleep, and snoring, *very* loudly. Oh, brother. Better put earplugs on the packing list.

* * *

"THESE ARE ALL fifteen-year-old suits," Travis said. "Only two of them have actually been in space. They've all been sitting in a warehouse for a long time."

We were all gathered at the ranch, beside the pool. The coffin boxes had been pried open. The space suits, a bright color Travis had called "Commie red," were packed in a substance Sam had called "excelsior," that looked like dried brown grass. Didn't the Russians have Styrofoam peanuts? Travis pulled one suit out of its box and brushed it off.

"Isn't fifteen years kind of old?" Kelly asked.

"Yes, and no." He didn't explain, and Kelly went on.

"And why weren't they ever used?"

"Obsolescence."

"Is that good?" Alicia asked. "I mean, are they—"

"Okay? They should be as good as new ones, mostly. I couldn't afford to buy the new model, chilluns. These'll have to do." He removed a helmet from one of the other boxes and twisted it into place. He stood and admired his work.

"What you should know about Russian engineering, crew, is that it often doesn't have the bells and whistles Americans usually design into their stuff. But it *works*. This kind of suit protected many a Russki behind during many a lonely man-hour. I'd stack 'em up against NASA suits any day."

I picked up what looked like an instruction manual from the scattered debris. Naturally, it was printed in Russian.

"Do you read Russian, Travis?"

"Passably well. We'll get one translated, and I'll check you out on all the Russian labels that are actually on the suit."

We helped him tie weights to the arms and legs of the suit and he snapped a fitting from the suit into an air compressor hose. Then we tossed it in the pool and started pumping it full of air.

Pretty soon the surface of the pool was boiling with foam, like we'd dropped in a giant Alka-Seltzer. Kelly turned away, grimacing. I think I may have groaned. I heard the freight train of history pulling away without me. *Good-bye, trip to Mars. . . .*

Travis kicked off his shoes and put his wallet on the patio table. He picked up a swim mask and put it over his head, then jumped in the pool. He was down only a short time, then came to the surface and clambered out, sopping wet but grinning.

"All the leaks are coming from the connector gaskets," he announced.

"This is good news?" Dak wondered.

"All according to plan, Dak. You know, the Smithsonian has dozens, maybe hundreds of space suits in the attic. They're mostly falling apart, there's no good way to preserve them. The plasticizers in these suit gaskets are simply going to bleed out eventually. All we have to do is change the gaskets and we're in business."

"Can you get them off the shelf?" Sam asked.

"No, they'll have to be custom-made, but it shouldn't be hard. I know an outfit in Miami can do it. Alicia, I'd like to put you in charge of—"

"Alicia's classes are too important," Kelly said. "Let me take it over, Travis. I'm beginning to have a little spare time, plus it'd be nice to do something with my hands other than type and move a mouse."

Jubal, Sam, Dak, and I loaded the empty coffins back in the U-Haul, and I took them to the dump, glad Mom had not seen them or the leak-like-a-sieve space suits.

AT THE END of the day we all took Travis to the warehouse to see *Red Thunder*. His reaction was gratifying: his jaw dropped as his neck craned up.

The cradle was finished, and the central tank had been upended, lowered into place, and braced, awaiting the six other tanks which would provide it with more support.

It looked weird, sticking up like that. The top was off so we could install the flanges and the openings which would soon hold the five Plexiglas windows of the cockpit, as Travis called it, or the bridge, as Caleb and Sam did.

And all of it painted a bright Chinese red.

Travis took it all in, then grinned at us.

"Ladies and gents," he said, "for the first time, I feel like we're going to Mars."

24

★ ★ ★

WE MOUNTED THE six external tanks over the next three days, and it was a perfect example of the learning curve. It took us all day to do the first one, but we did two the second day and the remaining three on the third. And there she stood, basically complete on the outside except for bolting on the tops of five of the tanks.

Tank one contained the air lock. We would enter that tank from the center, as with all the others. There was a deck there, with a hole and a ladder to climb down to the suit locker deck. There the five suits hung on simple racks. There were outlets to charge the suit batteries, and couplings to recharge the backpacks with compressed oxygen. Oxygen instead of the compressed air we'd be breathing aboard ship, because that's how the suits were designed, and because, even if we could reengineer them, carrying compressed oxygen gave us five times the suit time that compressed air would have.

In the floor of the suit deck was an airtight hatch and another ladder down to the lock itself. When we had that deck finished we all practiced climbing up and down the ladder, fully suited, and operating the locks by ourselves, as we might have to do in an emergency. It was tough going. But we'd never have to do it in full Earth gravity.

Outside the lock we built a platform large enough for four suited people to stand on, surrounded by a safety rail. Then we attached a ramp we could raise or lower with pulleys. It was ugly, but it was simple, and easy to fix if something went wrong.

Tanks two and five carried water and air. Compressed air was in ordinary pressure bottles, ten feet high and about a foot and a half across. The system was arranged so that one system could be entirely shut down without affecting the other, and either system would keep us alive for up to two months. It all fed into a system of fans and ducts and scrubbers. One of us would be awake and in charge of air control twenty-four hours a day, in four-hour shifts. We all had to practice on it until we knew what valve to turn for any possible situation.

Water was in big rubber bladders. We had debated mounting them up high, letting gravity provide our water pressure. But Travis pointed out we were going to have to bring water pumps anyway, in case we had to spend any significant amount of time in weightlessness, such as doing repairs on the ship or rescuing distressed *Ares Seven* astronauts. So down to the bottom they went.

The plumbing system of *Red Thunder* was about as basic as you could get: water bladder, pump, a T-joint and pipes that led directly to the cold water spigot over a deep sink, or to our Sears water heater and from there to the sink. The tap was the source for drinking water and bathing water. We were bringing enough clothes to change every day, but if we really felt we had to wash clothes we could do it in that sink.

Bathing would consist of running a measured amount of warm water into a bucket, then sitting on a stool in the bathing room—a prefab shower stall with a drain in the floor—and washing with soap and a washcloth. Alicia wrinkled her nose when we showed her that part of the plans, but said nothing.

But I thought she might mutiny when she saw the plans for the toilet.

"A hole and a bucket?" Alicia said, scandalized.

"We'll have a toilet seat over the hole," Travis pointed out.

"Oh, sure. And all the way to Mars and back, I'll have to put the damn seat down. Dak *never* puts it down, and I bet none of you do, either."

Nobody denied it, though Kelly got a case of the giggles which we all caught. Eventually Alicia laughed, too.

"Keep it simple, keep it basic," Travis said, over and over. "A flush toilet is too complicated, and it wastes water. Same with a shower."

He was right. We'd discussed all the possibilities before settling on the "one-holer." People who live in RVs and trailers have what they call gray-water and black-water tanks. Gray water is from the sinks and shower, and black water is from the toilet. We would have a gray-water tank, since all it needed was a pipe from the drain to the waste tank, in the bottom of tank two, and a valve that could be turned if we had to go into free fall, to prevent the water from backing up. As for the black waste . . .

"Down here we have an ordinary wire dirty-clothes hamper." Dak showed us when the plans were being finalized. "You put a plastic bag into the rack, you put down the seat, you do your business. Then you take the bag and sprinkle in some of these blue crystals, twist the bag, tie it off, and drop it down the glory hole."

"What's this?" Alicia asked, pointing to a square shape on the plans.

"Exhaust fan," Travis said. "Space stations smell bad. Be *sure* to turn on the fan when you use the toilet."

"With a flush toilet you wouldn't have so much of a problem," Alicia muttered.

Travis had suggested we simply dump the waste bags over the side.

"You'd have the Greens all over us when we got back," Dak told him.

"What for? We're not contaminating the Earth with this sh— . . . this stuff."

"Doesn't matter," I told him. "Believe me, Travis, my generation doesn't think logically about pollution. They'd hate us for it."

"That's right," Kelly said, and Alicia nodded.

Travis grinned. "You realize, anything we dumped overboard would be moving at solar escape velocity. Some of it will be doing three million miles an hour. I gotta admit, I'm kind of tickled at the idea that the first man-made object to reach the stars could be a bag of superfast sh—superfast doo-doo."

"Superfast doo-doo!" Jubal shouted, and slapped his knee. As usual when Jubal heard a good joke, he went around muttering it all day long.

TANKS THREE AND six held fuel and generators and batteries and fuel cells and heaters and air conditioners.

Me and Dak and Salty had debated a long time as to the best source of power. *Red Thunder*'s electrical needs were not enormous so carrying the means of producing that amount of power was not going to be a problem. But how to produce it?

I favored fuel cells. They are so elegant, it's hard not to love them. You put in oxygen and hydrogen at one end, and water and power come out the other. But Salty thought they were too prone to failure.

"So just carry a bunch of them," I suggested.

Dak liked the idea of generators.

"Talk about a proven technology," he said. "Those things, after me and Dad go over 'em, there's just no way they can fail."

And in case they did fail, Dak said, we just bring two.

Salty liked nicad batteries. I thought they were too heavy. Salty said nobody's supposed to worry about weight, like Travis said.

In the end, we took all three systems. Like everything else on *Red Thunder,* we wanted triple systems when possible, triple reserves when possible. Any of the three systems could have taken us to Mars and back.

Tank four was reserved for Sam and Dak's mysterious Mars Traveler, which none of us had seen yet. Dak said all we needed to do to the tank was mount a heavy winch in the top and line it with insulation, as we were doing to all the other tanks. He and Sam promised to have something to show us in two weeks.

* * *

THE CENTER TANK was living quarters.

At the very top was the bridge, Travis's domain. There was a second chair for a copilot. All of us except Jubal trained on it for a day, but none of us kidded ourselves that if anything happened to Travis we could just step into his shoes.

For navigation we had basic optical instruments and the simplest computer program we could find. With luck, you could shoot a few stars, type in a destination, and the computer would tell you where to point and how hard to push. It even worked that way in training . . . most of the time. But I crashed the simulator Jubal had set up the first five times I tried to land it. And I was the best of the three of us.

"Just don't get yourself hurt, Travis," Kelly told him one dismal night after we'd run through the results of the training program.

"Don't worry," Travis said with a grin. "I contracted to bring you kids back alive, and to do that I've got to watch my own backside, too."

Below the bridge were the other ships' systems. There were thirty-five flat TV screens on the walls, larger than the ones on the bridge, one for each of the cameras we had mounted inside and outside the ship. These were good-quality cigarette cameras, smaller than your finger, cheap, and practically indestructible. A few were mounted on motors, but most delivered a static image of the state of the ship. The control consoles for each of the ship's systems were here, and all four of our acceleration chairs. These were good, sturdy lounge chairs. The only problem I could see with them was they were so comfortable I wondered if I might nod off during an air watch.

The deck below that was the common room. One side was the galley, with a sink, an upright Amana freezer, and a refrigerator about the same size, both of them welded to the deck and fitted with strong latches. The freezer was full of high-end TV dinners from the local gourmet market, and the best brand of frozen pizza we could find. Travis told us the most frequent complaint from long-termers on space station duty was the quality of the food. We carried ice cream and Popsicles, too.

The fridge would hold cans of soda pop, and fresh fruits and vegetables. Alicia demanded we bring whole wheat flour so she could bake bread. I wondered if she'd find time for it, but why not? I liked fresh-baked bread as much as she did. So we packed some cold cuts and peanut butter and jelly, too.

We had a microwave oven and a radiant-heat oven just big enough to heat a frozen pizza or bake a few loaves of bread. Beside them would sit our espresso machine.

Opposite this little galley we installed a prefab breakfast nook. We bought it at a local building supply store, and it had a '50s diner look to it, with red vinyl padded seats and a Formica top. It would easily seat the five of us.

We carried playing cards, a Monopoly board, and dominoes. None of us but Travis and Jubal knew how to play dominoes. Travis promised to teach us, and I suspected they might be expensive lessons. I could end up back on Earth broker than when I left.

The deck below that was the one that contained the hatches to all five of the other tanks. We set up the infirmary there. At launch, and until and unless we needed it, the infirmary deck would be mostly bare. We carried enough folding cots to accommodate all of the Ares Seven if we had to. Alicia's medical supplies and instruments were in cabinets against the infirmary walls.

The two decks below were crew quarters, two "staterooms" to a deck. The captain and Jubal had the two on the upper deck, and below were the one Dak and Alicia would share, and my own lonely bunk. The rooms were small and without many frills, though we painted them warm colors to make them feel a little less like jail cells. Each contained an air mattress on a platform with clothes storage beneath, a bedside table with lamp and alarm clock, and a simple intercom and alarm bell.

We built from the bottom up. When a deck was finished the ceiling would be lowered into the tank and welded in place, becoming the floor of the deck above. These floors were made of metal grills. This made the ventilation system simpler, since air could find its way through the floors as well as the ducts.

When a deck was finished we installed insulation on all the walls—we used ordinary Owens-Corning, the kind with the Pink Panther printed on it—and covered them with big Styrofoam panels. All pipes and ducts and wires were exposed, for easier repair if that became necessary.

After two weeks we had capped one of the outer tanks and gained two days, putting us only three days behind schedule, with thirty days to M-day.

After another week we had capped two more tanks . . . but had had to remove the first one and tear out part of the air system, which was giving us no end of problems. We lost one of the days we had gained.

SIMPLY TO BUILD *Red Thunder* in sixty days would not have been a problem. But building it was not enough.

"Three parts to the problem," Travis drilled into us. "Construction, testing, and training. Construction is the *easy* part. We're not going to take off in a ship we don't know how to operate."

As the ship took shape we had to do exhaustive tests of each of the ship's systems, testing right up to the point of failure, and sometimes beyond. We had that demonstrated to us vividly when an air system broke down and we were unable to fix it with the tools we would have aboard. So, tear it out, design it again, build the new system, and test that to its limits. Each item that didn't work properly the first time and every time thereafter put us further behind schedule. Travis was uncompromising, and though we chafed at it, we knew he was right.

But training was the worst.

From the earliest Mercury days of manned space flight, training had been more extensive and more rigorous than almost any field of human endeavor. The idea being that, if you trained hard enough, you would know almost instinctively what to do in any given situation. Your response would become automatic, and you would remain calm because you'd been there before. It was proven, it was time-tested . . . and I just didn't think we had time for all the training Travis insisted on.

As if this weren't enough, we also had to train in the Russian space suits.

We had the manual translated, and by the time we were done we all had practically memorized it. We each had to log ten hours working in the pool with weights on our feet. That meant that another person had to be there to operate the rented crane to yank us out of the water if something went wrong.

Things did go wrong. The suits had been sitting on the shelf for a long time, which wasn't good for them. My very first training session, when I was supposed to be learning the use of a NASA-surplus zero-gravity power wrench, I spent the first fifteen minutes shivering as the suit cooling system brought me down almost to the freezing point, and when I had that adjusted right, my left glove sprung a leak and we had to abort.

We were at one of our regular Sunday meetings. Kelly was surrounded by stacks of paper and no less than three digital assistants, spread out on the picnic table at the Rancho. Each Sunday she handed each of us a small booklet detailing our every task, every movement for the coming week.

I looked around. Dak seemed to have lost weight, which he couldn't afford. Alicia wasn't smiling much. We had all been daunted to find how leaky the suits were.

"One more arm, and one more leg, and I think we'll have five completely sound space suits," she was telling us. She looked up at Travis. It was his money.

"Go for it," he said. But he didn't look happy. Donating the suits was turning out to be more expensive than he'd bargained for.

We spent an hour talking. When that was done Kelly opened the big cardboard box she'd brought to the meeting. She pulled something out of it.

"Bomber jacket?" Travis asked, with a grin.

"They had a special at Banana Republic," Kelly said. She stood up and put the jacket on. She looked great in it, but that was no surprise, she looked great in everything.

Dak and Alicia were out of their chairs, finding their jackets and putting them on. Kelly tossed one to me. I looked it over before putting it on. It looked used, but with leather jackets that was good. Somehow they stress the leather without weakening it, so it becomes supple and soft. I put it on and liked the feel of it, though it was far too warm for a Florida summer day. On the front, where a soldier would wear his medals, there was a name strip: GARCIA. Below that was an embroidered triangular mission patch. It showed the ship blasting in orbit around Mars, with *Red Thunder* written along the bottom. The patch was on the back, too, but larger.

"Did you do this?" Travis asked, pointing to the logo on the back of his jacket.

"I'm not that artistic. I've got a friend who's a graphic designer. Do you like it?"

We all did. Nobody had any objections to the jackets, either. They beat the hell out of NASA's tired old blue jumpsuits.

"Who's the friend?" I asked.

"A guy named 2Loose."

I was delighted. "You know 2Loose, too?"

"He did a mural on the new women's center," Alicia said.

Henry "2Loose" La Beck was an old classmate of mine, the Tagger King of Central Florida. In his outlaw days he must have painted a thousand walls and two thousand railroad cars. He did a little time for it, but often the owner of the violated building dropped charges after studying his work for a while, he was that good. Plus, he could run very fast.

Last I'd heard of him he'd cleaned up his act, gone legit, formed his own company and was doing pretty well. A lightbulb went on inside my head.

"Hey, how about we get him to paint *Red Thunder*?"

All I got at first were blank looks.

"It's already painted," Travis said.

"Yeah, but not like 2Loose can paint it," Dak said, with a grin. "He did some work on *Blue Thunder*. Just the pinstripes, I didn't want no Sistine Chapel ceiling."

"But he could *do* the Sistine Chapel," I said, "if you didn't mind God driving around in a low-rider and Jesus with spiky hair and tattoos."

"I like it," Alicia said.

"Me, too," Kelly laughed. "Let's ask him."

"Hey, wait a minute," Travis said. But we voted him down and, true to his word, this was still a democracy until we took off. So we decided to offer 2Loose the commission.

ANOTHER WEEK OF hard work, and we gained another day on the timetable.

It was becoming clear that the sticking point would be in the last week. Travis had scheduled a full-blown systems test for that week. For seven days, all of us but Travis and Jubal would be sealed into the ship, totally isolated from the outside environment. We would drink the stored water, breathe the canned air, and eat the frozen food, all the while we were training, training, training.

He was adamant that it had to be seven days.

"Seven days is already a compromise," he told us. "I'd be a lot happier taking a full month. The only reason I'm settling for seven is that *Red Thunder* is so powerful and so fast that we'll never be more than three and a half days away from Earth. I figure most things can be patched up well enough to last three and a half days."

WE GAINED ANOTHER day by cutting out hours of sleep. With three days until M-day minus seven, the day we had to begin the long-duration systems tests, we bolted down the top of tank seven, the central module, and *Red Thunder* was complete . . . from the outside. But we still had five days of work that *had* to be done before the test could begin.

On that day the Chinese *Heavenly Harmony* ship arrived at Mars and began its aerobraking maneuvers. Aerobraking had been used by all but the earliest unmanned Mars missions. Instead of firing rockets to achieve an orbit around Mars, a spacecraft would dip into the upper reaches of the Martian atmosphere. Friction would slow the ship enough that it would fall into a highly elliptical orbit; that is, one that looped far away from Mars—to what was called apoapsis—before curving back down to the orbital low point, the periapsis. Once there, it would dip into the atmosphere again, slowing more and making the orbit less elliptical. After half a dozen orbits of decreasing size the ship would settle into a circular orbit, and proceed to the Martian surface from there.

This all took time. The first long, looping orbit would take *Heavenly Harmony* a full six days. The next orbit would be four days, and so on. But who cared? Nobody was in a big hurry. The American *Ares Seven* was far behind.

"Maybe they'd hustle a little more if they knew we were here," Dak said, but his heart wasn't in it.

We were all watching the big television set in the warehouse, feeling defeated. On the screen, a million Chinese had packed Tien-an-men Square, shouting and chanting. Billions of firecrackers were going off. Dragon dancers snaked through the crowds. Somebody was waving a big sign, which the CNN anchorman told us translated as

THE EAST IS RED!
CHINA IS RED!
MARS IS RED!

"I'd like to give 'em something red," Dak muttered.

We had known this would happen, but it didn't lessen the impact. The Chinese were the first humans to reach Mars. But we kept bearing in mind that the first humans to reach the moon were Jim Lovell and the crew of *Apollo 8, not Apollo 11.*

"Travis," I said, "are we really going to lose . . . because of two lousy days?"

He kept shaking his head and I thought he wasn't going to answer. But when he looked up, his face was anguished.

"Manny, I made promises. To you, to your parents, and to myself. I think we need a full seven-day test. I can't back off from that."

"For myself," I said, "I release you from that promise. I think we won't know anything more after seven days than we'd know after five."

"Me, too," Alicia said. "Five days is enough."

"You want my vote?" Dak said. "I'm with them."

"I don't get a vote on this," Kelly said, "but I think they're right."

"Let 'em go, *cher,*" Jubal said quietly. "Two days . . . it don't signify."

Travis looked at him, and for a moment he seemed to be considering it. Then he looked down again and shook his head.

I caught Kelly's eye, and we got up and left the meeting.

FIFTEEN MINUTES LATER I pulled into the Blast-Off parking lot, driving Travis's Hummer. The goddamn old Blast-Off, how I hated the place now. For weeks my home had been in the warehouse, *Red Thunder* growing out on the warehouse floor. In another week *Red Thunder* would be my home, if I had to whack Travis on the head and hijack the ship and pilot it myself. One way or another, I was going. We'd come too far to stop now. I vowed I'd never spend another night in room 201.

We hurried into the lobby. Mom was behind the desk. I went behind it and flipped the switch that lit the NO in our NO VACANCY sign, and Kelly turned the window sign over so that it showed CLOSED.

"Mom, you've got to come with us," I said.

"Manuel, are you crazy? It's . . . three o'clock on—"

"Please, Mom, do this for me. I wouldn't ask you to if it wasn't important."

She started to say something, but she must have seen something in my face, because she nodded, and followed me.

Mom, Maria, and Grace got in the backseat and I took off for the Sinclair garage. I wasn't surprised to see Dak backing our rental truck out of the driveway, Alicia in the front seat and Sam in the back. I gave Dak the high sign, and he grinned and returned it.

Fifteen minutes later we all arrived at the warehouse. Once inside they all had to stop and stare. None of them had seen *Red Thunder* in her completed state, and she was an awesome sight to behold . . . unless you burst out laughing.

We herded them to the ramp and up onto the platform and then through the outer air-lock door. I showed them how it worked, how strong it was. Then up the ladder through the inner pressure door in the floor of the suit room. The five suits hung there, chubby and bright red, all with the Red Thunder logo prominent on the chest and backpack. The room had that new car smell. It was a rich smell. It was a smell that somehow seemed to inspire confidence. I hoped it was working on Mom and Sam.

Then up the ladder again and through the submarine-type hatch into the central deck of the central module.

"This is our radiation shelter, too," I told them. "It's shielded by the other modules, and by a layer of polyethylene plastic. That's what they use on atomic submarines to shield the reactor compartment."

Down the ladder to the staterooms, which looked pretty good in the low lamplight, as good as the accommodations on a budget cruise ship. Then up again, to the common room, to the systems control deck, and finally to the cockpit. I stood by and let them look out the windows, see the pictures on the monitor screens. It all looked very professional, very competent, I thought. If I was buying a brand-new spaceship, would I buy this one? I asked myself. Damn straight I would. I had had a part in every rivet, every weld. Give me time, I could take her down to the last nut and bolt and put her back together. With my eyes closed. Would this ship take us to Mars and back? I would bet my life on it. I *wanted* to bet my life on it.

I looked out the window. Travis stood down there, looking up at us, his arms folded across his chest.

"I PROMISED I'D not cut corners," Travis said, when we were all gathered at the foot of the ramp. "Shaving two days off the systems test is cutting corners, in my book. It's as simple as that."

"You said we'd never be more than three and a half days from Earth," I pointed out. "Five days is well over that margin."

"I said seven days; I said no cutting corners. I stand by that."

Nobody said anything for a time. I didn't plead with Mom, and Dak said nothing to Sam. What we wanted was plain enough, and both Sam and Mom could see it.

I tried to read her face. That was never easy, but she didn't look as stony as she had in the early days. It was clear that Maria would vote to go ahead, if she had a vote, but she kept properly quiet about it.

"Betty," Sam said, "I'd like to have a word with you in private, if you don't mind."

"Sure, Sam." They moved off, both looking tired. We all stood there silently, watching their backs. At one point Sam put his arm over Mom's shoulder, and she seemed to lean into him a little. God, how hard her life had been, how little she had ever gotten in return for her backbreaking labor at the motel. For a moment I wanted just to shout to them, *I'm sorry, I give up. I can't ask you to approve of this crazy thing.* After taking them on the tour, watching them looking at the preposterous ship standing there, I had never felt less confident of our safe departure and return.

After five minutes they came back. Sam looked straight into Travis's eyes.

"Travis . . ." He had a hard time getting started, then he stiffened his back. "Travis, we're voting with the kids. Five days, seven days . . . if it works, we think you should go."

Travis returned the stare, never blinking.

"I think five days ought to be enough. I think it will work. But it reduces our safety margin to a point that I'd be willing to risk *my* life . . . but not those of your children. Not unless you approve."

"You'd go?" Mom asked, staring straight into his face. "If you could run the thing yourself, you'd go?"

"I actually considered it . . . but I knew Manny and Dak and Alicia would kill me. And I need them. I'm the pilot . . . but they're the ones who built it, and they know how to run it better than I do."

"Okay, Travis. You do your five-day test. If it works, then y'all go ahead with what you have to do. Me and Sam, we give you our permission."

BEFORE MOM AND Sam left, Mom took me and Dak aside.

"I thought you ought to know what your daddy said to me, Dak," she said.

"Yes, ma'am?"

"You're old enough, you can call me Betty, Dak. What he did, your dad . . . he was in favor of letting y'all go. He knew he'd lose a lot of your respect if he put the hammer down on the project, anyway."

"Never," Dak said. "He could never lose my respect."

"Of course not. I put it badly. But the two of you, you'd lose something if he couldn't trust you to know whether this thing was safe or not."

Dak said nothing, still looking defensive.

"What he did was, he realized that if he just stood there and said he would let you go, then the whole load drops on *my* head. Now, *I'm* the one who either screws up the whole thing, or gets pressured into a decision I can't live with. So he told me the vote was going to be unanimous, one way or the other. If I voted no, he'd try to talk me out of it but if he couldn't, he'd vote no, too. If I voted yes, he was with me. Dak, I think it took a lot of love to put it that way. I just wanted you to know how special your daddy is."

"Yes, ma'am. He is."

Mom hugged me, then hugged Dak. We watched them pull out and down the road until they turned the corner out of sight. Then Dak and I turned to each other. He grinned, and I did, too. He held out a palm and I slapped it.

Red Thunder was still alive.

2LOOSE LA BECK was a little squirt, barely over five feet tall. He still looked and dressed like a gangbanger, something he never really was, but now he drove a two-year-old Mercedes, possibly the only bright orange Mercedes low-rider in Florida . . . or the universe, for that matter. There were elaborate murals on the hood and the trunk. The car had a sound system that could peel the paint off a house at one hundred yards.

Now he stood with his hands in his back pockets and looked up at *Red Thunder*. I'd have to say he looked more than a little dubious.

"I don't know, dude," he said. "I ain't supposed to paint no railroad cars."

"These aren't railroad cars now," I told him. "We cut off the wheels."

"I don't know," he said again. "I painted plenty of railroad cars in my taggin' days. But I ain't never painted one standing on end, dig? It changes everything. Screws up the proportions."

"You can handle it, 2Loose," Kelly said. "We'll pay you ten thousand dollars."

2Loose didn't quite sneer.

"I couldn't touch it for no less than twenty grand, friends. 2Loose has come up in the world. Everybody callin' me an artist now, not a stinkin' tagger. They put some of my stuff in a museum show, can you dig it?"

"Yeah," I said, "but how many people see it there? A few thousand? 2Loose, this thing is going to be seen by millions."

"That don't matter, I don't care how many people see it. The boxcars I used to paint, they'd paint 'em over before hardly anybody seen 'em. I don't care, man. I seen 'em, even in the dark." He paused a moment, still looking up at the ship. "How you figure millions of people? What *is* the damn thing, anyway?"

So we fed him the cover story of how this would be a prop in a major motion picture. He was pretty good, acting nonchalant about it, but I could see the hunger growing in his eyes. *Hollywood!*

"Fifteen thousand," Kelly said. "My final offer."

"You got it. When do I start?"

HE AGREED TO come back the day four of us would climb into the contraption and see if it could keep us alive for five days. It was a scary five days.

Who should show up that very evening but Mr. Strickland, old "ferraristud" himself. He came barging into the building like he owned it . . . well, come to think of it, he *did* own it, but a landlord's supposed to knock. He came with his entourage of three, Strickland being the kind of man who hates to be alone. One was his secretary, a former Miss Montana, one was his accountant, and I never did catch what the other one was, except Strickland shouted at him twice while he was there.

There's no love lost between the two of us, but he's not the kind who will flat out admit he hates you. No, he stretched out his arm with his big salesman's grin, and I reluctantly shook his hand, trying to forget all the nasty lies he had told Kelly about me, trying to break us up. When he patted my back I always felt I ought to check to see if he'd left a knife there.

"What are you doing here, Father?" Kelly snarled. "I told you not to come here."

"Don't I get a hug and a kiss, Kitten?" Oh, lord, how Kelly hated that nickname.

"Is it your birthday? Is it Christmas? I told you, you get two hugs per year, and after this I'm going to rethink the one on your birthday."

Strickland laughed, but I think she hurt him a little. I think it's likely that he did love her, in his way, which was to dominate her life, to make her an extension of himself. But fate had dealt him the wrong daughter. Kelly would never stand for that.

She went back to her office, walking with her back stiff and straight. It fell to me and Dak to give him the grand tour, which was the only way we'd get rid of him.

We just showed him the center section and the air lock, which we couldn't avoid. The others were full of water bags and air equipment, all of it working, which could raise awkward questions. Another dead giveaway, if anyone noticed, was that a spaceship set would have walls that could be moved so a camera could shoot from farther back.

Strickland didn't notice, and I breathed a little easier when I could be sure he had swallowed our cover story. Our biggest advantage in preserving our secret was that no sensible person could look at *Red Thunder* and deduce we were going to fly in it. She was too big, too awkward, and she had no engine.

We got rid of him as soon as we could, and I hurried to Kelly's office, knowing how badly he could affect her.

I found her on the phone, and she seemed to be doing fine.

"Who're you calling?"

"Locksmith. I'm changing the locks on all the doors."

Sounded good to me.

THE NEXT DAY we got another visit from the FBI, Agents Dallas and Lubbock.

I was closest to the door when the bell rang, so I went there and saw them on the television screen. My heart skipped a beat . . . but as I turned the camera, I couldn't see any SWAT team or uniformed Daytona police. I couldn't see anyone at all except Dallas and Lubbock. I called Travis and told him who was here. He was at my side within a minute, and everybody else was following him. He smiled at me and opened the door just enough to slip outside. The rest of us clustered around the little television screen.

There wasn't much to see. Travis did his loud redneck act, and the agents stood rigid as mannequins. Their lips barely moved when they talked.

Then they were getting back into their Feebmobile and driving away. Travis watched them, waved, then came back through the door. He was drenched in sweat. He pulled at his shirt, getting the cool air of the warehouse circulating.

"Man, could I use a drink." Alicia ran to get him a cold lemonade.

"They're pissed off, boys and girls," he said. "They must be, to tell me about it. Whoever's in charge of the search must be one stubborn cop, because now he's got his agents going back over old ground."

"They told you that?" Dak asked.

"Not in so many words. But FBI agents see themselves as an elite. They're not supposed to have to pound the pavement like beat cops. They were hot—the air conditioner in their car broke down—and they're tired, and they're fed up with the FBI and the search for a flying saucer. So they said a few things they normally wouldn't have. They're looking into my neighbor now, the Jesus freak. He hasn't let them in to tour his compound—and why should he? He's no David Koresh, but he hates guv'mint men."

"So you think we're okay?" Kelly asked. Alicia came back with a tall glass of lemonade. Travis drank half of it at once.

"Okay? I won't feel okay until we're out of the atmosphere."

M-DAY MINUS FIVE, and the four of us went up the ramp, into the lock, and sealed it behind us. For the next five days we'd eat, drink, and breathe only what was stored inside *Red Thunder*. We were all pumped.

We didn't stay that way too long. There were tests to run, drills to go through. Each of us had to be checked out on getting into a suit and down the ladder to the lock. Then the hours began to stretch. Soon we broke out the Monopoly board there in the systems control deck and began a game we figured would last the whole five days.

We should have known Travis wasn't going to let us just sit and vegetate, not when there was more training he could hit us with.

At hour thirteen an alarm bell began ringing on every deck, and a voice began intoning, "Pressure breach, Module Two, this is not a drill, this is not a drill." It was Kelly's voice, stored in the computer. Somehow, that made it even scarier. We knocked the Monopoly board over scrambling to our assigned stations.

Tank two was my department, so when we got to the center crossroads Dak grabbed the emergency suit from a locker as I leaned in and closed and dogged the outer air-lock hatch. I could hear a whistling sound but didn't feel any rush of wind. We'd had *Red Thunder* dogged down tight with an overpressure of one-quarter of an atmosphere for a full week, using the main air lock to enter and leave, and she'd been tight as a drum.

Dak had the emergency suit unzipped and held up in front of him with the zippered side to me, just as we'd practiced a dozen times. This suit was another Russian surplus item Travis had brought back from Star City, not nearly as expensive as the other suits had been. He had bought four of them. It was nothing but a clear plastic bag in the shape of a human being, one size fits all. There was a small oxygen bottle mounted on the chest. The hands were mittens instead of gloves. When you were inside one, you looked like somebody's dry cleaning, in a plastic wrapper.

The Russians had developed these suits for space stations. The idea was that you could don one in fifteen seconds and then have about thirty minutes to deal with an emergency after you'd lost all cabin air.

Or, if there was nothing you could do about it, and if you weren't in direct sunlight and being roasted like a chicken wrapped in tinfoil, somebody in a proper suit could carry you to a safe environment. There was a handle right on top where your rescuer could grab you like a caveman dragging his wife by the hair.

I stepped into the suit legs and Dak shoved the thing over me. I turned, and he zipped it. It was uncanny, I knew we were in no danger, we were still right on the ground in Florida, but my imagination was running away with me. My heart was pounding.

"Twenty-six seconds," Dak shouted. We'd never managed the fifteen seconds the Russians claimed. Alicia was our record holder at nineteen seconds.

I twisted the valve on the oxygen bottle and the suit blew up until I looked like the Michelin Man. I put one foot into the air lock, then the other foot, and crouched, the air-lock chamber being only four feet in diameter. Dak closed the hatch behind me, and I heard him latch it tight. I slammed the CYCLE button with one hand, and in a moment the green light came on, signaling that pressure was equalized inside the lock and on the other side. The pressure gauge was reading about 1.20 atmospheres, when it should have been 1.25. Temperature was seventy-five Fahrenheit, exactly where it should be.

I opened the inner lock, swung out onto the ladder. There was a locker there, and I opened it and got a pack of sticky patches and a smoke generator. I broke the generator and held it steady. The smoke drifted down, slowly, so down the ladder I went. I followed the smoke all the way to the bottom of the tank, the whistling getting louder as I descended past the big tanks of pressurized air. I reached the water bladder and stood on the bottom deck. Beneath was our gray-water tank. The smoke was moving more rapidly now, swirling around until it found the breach. I got on my knees.

The hole was perfectly round. Somebody had drilled it.

A cigarette camera lens poked through the hole. Faintly, from outside the ship, I heard Travis's voice.

"I make it three minutes and fifteen seconds," he said. "Some of you might actually have lived."

I shoved the camera back, heard Travis laugh. I took the patch I'd brought and peeled the backing off the sticky side. It was made of hard rubber, about the same flexibility as a car tire but more resistant to heat and cold. The patch stuck in place. It was only an emergency measure, we had better patches and the tools to apply them, and I'd do that as soon as I caught my breath.

I tried to be angry at Travis, but what was the point? The systems test was the perfect time to throw real-world problems at us, things we'd drilled on using computer simulations. But no simulation could really duplicate the real world.

And did he ever throw problems at us. There were a hundred practical jokes hidden in *Red Thunder* now, a whoopee cushion under every seat, so to speak. Travis could activate them from outside and watch us with the cameras that covered every inch of the ship's interior except the staterooms and heads.

So we got too hot and had to fix it, got cold enough that frost formed on the walls and we could see our breath, and we fixed that. We fixed problems, large and small, about once every three or four hours the entire time we were there. It was exhausting.

But we *fixed* them. We fixed every one of them.

THEN, ON THE fourth day of the test, twenty-four hours to go, trouble came at us from an entirely unexpected direction. "Like it always does," as Travis never tired of reminding us.

The phone rang. I picked it up, and it was Travis.

"Y'all have to come out now," he said. "I just got a call from your mother—"

"My . . . what's wrong? Is she—"

"She's fine, Manny. But we got trouble. We all need to be together to talk it over. Come on out, leave all systems running, we should handle this in an hour or so."

We met Travis at the bottom of the ramp. He wouldn't discuss the problem, just told us all to pile into the Hummer, and he took off for the motel.

Everybody was gathered in room 101 when we got there. Mom, Maria, Caleb, Salty, Grace, Billy . . . and somebody I'd never seen before, sitting on a chair at the far end of the room. He was short and chubby, red-faced, mostly bald. He wore a wrinkled Hawaiian shirt and it was soaking. He was smoking a cigarette and he didn't look happy.

"You!" Kelly shouted as soon as she saw him.

"In the flesh, Kitten," the guy said, with a mean smile.

Mom had handed Travis a business card when we arrived. It said:

SEAMUS LAWRENCE
"Seamus the Shamus"
Private Detective

There were phone, fax, and e-mail numbers in the lower left corner.

"He's a private detective," Kelly told us. "My father has had him tailing me, off and on, since I was fourteen. God*damn* you, Lawrence!"

"Is that any way to talk to an old friend?" He was trying to be glib, but he had to be intimidated by the hostile faces pressing in on him. He took a puff on his cigarette and looked around for an ashtray, shrugged, knocked the ash off onto the floor. I moved over closer to Mom. She was holding her .22 target pistol at her side.

"Is that a bullet hole in his shirt?" I asked her. He must have heard me.

"She shot at me!" he said, and he couldn't quite keep the fear out of his voice.

"If I'd shot at you, Mister Private Dick, I'd of hit you. I shot at that parrot's eye. I can put a round through your eye, too, if you give me any more trouble."

He looked down and sure enough, the bullet had gone through a loose fold of cloth, precisely through the eye of a red and blue macaw. This evidence of her accuracy didn't seem to reassure him . . . and it shouldn't have. Mom was capable of putting a real, nonlethal but very painful hurtin' on him with that little popgun.

"He came in an hour ago," she told us, "handed me that silly card, and said we had to talk about some people was planning to go into outer space."

"Unbelievable!" Travis said.

"Said to get Kelly here, pronto. Said for a hundred grand—that's what he said, 'a hundred grand'—somebody's daddy didn't have to find out about it."

"After all these years, you'd sell out my father?" Kelly sounded scandalized.

"He's sort of pissed," Lawrence said, defensively. "On account of I ain't been able to dig up dirt on your sp— . . . on your boyfriend there."

"It was real smart of you not to finish that word, Mr. Lawrence," Mom said, and you could feel the tension in her trigger finger when she said it. Lawrence sure felt it; he couldn't take his eyes off the gun, slapping dangerously against Mom's thigh.

"Unbelievable," Travis said again.

"What do you mean, Travis?" Alicia asked.

"Unbelievable anybody could be so stupid!" He looked around at us. "Don't you see it? Your dad got a tour of *Red Thunder* just a few days ago, and the thought never entered his mind that it could fly. Because your dad is smart, whatever else he is. He knows a spaceship has to have a big, *big* engine to take off. *Anybody* with any sense takes a look at *Red Thunder*, they know instantly it couldn't be a real spaceship. Hell, I could have given those FBI agents the tour, and they'd never have guessed, either."

"But it *can* fly," Dak pointed out.

"Exactly! But to believe it can fly, you have to either postulate an entirely new technology, or be so stupid, be so totally clueless as to how things work . . . it's beautiful when you think of it. He's so dumb he stumbled onto the truth."

"Hey," Lawrence said, but it was halfhearted.

"I got a rule," Travis said. "I've never had to use it so far in my life, but I think it's a good rule. Never pay ransoms or blackmail."

"I like that rule, too," Mom said.

Travis had his back to the prisoner, and we all saw him wink.

"Then I guess we gotta kill him."

For a moment I thought he'd gone too far, the guy looked like he might have a heart attack. He started babbling about how he'd go away, forever, forget about the whole thing, he'd leave town, he'd leave the state. He'd do anything.

We all watched him until he ran down.

"Maybe we don't have to, Travis," Caleb said. "All we gotta do is hold his sorry ass for twenty-four hours, then what can he do?"

"That's kidnapping!" Lawrence said, then realized what the alternative was. He babbled again about how he'd be happy to stay here, he wouldn't cause any trouble.

Travis went outside and everybody but Caleb followed him. Kelly spoke first.

"Travis, he's a drunk, he . . . oh, sorry."

"No offense taken. I was thinking the same thing. Get him liquored up. Alicia, you got anything in that drug cabinet we could use as a Mickey Finn?"

"A what?"

"Something to knock him out for a while."

"Oh, sure. No problem."

"Okay. Caleb can watch him. He won't need a gun, Betty, Caleb could take that pathetic loser apart with his bare hands. Give him all the booze he can drink, pop some pills in it. Dump him in an alley someplace, later. What's he gonna do? It'll be his word against all of us."

"That's what we'll do, Travis," she said. "He really burned me up. No way I was going to let the likes of him stop y'all."

"Mom!" I said.

"You know I'd be happier if you didn't go, Manny. But not this way."

I gave her a big hug.

AND SO WE returned to the warehouse, with one more night and a day to spend inside. 2Loose had erected scaffolds around the ship and hung tarps around it.

We climbed the ramp and sealed the outer air-lock door, cycled the lock, entered the ship interior. The Monopoly game was as we'd left it.

Other than our cans of Coke having grown warm, it was as if we'd never been gone.

TRAVIS DIDN'T THROW us any more emergencies.

"I feel dirty," he told us over the phone. "It's so easy to humiliate a man, especially when he's down. So easy. I'm not proud of it."

"That's something," Dak said. "You don't take pleasure in it."

"But I did, when it was happening."

"So did I," Kelly said. "Anyway, it had to be done."

"Jubal wants to know if he can stay with y'all for a while," Travis said.

"What, he has to ask?" Alicia said. "Send him in."

So Jubal joined the Monopoly game for an hour. He seemed unusually quiet, sweating a lot, very nervous. I hoped it was just opening night jitters, anticipation. I know I was feeling it. He couldn't be worried about the trip. Could he?

We slept, we woke up, and we sweated out the last hours until six P.M., when we swung the door open and came down the ramp. Mom was there, and Jubal, and Grace, and Salty, and Maria, and Sam. There was a big flat cake with a little model of the ship standing on it, and the logo of Red Thunder spelled out in red icing. Maria, who had baked it, cut it and we all had a piece.

"Where'd you get the model?" I asked.

"Oh, we got ten thousand of 'em," Mom said. "Didn't Kelly tell you? We're going to merchandise the hell out of this trip." I looked at Kelly.

"Well, I've got to have something to keep me busy while y'all are gone, okay?"

"Fine with me, Kelly," I said.

Then 2Loose gave us a tour of his masterwork. All the scaffolding and canvas had come down while we slept, and his masterpiece rose high in the air before us.

He had rendered the Six Days of Creation, from Genesis.

The first tank depicted the dividing of the light from the darkness, and I had almost been prophetic. God wasn't in a low-rider, he was doing a wheelie on a big Harley, and the Light was coming out of one tailpipe and the Darkness from the other. Shapes loomed in the big white and black clouds.

Tank two, the creation of the Firmament, which means Heaven, I think. How would a Cuban/French-Canadian maniac render Heaven? With lots of gold and lots of blue, and angels partying to boom boxes on Miami Beach.

On the third day God separated the waters from the dry land. Raging seas, towering mountains. "Let the Earth bring forth grass, and herb yielding seed after his kind, and the tree yielding fruit after his kind . . ." He showed all that, and in the foreground was a brightly colored jungle.

Tank four, the creation of the sun, the moon, and the stars. That may have been the most gorgeous panel of the six, stars whirling and exploding, the sun high above all.

Fifth day, creation of animals. Great whales, winged fowl, plus a lot of animals Noah must have forgotten to bring along on the ark.

And on the sixth day . . . created He the crew of the *Red Thunder*. That's right, the six of us—2Loose not knowing Kelly wasn't going, not knowing, in fact, that *any* of us *were* going, but one look at the last picture and you knew some vibe from our crazy little ship had touched his artist's heart and told him the truth.

We were standing together, smiling, wearing our brown leather bomber jackets. Travis in the back, a hand on Kelly's and Alicia's shoulders, Jubal in a place of honor down in front of us.

"My goodness," Alicia said. "This is really . . . something."

"Do y'all like it?" 2Loose asked anxiously.

"You done good, amigo," Travis said, slapping him on the back.

"We got our money's worth," Kelly said.

"What, you paid for this?" Travis asked.

"Shut up, Travis. It was my money, okay?"

Then it came time for somebody to smash a bottle of champagne over her . . . well, she'd have to sit in a cherry-picker to hit *Red Thunder*'s bow, so we settled for one of the landing struts.

Travis handed the bottle to Kelly, who looked surprised. But she took it.

"I christen thee, *Red Thunder,*" she said, and choked up. She cleared her throat. "Bless all who sail in her." She swung the bottle, hard, and we all applauded.

"And I think that'll be my exit line, my friends," she said. "I won't be at the launch in the morning. I don't think I could stand it."

My throat was burning as I tried to hold back the tears. No one had anything to say, but Mom put her arms around Kelly and hugged her tight. Jubal went to her and hugged her, too. Then Kelly came to me, and we kissed. Her eyes were full of tears, which she blinked away.

"Come back," she said.

"I will."

And she turned and headed for the door, never looking back, just raising one hand in a small wave as she left.

The three of us were glaring at Travis, and he looked back at us defiantly.

"Okay, I'm the bad guy. What was I to do? You all heard my reasons."

"Nothing, Travis, nothing," Mom said. "You did what you had to do."

I was still far from sure of that. And about 49 percent of me wanted to run after her, tell her I wasn't going unless she went . . . but I didn't think she'd respect me for it. I had to take her at her word, and she had said *go.*

"Now everybody get some sleep," Travis said. "Bright and early tomorrow morning we lift off. Nothing short of a hurricane's going to stop us now."

I'd grown so superstitious about the project that I actually checked the weather report, though it was too early in the year for hurricanes. Sure enough, none was in sight.

And I knew I wouldn't be able to sleep that night.

But I slept.

PART THREE

"JUBAL WON'T BE going with us," Travis said. I had just taken a bite of a Krispy Kreme, and suddenly I didn't want it.

It was four-thirty A.M. Dak and Alicia and Travis and me were sitting around a table that was looking very empty without Kelly and Jubal. The big doors leading out to the dock were open now, for the first time. *Red Thunder* was hooked to the overhead crane, and the leased barge was tied to the dock.

"Is he sick?" Alicia asked.

"Not really." Travis sighed. "We decided a few weeks ago that he couldn't go. He didn't want y'all to know. He was afraid you'd not like him anymore."

"That's ridiculous," I said.

"That's what I told him, too. But you know Jubal. Once he gets an idea in his head, there's not much chance of convincing him otherwise."

"What's the problem, Travis?" Dak asked.

"Jubal . . . friends, it was always an iffy proposition, Jubal getting into that thing." He jerked his thumb in the direction of *Red Thunder*. "Jubal doesn't even fly. He's afraid of flying and, worst of all, he can't stand small, closed spaces. Maybe you never noticed it, but Jubal doesn't go aboard the ship. Claustrophobia. If it was just claustrophobia he might have made it. But you add in the other phobia, it was just impossible. He could barely handle one hour the other night."

"Where is he now?" I asked.

"That's another thing. The main reason I wanted to take him with us is that he knows too much. The only place I could be sure of protecting him would be aboard ship. But that's impossible. Jubal is going underground, people. Caleb left with Jubal last night. He's taking him . . . I don't know where. What I don't know, I can't tell. But even if I knew I wouldn't tell you.

"Jubal's only hope is for us to get to Mars and back, and I'm afraid that, after we get back, all of you will have a lawyer as a constant companion for a few days, or weeks. Until it becomes clear to whoever might want to arrest us on some national security charge, suspend *habeas corpus* . . . till it becomes clear they can't get away with it."

WE HAD RAISED *Red Thunder* with the overhead crane and were inching it along the rails toward the barge when the rest of the liftoff party arrived, everyone in the know except Caleb and Jubal. Dak was up in the crane cab, sweating blood as he moved it at dead slow speed, just as he'd drilled a dozen times with our extra tank car, which we'd filled with cement to simulate the mass of the ship.

Everyone gathered outside as Dak swung the ship out over the barge. Then three of us jumped down to the barge and pulled on the ropes attached to the landing struts until they were centered on the stress gauges, where we'd reinforced the deck of the barge. Dak eased it down. There was a loud creaking sound that nearly gave me a heart attack, but then she was down and sitting pretty as can be as the sun broke over the horizon and the first red rays shone on 2Loose's masterpiece.

We were all wearing our bomber jackets, even Mom and Maria and

Sam. Every time I looked at them I thought of Kelly, how she should be here. I was being swept by an emotional whirlwind, feeling cheated, alone, abandoned, and about to burst with anticipation because the big day was finally here.

Dak got the ship perfectly in position, and we detached the hooks. Dak rolled the crane back into the warehouse and hurried down to ground level.

Aunt Maria had a video camera, making a record of what could become an historical moment. Grace was snapping pictures with an old Pentax.

"Where's Seamus the shamus?" Travis asked Salty at one point.

"Sleeping peacefully in a back alley behind a bar," he said. "He'll wake up in the drunk tank several hours after you've gone, and then he can tell his story to anybody he wants to. By then, you'll all be famous."

"Yeah." He looked around. "It's a shame we have to be so quiet about this," Travis said. "We ought to have brass bands, ticker tape, crowds of gawkers. They make a bigger fuss than this when a liner leaves Miami for a four-day cruise."

We were all standing around, awkwardly, wondering how to say good-bye when you're off to Mars. *Mars,* for cryin' out loud.

Dak and I got hugs from Sam and Mom, respectively.

"You come back, now," Mom told me, and gave me a last hug.

We all got together for a posed picture at the foot of the ramp, then Travis gave the high sign to the captain of the tug we'd hired to tow the barge out about five miles from shore. Seas were calm, winds low, a perfect day for a launch. Sam and Salty cast off the lines holding the barge to the dock . . . and we were moving.

Our good-bye waves were cut a little short, though, when a plain white sedan came around the side of the warehouse, going way too fast. It stopped, and Agents Dallas and Lubbock got out.

"Uh-oh," Dak said. We were maybe two hundred yards from the pier, heading into Strickland Bay. From there we'd have to weave through several palmetto islands, go under a four-lane freeway bridge, then through Spruce Creek, Ponce de Leon Cut, then cross the Halifax River, go through the inlet and out to the open sea. We figured about an hour to the inlet, give or take.

But Dallas and Lubbock could change everything.

"I wonder what the hell happened?" Travis said, watching the agents through his binoculars. "Are they on to us, or do they just have more questions?"

"Pretty early for a routine interview, isn't it?" Alicia asked.

We all watched as the agents hurried up to our shore party, and we could see they were pretty pissed about something. They were shouting at all of them. Dallas—or was it Lubbock?—was standing almost toe-to-toe with my mother, and Mom didn't retreat an inch. I found I was gritting my teeth. *You touch my mother, you slimy bastard, and I'll—*

Travis's and Dak's cell phones rang almost simultaneously. I could see Sam and Salty trying to keep their backs to the agents, letting Mom distract them. Travis picked up and nodded a few times.

"Thanks, Salty," he said. "Don't resist. But if you get a chance, get your butts out of there. I think they'll be too concerned about us to pay you much mind. Get back to the motel, all of you." Travis hung up.

"They may be on to us," he said. "We'll just sit tight and keep moving."

We watched as the agents abandoned their argument with Mom and hurried back to their car. Our friends and family faded back through the huge warehouse doors. I saw the street-side door open and all of them hurried through.

Maybe somebody just made a connection between Travis Broussard, whose neighbor reported a flying saucer, and Celebration Broussard, in Everglades City. Sure, but the Gulf Coast from Florida to Southeast Texas is lousy with Broussards. There were three other Broussard families, no relation, in Everglades City alone.

But it really didn't matter that morning. The only thing that mattered was, What are they going to do about it?

We found out within fifteen minutes. A Coast Guard helicopter came roaring toward us.

"That tears it," Travis said. "Everybody board ship. Secure all airtight hatches."

We moved quickly, up the ramp, which I stayed behind to close and seal. The ramp seemed to move slower than it ever had. Then I went up through the suit room, into the central module, dogging the door behind me, making sure the green light came on. *This is not a drill!* kept sounding in my ears. *This is not a drill!*

I found my acceleration couch and buckled in, semireclining, and put on my headphones. All the instruments I needed to see were on a movable panel, dozens of tiny television screens, three computer screens, switches, a trackball, gauges, red- and green-light pairs. Everything was showing green.

"Dak, get me the Coast Guard freak," Travis said.

"Comin' at ya, Cap'n Broussard," Dak said. I saw the rows of numbers flash onto his screen. Meanwhile Travis had switched to a marine band to talk to the tugboat.

"Captain Menendez, take us to the middle of Strickland Bay and cast us off. Then withdraw to a distance of one mile."

"We're almost there already, Captain. I will do as you order."

I was going nuts, not having a window to look out of, and I think Dak and Alicia were, too. For a moment I couldn't catch my breath, thinking of living in this little tin can for the next three weeks. But the feeling passed.

We could hear a big racket outside, the helicopter hovering close, and somebody speaking though a bullhorn. Travis tuned the Coast Guard frequency.

"—are ordered to cut your engines and prepare to be boarded. I repeat, tugboat and barge, you are ordered to—" Travis's voice cut her off.

"Coast Guard helicopter, this is private spaceship *Red Thunder*, aboard the barge. My countdown clock is running, and it is T minus one minute thirty seconds and counting. We have broken no laws, but you are welcome to board the tug or the barge after we lift off. Until then, I advise a distance of one mile, as the exhaust produced by this ship will be very large, and could endanger you. Over."

There was a long, long silence.

"Private spacecraft *Red Thunder,* this is Captain Katherine O'Malley, United States Coast Guard. I think we'll take our chances with your . . . your exhaust. Prepare your ship for boarding. Over."

"Crew," Travis said, "there are two Coast Guard cutters headed our way. Captain Menendez should be severing the lines in . . ." There was a slight lurch as the lines fell away from the barge and we were quickly dead in the water.

"Captain Broussard, this is Captain Menendez. What's going on? You told me this wasn't illegal."

"It's not, Captain. I'd advise you to let yourself be boarded, as you've done nothing wrong and have nothing to hide. *Hasta la vista."*

"Hasta la vista to you, too. And good luck . . . wherever you're going."

"Will do." There was a click as Travis switched channels. "Well, boys and girls, looks like it's put up or shut up time. Are you ready?"

"Go for it, Captain," I said, happy to hear no quaver in my voice.

"Let's go," Alicia said, and looked over and grinned at me. She reached over and took Dak's hand. Dak smiled.

"Banzai!" Dak shouted.

"Up, up and away . . ." Travis muttered.

For the first few seconds nothing much happened. I kept my eye on the three strain gauges, registering the weight of *Red Thunder* on each of her three legs. The numbers began to go down. And a loud roar was building outside.

"Look at that helicopter skedaddle!" Travis shouted. He turned one of our cameras on it. Sure enough, it had turned and fled as if we were a bomb . . . no point in thinking about that.

The roar built. The strain gauge numbers fled quickly across my screen.

"Almost there . . . ," Travis crooned. I tapped a key and watched Travis sitting there surrounded by his controls and instruments. He had on an expression almost painful to watch, made of equal parts worry and euphoria at finally going back into space.

There was a lurch, and the ship seemed to lean a bit before Travis corrected. The roar now was a living beast, a truly amazing noise.

"Crew, *Red Thunder* has left the planet," Travis said, and the three of us cheered. One second later the ship lurched hard to the left, and Travis said something you don't ever want to hear a pilot say: "Oops!"

"What is—" That was Alicia, gripping the arms of her chair. But the ship righted itself. I switched to an external camera, looking down from the top of the ship. The superheated steam obscured most everything . . . but I could see some of the water surface, being dashed to oblivion by the power of our drive.

"Where's the barge?" I asked. Travis laughed.

"That baby crinkled up like a potato chip and went straight to the bottom."

Damn. We didn't own that barge, we leased it. Oh, well.

"Hang on to your hats, friends. I'm outta here."

I quickly realized the noise I'd heard before was like a kitten purring. When Travis opened the throttles for a full two gees the sound became unimaginable. I think it might have deafened me if I hadn't been wearing headphones.

On the screen I saw the water dwindle away. Two Coast Guard cutters came into view, then the borders of Strickland Bay, then the freeway bridges. The bridges were bumper to bumper with stopped cars. I could see people standing on the roadway.

Two gees is not bad. Imagine someone your exact size and weight lying on top of you. Not pleasant, but not really painful, either.

On a VStar flight acceleration built up gradually as fuel was burned while thrust remained more or less constant. Near engine shutdown, VStar passengers experience up to five gees. Our two gees would be constant, falling off only as we left the pull of Earth's gravity behind. Here at the launch, one gee was from gravity, and one gee from our acceleration.

In moments I could see the whole city of Daytona on my screen. Then the whole county, then the whole state of Florida. Another camera showed the sky turning a darker and darker blue, then black. The roaring of the engine faded to a grumble as the air thinned into nothingness.

My God, I was in space.

IT DIDN'T TAKE long before the gee forces fell to one and a quarter.

"Okay, y'all," Travis said. "I want an inspection, top to bottom, see if everything survived the strain. Get it done quick, and you can come up to the bridge. And move carefully! We'll be heavy for a while yet."

One point two five gees was sort of like carrying a big backpack, it would have been easy to hurt myself if I got frisky. Before I opened the tank six interior air lock I checked the two pressure gauges, one for the interior of the small internal lock, one for the air-lock/space-suit module. Both gauges read a perfect 15 psi. I opened the hatches and swung out onto the ladder and down to the suit deck.

I immediately saw that one of the suits had fallen from its rack. It was lying there, facedown. I wasn't too worried. The helmet material was the stuff they use in "bulletproof" windows, and was guaranteed to withstand a .45-caliber slug.

I was about to bend down and pick it up, when the suit moved.

I jumped a mile, even in the high gravity.

"Oh my god. Kelly?"

She rolled over and sat up. I could hear her saying something, and helped her work the fittings of the helmet. I didn't know whether to be happy or horrified. But pretty soon happy won me over. I had even started to laugh as I pulled the helmet off.

"I can't believe you—Jesus! What—" There was blood running from her eyebrow and down the left side of her face, into her mouth, over her chin.

"I'm okay, I'm okay," she said. "Hurry, help me get out of this thing!"

"But . . ."

"Hurry!" I asked no more questions, and in a minute I had it off her. She wore jeans and a T-shirt, just like I did. She scrambled for the ladder and started up. There wasn't much I could do but follow.

When she reached the crossroads deck she headed down, past

Travis's quarters and the room that would have been Jubal's if he had come, then down again . . . and into the head. She slammed the door, and I could hear her laughing in relief.

"I've been in that thing *all night,"* she said.

I heard someone coming down the ladder. It was Alicia, looking confused.

"Kelly," I said, and grinned at her. Her face lit up.

"Oh, boy. Travis is going to be *so* pissed. . . ."

BUT HE WASN'T, not nearly as much as we had feared.

When she followed me up the ladder onto the bridge he did a double-take worthy of Laurel and Hardy, then buried his face in his hands. When he looked up he had a small smile on his face.

"I should have known," he said. "I should have checked."

"Listen, Travis, you're off the hook with my father. I mean, he's going to hit the roof, sure, but he was going to do that anyway when he finds out how much of my trust fund I've spent. I'll take full responsibility. You didn't—"

"If I had a brig, I would throw you in it."

"Aw, c'mon, Travis," Dak said. "She outwitted you, fair and square."

Captain or no captain, Travis knew he was outvoted on this one. It wasn't until later I wondered . . . was it a total surprise to him? He didn't search the ship before launch, and anyone who knew Kelly might have been suspicious at how little fuss she had given him about being left behind. Had he been giving her the opportunity to take matters into her own hands, so he could wash *his* hands of responsibility for her?

Yeah, but *I* knew Kelly pretty well, and *I* never thought of it. My only excuse is, I was so busy I never had time to think of it. When, just for a moment, I felt a little hurt that she hadn't even confided in *me*, I reminded myself I hadn't thought of helping her stow away, and I *should* have. I really *should* have. I felt lousy about that.

Alicia had examined her before we went to the bridge, cleaned up the blood and the wound, which turned out to be just a cut above the eyebrow. She shined a flashlight into Kelly's eyes, pronounced her fit and healthy, gave her two aspirins for her headache.

"I fell off when Travis stepped on the gas, but before he reached the full two gees," she told us. "A good thing, too. I hit hard enough at a gee and a half, or whatever it was. I wouldn't recommend two gees in the prone position. . . ."

One drawback to blasting at one gee all the way to Mars is that it was hard to see where you'd been. Naturally we all wanted a look at the Earth. In a free-falling ship like the Chinese *Heavenly Harmony* you could just swing the ship into any attitude you wanted. But we couldn't do that on *Red Thunder*, because while we were thrusting we had to keep the nose pointed toward where we were going.

There were five round windows on the bridge, one at each point of the compass, and one overhead. We could see where we were going, but not where we'd been. Where we were going was nothing but a bright, reddish star. The window that faced the sun was polarized almost to black, to prevent burning and blindness.

But Travis was able to angle the ship slightly by reducing the thrust of one of the three Phase-2 thrusters beneath us, enough that we could crowd close to the window and see a piece of the Earth. We were all astonished at how small it had become.

"We're past the moon's orbit already," Travis said. "Sorry to say the moon's way over on the other side of the Earth right now, so we can't see that, either. And in another few hours the Earth's going to be just a real bright star."

I felt the hairs rise on the back of my neck. So amazing to realize that, already, we were further from the Earth than any humans had ever been, except the crews of the *Heavenly Harmony* and the *Ares Seven*. . . .

"Kelly," Travis said. "Did you figure out how you're going to leave the ship when we get to Mars?"

"Sure. I got my own suit. I put Jubal's suit in . . ." She frowned. "Where's Jubal?" She was as shocked as we had been when Travis explained it to her. "His suit is aboard. The suit I was hiding in is mine."

"All those 'defective' pieces then . . . ?"

"A few were actually defective. But I bought my suit piecemeal, an arm and a leg at a time. And I used my own money. Believe me, I was tempted to charge it all to you, after the way you've treated me."

"I told you—"

"I know. Your reasons were good. But you're off the hook, and I'm here, and that's the way it had to be. So can we bury the hatchet?"

"I don't have a hatchet, Kelly."

"Uh-oh," Dak said. "Friends, we got a problem."

Travis hurried to the window, where Dak had been pressing his face close to get a last look at Earth before Travis straightened the ship again.

"What?" I said. "What problem?" My stomach tightened.

It was our "high-gain antenna." That's what we called it, anyway, though it had started life as a satellite dish and had sat for many years in Travis's yard, obsolete and rust-streaked. It was mounted on a tripod mast that looked out over Module Five, and motorized so we could fine-tune the aiming. One leg of the tripod had twisted a little, enough to make a stress fracture at the base, where it was welded to the body of the ship.

Travis sent Dak down to the systems control deck where the controls for the dish were part of his duties. Gingerly, Dak tested the motors: azimuth, altitude, skew. The dish moved okay, but with each move a small bouncing motion was introduced that made the weak weld open and close about a quarter of an inch.

"We do that too much, we'll snap it off like a dry stick," Travis said. He sighed. "Dak, we'd better listen for a bit while we still have it, okay?"

"Roger, Captain. *Calling Planet Earth . . .*"

After a few minutes of fiddling Dak picked up a strong signal. He frowned as he listened, static filling the television screen in front of him, then he grinned.

"It's CNN," he said, and we saw two familiar anchorpersons, Lou and Evelyn. The banner beneath them read, THE FLIGHT OF *RED THUNDER?*

"CNN has been unable to confirm the existence of a . . . as incredible as it may sound, of a home-built spaceship called *Red Thunder*, currently on its way to Mars at a speed almost impossible to believe. Here's what we do know.

"At a little after seven this morning, Florida time, *something* lifted off from Strickland Bay in Daytona. It had been sitting on a barge, being towed toward the open sea, when a Coast Guard helicopter and two cutters intercepted it. We have been unable to get a comment from the Coast Guard, or for that matter, any government agency to confirm or deny this report, but we do have video."

Whoever they bought it from had a good camera. We watched great clouds of steam billow from *Red Thunder*. It lifted, hovered . . . then began to rise . . . and rise, and . . . then it was screaming into the sky.

"Will you look at that," Dak breathed. I think we were all astonished at just how quickly the ship dwindled into the sky.

"Simultaneous with the liftoff, we received a press release via the Internet, and a website address, claiming to be from the families of the people aboard the ship. The release claims this ship, this *Red Thunder*, has a crew of four, headed by a man named Travis Brassard . . . no, sorry, I'm told his name is Broussard. Travis Broussard."

"Damn right, you idiot," Travis said, as his picture filled the screen. It was one taken by Grace, as were all the following pictures. He had a smile in this picture that reminded me of Bruce Willis, though Travis doesn't look much like Willis.

"We have confirmed that Broussard is an ex-astronaut, a former VStar pilot who has made numerous trips into space. We have a crew on the way to his home."

"Good luck," Travis said. "Nobody home there but a lawyer with a copy of the Fourth Amendment to the Constitution. The cops better have a search warrant . . . not that there's anything to find. The place is absolutely clean."

Then Dak's picture came up.

One by one we were identified, an unlikely rogues' gallery. I thought I looked pretty foolish, but then I always dislike pictures of myself.

Then there was a photo of the six of us, Kelly and Jubal included. We were in our bomber jackets, posed almost like 2Loose's portrait of us on the side of the ship.

"Also involved in the project are a Kelly Strickland, age nineteen, and Jubal Broussard, Travis Broussard's cousin." I was surprised that picture had been released, and looked at Travis. He shrugged.

"Kelly approved it," he said. "Her dad had to find out sooner or later."

"I wish I could watch when he finds out I'm here," Kelly said with a giggle.

"As for Jubal, there's no point trying to keep him a secret. Too many people know about him. But everybody in the family has been instructed to describe him as . . . well, as retarded. Most everybody *outside* of the family thinks he really *is* retarded." He looked at the ceiling, pursing his lips. "Sorry, Jubal," he muttered. "You know Jubal doesn't lie too well . . . but I'm hoping, first, that nobody finds him. If they do, Jubal's been told just to act confused, not to answer any questions at all, that way he doesn't have to lie. He can handle that. Hell, he *will* be confused, no acting necessary."

"You figure they'll think it was you, invented the drive?" Dak asked.

"Not for long, if they get a look at my physics grades at college. But I think they'll be inclined to postulate a seventh person, a Dr. X, as the mastermind. They can look for him all they want, since he doesn't exist."

"We here at CNN have been trying to contact *Red Thunder* since first reports came in," said one of the anchorpersons, and got our attention at once. "We *have* confirmed that, when it last appeared on the weather radar at a local television station in Daytona, the ship was accelerating at a constant speed. We have also been told by an anonymous source that tracking radar indicates the acceleration has continued unabated."

The screen showed a huge satellite dish, and the announcer continued.

"We have aimed our largest transmitter at the spot where we believe *Red Thunder* would be if it continued to accelerate at the same rate—and I emphasize that all our scientific consultants tell us this is impossible . . . still, if you can hear us out there, *Red Thunder*, please transmit on the frequency that should be . . . there, at the bottom of your screen. We want to tell your story to the world."

Travis grinned at us.

"That sounds like our cue, lads and lassies. You ready to speak to the world?"

"Wait a minute, wait a minute," Dak said, gesturing frantically. "Look!"

The scene had changed . . . to a close shot of the Blast-Off Motel sign. The camera pulled back, and a black woman moved into the shot, holding a microphone, pressing her ear with one hand, obviously trying to hear her producer over an earphone. Then she smiled when she realized she was on the air, live.

"Lou, Evelyn," she said, "this is La Shanda Evans reporting from the Blast-Off Motel here on the beach at Daytona. The Blast-Off is a local institution around here, dating back to the early days of the space program. There was even a suggestion a few years back to declare the sign a national historic site, though nothing came of it. Lately it's fallen on hard times, and today it doesn't seem to be open at all."

The camera panned to the door, and sure enough, the CLOSED sign was prominent in the window. I could see people inside. Evans knocked on the door, and Mom opened it a bit.

"Mrs. Garcia, we'd like to have a word with you, if we could."

"Uh . . . not yet, okay? Like I told you, we'll have a press conference in about an hour, as soon as the people aboard the ship send back their first messages." She glanced at her watch, and I could see the worry on her face. I glanced at my own watch, and saw we weren't really late, yet. But it was only a few minutes.

"Travis, we—"

"Just a minute, Manny. Just a minute."

The door was locked again, and the camera came back to Evans.

"Well, you heard it, Lou. We're waiting for word from this alleged *Red Thunder,* which I guess is your department. We were the first on the scene, about half an hour ago. But everybody else is arriving now, and it promises to be a bigger media zoo than the 2000 presidential election."

The camera turned to the parking lot, where people were running around and no less than three satellite trucks were setting up. There was police tape around the lot.

"So that's the news from here, Lou and Evelyn. Oh, one more thing. Before Mrs. Garcia shooed us away fifteen minutes ago, I was able to buy this from her. Apparently it is a model of *Red Thunder.*" She held up something and the camera zoomed in on it. It was a small plastic image of *Red Thunder* in a clear plastic snow globe. Evans shook it and the plastic snow swirled. I looked at Kelly, who was grinning.

"Might as well make as much as we can off of this," she said, unabashed.

"Nineteen dollars and ninety-five cents," Evans said. "I've got a feeling these are going to be collector's items, one way or another."

The scene cut back to the CNN center. Lou was laughing.

"Pick one up for me, will you, La Shanda?"

Dak hit the mute button.

"Ready to do the press conference, folks?" he asked.

Nobody was real eager, but we had to make ourselves famous, right? Though, from what we just saw, we were already well on the way.

Dak adjusted our antenna. I broke out the wide-angle TV camera and clamped it to the brace on the wall, then aimed and adjusted it by looking at the picture on the main screen.

"CNN, can you read me?" Dak was saying. "CNN, this is private spaceship *Red Thunder,* calling CNN."

"Don't forget about the time lag," Travis said. "It should be about four seconds—"

"*Red Thunder,* this is CNN. We are receiving your audio signal. We are not getting any television signal."

"That's 'cause I ain't sent it out yet," Dak muttered, and flipped a switch. After a short pause, the technician's voice came on again.

"Got it! Tell Lou—"

I looked at the TV with the incoming signal. Lou was looking excited. He waved at Evelyn, interrupting her. Dak turned up the sound and beckoned us all over to the wall. Soon I could see us all assembled on our TV screen, Dak seated at his console, the rest of us standing against the wall, like a police lineup. Dak turned up the volume.

"—word coming in that we've acquired a signal from this alleged

Red Thunder. We should have the picture up in . . . here we go. Is this the . . . ah, the private spaceship *Red Thunder*?"

Travis held up his microphone and cleared his throat. Dak winced; amateur hour.

"Yes it is, Lou, private ship *Red Thunder,* on our—"

". . . I'm not getting anything, what . . . hello, I'm hearing you and we see the picture now. To whom am I speaking? Hello? Hello?"

"You've got to remember the time lag, Lou," Travis said. "It's about four seconds now, we're a bit beyond the orbit of the moon. The best way to handle it is to say your piece, then say 'over.' Okay? Over."

Four-second pause.

"Yes . . . yes, I understand. Ah, is this Travis Broussard? . . . oh, right. Over."

"This is Captain Travis Broussard, master of the private spaceship *Red Thunder,* currently blasting at one gee, constant acceleration toward the planet Mars. Over."

Four-second pause. I watched the CNN feed instead of our own screen. CNN had us in three-fourths of the picture, with anchorman Lou's image down in the lower right-hand corner. We looked pretty good. My hope was that Travis could handle all the talking. Or Kelly, she was a good talker.

"Thank you for talking to us, Captain Broussard. You say you're aboard a private spaceship. How is this possible? Over."

"It's possible because these kids . . . these young people you see around me worked their butts off all summer long to build it. If you go to 1340 Wisteria Road in Daytona you'll see the warehouse where we built it. You're welcome to go inside, just show your credentials to the security guards.

"And it's possible because of a revolutionary new technology that gives us almost unlimited power. Power to go anywhere in the solar system in only days or weeks, not months or years. Power to reach the stars. Or, back on Earth, the means to reduce our use of coal, oil, and nuclear power. Over."

Four . . . no, almost a five-second pause.

"Captain, our science consultants here at CNN are telling us your 'revolutionary new technology,' is that what you called it? They're saying it's impossible. Over."

"That's what I would have said, too, a year ago. But ask your technical people where this signal is coming from. Over."

"They say it's coming from outer space, and a long way off," Lou admitted.

"You're going to hear a lot of denials about this today, Lou. It's inevitable. But it's the truth, we are on our way to Mars, and we'll be there in just over three days."

"That doesn't seem possible. That . . . wait, if you can get there in three days you'd be ahead of the Chinese lander, isn't that right? Over."

"That's right, Lou. They should still be doing aerobraking maneuvers when we land. By the way, we seem to have damaged our main antenna during launch, so it's possible we won't be able to communicate with Earth all the way there and back. I'd like to warn you, and especially our families, that a sudden loss of signal does not mean we've blown up. Over."

"I'm sure that would look terrible to your loved ones," Lou said, then he frowned. "But it occurs to me that a 'loss of signal' would be a very convenient way to cover any weaknesses in your story if, for instance, you were actually transmitting from a clandestine location here on Earth, relaying it through a very small, very fast rocket in the direction you claim to be going. Over."

"You're very sharp, Lou. I can't disprove that theory just now. You'll—"

"It's not me, I'm no expert, this proposition was . . . oh, sorry, I should have waited . . . well, our science adviser is on his way to the studio and he suggested that theory to explain what seems flatly impossible to everyone we've talked to. Over."

"As I was saying, I can't disprove that. But you'll all know for sure soon enough. Now, I'd like to introduce you to my crew, starting with . . . wait a moment, Lou. We're just seeing your new picture, give us a moment."

What we were seeing was the scene from the Blast-Off, down in the left-hand corner of the screen.

It looked like Mom had let a camera crew into the living quarters. I saw Mom, Maria, Sam, Salty, Grace, Billy . . . and Caleb, back from wherever he had hidden Jubal. Some of the neighbors were in there, too, looking amazed and happy. Everyone was gathered around the television set and you'd have thought we just won the World Series and the Superbowl all at the same time. There was laughing and crying, everyone was holding long-stemmed glasses of champagne.

I came within an inch of waving at the camera, like a three-year-old.

"We're switching live to the Blast-Off Motel," Lou said.

"Thanks, Lou," La Shanda Evans said. "We've been invited into the motel office to share this moment with the friends and relatives of the *Red Thunder* crew. Let's see if I can get a word. Betty! Mrs. Garcia, can I get a few words with you? Would you like to say a few words to your son?"

Mom made an effort and calmed down. Then she looked right into the camera.

"Manny, hon . . . I just want to say . . . I'm so proud of you I could just bust."

Oh, my, did I ever wish that camera was not on me. I fought back the tears as Travis handed me the mike.

"I love you, Mom," I said. "And don't worry, we're coming back, all of us." I handed the mike back. In five seconds we saw everyone in the room react, first with a respectful silence as they heard the first part, then with cheering.

There was more. Dak got to talk to his dad for a moment, and Kelly and Alicia were introduced by Travis. Then Travis got the mike back. He paused for a moment, looking very solemn.

"I have one more thing to say," he began, "and then we'll take you on a tour of the good ship *Red Thunder.*

"I spoke about the radical new technology that is making this trip possible. It really will revolutionize every aspect of our daily lives. The potential good things that can come from this technology are too numerous to mention. I'm sure I've not even thought of a fraction of them.

"But as with any powerful new science, there is great potential for harm, even for disaster. This is not the time or place to get into details, but we have decided that this new science is too much power for any one nation to possess. It is also too much power for *all* nations to possess. . . . So which will it be? How can this new power be managed?

"I don't know. I haven't got a clue. We've been sorely tempted just to destroy all knowledge of how this new source produces power . . . but I don't believe that will work. What one man has discovered, another will eventually discover.

"All I'm sure of is that it is *way* too much power for one man, or a small group of people, to possess. We have to figure out a way to bring this miracle of free power to humanity without destroying humanity in the process. I don't want this responsibility, none of us here do. And that is why we are undertaking this journey, to become a voice that people will listen to.

"Right about now videotapes should be arriving by messenger at the *New York Times*, at the *London Times* and the BBC, at fifty media offices around the globe. These tapes will show some of the things that can be done with this technology—which we've been calling the 'Squeezer,' or 'Squeeze' drive. I want to urge the people of the world to study this information closely. It is vital that you do.

"Sorry to go on so long, Lou. We're going to start the tour now. Feel free to ask questions if you want to. Over."

Of course no newsman in history could ever have restrained himself with an invitation like that. Lou—while probably estimating the size of the raise he was going to get and already mentally polishing his Pulitzer Prize—had a thousand questions.

We ran the tour by simply switching from one camera to another as we moved from room to room. We also showed some outside shots. It took about an hour.

Midway through the tour, a phone rang. We all looked at each other. Kelly felt in her hip pocket and pulled out a cell phone. It rang again.

She retreated down the ladder to the lower stateroom deck. I followed and watched as she opened the phone.

"Hello? . . . I don't believe it. Can't I get away from you *anywhere*?"

I mouthed *Daddy?* and she nodded. Then she laughed.

"*Turn this thing around?* You've got to be out of your mind. . . . No, you will not, Father, Travis didn't shanghai me—in fact, I had to sneak aboard. . . . Don't mention it again, Father, or . . . Okay, you asked for it. Are you in your office? Good. Look in your bottom left desk drawer. . . . Got it? That's just part of what I know about you. Do you want to see any of that on the front page of the *Herald*? . . . Oh? Then stop shouting about putting Travis in jail. What . . . what do I want you to *say?* How about, 'I'll pray for you.' How about just, 'Be careful.' . . . No, I didn't think so. Okay, Father, but I'm coming back, in spite of you." She snapped the phone closed, then turned and went into the head. She opened the glory hole and dropped the phone in.

She smiled at me . . . but the smile broke apart and she started to cry. I took her in my arms and let her get it out. At that moment I stopped feeling sorry for myself that I didn't have a living father. How much worse to have a father who was so hateful?

An hour later, when I used the head, I could still hear the phone ringing, way down at the bottom of the chute, among the crumpled plastic bags of urine.

27

★ ★ ★

OF COURSE NO cell phone could have reached us where we were when Kelly got her call. We told Travis about it and he theorized Mr. Strickland must have a friend at CNN, and had piggybacked the phone signal onto the signal the network was sending to us.

"Whatever else he is," Travis said, "you gotta give him top marks for resourcefulness."

"I knew that already, believe me," Kelly said.

After the grand tour of the ship, things settled down a lot. We could have given nonstop interviews, since every news outlet on the planet had requested one, but we'd soon have been repeating ourselves. How many ways can you answer "What does it feel like, being out in space in a home-built contraption? " So we said we were too busy and scheduled another live report in twelve hours.

Too busy? It was a lie.

On a long trip, whether you're headed to Mars on a spaceship or sitting in an Amtrak train from New York to Los Angeles . . . the main thing you experience is boredom. Actually, the trip to Mars was *more* tedious. On the train there would be changing scenery. While you really couldn't beat the view from *Red Thunder*'s ports, it never changed.

Once Earth had dwindled to a bright star and while Mars was still just another, bright reddish star, the starry background was fixed. It was hard to believe you were moving at all, much less streaking along at the fastest speed humans had ever traveled.

So what did we do? We played Monopoly and watched television.

Soon all the networks were beaming their signals to us. Dak set it up so we could monitor a dozen of them on a picture-in-picture screen, like an animated quilt, and when we saw something interesting he'd throw that image and sound onto a big screen.

The two most critical systems, navigation and air, ran automatically on computer control and we only needed to monitor them. Travis was technically always on duty while the ship was in motion, but the autopilot was proving to be perfectly reliable, so he could sleep with an alarm bell beside his bed that would sound if the computer lost the star it was fixed on. The star was never lost, and Travis slept soundly.

We did stand four-hour watches on the air system, but it didn't interfere with the Monopoly game, since the control console could be run with a remote from the common room deck. All the lights stayed green.

Television went to work on us.

We've all seen it. A celebrity is murdered, or accused of murder. A powerful politician is caught in a scandal. A certain story catches the interest of the public. Suddenly ordinary people are caught in the media spotlight. Suddenly your entire life is under a microscope. The media wants to know it all, the good and the bad, but most especially the bad. Few of us are so blameless as to withstand that spotlight.

Kelly, through our new best buddy, Lou the Anchorman, tried to contact her mother, but got only a busy signal. Then her mother arrived at the Blast-Off and had to fight her way through the cameras and mikes until Mom let her into the lobby. The cameras caught them through the windows as they hugged. Then, of course, the media got to listen in as Kelly and her mom talked, briefly. Her mom was worried sick, of course, but there was no nonsense about turning the ship around.

Mr. Strickland, with the sure business sense of a barracuda, decided to jump on the *Red Thunder* bandwagon with both feet, both arms, and his big fat ass, all at once. When the news crews arrived at Strickland

Mercedes-Porsche-Ferrari, banners were already going up: HOME OF *RED THUNDER* CREWPERSON KELLY STRICKLAND! When Strickland was interviewed you'd have thought he built *Red Thunder* single-handed. He even managed to brush away a tear when asked how he felt about his daughter going into space with this possibly crazed ex-astronaut.

"I have the highest confidence in Captain Brassard," he said, and if I hadn't known better I'd have believed he and Travis "Brassard" were the best of friends. "I'm sure he'll bring my precious daughter home safe and sound."

With a smile that wasn't pretty at all, Kelly asked to be connected to our law firm, and told one of the shysters there that she had reason to believe Strickland Mercedes-Porsche-Ferrari was in violation of the law, displaying a trademarked term without permission. She had copyrighted and trademarked everything with the remotest connection to the Red Thunder Corporation, and at that very moment injunctions and summonses were being prepared and served on the dozens of souvenir stands and T-shirt shops and the single car dealership that were seeking to profit from our enterprise.

"We intend to sue for damages when we return," Kelly told Lou, and soon the news was being told to an audience of about two billion, planetwide. A camera crew showed the forced removal of the banners from the car lot of Strickland MPF. The camera caught, for a moment, an unguarded expression on Strickland's face as he hurried back into his building with Miss Iowa.

When the media is looking at you that hard, people you hardly know show up. Dak's mother showed up at the Blast-Off.

What better boost could one imagine for a singing career that had floundered for almost as long as Dak had been alive? It was as if the brother of a no-talent singer was suddenly elected President of the United States.

She didn't try to fight her way through the crowds like Kelly's mom had. She lingered there, with her perfect hair and makeup and teeth. She projected concern for her darling son. She was praying for Dak's safety, and appearing nightly at the Riviera Room in Charleston, South Carolina.

But by then the media had already started to grow some teeth. She had no good answer when asked why she hadn't visited her son in twelve years, and she retreated into the Blast-Off. She emerged about fifteen minutes later, not nearly so eager to talk to reporters. But the next day she canceled her gig at the Riv and moved up to a club in Atlantic City. She never did try to talk to Dak. Must have slipped her mind . . . or maybe she had a pretty good idea of what Dak would say.

Much about Travis clearly had the media frustrated. Vast as his clan was, they were unable to locate a single person who would go on camera and talk. The biggest potential story there was obviously the guy with the white beard, painted on the side of the rocket ship, but no Broussard was talking about that except to say, off the record, that cousin Jubal was mildly retarded. Jubal was being kept hidden because things like this would upset him. Which was exactly what Travis had told them all to say.

But the juiciest story about Travis was that his ex-wife was one of the Ares Seven, en route to Mars in the *Ares Seven*.

The crew of the American ship held a press conference when we were about a day out from the Earth. They could barely conceal their irritation, though the public face they had obviously been told to put on was that if, *if* this ship existed, and was crewed by Americans, then we wish them the best of luck. After all, it doesn't matter who gets there first, the important thing is that people are going to Mars.

Holly Broussard Oakley seemed baffled. It must have been nightmarish for her, a few weeks away from landing on Mars only to find that her ex-husband might be waiting for her when she arrived. We all felt sorry for her, even Travis.

But the worst for Travis was when they tried to bring his daughters into it. The question was immediately raised concerning how smart it had been to embark on a trip as hazardous as this while the mother, who had custody, was in a similar situation. A procession of talking heads discussed how traumatic it would be for the children to have both parents killed in outer space. School pictures of both children and live shots of the front door of Holly Oakley's apartment building and the girls' grandparents' house were shown. Television people, desperate for pictures, went so far as to pester neighbors as they came and went during the day. Being a reporter must be a very nasty job, if you have any human sympathy at all.

The story of Travis's emergency landing in Africa was told many times, and also of his landing in Atlanta. Sources who would not be named hinted there was more to that story than met the eye, and the reporters kept digging. I hoped they wouldn't find out, it wouldn't help my mother's peace of mind . . . but I knew by then it was best to be prepared for the worst.

The worst case was Alicia, of course. A father in prison at Raiford, for killing her mother? *Terrific* story. An old mug shot was dug up of a baffled-looking white man with unkempt hair and a cut lip, side by side with a picture of a smiling black woman. Court TV had covered the trial, so highlight tapes of that were shown, particularly the sentencing. About the only good news was that her dad had refused to talk to reporters.

At some point in all this TV watching I realized, with a bit of a shock, that I was the only one of us who wasn't getting shafted in one way or the other. Of all of us, I was the only one who didn't have "issues," as the school counselor used to say, with one or more of my parents. The only problem I had with my dad was that he was dead.

No such luck. They dug up the story of how he had been killed, gut-shot during a drug deal gone wrong. A reporter brought it up during an interview with my mother, and it looked like they'd sandbagged her, that question coming out of left field, because she looked stunned . . . then shoved the offending journalist out the front door.

"Oh, Betty," Travis moaned when he saw it. "Never attack a reporter, no matter how richly he may deserve it."

"Mom and her temper," I said, feeling all flushed and sweaty. Kelly took my hand and squeezed it . . . then rolled an eleven and landed on Dak's New York Avenue property, with a hotel. For once, Dak didn't whoop as he raked in his money.

"Let's lighten up, friends," Travis said. "We all knew this was going to happen. And not a one of you has done anything to be ashamed of. So don't be ashamed of the dark side of your families, okay? All families have dark sides. Believe me, when we get back, all will be forgiven and forgotten."

It wasn't all rotten. Lots of the sidebar stories made us laugh.

In the days after the launch, they must have interviewed every student and teacher in every school any of us ever went to. Our peers were behind us, 1,000 percent. It started getting embarrassing, hearing them all say how smart we were, how nice we were, how we were always ready to help out anyone who needed help, and how good a friend we had been, to a lot of people who we barely remembered at all. It was like a berserko school shooting—"He always did seem a little weird, he had no friends, hell yes, we all figured he'd shoot up the school one day!"—only in reverse.

We all cheered when they got around to interviewing 2Loose. The dude was good. He instinctively knew how to manage the news, and he was perfectly willing to spend all day in front of a blowup of his artwork on *Red Thunder,* explaining it to all the viewing audience. And he conducted interviews only in his studio, where people could get a load of all his other work . . . which was for sale.

BUT THERE WAS more news than just the tabloid-style fluff. It reminded us that what we were up to here had serious consequences, was a lot more than just a jolly jaunt to another planet.

Agents Dallas and Lubbock showed up at the Blast-Off about four hours after we lifted off, along with four or five other agents and a few local cops. The cops didn't look too happy, I felt they were strongly on our side. They were all admitted into the living room, which was already crowded with our friends . . . and a small, quiet man with a briefcase who had been sitting by himself in some of the previous shots. What followed might have been funny if we all didn't have such a stake in the outcome.

The agents clearly didn't like the presence of the television cameras, and liked it even less when the man in the suit identified himself as George Whipple, from our law firm, representing the Broussards, Garcias, and Sinclairs.

"We'd like you to answer a few questions for us," Agent Dallas or Lubbock said.

"Sure," Mom said.

"That is . . . down at headquarters," Dallas or Lubbock said.

"Are my clients under arrest?" Whipple asked.

"Er . . . no, but it might be easier if—"

"My clients will answer any questions you have right here," Whipple said. *Right here, in front of two billion people.* "If you arrest them, I will of course wish to accompany them. I advise them to answer no questions unless I am present."

The incident was basically over right there, though Dallas or Lubbock didn't give up immediately. But what were they going to do? Handcuff two men and three women and drag them away . . . charged with what? They couldn't mention any "national security" baloney. We'd stolen nothing, revealed no secrets to any foreign power. Whipple told us that he had found us in violation of only three laws. One, we had operated an experimental aircraft not registered with the FAA. Two, we had taken off without clearance from Daytona airport or anyone else. And three, we had set off fireworks without a permit. The people at the Blast-Off could only be charged with *conspiracy* to commit those crimes, "as shaky a legal house of cards as I've ever seen," Whipple said. "If I can't get all of you off for going to Mars and becoming national heroes, I'll never practice law again."

The agents and cops left the motel fifteen minutes after they arrived. The cops were grinning. Lubbock and Dallas were posted to the FBI office in Butte, Montana.

There was no comic element to the other big story, though. We had known China would not be happy to be beaten in the race to Mars. They had invested too much money and national prestige. Their loss of face would be gigantic, if we were to beat them there.

So the official line in China was, It's a hoax.

We watched the head of the Chinese space program go on television to denounce the whole story. He sounded angry, though I'll admit that people speaking Chinese or Japanese always sound a little pissed off to me, the way they spit out their words.

"That's our biggest problem right now," Travis told us. "We have to prove to the world, even to the Chinese, that we're not sitting in a television studio in Washington, making all this up."

"How we going to do that?" Dak asked.

"I've got a few ideas," Travis said, with a grin.

The grin died when we saw the rally of one million angry Chinese in Tien-an-men Square, burning American flags. A good many of those people marched to the American embassy and began throwing stones and firebombs. A Marine guard was killed before the Chinese Army pushed the crowd back. I thought Travis would climb through the screen and start killing rioters himself when that news came in, and we were all ready to go with him.

After that we turned the television off for a while.

IT HAD BEEN hard for me to imagine sleeping while hurtling through space at an insane speed. I hadn't counted on just how boring boosting through deep space at a constant one gee could be. It was exactly like the five-day drill, except then Travis was throwing emergencies at us.

Dak whipped us all at Monopoly, and nobody felt like starting another game. He was on air watch at the time, and when his watch ended it would be Alicia's turn.

Kelly yawned and got up from the table.

"Time to hit the sack, don't you think, Manny?"

"Go on, y'all," Alicia said, with a wink.

I followed Kelly down to our stateroom, and once inside she closed and bolted the door and leaned back against it.

"You've heard of the Mile High Club?" she asked.

"Everybody's heard of the Mile High Club."

"Well, my darling, we are about to join the Million Mile High Club. We may even be the first members." She joined me on the bed.

First members? Probably not, though nobody on the *Heavenly Harmony* or the *Ares Seven* would have copped to it. Both China and my beloved home country managed the news too strictly for that.

Even if we weren't the first, it was a night to remember. I think I got an hour of sleep, and then Alicia was knocking on our door because I was on air watch.

So a trip to Mars doesn't *have* to be boring.

ABOUT TWO HOURS from turnaround the whole ship rang like a giant bell. I was instantly on my feet, and we all heard the alarm sounding and Kelly's recorded voice.

"Pressure loss from Module One. Pressure loss in Module One. This is not a drill. This is not a drill."

I was the first to the crossroads deck, and I leaned in and pushed the inner air-lock door shut, and by the time I'd done that Kelly was there to help me into my short-term survival suit, as we had drilled. I had it on in seconds, and stepped into the lock. Kelly shut it behind me, and I heard her slap the metal to tell me it had been secured.

The pressure gauge in the lock was reading normal, and so was the one for the module . . . wait a moment, I saw it go down just a hair. It was enough that the inner door could not be opened unless I hit the emergency override switch, there in the lock.

Procedure was to activate my suit if the pressure was 10 psi or less. It was still a long way from that, and if it did begin to fall rapidly, if whatever puncture had been made suddenly grew, I could activate the suit in two seconds flat. So I overrode, and opened the inner hatch. I swung out onto the ladder and took two of the round patches stored there and a smoke generator, which I broke to activate, then held still to see which way the smoke drifted. It went up, so I followed the smoke up the ladder.

At the very top of the module the air was swirling a lot more violently than it had midship. But the pressure was still good, as the automated air system released more air to make up for what was being lost, something it would continue to do unless the losses reached a much higher level. I could see the smoke being sucked away into a tiny hole. Sprayed-on insulation had exploded inward like glass hit by a BB.

"We hit something," I said over the radio. "There's a breach, smaller than a BB. You think we hit a BB?"

"If we hit something that big, at this speed," Travis said, "it would have torn us apart. A speck of dust, or a very small grain of sand. Don't put the patch on until—"

"I've got the situation in hand, Travis. Sorry, I meant Captain."

"You're doing fine, Manny."

The thing cooled fast. I didn't risk touching it, but I put a patch over it and it held. The smoke stopped swirling. When I was sure it was securely in place I went back down the ladder, then up again with a silicone sealer gun, and caulked around the edge of the patch. Once, twice, three times for good measure. Vacuum did not suck the thick, gooey stuff in around the edges of the patch. Mission accomplished.

"Let's save this story until we get back," I suggested when I'd climbed back into the central module and as Kelly was helping me remove and fold the suit.

"Suits me," Travis said. "Kelly, make a note, would you? When we're building *Red Thunder Two,* we add an extra layer of steel outside the nose of the ship, with a foot or so of space between it and the hull. Then something like this hits us, all its energy will be soaked up by the shield."

"Red Thunder Two?" Kelly asked. Travis grinned.

"Sure. You didn't think this trip was going to be the end of it, did you?"

"Tell the truth, I hadn't thought that far ahead at all."

To say that Dak and I were eagerly looking forward to turnaround would be quite an understatement. What's the biggest attraction about space travel? When you think about it, much of a life in space has to do with restrictions, on just about everything. Your living space is more constricted than a submarine.

The one area where you are freer than you are on Earth is your freedom from gravity. Free fall. Weightlessness. Flying like a bird, bouncing around like a rubber ball. You can't possibly read about it, or see it, without wishing you could be that free.

Ironically, *Red Thunder* took that away. Not that I'm complaining. Months and months of weightlessness, or three days of one-gee acceleration and deceleration? I think anybody would opt for the three days.

But then there was turnover.

It was possible to turn the ship without turning off the drive, but it had never really been done before, and Travis, like all good pilots, was a staunch conservative. He would turn off the drive before turning around, and he would do it slowly, taking between ten and fifteen minutes. So for that amount of time, we would get to have fun in free fall.

We spent the last hour before turnaround tidying up the ship, since anything that wasn't tied down would immediately float when the drive went off. That could really be annoying since, according to Travis, "It is axiomatic that, in weightlessness, everything you will soon need will seek out and find the absolute worst hiding place possible, sure as bread falls butter side down."

The last thing that happened before turnaround was that Travis handed out plastic garbage bags. We laughed, and he just gave us a small smile.

Two minutes after engine shutdown, I was sick as a dog.

My only consolation was that Dak was blowing chunks, too. We each filled our plastic bags, and asked miserably for another. Ten minutes into turnaround I was cursing Travis, *Can't you get this over with faster?* By then I was into the stage where you've brought up everything you have, and still can't stop. The dry heaves.

How could it possibly be worse? Oh, *please.* The thing that made it *infinitely* worse was . . . Alicia and Kelly were having the time of their lives.

They loved free fall. They bounced off the walls, did midair aerobatics that would have made the Red Baron proud. From time to time they stopped laughing enough to apologize . . . and then the ridiculousness of the situation hit them again. I doubted I'd ever forgive them.

"Almost there, guys," Travis called from above us. "Don't get discouraged. Over fifty percent of people experience nausea on their first flight."

"Did *you* get sick?" Dak asked. I said nothing. I was at the point where simply hearing the word "nausea" was enough to send me into a fresh fit of barfing.

"Well, no. Luck of the draw, I guess. Okay. Everybody strapped in?

Now, look at the space over your heads. If there's anything floating in that space, it's gonna come crashing down on you in about ten seconds. Are you all clear?"

We reported we were clear. Travis eased the throttles up . . . and I felt myself settling down into the foam of my acceleration chair. There was a g-meter in my line of sight, just a needle attached to a spring, and I watched it creep toward that magic number of one gee . . .

And the whole ship shuddered, there was a huge *thump!* from somewhere aft, and Travis eased up on the throttles so fast we all would have been thrown from our couches if we hadn't been held in place with lap belts.

Instantly I was too scared to be sick. We all looked around, knuckles pale as we gripped the air rests.

"No alarm," Dak whispered. He was right. No bells clanged, no recording of Kelly told us *This is not a drill!* How could that be?

"No pressure breach," I said, scanning my boards for an indication of the problem. All my lights were green. So were everybody else's . . . then Dak noticed his signal-strength indicators for the various channels he had been picking up from Earth. All the meters were zeroed.

"The antenna," Alicia guessed.

"We lost the antenna," Travis called out from above us. "Has to be. I'm unbuckling now, take a look . . . yes, it's gone."

"What did it hit?" I asked.

"It hit a strut," Travis said. "Manny, I just flipped a coin and you're it. Come to the bridge, you are acting pilot for a while."

I unbuckled, my queasiness returning, and floated up to the bridge. Travis was out of his command chair, leaning close to a side window for a look at the strut.

"I don't see any damage from up here," he said, "but I'll have to go out and take a look." He lowered his voice, without actually whispering. "If something happens to me, you are in charge. What will you do?"

Throw up, crap in my pants, and have a nervous breakdown, not necessarily in that order, I thought. But I said, "Kill our velocity."

"That's locked into the computer," he said. "Just do what we'd already planned to do. That will bring you to a stop about a hundred thousand miles from Mars."

"Plot a course back to Earth," I said.

"Never hurry," Travis said. "Take your time. You'll have plenty of time. The tutorials for the navigation program are good. But before you do that, while your speed is low, send somebody out, Kelly or Alicia, to check the strut if I haven't been able to get a report back to you. You and Dak, you aren't rated for free-falling suit work until you've put in eight hours weightless without throwing up. Sorry, that's the way it has to be. You can *not* throw up in a suit. Okay?"

"Okay."

"Go on."

"Reduce speed to a few hundred miles per hour, relative to the Earth . . . enter the atmosphere tail first, engines firing . . . and burn up in the atmosphere, most likely."

"A negative attitude's not going to help you. If Kelly or Alicia reports the strut is damaged, land in the ocean. She should float."

"Blow the emergency hatch, deploy the rubber raft, and get the hell out of here," I said. The emergency hatch was the top of Module One. It was held on with explosive bolts. A standard airline inflatable raft would deploy automatically when the bolts were blown, and it would be up to us to abandon the sinking ship.

"You might consider a water landing even if the strut's okay, if you don't have confidence about easing her down on land."

"I don't have that confidence."

"Do what you have to do. Anyway, this is all just standard procedure, this briefing, you know that. I'll be back here in twenty minutes." He grinned.

Alicia poked her head through the hatch.

"Travis, we've been talking, we figure me or Kelly ought to go out and check the strut. You're the captain, you shouldn't leave the ship."

Travis sighed.

"There's wisdom in what you say. But the suits and the lock haven't been tested, and as captain I won't send any of you out in them at this point. I have more suit time than the rest of you put together. End of discussion."

Alicia looked like she was going to say something else, but remembered what she had agreed to. Dak joined her, and he had a suspicious look.

"How do you flip a coin in free fall, Captain?"

Travis took a quarter from his pocket and set it spinning in the air. We all watched it for a moment, then Travis clapped his hands together, trapping the coin. He moved his hands apart and the coin floated there, the "heads" side facing him.

I WATCHED ON a TV screen as Dak and Alicia helped Travis into his suit. I was glad we'd practiced it. When we began it had taken us the better part of an hour to get into one. After a lot of drilling, we could do it in ten minutes, with another five for systems check. Travis did even better, naturally. Kelly joined me on the bridge and we watched through more cameras as Travis entered the lock and cycled it. I saw the pressure gauge drop to zero, then the door opened.

We switched back and forth between a rear-looking stationary camera and the one mounted on Travis's helmet. Travis handled himself well, securing his safety line, then swinging out and over the strut, where he commenced his inspection. Pretty soon he located the impact area.

"That dish is headed for the stars, at about three million miles an hour," Travis said over the radio. "How long before it gets to Alpha Centauri?"

"Is this question going to be on the final exam?" I asked.

"Extra credit."

"A thousand years," Kelly said, and when I looked at her, she shrugged. "Just a guess," she whispered to me.

"Did you give her the answer, Manny?" Travis said with a laugh.

I hadn't even figured it out myself. But light travels 186,000 miles per second, which would be . . . eleven million and some miles per minute, 670 million miles per hour, a light-year was 5.8 trillion miles,

Alpha Centauri was about four and a half light-years away . . . the answer I kept getting was 1,004 years. How about that?

"Trick question," Travis said. "The answer is, never. We're not aimed at Alpha Centauri."

Travis moved along the strut quickly. I had another episode of the dry heaves before he got to the most critical area, the welds connecting the strut to the thrust cradle, and from there to the rest of the ship.

It was half an hour before Travis pronounced it good. Another twenty minutes to get inside and up to the cockpit. Five more minutes before he was satisfied we were ready to apply thrust again. And just a bit over an hour after the emergency began, that blessed, blessed thrust settled down on my abused stomach again. I felt like I'd gone ten rounds with the heavyweight champion of the world.

Travis got the ship stabilized on her new thrust vector, and then joined us in the common room.

"Aren't we going to miss Mars now?" Alicia asked. "I mean, we traveled more than three million miles while you were outside, if I understand right."

"You understand right. If I stuck to our original flight times we'd go way past Mars and have to come back. But I can compensate by applying just a bit more thrust. I haven't figured exactly what that thrust should be—that's one of the nice things about *Red Thunder*, she's very forgiving, you basically just have to aim at where you're going and blast, not calculate complicated orbits. If you go too far, you can just thrust your way back. But it'll be about one point oh three or maybe one point oh five gees from here to Mars, to bring us stationary a thousand or so miles above the atmosphere. You won't even feel it. In fact, it's one point oh five now. Do you feel heavy?"

I did, a little, now that he mentioned it, but it was only a few pounds, and that heavy feel could be just my abused stomach bitching at me.

It wasn't until then I had time to think about the consequences of what had befallen us with the antenna. We couldn't transmit or receive signals from the Earth anymore. We were out of contact, and would stay that way.

Suddenly outer space felt pretty lonely.

I TAKE BACK everything I said about the lack of a view aboard *Red Thunder*. When we arrived at Mars, Travis inserted us neatly into a close orbit, and Mars in all his glory filled half the sky.

The Red Planet was not as red as I'd expected. There were infinite shades of rust, then large areas of lighter-colored sand, vast deserts and deep valleys, volcanic mountains that cast a long shadow if they were on the day/night terminator.

If only I felt well enough to truly appreciate it.

We all floated in the cockpit, getting the best view we would have on the entire trip, and my mouth kept filling up with spit. Then I'd try to swallow, and my stomach didn't like that idea at all. I'd gag, and try to throw up again. I think Kelly, Alicia, and Travis were starting to find Dak and me pretty disgusting. The bastards.

We could have simply eased into the atmosphere without any orbiting at all, *Red Thunder* was capable of that, but the site Travis wanted to land on was on the other side of Mars when we got there, so we "parked" for an hour.

"Noctus Labyrinthus?" Dak asked. "I thought—"

"Elysium Planitia, what I told everybody during our last news conference," Travis said, with a grin. "A nice, flat plain where there's very little of real interest. An excellent choice to make a nice, safe, sane touchdown. But we ain't going there."

"Why not?" Kelly asked.

"Because it's boring, and because that's what I wanted the Chinese to hear. My children, the two greatest tourist attractions on Mars are Olympus Mons and Valles Marineris. The first is the largest volcano in the entire solar system. Almost seventy thousand feet higher than the surrounding ground. Compare that to Mauna Loa, Earth's biggest volcano, which is twenty-nine thousand feet above the ocean floor.

"Valles Marineris is the Grand Canyon of Mars, and it would stretch almost from New York to Los Angeles on Earth, four miles deep and four hundred miles across in some places. Either one would be a wonderful place to land."

"Then why the valley?" Alicia asked.

"Two big reasons. We're pretty sure we understand the forces behind Olympus Mons. There's no shifting of the crust on Mars, no continent-sized plates moving along fault lines. Volcanoes form because there's an upwelling of magma in the mantle. On Earth, the plates move over that hot spot, which is how Hawaii formed, a series of newer volcanoes popping every few million years as the plate slid over the hot spot.

"On Mars, the crust just sits there, and Olympus Mons just grows, and grows, and grows, over billions of years."

"Sounds great," I said. "Why don't we go there?"

"Because Valles Marineris is more likely to contain the answer to the most important question about Mars. Is there any water still there? The valley looks like it could have been formed by running water. But how long ago? Is any still left, frozen in the ground like permafrost in the tundra? The canyon's an obvious place to look." Then he smiled a little broader. "Besides, it's where the Chinese will land."

He called up a map of Mars on his screen. He jabbed his finger at a point just above the north rim of the Valles.

"Longitude ninety-five degrees, six degrees south latitude. I'll be able to eyeball the correct landing site, because we'll be able to see the Chinese pathfinders."

It was the successful landing of two out of the three "pathfinder" ships on Mars that had finally lit a match under the complacent butts of those in charge of America's manned space program. One of the ships had failed to respond to commands from Earth and zipped on past Mars and into oblivion. But the other two had landed within half a mile of each other.

"The Chinese *have* to land there, they've got no choice. So I will come down at the landing site they announced to the world. I'll find the supply ships and put down within a couple miles of them. And then . . . then, my friends, we've got them.

"We're going to hijack the Chinese mission."

And he explained his plan to force the Chinese to acknowledge our presence on Mars . . . and soon we were all grinning with him. It sounded foolproof to me.

Providing, of course, that we didn't kill ourselves during *our* landing.

TRAVIS FIRED A long burst to slow us out of Mars orbit, then we were weightless again for what felt like three hours but really wasn't nearly so long.

Once again the four of us were strapped to our chairs in the windowless control deck. There was a cruciform cursor superposed on our aft-looking cameras, the ones that would be giving Travis his only useful view of where he was going. The cursor was right on the knife edge of the western reaches of the Valles Marineris. Of course we were also using our radar to judge altitude, but radar was one of the weak points of *Red Thunder*. To keep our costs under one million—okay, in the final accounting we had spent more like $1,150,000 of Travis's and Kelly's money—the great majority of the ship was built with parts purchased off the shelf, from the tanks the ship was made out of, right down to our pressurized ball point pens, an item NASA had once spent almost three million dollars to develop. But good civilian radar equipment that would meet our needs was hard to come by. We wanted to be able to bounce signals off Mars and the Earth while still hundreds or thousands of miles away, and would need even more range if we had to find a crippled and lost *Ares Seven.*

Our radar equipment had been scavenged from an Air Force airplane graveyard, from the nose of an old fighter plane. It was the best we could do.

It seemed to be functioning well as we descended, the numbers flickering down rapidly on my screen. Ten miles. Nine miles. Eight miles. More and more detail appearing on the screen. I made myself relax, breathing steadily. Not for the first time on this trip, I wondered if I was really cut out to be a spaceman. My stomach was protesting all the changes in gravity as Travis nursed the big, awkward contraption down to her destiny on the Red Planet.

Three miles. Two miles.

The terrain undulated gently in a washboard pattern created by the dust storms that periodically swept Mars from pole to pole, and could last months. If one had been happening when we arrived we would have been out of luck, orbiting for no more than a week before we'd be forced to go home. But the air was clear as glass.

One mile. Half a mile.

"There they are!" Kelly shouted. I followed her pointing finger to a screen showing two regular shapes in the sea of shallow craters and rocks of every size.

"I see them," Travis said in our headphones. "Please don't holler so loud."

"Sorry," Kelly said.

One thousand feet. Five hundred feet. Travis meant to land us someplace where the Chinese might not spot us on the way down. It wasn't critical that we not be seen, but it would help. The Chinese were following the pattern of the Russians during the Soviet Union days, landing completely on automatic, just like the pathfinder ships. Communists apparently just hated to relinquish any control they didn't have to, so Soviet and now Chinese cosmonauts had to be content to let machines handle chores that our own "Right Stuff" astronauts would have claimed as their own.

"One hundred feet," Travis called out. "Picking up some dust. Fifty feet. Thirty feet. Fifty feet to starboard. Still thirty feet elevation." There had been a big rock at the spot Travis had been about to land on. He moved over, then again. Twenty feet. Ten feet.

"I have a touchdown signal on strut two, Captain," Dak said. Then, quickly, "Touchdown on strut one . . . and strut three."

"Cabin listing less than two degrees," I called out.

"Air systems four by four," Alicia shouted.

"Cutting power," Travis said, and the roar of the engines—not nearly so loud in the thin atmosphere of Mars—tapered off and died. I kept my eyes glued to the tilt-meter, which settled another degree, then half of a degree. If tilt exceeded five degrees I was to recommend another liftoff and touchdown . . . something Travis could of course see and do from his own instruments. But on a ship you back *everything* up.

The meter stabilized.

"We're down, guys and gals," Travis shouted from above.

Somebody should have thought to bring some ticker tape and confetti. We made up for the lack by cheering our lungs out.

We had made it. We were on Mars.

FIRST WE ALL had to crowd into the cockpit, wearing our bomber jackets and big, goofy grins. Kelly the shutterbug took pictures of us. The view was stunning. I'm a Florida boy who's never been anywhere. There was nothing like this in Florida. Not a speck of green to be seen anywhere. Rocks everywhere you looked, though this spot wasn't as stony as the places where previous Mars probes had landed. It was midday, and the sky was a pale pinkish on the horizon and a deep blue straight up. Wisps of high cloud so thin you could barely see them. Dust, I think, not water.

The external thermometer was reading minus eight degrees, Fahrenheit.

"Time to suit up, don't you think?" Travis said. He got no argument. We all trooped down to the crossroads deck and then down into the suit room.

I don't know if Dak and Kelly and Alicia were holding their breaths, as I was. We'd never discussed this part of the journey.

Who gets to be first? Who gets the headline in the history books, and who ends up in the fine print? Travis was the captain, so didn't he have the right to be first? But, being the captain, didn't he have an obligation to stay with his ship? And if he did, who would tell him? I wasn't eager to try.

"You kids get to be first," Travis said, and smiled at the guilty looks on our faces. "Sure, I've thought about it. But, plain truth, none of this would have happened without you four. And Mars belongs to the young. And . . . well, hell! Get your suits on before I change my mind and beat y'all out the door!"

We didn't need more prompting. We all set new records getting into the things. Then down into the lock, Travis sealing the hatch behind us. Final suit checks, buddying each other. Then cycle the lock, watch the pressure equalize with the breath of carbon dioxide gas outside, and open the outer lock door.

Dak deployed the ramp, made of metal mesh, impossible to slip on. We started down the ramp, suddenly shy about it.

We had talked about the famous "first words." Everybody knows the pressure Neil Armstrong was under, how they had a camera set up just to capture that moment, that first step, and all America was asking, "What will his first words from the surface of the moon be?" Armstrong must have worried about it. And once there, he blew it, though he always maintained he *really* said, "One small step for *a* man . . ."

I had toyed with the idea of something like, "Holy crap! We're on Mars." But I knew I didn't have the nerve for that, and it would have stunk to high heaven, anyway. But, gosh darn it . . . I don't think any of us were up to saying something like, "What hath God wrought?"

So I had an idea, and while we were still standing on the ramp I told the others about it. It was agreed to with no objections. We all went to the foot of the ramp.

"On my signal, kick off with the left foot," I said.

"Roger."

"Will do."

"Weeee're . . ." and we all stepped off.

". . . off to see the Wizard! . . ." We skipped ahead a few feet—skipping's not easy in a space suit, even at one-third gee—and then nearly collapsed laughing.

I swore a mighty oath the Chinese were not going to steal this moment from us. The truth was going to get out, no matter what.

We were the first!

WE HAD TALKED about running up a flag. All the Apollo astronauts did. We knew the Chinese planned to. But what flag?

We were all Americans, all proud to be Americans. But we were not, strictly speaking, an American mission. We had no connection to our government, and that's the way we wanted to keep it.

The United Nations flag? But Travis didn't have a very high opinion of the UN, and neither did Kelly. Dak and Alicia were like me, politically not very involved. We were willing to go along with Travis and Kelly.

"How about the state of Florida?" Dak had suggested, not very seriously.

"Looking at what Florida has done to the land," Kelly said, "I wouldn't trust those idiots in Tallahassee to run a mud puddle, much less a whole planet."

"Besides, they wouldn't be interested," I pointed out. "There's no beachfront land to screw up."

Travis suggested they use the flag of his old alma mater, Tulane.

"Do they have a flag?" Alicia asked.

"I could find out. Better yet, how about the flag of MIT? That ought to get you guys a full scholarship, don't you figure?"

In the end we decided to go flagless.

We set aside thirty minutes for just looking around, for getting used to the idea that we were really on Mars. "Gosh-wow!" time. Travis had put us down in a small valley. We walked up the gentle slope of the dune north of us and took a look around. Walking was easy in the .38 gravity, even with the pressurization that made space suits a bit hard to bend, even with the added weight of suit and backpack.

I'd hoped the trio of volcanoes in a straight line, Arsia Mons, Pavonis Mons, and Ascraeus Mons, might be visible in the distance. The map scale had deceived me. We were over four hundred miles away from them, with Olympus Mons another five hundred beyond that. From the rise we saw more of the same terrain we had landed in. The spectacular views in these parts were *down,* not up, and we wouldn't see it until we were standing on the edge of the Grand Canyon of Mars.

So we took a few pictures, or Kelly did, with her camera in a plastic box usually used for underwater photography. Then we went down to deploy our surface vehicle.

We had loaded it into Module Four. It was hard to believe that, a few months before, it had been Dak's pride and joy, *Blue Thunder.* All that was left of it was the pickup bed and body. Sort of like those "stock cars" they drive at Daytona, called Fords or Chevys, actually nothing but car-shaped Fiberglas shells surrounding an engine and chassis, built from the ground up.

Module Four had been pressurized and heated during our flight. Now Dak climbed up a ladder and found a control that released the 15 psi atmosphere inside. When that was done the simple plug-type door was pulled in and up by an ordinary garage-door opener. He stepped inside and handed out six metal tracks, which me and Kelly and Alicia fitted together into two corrugated metal ramps. We lifted one end of each track so Dak could fit them into slots on the module, then carefully aligned them.

Dak operated an electric winch and slowly, slowly, *Blue Thunder* came down toward us. When it reached the ramp Dak shoved it until its wheels were in the tracks, then we lowered it the rest of the way.

Its undercarriage had been greatly modified. A framework of steel and giant shock absorbers supported the truck body a full three feet above its wheels. But those wheels were just for getting it down the ramp. When we'd rolled the vehicle away from the ramp Dak operated a second winch, and the *real* wheels came down, like four pink donuts on a spike. They were earthmover tires, a bit over seven feet high.

But . . . pink?

"The only color they had in stock," Dak had said. "They'll do the job."

The job they had to do was to protect the rubber of the gigantic tires from freezing and flaking away, like his experimental tire had done. It turned out sixteen was how many electric blankets they needed, modified with zippers around the edges, to cover the tires. Each nestled in its own pink cocoon, like weird, flattened Easter eggs.

We got the wheels down and unwrapped, then jacked *Blue Thunder* up to the proper height, removed the regular tires and replaced them with the big ones. Each wheel weighed eight hundred pounds on Earth, but just three hundred on Mars. We could horse them around without too much trouble.

They call it a Bigfoot, at monster truck rallies. They are all descendents of the original Big Foot, made by some maniac a long time ago. They have only one use: to bounce recklessly over lines of junk car bodies as quickly as possible, preferably without killing the driver by turning over on him.

Only one use, until we took one to Mars, that is.

"It's perfect," Dak had said, when Dak and Sam first revealed their creation to us, back at the warehouse. "You've seen the pictures, Mars is scattered with rocks, lots and lots of rocks, any size you want. This baby will crawl right over any rock smaller than a Buick. Bigger than a Buick, I figure we'll drive around it."

"Isn't the center of gravity kind of high?" Travis had asked. "I've seen them turn over, on television."

"That's in a race," Dak had said. "Fools be driving those rigs way too fast. Keep it down to five, ten miles an hour, it'll climb over most anything."

"Yeah, but who'll be driving at five, ten miles an hour?"

"You're lookin' at him. I don't always drive like I did that night I almost run you over. Right, Manny?"

"Dak can be an extremely careful driver, when he wants to be," I said.

"And he damn sure *will* be, won't you, son?" Sam had glared at his son.

It took about two hours, Travis barking in our radios if he thought we weren't being careful enough, to reassemble *Blue Thunder.* I was glad we'd put in all that suit time at the bottom of Travis's pool. You don't dare get careless in a suit, not when there's nothing outside it but extremely cold, thin, poisonous gas.

Travis wanted us to come in for the night, but it was still several hours away so we talked him into allowing just a short jaunt. After all, we had to see if it worked as well on Mars as it had in the warehouse where we'd first seen it, didn't we?

So Dak climbed up into the cab, which had been completely stripped of doors, windshield, seats, roof, and most of its instrument panel. Dak had new instruments to look at, and simple plastic seats. He still had a steering wheel, but because space-suit boots were not very flexible he and Sam had substituted a hand control for the foot pedals. Push it forward to go, pull back to stop.

Alicia pulled herself into the shotgun seat, and that was all the seats there were, except a backward-facing bench in the bed. Kelly and I climbed up there and secured our safety lines to a pipe that ran just below the roll bar. Standing up was by far the best way to ride, and Dak had promised to take it slow.

Dak deliberately picked out some fair-sized rocks to climb and *Blue Thunder* performed perfectly . . . all in an eerie silence that was partly because of the thin air and partly because of the most important modification that had been made. Under the hood, where you'd expect to find an engine, there was now only two big tanks, one for oxygen and the other for hydrogen. The engine was sitting on the floor of Sam's garage, and *Blue Thunder* was now powered by four electric motors, one for each wheel. Beneath my feet, under the truck bed, were six fuel cells. *Blue Thunder* could operate with only two of them online, but today, as the Martian evening progressed, I could see a line of six green lights on Dak's dashboard.

"One mile, tops," Travis said over our radios.

"Gotcha, Captain," Dak said.

There was a computer screen on the dash in front of Alicia. It showed a map of our landing area, part of the extremely detailed map we had downloaded, free, from NASA. Alicia's job was to try to match the terrain with the real-time map *Blue Thunder*'s navigational computer was generating. That information was being fed constantly by our inertial tracker, which was accurate down to about one *inch*.

The shallow gully we had landed in was curving off to the west as Dak drove down it, and we tried several gullies on the map, sort of like moving a transparent overlay map over a more detailed topographic map. Alicia moved the cursor into a place that might be right, but the computer didn't like it. Again, same result. But on the third try the computer signaled we'd hit the jackpot.

"I've got our position now, Travis," Alicia said. "Uh . . . Dak, why don't you turn right here . . . I mean, west. Go up that slope, and there should be a crater, about forty feet wide, on the other side.

"West it is, hon," Dak said, and Kelly and I held on, though the safety lines held us securely, as Dak powered up a slope of about 20 percent.

"Just like four-wheelin' in the hills!" Dak chortled. He was having the time of his life. How many NASCAR drivers got to hot-rod around on another planet?

We got to the top of the ridge, a bit higher than the one we'd walked up, earlier, and down there at the bottom was exactly the crater Alicia had described.

"We'll call it Alicia Crater," Dak suggested.

"The hell we will," she said. "We get to name stuff? If we do, you better name something a lot more impressive than *that* after me."

"Okay, baby." Dak sounded so contrite that we all laughed, Travis, too.

He drove us along the ridge for a while, but Travis's voice came again, like a leash on a frisky dog. "I make you one point one miles from the ship right now, Dak. Time to turn around."

"Yassuh, boss," Dak said. "Manny, Kelly, can you see anything from up there?"

We'd been headed toward the Valles Marineris; the map showed it only 3.4 miles ahead. . . .

"I see a line, a little darker, maybe," Kelly said.

"Maybe," I said. "But the horizon here is confusing. Too close. We know it's there, the valley, but I wouldn't swear we're seeing it."

"Me either," Kelly agreed.

"Tomorrow is another day," Dak said, and brought *Blue Thunder* smartly around. We followed her outward-bound tracks for a short distance, then Dak went down through the next gully, up the crater wall, down to the inside, then up and out. We made about a quarter of a circle of *Red Thunder*, and came back home from the west.

We got out except for Dak, and we laid electric blankets on the ground in front of each of the wheels. Dak drove onto them, and in another thirty minutes we had the blankets laced around the wheels and plugged into ship's power. It was exhausting work, a lot harder than I'd expected, just like assembling the vehicle had been. Travis laughed when I mentioned it.

"Now are you glad I had your lazy asses out running every lousy morning?"

"I'd be even happier if you'd worked off that beer gut, Travis," Alicia said.

BACK INSIDE, WE all gathered in the cockpit to watch our first Martian sunset . . . the first Martian sunset ever seen by human eyes. We were the first!

The stars came out, much brighter than I'd ever seen them on Earth . . . well, from Florida, anyway. Hundreds of years of industrial revolution had filled Earth's skies with a lot of smoke and chemicals, the ozone layer seemed to be in trouble, and maybe the whole planet was warming up. . . .

It was impossible to worry about things like that while we watched the stars come out. But you had to wonder, would Jubal's miracle drive make it possible for humans to live on more than just one, vulnerable planet? If we could lift things on a large scale, it would be possible to have a self-sustaining outpost on Mars in only a few years . . . and then there were those wild-eyed dreamers who spoke of "terraforming," of changing the very nature of Mars to make it more Earth-like, to fill its basins with water and its air with oxygen. But even the most optimistic of those dreamers said it would be a project for centuries, not years. I'd not live to see it. I wasn't even sure if it was a good idea. Because . . . there were the stars, waiting out there. Some of those stars would have planets that were already Earth-like. Some of those Earth-like planets might already have intelligent life forms on them, but some may not.

I might live to see that. I really might.

Now the faint light of the sun from under the horizon faded out completely, and I realized what I'd been seeing before was nothing. Nothing at all. More stars in all their glory, endless thousands of them, and splashed across the sky like . . . well, like spilled milk, was the incredible immensity of the Milky Way, our galaxy, a hundred billion stars so thick you couldn't pick out a single one.

My arm was around Kelly, and I hugged her tighter.

I don't know how long we stayed there like that, but eventually Travis suggested we all get some sack time.

"Big day tomorrow," he said. "Luckily, we get an extra thirty-seven minutes." That was because it takes Mars twenty-four hours and thirty-seven minutes to turn once on its axis. We had decided to stick to Greenwich Mean Time for the ship's log, and to simply tailor our working days as morning, noon, and evening. There was little to be done at night, with the temperature just outside that clear plastic porthole already down to one hundred degrees below zero.

Of course, there were other things two people could do during off hours. Kelly and I retired to our room and did most of them.

Mile High Club, Million Mile High Club, and now the Mars Club . . .

We were the first!

THE NEXT MORNING, judging by the expressions on Dak's and Alicia's faces, we weren't the first Mars Club members by much. Suiting up, Travis looked at us one at a time, and shook his head.

"You guys are disgusting," he groused. "Don't you know we're making history here? Don't you have any—"

"Who says you can't make history in bed?" Alicia wanted to know.

"We made some history last night," Kelly agreed. Suiting up had to wait a few minutes until we all stopped laughing.

ONE OF OUR hard and fast rules was that *Red Thunder* was never to be left empty. Another was that Dak was the official driver of *Blue Thunder*, unless he chose to delegate it, and none of us figured he would. Only fair, I guess. It was his truck. Since we planned to use the truck every time we went out, it meant that the other four of us had to share the ship duty. We tossed a coin—slowly, in the low gravity—and Alicia drew watch duty the second day. She was disappointed, as we all would have been, since it was to be a big, big day, but she submitted gracefully.

Once outside we removed the heat blankets from the tires and inspected them all very closely. They seemed to have come through the incredible cold of the night without any trouble. All systems checks were nominal, as they say at NASA, all six fuel cells humming—or gurgling?—along most satisfactorily. We boarded, Kelly and I in the back again, and took off in search of the Chinese pathfinder landers.

They weren't hard to find. Our map was spot on, and we had marked the valley where we needed to be, a bit over four miles to the east of us. Dak got us there in no time, dodging around all Buick-sized rocks, as he had promised. We retired to a spot a few gullies back, parked, and waited.

We knew when the Chinese landing was to be, just about an hour from the time we parked. We hadn't been in contact, so we couldn't be 100 percent sure they'd be on time. That they would land *here* was a total certainty; that they would land at the appointed time about 98 percent certain, according to Travis. I had no reason to doubt him. But it was a nervous hour.

Actually, fifty minutes, because we spotted the ship with ten minutes of retro-fire still to go, way, way up there in the beautiful sky. It was leaving a faint contrail in the icy air, and it was an awesome sight. I choked up, thinking about four frail human beings in that little ship, descending into this awful vastness.

We had a surprise prepared for them. I almost felt sorry for them . . . I *did* feel sorry for them as fellow humans, but I had no sympathy at all for the cynical old men who had sent them here and who had arranged a riot that had killed a fellow American. May they all choke on their moo shoo pork.

"Come on, come on, baby." I don't think Travis was aware he was coaxing the descending rocket to a soft landing. Politics are forgotten at a time like that.

The ship was a simple cylinder, wider than any of our seven tank cars, but not much taller. The rocket drive would take up a lot of the bottom part. Those guys expected to be staying a long time in a habitat smaller than some jail cells.

It came down frighteningly fast for a long time, then put on a burst of energy that must have subjected the crew to a lot of gees, hovered at about fifty feet, then started easing down at about three feet per second. Another pause at the five-foot level, then it was bouncing on its big springs. We all looked at each other, and let out a cheer.

"I gotta hand it to him, that was one sweet landing," Travis said. "Yessir, whoever wrote that landing program was really good." And he laughed.

We set up a television camera with a long lens, so that it was just peeking over the slight rise we had hidden behind. We moved back to *Blue Thunder* and waited again, this time watching the image on the television screen, which showed the lower part of the Chinese ship. We figured they had orders to get out and onto the planet soon, just in case those lousy Americans actually existed and had not blown up halfway into their journey.

It took them a little over an hour. Then the lock door opened, a ramp was deployed, and a single cosmonaut came down it and, with no ceremony at all, stepped onto the Martian soil and set up a television camera on a tripod.

"I think we're witnessing a little white lie," Kelly said.

"How you figure?" Travis asked.

"That camera, they're going to send the picture from that as they all come out at once, and say that is the first human steps on Mars."

"I think you're right. Well, it worked for Douglas MacArthur." He saw our blank looks, and shook his head, as much as you can in a space suit.

"We know who Douglas MacArthur is," Kelly said—and she could speak for herself, as far as I was concerned, I had only a vague idea he was a general. "What's the story, that's what I don't know." So Travis told us how the general reenacted his "first steps" wading onto Philippine soil during the Second World War. He'd apparently made a promise, something like, "I'll be back."

Sure enough, five minutes later the door opened again and all four Chinese cosmonauts got together on the ramp . . . and just as we had done, kicked off in step so their feet touched the ground at the same time.

"Time to saddle up and go," Travis said. "Dak, you got a good idea where their camera is aimed?"

"No sweat, Captain."

So we boarded and Dak drove down the gully to a spot that ought to be right in the center of the Chinese camera's field of vision. Then he gunned it.

Blue Thunder was a little friskier than he'd counted on. We left the ground with all four wheels as we topped the rise, then settled back easily in the low gravity, and the Chinese cameras caught it perfectly. "Sorry, Captain," Dak said.

"What the heck. Go for it."

The terrain was almost free of rocks, so Dak moved at a speed he hadn't attempted before. He drove to within a hundred feet of the assembled Chinese and skidded to a stop. Old Glory, the Stars and Stripes, slashed back and forth from its mount on the end of our fifteen-foot radio antenna.

Their backs were to us, they were lining up to salute the flag they had just erected, when something told one of them we were behind them, maybe a reflection in his ship's shiny metal skin. He turned, jumped right into the air in surprise, and almost fell over coming down. He must have shouted, because the others turned, too, in time to see us clambering down from *Blue Thunder*.

Travis was in the lead, holding up a sign he had made that said CHANNEL 4 in English, Russian, and Chinese. The first guy—who turned out to be the leader of the expedition, Captain Xu Tong—switched channels. Almost at once I could hear excited chatter in Chinese, then Travis's voice booming over it . . .

"Welcome to Mars!" he said, extending his hand. Xu was still suffering from shell shock. He let Travis shake his hand, and then took my hand when I offered it.

It was at that point that the live television feed was cut, back on Earth . . . cut in China, anyway. But all of the television networks in the rest of the world were still sending out the signal for all to see. We lost a billion viewers at one stroke. That left only three billion watching. . . .

And that's what Travis meant when he said we were going to hijack their expedition.

AFTER THAT, RELATIONS between the two crews were surprisingly cordial.

The *Heavenly Harmony* crew had not been informed about the launch of *Red Thunder*, and they were furious about that. Not that they could do anything about it, or even dare mention it when they got home, but with us they could express their frustration.

After introductions were made we got down to the serious business of taking pictures of each other. Kelly used four rolls of film and Kuang Mei-Ling, the exobiologist who spoke a little English, shot at least that many. Then we were invited in for lunch.

The decks of the *Heavenly Harmony* were a bit wider than ours, but there weren't as many of them. Basically, it was command and control on top, common room one floor below, and sleeping quarters below that. They did have a tiny shower, which Kelly eyed hungrily as we were given the tour, but their toilets were chemical like our own, if a bit fancier.

So we sat down together and we were treated to some sort of noodle soup with chunks of pork and vegetables in it, along with bowls of rice. Luckily, there was no bird-nest soup or thousand-year-old eggs or sautéed ducks heads, or anything gross like that. We all cleaned our plates.

Travis then asked Captain Xu if we could send some short messages to our families back on Earth, since our own long-range radios were no longer working. Xu said he'd be happy to, but as we approached the television transmission desk one of the crew, Chun Wang, seemed to object. A few intense words were exchanged as we Americans busied ourselves looking around, not wanting to witness a family squabble. Xu won, though we weren't exactly sure what it *was* he won, and we all broadcast simple messages; we're safe, we're happy except we miss you . . . and *we were the first!*

Then we all boarded our separate chariots and headed south in search of the Grand Canyon of Mars.

The Chinese were awed by *Blue Thunder*, as who wouldn't be? It dwarfed the Chinese rover, which looked a lot like the Apollo lunar rovers, but with bigger wire-weave tires. There were four seats, all occupied. They trusted their automatic systems to handle things while they were away, and I couldn't argue with them. After all, the computer had landed their ship.

But we did have to pause a few times as the Chinese driver had to find a way around big rocks. Dak waited patiently for them, a smug smile on his face.

When we got there the Chinese geologist, Li Chong, leaped from the rover like an excited puppy and started banging on rocks with a hammer. He tried to be five places at once, dropping samples he was trying to stuff into plastic bags, picking up new ones. It must be incredible, I realized, to have an entire planet to study . . . and in this case, *he* was the first. The first rockhound on Mars.

As for the rest of us . . .

Never having been to the Grand Canyon in Arizona, or to any canyon, for that matter, I had nothing to compare it to. I saw incredible desolation. Incredible colors. Incredible immensity. I picked up a rock and hurled it out into space, and we all watched as it fell, and bounced, and fell some more, and bounced, until we lost it.

I noticed Chun Wang didn't seem to have much to do. Kuang Mei-Ling and Li hopped about like excited sparrows, and even Captain Xu seemed to have some geological training, helping gather samples. I didn't say anything about it, since we were all on the same suit channel. But later I mentioned it to Travis.

"Political officer," he said. "Commissar, or whatever the Chinese call it. He's a Party member, here to keep the others in line. Standard operating procedure on a Chinese vessel. Did you see how nobody talked to him much, at lunch?"

Now that he mentioned it, I had noticed that. Chun seemed to sit off to himself somehow, even at the crowded table. The other three had virtually ignored him.

"Some sort of social dynamic going on there. Mei-Ling is married to Captain Xu, and I figure that's put a lot of strain on Chun and Li. And

Chun seems to be largely frozen out by the others. People problems, Manny. It was always in the cards that people problems would be at *least* as big a hurdle as engineering problems on a trip as long and as cramped as they're on."

GOOD MANNERS DICTATED that we invite the Chinese aboard for a meal, so Travis did. We arranged it for Day M3, our third day on Mars, the second day for the Chinese. I drew the short straw that day and watched through the ports of the cockpit deck as the two vehicles headed off for the Valles again a few hours after sunrise, feeling a bit lost and abandoned. They would be back around midafternoon, a time dictated by the capacity of the suit oxygen tanks, and our stamina.

"Let's face it, friends," Travis had told us. "The five of us are not going to be contributing a hell of a lot to our knowledge of Mars, unless we stumble over a dinosaur bone or an abandoned city or a giant face, or something. There's no point in working sunup to sundown."

I hadn't given a lot of thought to what we'd do when we got to Mars. None of us had, we'd all been far too absorbed in the task of getting here at all.

But what the heck was I doing here, really? Why me, and not some infinitely more qualified scientist? I could walk right over some geological formation or group of rocks . . . or even cleverly camouflaged lichen or moss or some more alien form of life, blissfully unaware of its importance.

I had no business here. None of us did, except maybe Travis. Sure, we had worked our butts off, labored all summer to build the ship to get here, but the Chinese all held doctorates. Even Chun, the chief Commie, was an M.D. How bitterly ironic it must be to them for a group of barely educated kids to get here first.

Before long I'd worked myself into a blue funk. I prowled the kitchen, looking at the food we'd brought. Frozen pizza. Infantile! Would the Chinese eat pizza? That's the kind of thought I occupied myself with as I waited eight hours until the tiny caravan reappeared from the south. I helped people out of their suits and we all gathered in the common room, quite crowded with nine people in it, four of them on folding chairs.

It turned out pizza was okay.

"We have many Western rapid-food places in China now," Xu explained. "Most of us have eaten at them at one time or another."

Chun didn't care for pizza, but smiled broadly when we showed him a Hungry Man Mexican dinner, with enchilada, tamale, and refried beans.

But the real hit of the day was Alicia's food.

That's what we'd been calling it, to bug her, but we'd all eaten our salads and fruit along with our frozen dinners. But the Chinese . . . you'd have thought they'd been stranded on a desert island for a year with nothing to eat but thistles and rats. Well, maybe that's not a good example. For all I know Chinese may *like* thistles and rats, they seem to eat just about anything. But they almost drooled when they saw the fresh Florida oranges Alicia had brought by the bushel basket. And grapefruit, and tomatoes, lettuce, fresh broccoli, tons of other stuff.

Mai-Ling, Li, and Xu each ate a slice of pizza, I suspect just to be polite, and Chun ate half his dinner, then they attacked the fruits and vegetables. Their own supplies had been used up months ago and they were down to the basic rations for the rest of the trip: rice, noodles, canned or frozen vegetables and meats.

"They lost a lot of face yesterday, over dinner," Travis told us later. He and Xu had developed a rapport quickly. Somehow Commissar Chun's suit radio had developed a slight glitch, it wouldn't receive channel four anymore . . . tsk, tsk, how unfortunate . . . so Travis and Xu had spent a lot of the day talking about things Chun shouldn't hear.

"Of course, the whole nation lost face big-time when we beat them here, but the *Harmony*'s crew doesn't feel too upset by that because it wasn't their fault. But setting such a poor table . . . of that they were very ashamed."

"I didn't think it was so bad," I said.

"I didn't either," Travis said. "Space rations, what did they think we expected, Peking duck? Go figure, huh? Anyway, Chinese culture is different."

"Must have lost heap big face today, eating them oranges," Dak said.

"Yeah, but they didn't mind it so much. Good work, Alicia."

We were gathered in the common room at the end of the day. The others were all pleasantly exhausted from the day's work. Me, I was wired as a two-dollar junkie, having done nothing all day but worry and fret. But it was good to sit with everyone and talk about the day's events. The one we talked about the most concerned Commissar Chun.

After dinner, when it came time to reciprocate on the tour we'd been given of the *Heavenly Harmony,* Travis caused an international incident, of sorts.

"Captain Xu, are you a member of the Chinese armed forces?" Travis asked, knowing Xu wasn't. He then turned to Chun. "Doctor Chun, you being the political officer of the *Heavenly Harmony,* I must respectfully decline to show you my ship above the level of this common room. There are things up there I must not allow the representative of a foreign power to see. I'm sure you understand."

Xu started to smile, quickly concealed it, and translated for Chun.

Chun snapped off some choice comments which Xu did not translate, then told us he would wait for us outside. Travis also declined to let Chun off *Red Thunder* until we all went, pointing out that he didn't want Chun getting a close look at the Squeezer drive, either. Chun nearly exploded. Again Xu didn't translate, he didn't really need to.

"Manny, would you keep Doctor Chun company for a while?" Travis asked.

"Sure." Damn Travis. What was I supposed to do if Chun objected? Wrestle with him? Hit him over the head? I was ready for anything as the others went up the ladder to the control deck, but Chun just sat down in his chair. He looked at me, smiled vaguely, then began moving bits of orange peel around on the table in front of him. I'd never seen a man so tired, so depressed, in my life.

I almost felt sorry for him. I mean, I'd been getting the shivers a few hours ago just being alone on good old, homey *Red Thunder,* with my friends only a few miles away, and Alicia said she'd felt the same way on her first watch. Chun's nearest friend, assuming commissars have friends, was over *one hundred million* miles away.

And it was all baloney, anyway. Secrets? Rubbish. There were no big secrets in the controls of *Red Thunder.*

"I couldn't resist needling him," Travis admitted that evening. "Did you see how he tried to walk under the ship, get a close look at the drive? Oh so casually, like strolling in the park . . . well, I casually just happened to get in his way."

"Might have been crueler, you *let* him see the drive," Dak said. "What's he gonna make of it, anyway?"

"You've got a devious mind, Dak," Travis laughed.

Later I bought up what I'd spent part of the day thinking about, our lack of qualifications for exploring Mars.

"What can I say, Manny?" Travis asked. "You're right. None of us can say we 'earned' the right to be here, to be the first. But that's just the luck of the draw. If we were going to be the *only* ones here, I'd say this was nothing but a publicity stunt. It *is* a publicity stunt, remember. But it's in a good cause, and believe this: In a year, hundreds of geologists are going to be crawling all over this big ball of rock, and we led the way. Jubal made it all possible, and we did it. If you're worried about what they're going say about you in the history books, just remember that."

THE NEXT DAY, Day M4 for us, we rendezvoused at the canyon edge and then took off to the east, stopping every quarter mile or so for Dr. Li Chong to take more samples. This time I got to ride shotgun, it being Kelly's turn to mind the shop while the rest of us were out joyriding. Alicia and I both warned her of the loneliness, and how it could sneak up on you and make you feel panicky.

"Don't worry, I'll just smoke a little more weed," she said, and for a moment I thought she was serious. Then she shoved us both toward the air lock, swearing she'd be just fine, she could take care of herself.

We came to a part of the Valles that didn't look that different from any other part, at least to me, and Li had Captain Xu stop. Dak pulled up next to them, and we watched Li go to the edge and stand there, hands on hips, looking down.

"What's he want?" Dak asked.

"The . . . the striations, the layering," Xu told us. "He was looking for a formation like this, but it is too far down, too steep. He is frustrated because of this."

We all got out and looked down to where Xu was pointing.

The previous night I couldn't sleep, so I went to the commons and cranked up the DVD reader. We'd brought along a pretty respectable reference library. I found some encyclopedia articles about the Grand Canyon in Arizona, and read and looked at pictures until I finally began to yawn.

It was easy to see that the Grand Canyon and the Valles Marineris didn't have a lot in common other than both being deep and wide. The book said the rocks near the bottom of the Grand Canyon were about two billion years old. You could see the layering, like a million-layer birthday cake, from different stuff that settled out during different epochs. Then the land got shoved upward by the movements of the crustal plates, and erosion had begun.

Had Valles Marineris been formed like that? Nobody knew for sure. If it did, where did all the water go? Boiled off into space? Sunk into the ground? How much water? Enough to be useful if humans decided to come here in large numbers?

Most geologists—or areologists, as some preferred to be called—believed the Valles had been eroded by running water, just like the Grand Canyon.

That was about as far as I got. So I knew what Dr. Li was talking about, in general terms. The layering here was different. But it all boiled down to . . . or more probably, *froze* down to . . . water. So far Li had not found moisture-bearing rocks or soils, which was what he wanted to find.

"Down there at the bottom, you see it?" Li said, translated by Xu. "Layering, which was caused by a very ancient sea of water. Then . . . farther up, several more areas of layering, suggesting that seas once again covered this area, at very long . . . intervals. The water returned. The water must still be here . . . somewhere."

We could see the layering he was talking about a long way down the slope, which was about sixty degrees.

"One theory . . . which Li likes very much, is that water is still present about two hundred meters down. Pressure might keep it from freezing at that depth. As the pressure builds up, water might be forced . . . what is the word? . . . laterally along rock strata. Then, at a place like this, that layer has been eroded away. The water is forced into the air, where it freezes. A plug forms. When the pressure is sufficient, the plug blows out, and a slurry of rock, ice, and some water sprays outward, forming an apron of debris much like what we see spreading away from that layer below us, about two hundred meters down. Li wishes he could take samples from that area."

"Well, heck," Dak said. "Let's just lower him down and let him chip some off."

When Li understood that *Blue Thunder* was equipped with a powered winch and a thousand meters of heavy-duty poly rope, I thought he would hurt himself dancing around. Travis was dubious, but I think he was interested in helping the Chinese regain some lost face, so he agreed.

We secured Li to the rope and he went over the side, walking backward. In fifteen minutes he was down. He chipped for a while, and then our radios were filled with his excited chatter. Xu smiled hugely at us.

"He has found ice!" he said. "Just where he expected to find it."

So, in the end, the crew of *Red Thunder* did get to do its little bit of discovery. Short of finding actual Martian life, it was as exciting a result as anyone could ask for.

WHEN WE GOT back, Kelly was in tears. I just held her for a while, until she could stop shaking and get herself back together.

"I feel so dumb," she said. "Acting like I'm six years old or something."

"That's just how I felt," Alicia said.

"With me, it was more depression," I said.

"Why didn't you call us on the radio?" Travis asked her. "We'd have come back and got you, made some other arrangement."

"That's why. You would have come back. I kept telling myself I'd be okay, then I'd start shivering again. Couldn't stop." She blew her nose. "I almost decided to come looking for y'all. Follow the tire tracks."

"That's crazy, Kelly," Travis said, not unkindly.

"That's what I'm telling you, Travis. I was out of my mind. I've never been so scared in my whole life."

Travis told us that, starting tomorrow, we'd operate on the buddy system all the time. No one would be left alone. Since he was adamant about having someone aboard ship at all times, that meant that only three of us at a time could go exploring.

"What the heck," Dak said. "I'll take my turn, too. Any of y'all can drive *Blue Thunder* . . . well, about half as good as me, and since I'm twice the driver I need to be, that ought to be all right."

Alicia hit him with an apple core.

30

IT WASN'T UNTIL the next morning, Day M5, that we realized Travis hadn't meant to include himself in the buddy system rotation.

"I can handle it, don't worry about me," he said.

Debate was allowed aboard *Red Thunder* until Travis cut it off. So we were still arguing about it when somebody knocked on the door. Whoever it was must have been pounding on the side of the ship with a wrench or something.

"I wonder who that could be?" Kelly asked.

"Marvin the Martian?" I suggested.

It was still half an hour until the Chinese were due to join us for another day of exploration. Travis frowned and looked at his watch. Alicia tapped a few keys on her board and we saw a view from one of our outside cameras. There was a single Chinese standing on our threshold platform. We could see the Chinese rover parked a few feet from the ramp, and no one else was in it.

"Who's that knocking at our door?" Dak asked.

"Captain Xu, Mr. Sinclair. Captain, may I come in? This is an emergency."

We all looked at each other, then Travis shrugged and made his way down to the air lock. We heard it cycle, then voices too indistinct to hear. Travis shouted, "No!" and the rest of us scrambled for the ladder.

"It happened about eight hours ago," Xu was saying. Travis looked at us.

"Xu says the *Ares Seven* blew up."

Though the news was not entirely unexpected, it was still shocking to hear it.

"Apparently the crew had some warning," Xu went on. "They declared an emergency and within two minutes telemetry ceased. But Ms. Oakley had indicated that at least three of the cosmonauts were still alive."

"Holly's alive," Travis breathed.

"Well . . . that no longer seems likely."

"Likely or not, we're going after them," Travis said.

This time it was Xu's turn to be shocked. *Red Thunder* could fool longtime astronauts that way, at first. It could take them a while to realize, on a gut level, just how much Jubal's baby had changed all the rules of space travel.

"Yes . . . yes, of course. If there is anything, that is, if I can help in—"

"Do you have any kind of maneuvering unit, a suit jet or a low-powered rocket unit we could use for an EVA if we can find—"

"Pardon me . . . what is this EVA?"

"Extra-Vehicular Activity—one of those NASA jawbreakers, this one means stepping outside the ship for a bit."

"Yes, we have such a device, and I would be happy to give you one."

"Can we go get it? Now? Time is critical."

"Certainly."

"Crew, I hope to lift from here in no more than one hour. Batten down all the hatches, secure everything, you know the drill. Captain Xu, let's go."

"I can get *Blue Thunder* stowed away in about an hour, Cap . . ." Dak saw the sad look on Travis's face, and the air went out of him. "Sorry, Captain, I wasn't thinking. I just hate to abandon her. Captain Xu, you're welcome to use her when we've left."

"Drive it about half a mile away and leave the keys in it, Dak," Travis said. He was kidding about the keys. "We'll come back in a few months and pick her up."

Dak brightened at that thought, and joined Travis and Xu on the way to the lock.

DAK CAME BACK in a foul mood.

"One of the electric blanket connections was loose," he said. "One of the tires turned into black confetti. She's not going to be any use to Captain Xu or anybody else, and I didn't bring a spare." He kicked a chair in his frustration.

Travis and Xu came back with the space propulsion device.

"Somebody at NASA or some branch of government figured out we were the only possible hope for the *Ares Seven,*" he said. "So they sent the last telemetry from the ship to Captain Xu. It'll give me a pretty good idea where to look for them." He held up a silvery DVD. "Thanks, Captain."

"I was glad to help. But I must mention another problem." It took him a while to get going, and I could only imagine how much this was costing him in face.

"Comrade Chun has . . . has suffered a mental breakdown. We received orders not to pass this information on to you. I felt the origin of the orders was dubious, not through the proper chain of command of the space agency. Chun ordered me to . . . to destroy your ship, or disable it in some way. He became violent, and had to be restrained."

He looked down at his feet for a long time, and none of us said anything. Destroy our ship? Had they brought explosives along? Then I remembered that part of that day's agenda was to set off charges and study the seismic vibrations, like wildcatters did when searching for oil. *Red Thunder* was tough, probably tougher than those Chinese murderers back in Beijing realized, but like any ship there were vulnerable places, and it wouldn't take much of a charge to weaken or destroy them. That son of a bitch!

"We face a very long sojourn here on Mars," Xu finally went on. "I was wondering if it was at all possible . . . to . . . for you to carry Comrade Chun back with you and hand him over to the authorities, or to your Chinese embassy. I . . . I don't know how we are going to guard him and restrain him during all that time. And since you will be back on Earth in just a few days . . ." He seemed unable to go on.

Travis put his hand on Xu's shoulder, looked into his eyes, and shook his head.

"Can't do it, friend. I'm not going to have my people guard him twenty-four hours a day, no matter how short the trip is."

"Yes, of course. I'm sure I'd feel the same way. Then, failing that . . . do you have anything aboard ship that would be helpful in restraining him? It appears that we left Earth without a single pair of handcuffs." His small smile was ironic.

"That, we can do. Though we somehow forgot the handcuffs, too."

We gave him half a dozen rolls of duct tape and a spare coil of poly rope. They hadn't brought any duct tape, believe it or not. One good rule for living, in my opinion, is to never go beyond the city limits of your hometown without a roll of duct tape in the trunk and a Swiss Army knife in the glove box.

"I don't think you'll have to sweat out the whole time here, though," Travis said. "Plenty of others ought to show up in the coming months. Hell, I'll come back and get you myself if no one else will." He paused a moment. "I don't know how much hot water you're going to be in over this business, Captain Xu, but if I come get you, I'll take you back to wherever you want to go on Earth. You know what I'm saying? Anywhere."

Xu smiled. "I understand perfectly, and thank you. Unfortunately, I have a very large family, many relatives, and could not go abroad without them. And, I must say, I love my country, though not always those who govern it."

"Well said. I've enjoyed knowing you. Give my love to Mei-Ling and Dr. Li."

We all seconded that, and shook his hand.

Fifteen minutes later, just long enough for Xu to get out of the way, we raised ship for an unknown destination.

* * *

WE BOOSTED FOR about four hours. Turnaround—and, *hallelujah!* I didn't feel half bad—then boost again for another four hours. Then weightlessness.

Dak was still sick. I wasn't tempted to giggle, not even for a second.

I don't know how to describe the problem Travis had to solve for us to have any hope of finding the *Ares Seven.*

Up until she blew, she was continuously sending back information as to her position, and we had the last seconds of that. She had slowed down below solar escape velocity so, undisturbed, she would swing way, way out into the cometary zone and return to the inner solar system in about a thousand years.

But the explosion itself would certainly have provided enough energy to alter her course. All Travis could do was to try to bring *Red Thunder* to rest in the area where she should be if we extended her orbital parameters from the time of the explosion.

We had good orbital mechanics software. We had middling-to-poor navigation optics to tell us our precise position. We had good data from Earth. We had poor-to-bad radar for the final stage of the intercept. Good news, bad news, good news, bad news.

But in the good news column I would put the fact that Travis Broussard had proved himself to be the best seat-of-the-pants spaceship pilot in the history of man in space. If anyone could get us there, if anyone could find that ship, I was betting on Travis.

He brought us to what seemed the most likely area and velocity. We set up, and we waited, like a traffic cop waiting for a speeder to come by. But we couldn't wait for too long, the situation was too dynamic.

Casting around for a sighting involved a lot of starting and stopping. As time wore on Travis grew less gentle with us, going from weightlessness to three gees, the maximum Travis felt he dared subject *Red Thunder* to. It got to where I was looking forward to free fall, at least it afforded ten minutes of stability. Dak was still very sick, trying to ignore it, and even Kelly started to look a little green.

We did this for two hours. Travis seemed ready to go on with it until hell froze over or we ran out of gas. The rest of us grew increasingly discouraged. We realized Travis was, too, when he started shouting down to us, asking if we saw anything, when he had to know that if we did we'd shout it out instantly.

Normally I was in charge of the radar. I still was, but we had the radar display up on all four of our screens. What else was there to do? We stared at our screens until our eyes hurt, and saw nothing at all.

Then, on the thirteenth stop, just as Travis was about to boost again, I thought I caught a flicker on the edge of my screen, from the corner of my eye. Could it have been the ship, or a piece of it, drawing the shallowest possible chord through the spherical volume of space we were searching?

"Did anybody else see that?" I asked.

"See what?" Travis bellowed from above.

"I thought there was a flicker," I said. "Nobody else saw it."

"Heading! Give me a heading!"

I gave it to him, and instantly the ship started turning to point to it. Then three gees smashed into us again. Dak groaned, and couldn't get the barf bag to his mouth with arms suddenly turned to lead, but it didn't matter, he didn't have anything to bring up.

"I see it again!" I sang out. There it was, flickering . . . and another, and another.

"Four . . . no, five blips."

"I see seven," Alicia called out.

"It's the debris field," Travis shouted down to us. "Now we have to figure out which ones are worthless."

We wanted to find big chunks, but the biggest might not be the prize we were looking for. It all depended on the size and shape of the explosion, and where people were when it happened. The first three objects we found turned out to be heavy parts of the engine.

"Stands to reason those would be thrown the farthest, right?" Travis said. Nobody responded. "Well, anybody have any better theory?"

"Sounds good to me, Captain," I said. I was staring at a screen with maybe a hundred twinkling blips, some of them flashing every second or two, some waxing and waning over a period of minutes as they rotated. *Red Thunder* was drifting through the debris field. It was dangerous to go through it any other way. Already we'd heard two loud clangs as fist-sized hunks of stuff hit us.

After spotting and rejecting a few dozen objects Travis was getting frustrated again. "Can anybody help me out here? Anybody got any ideas? Crazy ideas, stupid ideas, out-of-left-field ideas . . . any idea at all. I promise I won't laugh."

Nobody had one. But I was studying one blip we were slowly moving away from. Actually, I was wondering if it might be more than one blip, connected in some way, from the way the reflection changed. Stupid idea? Well, he asked for it.

"Travis, I've got something interesting," I said, and gave him the position of the triad of blips. Instantly *Red Thunder* began to rotate again.

"I don't see it," Kelly said, softly enough that Travis wouldn't hear. I moved the cursor over the trio and highlighted it in red. Kelly chewed her lip. "Might be something. Can't hurt to go look."

"Bingo!" Travis called out two minutes later. "Manny, come look."

I unbuckled and floated up to the cockpit. Out the window I could see the object, about three miles away. Actually, three objects of various sizes, all rotating around a common center of gravity. I couldn't see what was holding them together.

"Wires," Travis said, reading my mind. "Unless I'm mistaken, two of those chunks are parts of the living quarters. Those two are worth a look, don't you think?"

"Sure do."

"Okay, go below and strap in again, I'm going to get us to about a hundred yards, more or less. Take me about five minutes."

I knew that was headlong speed in space, where it typically took a VStar several hours to close the last few hundred yards with a space station. I also knew *Red Thunder* was not famous for fine control. The Squeezer engines were great for raw power, but it was hard to release just enough energy to get you where you're going without getting yourself into trouble. But once again, I'd bet on Travis.

And because I knew Travis all too well by this time, the first thing I did when I got to the control deck, even before strapping in, was to incite the crew to mutiny. I quickly determined they were all with me, so I strapped in and sat tight.

As soon as we were where Travis wanted us to be, he called out.

"Dak, I flipped a coin and you're it, in control until I get back."

"I don't think so, Captain," he said. Travis stuck his head down through the access hole and frowned at Dak.

"What's the problem?"

"This isn't right, Travis," I said. "You shouldn't be going over there."

"I've got more suit hours than—"

"We know that. And if something happened to you, we might as well just open the hatches and suck vacuum," Dak said. "You're the only one can fly this thing, probably, and the only one who can land her, for sure."

"What is this? Are you saying you won't take control?"

"If you order me to, I will. But we want you to see you shouldn't give the order."

"This is what you all think?" He got nods from all four of us. For just a moment I thought he was going to dig in his heels, but then he swung himself down to the control deck and hung there, and rubbed his face with his hands. He was probably feeling as tired as I was, and I was exhausted.

"All right, I'm trapped. I think I'd rather cut off my right arm than send one of you kids out there to handle this . . . but I guess it's what I signed up for when I raised ship without a trained copilot aboard. Alicia, you suit up, the sooner the better."

"Right, Captain," she said, and started unbuckling.

"Hey, wait a—"

"Sorry, Dak, you asked for it. You're still far too sick to go, under any circumstances. My intention was to have Alicia go with me. Whatever we decide, Alicia *has* to go. It's what she trained for. If anybody's hurt over there, there's not much I can do for them. But Alicia can. And because of the buddy system we started this morning, Kelly goes with her."

Kelly was way ahead of him, already unbuckling. And now it was my turn to squawk. Travis cut me off just as abruptly.

"I probably like it even less than you guys do. My generation, we were taught that it's always a man who goes into the dangerous situation. You mean to tell me twenty-first-century men are still overprotective of their women?"

Neither of us had anything to say in our defense. Yes, I did feel protective of Kelly, and Alicia too, for that matter. But Travis had us trapped. It was true, Alicia had to go. It was true, Kelly was the only possible buddy, as Dak and I were still far from sure of our ability to do the job without filling our helmets with vomit, though I was doing a lot better than Dak was by then.

We all followed the girls onto the suit deck. Dak and I helped them get suited up, Travis carefully keeping his back to us. He was putting together a tool kit with some of the things they might need, just a heavy-duty canvas bag with a drawstring.

"For once in my life, I'm not sure I want to be a feminist," Kelly whispered. "Manny, I'm real scared."

"Just say the word, and you don't have to go," I said, meaning it. I'd fight Travis with my fists, if I had to.

"*You* wouldn't say the word, would you? Be honest."

"No. No I wouldn't."

"And you'd probably be almost as scared as I am."

"Probably more."

I noticed that Travis was suiting up, too. He smiled at me.

"Somebody has to go outside to help them with the crossing," he said, "and I don't figure that'll be too dangerous. But I want both of you to suit up, too, all but the helmets, and keep those with you. Should have thought of it before, there's too much stuff flying around out there, we could get a puncture."

And with that, the three of them put on their helmets—a last kiss from me to Kelly—and entered the air lock.

Dak and I watched it cycle as we suited up, then hurried up to the cockpit. We got there in time to see the three of them float up to the portholes, tethered together and also tied to a safety line that was attached to one of many hooks welded to *Red Thunder*'s side for that very purpose.

"Kelly, you go first. I'm going to be here to belay you when you get there. You see that shred of aluminum about twenty feet from the biggest piece?"

"Yeah, I think so."

"That looks like the center of gravity. You get to that, you can hook your line and not start spinning. Then I'll send Alicia over. Now, this dingus right here."

He was holding the Space Maneuvering Unit Captain Xu had loaned us. It looked like bicycle handlebars with a big thermos attached.

"You're going to start off with just a simple kick against the side of the ship. You hold the SMU like this. See? Over your head. Hang on to it, but do *not* use it to speed up or slow down. Use it for course corrections only. You hit this button with your thumb. Don't hold it down, or I'll reel you back in and have you do it again. Okay?"

Kelly nodded. I figured she was too scared to talk.

Travis tied the SMU to Kelly's suit so it wouldn't be lost, tied the tool kit around her waist, then he picked her up and swung her into a position about six feet from the side of the ship. She flailed around in panic for a second and my heart leaped into my throat. Then she settled down, facing Travis, and he put her through a series of familiarization drills. At first she held the control down too long and shot out to the length of her safety tether, which was about twenty feet long. Travis pulled her back, talking softly and calmly the whole time, and positioned her again. She quickly learned how to point the thing to get to where she wanted to go.

"I never felt so useless, man," Dak said, and I could only agree. How did this happen? Kelly and Alicia had never dreamed of space, like Dak and I had. So why were our girlfriends out there, and us in here?

After about twenty minutes of drills, Travis judged Kelly as ready as she'd ever be. So he positioned her with her feet against the side of *Red Thunder* and told her to jump. She jumped.

At first it looked good, she seemed to be headed right toward the center of gravity of the *Ares Seven* wreckage. But Travis, who had a better line of sight, told her she was bearing off to her right, and Kelly tried to correct. She held the button down too long, and it looked like it twisted in her hands. Whatever happened, she lost the SMU and began flailing around again.

"Oh God, oh God," she was whispering.

"Kelly, get the SMU back. Just pull in your left arm. That's right. Now you've got it. Now aim it directly away from your chest and just touch the button."

She was still swinging out in such a way that she'd eventually wrap herself all around *Red Thunder*, but more slowly.

"Do that again. That's right. And again. Once more."

Now she hovered motionless at the end of her tether. I checked something I hadn't remembered up to now, which was the telemetry from her suit. Her heart and breathing rates were way up. The heart rate slowed some as Travis pulled her slowly back to us. I could hear her sigh as her boots touched the hull again.

"Not bad," Travis said. "I never expected we'd get it on the first try. You want to wait a bit, catch your breath?"

"No, let's get it over with."

She jumped again. This time she looked off course right from the start . . . but this time she did a lot better with the SMU, got herself almost lined up, overcorrected, corrected again, and with about ten feet to go was only a few feet off the optimal location. Travis snubbed her safety rope and then coached her through the last feet with tiny bursts from the SMU. It took her a full minute to cross that last few feet, but when she finally was able to reach out and grab that collection of tight cables I heard her laugh, sweet music to my ears.

"Good. Hook your second safety rope to something . . . that's good. Now unhook the first line and clip it to the wires right in front of you. Got it."

Travis pulled that line almost taut, and clipped his end to a ring.

"Now Alicia's coming over."

It was easier, because all Alicia had to do was clip her line to the first rope with a snap ring, and pull herself across.

"Just pull a few times," Travis told her. "It should take you a full five minutes to get across. Okay?"

"Got it."

One hand on the rope and one carrying her pressurized "black bag" of medical supplies and instruments, she shoved off.

"Oh, man, I don't like this, I don't like this."

"Closing your eyes might help," Dak told her.

"Dak, stay off the line, please."

"Let him talk, Captain? It helps me, some."

"Right. Sorry, guys."

"No problem."

"Dak, could you just talk to me?"

Dak hurried down to the control deck, talking all the way, and came back again in a few seconds with a CD. He stuck it in the player and soon one of Alicia's favorite songs was filling our ears. I heard Alicia laugh, then she started singing along.

"Open your eyes now, Alicia," Travis said when she was almost there. "Got it? Just tighten your grip on the rope, that should do it." It did, and in a few seconds Kelly had grabbed Alicia's hand and they were securing themselves.

"Now what?"

"What looks promising?" Travis asked. There was a long pause.

"Nothing," Kelly admitted. "I don't see any lights, or anything like that."

"That's okay. Keep looking."

"It's pretty dark."

"Turn on your headlight."

"My . . . oh, well, duuuh! Forgot all about it." All the suits had krypton lights mounted over the faceplates, not that different from automobile headlights, though when one proved to be defective we had to order a new one from Russia.

We saw the lights go on from both their suits.

"I think I know where you are," Travis said. "Dak, Manny, bring up that schematic on the *Ares Seven*. Check me, but doesn't it look like they might be where C deck used to be?"

We brought it up on Travis's screen, twisted it a few times, and then it fell into place. Dak pointed to a large oxygen cylinder on the schematic, then to a big tank just above Alicia's and Kelly's heads.

"I think you're right, Captain. Kelly, Alicia, if we've got you located right, the main air lock ought to be on the side facing away from *Red Thunder*. Turn to your left a little, Kelly . . . a little more . . . there. What you're lighting up now looks like it might be the descent ladder and what's left of a landing strut. See it?"

"Yes. But . . . there's a lot of wire here, it's a real rat's nest."

"Don't get caught up in the wires," Travis said.

"I'm staying clear. But that puts the air-lock door on the other side of all that wiring. I don't think we can get through unless we cut some of it."

"Don't!" we all three shouted at once. Kelly laughed.

"We're not making a move until we've discussed it, don't worry."

"Ideas?" Travis called out.

"Get them back, circle around the ship, send 'em over again," Dak said.

"Cut some wires, see if we can get through that way," Alicia said.

There was a long silence.

"I've gotta go with Dak," Travis said. "Come back to the tether rope and I'll haul you back."

"That's going to take hours," Kelly said. "If anybody's in there, they could be running out of time."

"If nobody's in there," Travis said, "you're risking your lives for nothing."

"I think somebody's in there," Alicia said.

"Me, too. And don't call it female intuition. Somebody's in there."

There was another long silence. Travis sighed.

"One wire at a time. That's a terribly dynamic situation you've got over there. Cut the wrong wire, it could all go flying apart."

"Then you'll just come and get us, right?"

A pause. "Sure. Just take it slow, okay?"

"Got it. Now, where are those wire cutters? Oh, Alicia, can you . . . I just lost that hammer with the red handle, Travis. Sorry, it just floated up . . . let me see if I—"

"Let it go!" Travis snapped. Then he muttered, "I should have tied the damn things together. . . . Kelly, don't worry about it. Worse comes to worst, you can use just about anything as a hammer."

"I've got the wire cutters. I'm tying them to my suit . . . closing the tool bag. Now, Alicia, which one should we cut first?"

"That one right there."

"Cutting a thick, green wire . . . now. . . . Well, that worked out okay. Pull it to one side, Alicia . . . there. Now, cutting a thick, *gold* wire. . . . There."

She cut six wires and pulled them out of the way before she got the wrong one. As soon as she snipped it everything started to move.

"Move back, Alicia!" Kelly warned, and they moved . . . and the smallest of the three orbiting pieces of the *Ares Seven* pulled itself free and began to spin off into oblivion. It all happened soundlessly, but my mind supplied the shriek of straining metal and the sound of snapping guitar strings as smaller wires, unable to take up the burden once borne by three or four wires, snapped and popped like cracking whips. Kelly and Alicia turned their backs to the mayhem. I saw one snapping wire slap itself across Kelly's backpack. Then the two remaining pieces of the ship parted company and began drifting apart . . . and the safety tether was tied to the wrong piece.

Travis took it in, saw the wayward hunk of junk about to pull the line taut, and he reached down and pulled the free end of the rope, which he had tied in a slipknot in case of this very situation. The rope whipped through the eyebolt and was gone.

"Had to do that," Travis said. "*Had* to do that, it was about to get pulled into a spiral . . . it would have—"

"Wrapped itself around *Red Thunder,*" I said, "and crashed into us."

"Too right. Kelly, check your suit systems, right now!"

". . . five by five, Travis." They were still tied to the big piece, and now they could see themselves drifting away from us. "You'll come get us, right? I mean . . . soon? I don't like this very much."

"I'm coming in right now," Travis assured her, and he had already moved out of my range of vision. We heard the lock cycling, and Travis made it to the bridge in record time, frost forming on the very cold surface of his suit.

Dak and I went below and strapped in. We felt a few gentle shoves as Travis turned the ship, using the small thrusters not very different from the SMU. Then a mild kick in the pants as he fired the main drive. Two minutes later, another firing of the main drive, then the slightest burp, and when Dak and I scrambled up into the cockpit we could see he had brought *Red Thunder* motionless with respect to the wreck and the girls, an incredible piece of computerless flying that proved once more that nothing would ever substitute for a skilled pilot at the con, no matter what the Chinese said.

"All right, guys," Travis said wearily. "Your point has been proven. I have to stay here at the controls. Manny, I want you to—"

"We see two space suits!" Kelly said. Travis was instantly at the porthole beside us. From where we sat, the girls seemed to have moved to the other side of the ship. We could see their lights from the reflections on shiny surfaces, but not the lights themselves.

"Didn't I tell you not to move around?"

"Actually, you didn't, Travis, but we didn't move much. This hunk of junk has picked up a rotation. We've turned away from you. I'm approaching one of the—"

"*Please* stay put, Kelly."

"I'm barely moving. I . . . oh my God. Don't be sick, don't be sick, don't be sick."

"Captain, there's somebody in the suit," Alicia said. "Don't look at him, Kelly."

"I'm okay. I'm okay."

"The . . . ah, one arm is torn off at the elbow. Hard to tell if he died of loss of blood or freezing or anoxia."

"Don't be sick, don't be sick, don't be sick . . ."

"Can you tell who it is?" Travis said softly.

"Captain, the face is . . . it's not pretty. I'm not even sure if it's a man."

"Roger."

Kelly seemed to have controlled her stomach. As the wreckage slowly turned toward us again, rotating at about one turn in three minutes, we could see them again.

"The air-lock door is free now, Captain," Kelly said. "Can you see it?"

"We see it. I'm sending Manny out to throw you another line."

"Captain," Alicia said, "I suggest you wait on that. You're not going anywhere, right? I mean, now that you're with us again."

"That's right."

"Well, when Kelly lost the hammer I got to wondering what we might need that we didn't bring with us. Why don't we wait until we've looked at everything? I don't think we want to make that crossing any more than we have to."

"I concur, Alicia, now that you mention it. Good thinking."

"We're approaching the air-lock door now."

There was silence for a while. Travis put his hand over the microphone.

"Boys, you're never going to find women with more courage than those two. And they're smart and beautiful, into the bargain. You better marry them."

"I've been giving it a lot of thought," I said, and Dak grinned.

THEY MADE THEIR way to the air lock. There was a small window set into the door at head height, and it was cracked but not exploded.

"Look at this," Kelly said.

"What?" Travis, Dak, and I said at the same time.

"Frost, Captain. Even a couple little icicles."

"Condensation," Travis said, excited.

"Gotta be," Alicia said. "I think there's still air in there."

"If we can get the door open," Kelly said. "I'm punching the button . . . nothing. Trying again. Nothing. Should we whack it upside the head, guys?"

"Always worked for me," Dak said.

"Whacking . . . nothing. Whacking again. Nothing. Alicia, can you get that torqueless power wrench out of my bag? Don't let anything float away. Damn, what we need for this job is that eight-dollar hammer I lost, not this four-hundred-dollar piece of NASA surplus. Isn't that always the way?"

She was talking a lot, not only to calm her own nerves but because we'd asked her to. Describe everything, Travis had said. In great detail.

"No action on the door, Captain."

"Kelly, hit it again, then put your helmet in contact with the door."

"Why, Captain?"

"Sound can carry through metal but not through vacuum. It's possible somebody in there hears you knocking on the door."

Any science-fiction reader would have known that, and once again it came to me, hard, that space was *my* dream, *Dak's* dream, not theirs. *We* should be over there, risking our lives. Why is the universe so unfair, so perverse?

"Yikes, that really rang *my* bell," Kelly said.

"What happened?"

"Had my helmet against the door when I whanged on it, like a dummy. Hitting again, three times." A short pause. "Yes! Yes, I heard three taps! There's somebody in there! But how are we . . . wait a minute, what's this?"

"Tell us, Kelly, tell us!"

"The door is rotating. It's half open . . . three-quarters open . . . stopped."

"I can feel somebody pounding on the door," Alicia said. "Put your hand on it. Feel it? Somebody's in there for sure, Captain. And it looks like the door cycling switch works from their side."

"Alicia, don't go in, we don't know if—"

"Sorry, Captain, I've got to go in."

"Me, too," Kelly said.

"We're both inside the lock now."

"Kelly, Alicia, I want you out of there in no more than five minutes, with a situation report. I doubt we'll be able to hear you once you get inside. *Five minutes!* Got it? Or all three of us come looking for you."

"Got it, Captain. The cycling button in here works. The lock is rotating. . . ."

And then there was silence.

31

★ ★ ★

THE AIR LOCK on the *Ares Seven* was a barrel type, maximum capacity: two suited astronauts. There was an inner pressure door which you pulled closed behind you. Then the barrel rotated until the one doorway in it faced the outside. It had been designed for use on Mars, when people would be coming and going frequently.

There was a manual crank to turn it, too, which now jammed when it was almost fully opened. But it still could be cranked, in both directions. We didn't know that at the time. We thought the lock was still working electrically.

So Alicia and Kelly went inside, and we waited. Five very slow minutes. Then we saw a light from the far side of the ship, which had rotated the lock door away from us.

"Good news first, Travis," Alicia said. "Holly is alive, and she's not hurt."

Travis bit his lip and turned away from us for a moment.

"The guy we found was Dmitri Vasarov. There was an indication of trouble and three people got into suits to check out the engine. That's when the explosion came. Holly doesn't know Vasarov was crushed, and we didn't tell her. She's . . . well, she's sort of in shock. She saw

Welles and Smith flying away from the ship after the explosion. Smith was alive. She was struggling. Welles . . . she's sure he's dead. He was almost cut in half.

"About, Smith, Captain. Should Kelly and me come back to the Big Red, and we go looking for her first? If Manny brought over a bottle of air these people in here would be good for another day or two, easy . . . if it doesn't blow out."

"Negative, Alicia," Travis said. "She's dead now. Her suit would have run out of air a long time ago."

"God, that's awful. What a horrible way to die."

"Actually, Alicia, a few people have accidentally drifted away from a space station, thought they were dead, then got rescued. All of them said the same thing. After a short time of panic and fear, they achieved a feeling of peace. I wouldn't know about that, but let's hope that's what happened to Smith."

"Amen."

"So what's the situation in there? Four survivors?"

"Three. They have the body of Marston, the M.D. Why couldn't *she* have survived? She could have handled this so much better than me."

"Don't think that way. So you've got injuries?"

"Just minor bruises and abrasions on Holly and Cliff Raddison. Cliff might have a fractured arm. Have to x-ray him to be sure.

"Things are a real mess in there. Captain Aquino smashed his head and got his leg caught somehow. He's got a compound fracture of the left femur, real bad. He lost a lot of blood. Holly and Cliff stopped the bleeding. He's delirious most of the time. I only stuck around long enough to give him a shot of morphine—and I've got to be sure to thank Salty for getting that for us. Then I came out here so you guys wouldn't worry."

"What do you need, Alicia?" Travis asked her.

"Okay. First, space suits. Three of them. I think we can use the empty suit we saw next to Vasarov's body. But we'll need two more."

There was a short silence as the three of us in the ship worked it out. Like that old logic problem: *You have a fox and a goose and a bag of grain to get across a river . . .*

"They can have mine," Dak said bitterly. "All the use *I'm* getting out of it . . ."

"We're short a suit," Travis said.

"You're forgetting, Travis. Manny can bring over Dak's suit . . . and Jubal's."

"Jubal's suit is aboard?"

"Kelly told me she stowed it in a locker. The problem is . . . can Jubal's suit fit on Holly, or Cliff, or Aquino?"

"We'll make it fit, by God," Travis said. "Dak, go get it ready."

"Captain, it's *cold* in there," Alicia said. "About ten below zero, and falling. Is there any way we can heat the place?"

"Is there any power available?"

"That went out completely not long before we arrived. Cliff and Holly have been sitting in there in the dark, wrapped up in what clothes they could salvage. They were conserving the one flashlight they found, using their little bit of power to run a heating element. They're in danger of frostbite."

"Just a minute, Alicia. Guys, any ideas?"

I didn't have one. We'd backed up the heating system on *Red Thunder,* just like we'd backed up everything. I could have torn out a heater, but there was no power on the wreck to run it. A simple catalytic tent heater would do the job. We hadn't brought one.

"A long extension cord?" Dak suggested.

"We don't have anything that long," I said.

"The only thing we can do is to hurry, then," Travis said. "But we've got to hurry *slowly,* okay? I mean, think before you move. I'm not going to lose you, any of you, including the *Ares* survivors."

"Roger. The wreck is leaking, and we don't like the looks of that lock window."

"So what do you need?"

"Jubal's suit, and Dak's. A big bottle of air. Flashlights, the more the better. Some whole blood, a couple pints. I can't recall Aquino's type, but it's in my medical file. And patching material, lots of it."

"Roger," I said, and took off.

* * *

SOMEHOW I WRESTLED all that stuff out of *Red Thunder*'s air lock, all tied together.

Along with everything else I'd brought enough yellow poly rope to outfit a Boy Scout Jamboree. I got everything tied to an eyebolt so it wouldn't drift, and started casting. I figured it would take a few false starts before I got the hang of it. I was right. But on the fourth try, just as Kelly was coming out of the lock, I got the weighted end of the line dead center. Kelly only had to reach out and grab it. She tied it off, and I attached the bundle of junk to it. She pulled it across, hand over hand at first but then just letting it drift, because though it was weightless, it still had considerable mass, something you could never forget out there or you could get crushed.

When she had the stuff I pulled the rope back, tied it down, then pulled myself along it. *First you take the goose across the river because the fox won't eat the sack of grain . . .*

It took me three minutes to cross, but in only one minute I experienced what Travis had talked about. At first I was scared. Dear Lord, it was empty out there! Just two little specks tied by a thin cord, and me in the middle. But very quickly I experienced something like rapture. Somehow, in all this vastness, my fear was so insignificant, so primitive and unworthy an emotion for this starry cathedral, that it just went away. So be it, I thought. Amen. This place is inimical to life, tries every second to snuff it out . . . and I didn't mind. Oh, I wasn't eager to die, but for the first time I could remember, I wasn't afraid to die, either. I smiled, then I laughed.

"Manny? Problem?" It was Travis.

"None, Trav. Kelly, did I tell you I love you?"

"Not today," she laughed, "but it's been a busy day."

"I love you. Will you marry me?"

"Yes. Yes, Manny, I will."

"Duly witnessed and recorded," Travis said. "Dak, have a cigar." I could hear Dak laughing in the background. I drifted along the rope and into Kelly's arms. You can't kiss in a space suit, and even hugs leave a lot to be desired, but we did the best we could.

AFTER WE'D CYCLED Jubal's and Dak's suits through the lock Kelly got in and I shoved everything else in with her. She knocked on the wall with a wrench and the barrel of the lock began to turn. She smiled and waved at me, then she was gone, and the cracked window rotated into my view. I could see why they were worried. What Alicia had described as little icicles had grown into white starbursts a foot long, what I guess you'd call free-fall icicles. I had to knock them away with my glove before I could get to work.

Anybody in Florida knows what to do when there's a hurricane alert. I'd lived through two near misses. Each time Mom and Maria and me had taped up the windows. This won't stop them from breaking, but it stops them from shattering in such a spectacular way. This window was about to get a total taping with our alternative patching material, duct tape.

We'd tested, and found that ordinary gray duct tape stood up to cold and vacuum for something between six and eight hours, after which it could turn brittle and lose its gumminess, or adhesive qualities, whatever you want to call it. I had a big roll of it tied to my belt. I started peeling off three-foot strips and pasting them over the window.

Not a fun job. If you've ever been frustrated trying to lift up the end of a roll of sticky tape, try it wearing mittens. If I ever order another space suit, I'll be sure it has something that can be used as a thumbnail.

I struggled for ten minutes, strips of crumpled duct tape clinging to my suit, feeling like Br'er Rabbit fighting with the Tar Baby. I covered the whole surface of the window with long strips, much longer than needed to cover the one-foot diameter circle. Then I put on another layer, at right angles to the first, and for good measure, a third layer, diagonally. Then I knocked on the metal of the hull and the lock rotated. I got in, and repeated the process on the inside of the window. When I was satisfied I knocked again, and the inner lock door was opened by Kelly. She had her helmet off and her nose was red and dripping a little, and she was the prettiest girl I'd ever seen.

I got quick introductions to Holly and Cliff. Both were shivering uncontrollably, though wrapped in layers of cloth. I had brought a couple of big fluorescent camp lanterns, which we switched on. They gave out a ghastly light, making our skin look like sour milk, except Cliff's, whose dark skin looked almost bluish.

First order of business, get them into suits.

There is no such thing as a one-size-fits-all space suit, but the Russians had come about as close as possible. The torso can be expanded and the arms and legs lengthened or shortened a full six inches. This was accomplished with a design a lot like those bendable plastic soda straws, a bellows arrangement. We figured to fit Captain Aquino into Jubal's suit, as he was a short man, like Jubal, though not nearly so bulky.

Captain Aquino almost proved to be my undoing. I guess I hadn't realized that "compound fracture" meant a sharp point of bloody white bone sticking right out of the meat of his thigh. I felt sick, quickly removed my helmet just in case . . . and the cold slapped me in the face so hard I was shocked right out of my nausea.

I was breathing hard, and so was everyone else. The air felt thin and sour. But I'd brought an alarm that would scream if the oxygen content fell to dangerous levels, and so far it was silent.

You don't really know what chaos can be until you've seen it in free fall. Things were drifting around, things as small as tiny frozen droplets of water and blood, and as large as tables and chairs. You could shove them into a corner but they'd just drift right back out again. One of the things that kept floating about and getting in the way was the body of Dr. Brin Marston. Aside from some blood coming from her mouth she seemed almost unhurt. She did seem to be bent backwards more than normal.

"She died peacefully," Holly said to me. "She never woke up. After an hour she stopped breathing."

Holly Oakley was in shock, like Alicia had said. I had to stifle a laugh that would have been horribly inappropriate. But think about it. She's sitting in total darkness, she and Cliff. They know they are doomed. They know the air is going to kill them in a few hours, the only question is how. By getting too cold, too thin, or too oxygen-poor? Then there's a knock on the door, and who is it but your ex-husband, the one your lawyer screwed so badly in the property settlement, the alimony, and the child support.

For the record, Travis said the property settlement had been more than fair, she had never asked for alimony, and he'd never begrudged a nickel of the child support.

Now she seemed to be only partially aware of what was going on. Kelly was helping her into the suit Alicia had brought in, the one that had been on the rack beside Vasarov's corpse, and it was like dressing a toddler. Holly's attention wandered, often to the body of Dr. Marston.

"Manny, can you do something with her?" Kelly asked, jerking her head toward Marston. I shoved the body against a wall, then tied one of her legs to a stanchion. I tried to close her partially opened eyes. Big mistake. Her eyelids were frozen in that position.

Cliff had managed to struggle into Dak's suit. He was about the same height as Dak, but quite a bit huskier. "It's going to cut off the circulation in my legs," he said, teeth chattering, "but I can handle that if I have to."

"It'll only take ten, fifteen minutes," I told him. I showed him how to adjust the systems on the Russian suit. He sighed as the heating elements warmed up.

"God, I hate being cold," he said. Then we both went to help Alicia.

I really had to hand it to Alicia. Liquids won't drip in free fall, so how do you make an I.V. work? She had brought some broad rubber bands. By winding them a few times around one of the bags of type B positive blood I'd brought over, she could produce enough pressure to force the blood into Captain Aquino's veins. But that was about all she could do for him until we got him over to *Red Thunder*.

"Setting the bone will be easier once we're under way," she decided. "Right now, I want to disturb that wound as little as possible, or he'll start bleeding again." She got a big pad of sterile gauze and packed the wound, then wrapped it tightly in sterile tape. The gauze turned red almost immediately.

"Let's get him in the suit, pronto," she said.

We got the body of the suit on him, the I.V. tube nestled against his chest. Got the arms and gloves on, then one leg. Then, very gingerly, eased the other leg over the wound. Aquino began moaning and tossing his head, so Alicia jabbed him with more morphine. We got his helmet on and turned on all suit systems. All lights were green.

But not on Holly's suit. No sooner had we buttoned her down and turned the suit on than we got a big red light for pressurization. A quick inspection found two holes one inch across in the right lower leg. Something had passed right through the tough fabric.

"Okay," Alicia said. "We'll get Cliff and the captain across, then I'll come back with Kelly's suit. It should be a pretty good fit."

"No!" Holly grabbed my arm and squeezed hard. Her eyes were wild. "I can't stay here in the dark, alone. Please don't make me do it."

"It won't be dark," Alicia soothed.

"I can't do it."

"I'm not sure this place will stay pressurized much longer," I said.

"You're right. Okay. Do you think we can patch it so it will hold?"

"Yes." I sounded surer than I felt . . . but the duct tape hadn't failed us so far.

So we wrapped tape, round and round and round some more. We used the rest of my roll, making a thick, tight band from her knee to her ankle.

It should hold, I thought. It *had* to hold. We couldn't bring her dead body to Travis after coming so close.

I'm not a praying man, but I prayed. *Please, just ten minutes. Let it hold for ten minutes.*

SINCE AQUINO SEEMED to be more or less stabilized, we moved Holly up to priority one. I crowded into the air lock with her and I pressed the button . . . and nothing happened.

"Please don't tell me it's stopped working *now!*" I shouted.

"Calm down, Manny," Kelly said over the suit radio. "It only works on manual now. Alicia is cranking it . . . there it goes."

It seemed slower than it had when I entered the ship, a thousand years before, but it was turning.

We had worked it all out before we got into the lock. As soon as there was enough space, I squeezed through the door and snapped onto the lifeline attached to *Red Thunder.* No time for any rapture during this crossing. I pulled myself along, talking on the radio the whole way, alerting Dak and Travis that we would be in a hurry when Holly came over. I only started slowing myself when I was twenty feet from the ship. I soaked up my momentum with my legs, got turned around just in time to catch Holly as she came speeding along the line. I quickly unsnapped us from the crossing line and attached us to the line leading back to *Red Thunder*'s air lock. Hand over hand, with me in the lead, we made our way around the ship.

I got her in the lock and started it cycling. Elapsed time: five minutes flat. *Okay, God, we didn't need the whole ten minutes, so hang on to the surplus and let me use them for the rest of this stunt.*

I looked back at the wreck and saw Alicia starting across, hauling Aquino at the end of a short rope. Trying to hurry slowly, I pulled myself back to the crossing rope and waited for her. *You go back for the fox, row him across the river, bring back the goose . . .*

When she was safely on her way to the lock I pulled myself across the gap once more. The lock was just finishing its rotation, bringing the taped-over window into view again. I didn't like the looks of it, I thought it might be bulging. It stopped. Cliff would be letting it flood with stale *Ares Seven* air. It bulged even more. Nothing I could do about it, it would hold or it would not.

Then I thought about it some more. I pictured it . . .

"Kelly! You and Cliff get away from the door, it might—"

That's when Cliff pulled the inner door open, and the patch gave way, the tape-wrapped circular window hitting me square in the face-plate. Some of the remaining adhesive glued the patch in front of my face for a second, until I yanked it away.

It all lasted only a few seconds, with small objects being shot through the hole by the escaping air like weird grapeshot. I stayed off to the side until the eruption died down. I pulled myself around to look through the hole, but something was blocking it.

Somebody's spacesuit backpack.

Cliff was breathing hard. "Manny, Kelly got sucked into the air lock. There's a bunch of junk jammed in there with her. I'm clearing it away as fast as I can, one minute, I think. Two minutes, tops."

I couldn't see anything but the red fabric covering Kelly's backpack. But then some snow began to drift out of the hole.

"Something hit me pretty hard in the side," Kelly said. "I'm trying to get my hand around to it . . . there's a clear fluid leaking, Manny. Not blood. Clear. I'm . . . I'm scared, Manny. I feel like I'm buried alive."

There she was, inches away from me, and there was nothing I could do.

"We'll have you out in just a minute, honey," I said.

"I'm starting to feel . . . kind of cold. It's suit coolant leaking, isn't it, Manny?"

"It must be. Even if you lose it all, you can't freeze that quick, babe. I'm going to set a new Olympic hauling record. I'll have you back safe and sound in Big Red before you know it." But was her voice fainter? And if it was, was it because she was speaking softer . . . or because the air was getting thin?

"I've got it cleared, Manny," Cliff said. I could see Kelly's backpack move away from the empty porthole. "I'll squeeze in here, and you crank us around."

"Me . . . crank what?"

"The manual lock turner," Cliff said, a little impatiently.

"What . . . where is it?"

"To your left . . . are you oriented with your feet aft?"

"Yes."

"To your left, two feet away, a red arrow should be pointing to the hatch cover for the manual control."

"Got it." I grabbed the hatch cover handle and pulled. And I pulled myself right off the ship. In free fall nothing can be pulled, twisted, raised, or lowered unless you are tied to or braced against something that will give you leverage.

I planted my feet against the side of the ship, reached down, and pulled. And pulled, and again, and again.

"Hatch cover is jammed," I said. "I'll try it—"

"Never mind, no time. I'm out of the lock now. Cranking it around . . ."

The empty hatch window rotated away from me, and in about a minute the inner door appeared, and the instant it was open enough I reached in and grabbed one of the shoulder straps the Russians had put there for exactly that purpose, hauling a wayward, disabled, or dead cosmonaut without damaging the suit.

. . . You leave the goose, then row back and pick up the sack of grain.

A fine mist was coming from a small tear in the fabric of her suit, freezing almost instantly. Now I saw some blood mixed in with it.

"I'm cold," Kelly whispered. "I'm real cold."

How much air was she losing? In the time I had to get her across she would not freeze to death. But she could die very quickly with no air. I looked at the system lights on the forearm of her suit. Oxygen pressure was green, but for how long?

There was what seemed like several miles of rope between us and *Red Thunder*'s air lock. Actually, it was three ropes. Twenty feet along the wreck from the lock to the crossing line. The line was a hundred yards long. Then there was the line from *Red Thunder*'s cockpit to the air lock aft, about fifty feet. Too long.

Sometimes you can't hurry slowly, you just have to act. I worked it all out in seconds, then I planted my feet against the hull by the lock and *jumped.*

At first I thought Kelly's weight on my right arm had pulled me off course. My target was the titanium thrust ring Caleb had worked so hard on, so long ago. The last of the three ropes was tied to it. If I could snag the ring or the rope, I'd have saved two, maybe three minutes. If I'd aimed badly, I had killed Kelly. If we both soared off into space, Travis would come get us. I'd be alive, but Kelly would certainly be dead. I had plenty of time to work that out as we flew between the two ships.

Though it was the fastest crossing I ever made, it felt like the longest. How fast were we going? Fifteen miles per hour? Thirty? Probably not. But there was a threshold speed, beyond which my hand would not be able to stay closed when I grabbed the ring.

If I was even close enough to grab it.

Then I saw I would be close enough. I reached out.

"Try to hook your elbow through the ring," Travis said.

Elbow . . . I was going to be close enough. I held out my free arm and let the ring hit me, instantly curling my arm. It was almost pulled out of its socket as my body and then Kelly's pulled at me, swinging around the ring.

My arm was forced straight out and I lost contact with the ring. *I've missed. I've killed her.*

Then I opened my eyes and saw I was floating motionless relative to *Red Thunder.* I shoved my feet against the thrust ring and swung us both into the air lock.

"I think I'm burned," Kelly said, even fainter than before. "It hurts."

"Almost there." I slammed the emergency button and air flooded the lock, silently at first, then becoming a scream, louder and louder.

I realized it was Kelly screaming, incoherent at first, holding her hands to the sides of her helmet.

"Ow, ow, ow! Hurts, hurts, it hurts, Manny!"

Alicia pulled herself headfirst down the ladder leading to the suit room. We both helped Kelly out of her helmet, then her suit.

The worst pain was coming from her ears. There had been very little pressure when I pulled her into the air lock. Getting so quickly to 15 psi hadn't done her eardrums any good. But it got better quickly, though Kelly continued to yawn for the next hour.

She had first-degree burns on her right leg and arm, the parts most exposed to sunlight during our crossing. The sun is *that* hot out there, heating a suit with lost coolant in only seconds. Her only other injury was a gash in her side, from whatever piece of junk had slammed into her and holed her suit.

"Not much more of a hole and you'd never have made it," Travis told her after he'd examined her suit. "You were lucky."

"Lucky to have found Manny," she said. "Smart to have kept him." She kissed me. I suppose I should have said something like, "Aw, shucks, it weren't nothing." But I was pumped up with emotion, fear, joy, and love all swirling around in my heart. And it *had* been one amazing feat, if I say so myself.

I was so full of myself that it was a full ten minutes before I gasped and said, "What about Cliff?" But at least I remembered. Alicia was too busy getting Aquino settled in the bed that would have been Jubal's, but the others didn't have any excuse.

"That's right," Kelly said. "There's no manual crank inside the lock."

"I'd call that a design flaw," Travis said.

"Whatever, I've got to go back and get him out," I said, suddenly more tired than I'd ever been before. But there it was. Travis couldn't go. Alicia had to tend to her patients. Kelly's suit was ruined, and Cliff was wearing Dak's. . . . *Leave the grain with the fox, row back and pick up the goose.*

I had to cross once more.

32

★ ★ ★

I KNOW PEOPLE have slept in space suits before. I never expected to. But I almost did, on my last there-and-back crossing. I wished I'd had a cup of coffee first . . . but Cliff couldn't wait. Not a hundred million miles from home.

I went back to the *Ares Seven* with a crowbar and on the third attempt, popped the air-lock manual control access hatch open. I cranked the lock around and Cliff came out. I thought he might have to carry me across, but I made it.

"I sure hate to leave Brin and Dmitri back there like that," Cliff said.

"Can't be helped," Travis said over the radio. "Captain Aquino is too urgent, he's in critical condition. Anyway, we or somebody else can come back to the ship and get them, if their families want the bodies. I doubt anybody will ever find Welles and Smith, though. Too small a target in too big a solar system. Space will have to be their graves. I wouldn't mind that, myself, when I die."

Once we'd broken out and set up two extra acceleration seats—just two cots with lots of foam padding—Travis got us in the right attitude and started blasting toward the Earth. We were close enough to Mars when we found the *Ares Seven* that this return trip would take just about as long as the outward leg had.

With the acceleration back, Alicia got to work on Aquino. She had brought a collection of CDs on advanced first aid. We all watched with her as trained EMTs set the "femur" of an amazingly realistic dummy. Then Dak and Alicia went into his room and set the bone. That was fine with me. Even the video had freaked me out.

She had been right about Cliff's arm. The X ray showed a small break of the ulna that was causing him pain and swelling, but wasn't urgent. "I played a whole quarter with worse than this, back in my football days," he said. She secured and protected it with an inflatable splint, gave him a shot of morphine and a sling, and discharged him, giving him a bottle of pills on his way out of the infirmary.

"Take two of these and don't call me in the morning," she said. "Heck, take four of 'em if you want to, whenever it hurts."

She treated Kelly's mild burns and taped up the small wound in her side.

Holly was still not doing so great, so Alicia calmed her down with a couple Percodans, tapered the dose down over three days until she was back to normal . . . or as normal as she'd ever be again. We all figured she'd never go back into space.

While this was going on Travis was beaming around at all of us, hugging us, slapping us on the back like a happy father at a Little League game.

"Y'all did a miracle," he told us. "You gave me a lot more gray hairs, but you pulled it off. If they don't strike some kind of special medal for y'all when we get back, I'll kick my congressman's ass all the way from Washington to Key West."

Washington to Key West. It reminded me of a problem we had not completely solved yet. Where do you land an outlaw, independent spaceship, crewed by people who might be heroes, or might be subject to arrest or worse sanctions by government agencies both open and covert?

"Washington," Dak said, at what *had* to be our final discussion on the subject, since we were only about twelve hours from landing. "Put her down right there on the Mall. Show 'em we ain't fooling around. Public as can be. Right?"

"Miami International Airport," I said. "It's public, and people can be kept back and out of danger."

"And it's too dang easy to seal it off completely," Travis said. "Put out a story that we all died from poison fumes or something. Carry us away to Cheyenne Mountain in helicopters."

"Black helicopters?" I asked. Travis ignored it.

"Lock us away behind the fifty-ton blast doors. The spooks work us over with drugs and bright lights in our eyes. When they find out we really don't know how to build the Squeezer drive, we're dumped in shallow graves in the piney woods."

"You really think they'd do that?" Cliff asked.

"No. Mostly, I don't think so. So I don't plan to give them a *chance* to do it. Part of me, what I'd like to do is land her at Edwards Air Force Base, in California. Miles and miles of desert, plenty of room for error, nobody to get hurt if something goes wrong. Or the VStar landing strip on Merritt Island, right at the Kennedy Space Center. They're all too isolated. No witnesses but the ones the government allows in.

"The other part of me wants to set her down on the pitcher's mound at Yankee Stadium during a game. The middle of Central Park. Coney Island. Someplace with a million witnesses."

"You land at Coney," Dak said, "people will start lining up to ride it."

Travis shook his head. "To a pilot, the only thing worse than falling out of the sky is to fall out of the sky and *hit* somebody. What we need is lots of people, but not too close. Say, half a mile for the closest people. That way, something goes wrong, I've got a fighting chance to steer us to a crash landing where nobody's standing."

"What about the exhaust?" Cliff asked. "Is half a mile enough?"

"Should be. The exhaust is hot, but not toxic." We had been filling Cliff in on the story of *Red Thunder*. Though NASA had not tried to hide our existence from the Ares Seven, they hadn't exactly been full of information.

"If they actually end up making a movie about you guys," he said, laughing, "you can bet they'd build a mock-up of your ship and turn it into a ride at Orlando."

"That's it!" Kelly shouted. We all looked at her. "We land at Orlando!"

I got it, and grinned at her. Then Dak got it, and Cliff, and finally Travis.

"Maybe," he said. "Maybe."

TRAVIS SLIPPED US into a fairly low orbit around the Earth.

Dak didn't get sick. He had done okay at turnover, too. It cheered him up, but only a little. We were all aching to get down, Alicia most of all. She had stabilized Aquino, but he was still in critical condition. She had little patience with Travis's decision not to land immediately.

"I don't believe in those spooks you talk about, and this man needs better care than I can give him. *Now!*"

We managed to cajole her for a while. Travis promised we wouldn't remain in orbit more than six hours, tops. Then he'd set *Red Thunder* down, one way or another.

Suddenly we were busy again. This close to Earth we didn't need the lost dish to transmit a signal the people on Earth could pick up. Calls were coming in from all channels, wondering if we were *Red Thunder.* At first we just let the phone ring.

Kelly logged on to her ISP and went to the websites of the various theme parks south of Orlando. In five minutes she had a map that showed what she wanted.

"Lot G," she said, pointing to the map. "The 'Goofy' lot. It's the biggest parking lot in all the parks. Look at the scale, it's almost a mile across."

"Almost," Travis said, still dubious. "And that monorail runs right through the middle of it. What time is it? Eastern Daylight."

"Almost noon," Dak said.

"We give them two hours," Kelly said. "Make up your mind, Travis. You wanted a big, empty space with lots of people to witness the landing. And I hate to put it this way, but if we crash on top of people, we'll all be dead and not have to worry."

"Are you an atheist, Kelly?"

"I'm an ex-Baptist, that's all I'll say."

Travis thought about it for a moment, then nodded.

"Best we're going to do, I guess. Now all I have to do is get the President of the United States on the phone."

"Already did, Travis," Dak said, beaming. "I've got her on hold. Don't look at me that way. She called *us,* okay?"

"Okay, Dak. Now put this signal out to everybody. *Everybody.*" He sat in Dak's chair and took a deep breath.

"Good morning, Madam President," he said.

"It's just afternoon where I am, Captain Broussard."

"And where is that, Madam President?"

"I'm aboard *Marine One.*" The picture came on, and we could see her sitting next to a window in a helicopter. "I hate flying in these things. I don't know how you people would dare to fly all the way to Mars. I congratulate you all. Captain, is this line secure?"

"No, ma'am, it is not. We don't have scrambling capability, never figured we'd need it." Actually, there were scrambling programs in many of our computers; the White House or one of their spook agencies was bound to have a compatible program. The President must have known that, but ignored the lie, like the former diplomat she was.

"Very well. I'm on my way to Andrews Air Force Base, should arrive in five minutes. Many members of your families and other loved ones are already en route to Andrews in a gover— . . . in a chartered jet. I would like you to land your ship there. We intend to hold a 'welcome back' ceremony."

We all had the same reaction when she mentioned our families: Hostages.

I'm ashamed to have harbored that thought. But the government ought to be ashamed, too. How did it happen that most of us don't trust our government not to trample on the Constitution, under the umbrella of National Security?

"I presume our lawyers are aboard that plane, too, Madame President," Travis said. One of the things he'd stressed the most to our friends and relatives was that, until *Red Thunder* returned, your lawyer is your Siamese twin. The only way our lawyers would *not* be aboard was if our families had been arrested by force, in which case our legal brigade would earn their outrageous hourly charges by raising a stink in the media bigger than this media-happy country had ever seen.

"Yes, I believe they are aboard."

"It's a kind offer, ma'am," Travis said. "And please forgive me, but Andrews is on your home grounds. It's your stadium, your ball, and your bat. We intend to land a little closer to our home turf."

"What do you propose?" Diplomat or not, she looked a little pissed when she said it. I guess Presidents don't hear the word *no* very often, or even *no, thank you.*

Travis told her, and she was shaking her head before he got very far.

"Out of the question."

"I'm sorry, I guess I didn't state my intention clearly. We are going to land in that parking lot. I'll be in position to land in another two hours. That should give you plenty of time to do a few things:

"Clear that parking lot. Change the course of that government jet, have it land at Orlando and then fly our loved ones by helicopter to Lot B, that is the 'Bambi' lot, which is the closest point people should be allowed to approach our ship until I broadcast the all clear. I don't want to see any soldiers. Local police only."

"Is that all?" Her voice had a definite edge to it now.

"No, ma'am." Travis grinned. "I'd like to respectfully extend to you an invitation to witness the landing, the return of the first men and women to walk on Mars."

The President looked stricken when Travis said "Mars."

"Oh, my God," she whispered. "Please forgive me. In the heat of the moment, I forgot to mention the very first thing I should have told you. A few days ago our Mars mission, the *Ares Seven,* suffered some sort of onboard explosion. We've heard nothing from them since, and we—"

"It's not a problem, Madame President. I have some good news to report to all Americans, and people around the globe. We found the *Ares Seven.*

"There is some bad news, too, I'm afraid. Astronauts Welles, Smith, Marston, and Vasarov died of their injuries before we could get there.

"But we rescued Holly Oakley and Cliff Raddison and Bernardo Aquino. Aquino was badly injured, and I'm sure his life was saved by our medic, Alicia Rogers. But he is still in critical condition. Please excuse my abruptness, but there is a lot we need to do before the landing, in two hours' time. Good-bye."

Travis looked happy. It must be a heady feeling to put the President on hold, refuse an order, and hang up on her, all in the space of ten minutes.

TRAVIS WAS TELLING another lie when he said we'd be very busy over the next two hours. He had already plotted our landing trajectory, a matter of five minutes of computer time, almost all of that feeding in the data.

Dak and Cliff and I had nothing to do at all. Holly and Alicia were standing their vigil by the still-unconscious Captain Aquino. Holly had started doing that about twenty hours into our return, when she was getting over the effects of her living nightmare. Was there something going on there? Oakley and Aquino? *Ares Seven* had been in space a long time. But it wasn't my business.

Kelly was the only one of us with lots to do. She was on the phone right up to the point we had to strap in. She visited the New York Stock Exchange to check up on Red Thunder, Inc., which was trading up almost 100 percent before the exchange suspended trading to let things settle down. I hadn't even known we had stock to be traded, much less that I owned a big chunk of it. I'd been too busy building and training.

The document presented in the Initial Public Offering was interesting, though. As a corporate statement of purpose there were just two things: "To construct and launch a manned vehicle to take human beings to Mars and return them safely to the Earth" and "To promote, publicize, and in any other manner to exploit the trademarked and copyrighted symbols associated with the ship and its crew and its mission, in any medium whatsoever."

While I was loafing through my last few hours in space, Kelly was determining what kind of sneakers I'd be wearing for the next year. She had Nike and Adidas in a bidding war. While the ship was still building, Kelly had made the acquaintance of the publicity and promotions departments of dozens of companies who relied heavily on advertising to sell their stuff . . . and who doesn't? She had pitched it as a motion picture tie-in, naturally, and had to be careful not to get anybody *too* interested in our phantom flick. Then, the day before launch, she had e-mailed all those people . . . *you may recall our conversation of August 9* . . . telling them to watch the skies the next morning.

After launch—a thousand years ago, it seemed, and in a previous lifetime—she had worked the telephone until we lost the dish. She even inked a few deals by fax, all subject to our safe return, of course.

We were all going to be on the Wheaties box, if we lived. . . .

TRAVIS BROUGHT US almost to rest ten miles above Orlando, and began our descent at a speed not much greater than the express elevators at the Empire State Building.

"I've never eaten a single flake of Wheaties in my life," I told Kelly.

"You'll eat a whole bowl of it in a few days," she assured me.

We watched on the screens as the grid of lines below us resolved into streets, and buildings. Then we could see the maze of freeways snaking their way through America's theme park heaven. They were all gridlocked, no one moving an inch anywhere. But they didn't seem to mind. They stood on their cars, beside the road, or behind yellow police tape, facing an almost solid line of squad cars from every community close enough to get there in two hours. A dozen helicopters were parked in Bambi Lot, one of them *Marine One.* Dozens more hovered at a safe distance, their telescopic lenses sending the picture back to networks all over the world.

Travis brought *Red Thunder* in like he did it every day.

"Touchdown on strut one!" Dak called out. "Touchdown three! Touchdown two! We're down, Captain."

"Shutting down engines," Travis called back.

But the engine noise did not die out. *Red Thunder* was still shaking.

"Manny, Kelly," Travis said. "Get down there and see what the problem is. And *hurry slowly!*"

We did, and Alicia and Dak joined us. We entered the lock, overrode it by pulling the big red, recessed handle, and the outer door opened. We smelled the fresh air of Earth again . . . the fresh, *hot* air of Earth. The ship had heated the landing zone, buckled some of the asphalt. We lowered the ramp and looked out.

The roaring sound got louder. It was the crowd, half a mile away, a million people who had bought a ticket to a fantasy and got a glimpse of a dream come true instead.

We were home.

TEN YEARS LATER

FOR THE NEXT five years *Red Thunder* sat right there, where Travis had put her down. They built a geodesic dome over her with a fantastically detailed diorama and they covered the asphalt with sand, gravel, and rocks, every grain of it imported from Mars. Goofy had to find himself another parking lot.

We were all there at the opening, and I watched with a creepy feeling as the ramp lowered and four lifelike robots walked down the ramp and started to sing . . . not "The Wonderful Wizard of Oz." The copyright holders kicked up a fuss, because we hadn't landed in *their* parking lot. So they sang "When You Wish Upon a Star." I wish we had sung that, too. And I wish we'd sung better. On the tape, we were plain awful.

After five years Red Thunder, Inc., donated the ship to the Smithsonian, who installed it under a glass pyramid right out in front of the Air and Space Museum, watched over by the *Wright Flyer, The Spirit of St. Louis,* Chuck Yeager's *Glamorous Glennis,* Alan Shepard's *Freedom Seven* Mercury capsule, and *Apollo 11*. Rare company, but the magnificent old bird deserves it.

* * *

IN THE EVENT, we had no trouble with the government. Is that because of the precautions we took, or do they exist only in the minds of paranoid novelists and screenwriters? The actions of some of the agencies we *do* know about scare me plenty.

What dealings we had with the government were open and friendly, mostly, though some voices were raised suggesting we ought to turn Jubal's creation over to the government, if we were patriotic Americans. But the image of the American flag rising over the sand dunes of Mars, spoiling China's moment of glory, was too firmly fixed in the American imagination for that point of view to last. When we testified before the Joint Committee of Congress there was not a breath of reproach in the air. We were honored guests invited to share our story with the world.

The first year was a whirlwind. In some ways it was more stressful than the trip to Mars, at least to someone like myself, camera shy and not fast with a quip, like Dak and Kelly and Travis. We rode in a ticker tape parade down Wall Street in New York, and in a parade I enjoyed a lot more through the town of Daytona, local kids who had made good. The parade ended at the racetrack, the Holy of Holies in Daytona, where we were given trophies with checkered flags on them. The little stock cars on top of the trophies had been unscrewed and replaced with *Red Thunder* models.

We could have paraded down the main street of every city and town in America if we'd accepted all the invitations.

If somebody wanted to use our images to sell something, or put us on their product, we researched them carefully . . . and then charged all the market would bear, which was *plenty.* Banana Republic sold thousands of *Red Thunder* leather jackets, and we got a piece of each one. We wore Adidas "Red Thunders" and ate Wheaties, though I only ate the one bowl. Nothing against Wheaties, I just don't like cereal.

We made a lot of money. More than I ever dreamed possible. I never felt like we degraded ourselves. But it's odd and not exactly pleasing to see something that resembles your face on the muscle-bulging body of an action figure toy.

One of the things that left a bad taste in my mouth was the movie, which hit the cineplexes a year to the day after our return. It did okay, but not as well as expected. There were several reasons for that, one being that they didn't wait until they had a good script. The twerp who played me didn't look a bit like Jimmy Smits, but the girls loved him. The animated television series about us was *much* better, it ran for seven years.

Then there was the undeniable fact that, in Hollywood terms, the *real* story of a *real* pioneer trip just didn't measure up to the likes of *Star Wars,* or any of hundreds of outer space adventures full of blazing ray guns and weird aliens.

And the public was just getting tired of us. I was sure getting tired of *them.* When your face is on magazine covers and television screens as mine was, you can't go anywhere without being recognized. You never get a moment's peace.

So after the first anniversary we mostly withdrew from the public eye. You can never really erase your celebrity, once you've gotten it or had it thrust on you, but you can stop catering to it. I'm not complaining. Celebrity is a small price to pay for freedom from financial worries.

FAIRY TALES END happily ever after. Real life never does. We came a lot closer than most. It's just that things don't always work out the way you had imagined. But sometimes the alternative is just as good.

Things didn't work out as planned for Dak and Alicia. They had a falling-out and they parted company. But since Alicia remained friendly with Kelly and Dak was still my best friend, though growing more distant with each passing year, they see each other fairly frequently and they get along.

Dak never recovered from the humiliation he felt as the champion puker aboard *Red Thunder.* No one ever blamed him for it, but he punished himself. For the first year he made public appearances with the rest of the crew, but when we got tired of the celebrity rat race, Dak was not. So he started touring the sports venues of America, anything from football games to tractor pulls, riding into the arena on *Blue Thunder,* which had been retrieved and restored to diesel power. It was quite a show. When he tired of it, he donated it to the Smithsonian, to be put in the crystal pyramid with Big Red.

He took up racing, mainly motorcycles and pickups, but he'd drive almost anything that went fast. Kelly says he's still proving himself, over and over, and she's probably right. But he seems happy, and that's all I care about.

He and his father devote much of their time to their speed shop, not only building their own cars but working on and designing others. I always ask Dak if he's ready to join the NASCAR circuit, and he always scoffs. NASCAR is "the last white good-ol'-boy club left in America," he says, and stock cars are "the fastest billboards on the planet."

On Sam's first birthday after the return, Dak bought him a classic Harley. I bought Travis's Triumph. Weekends when we can get together, we drive all over Florida with Dak on *Green Thunder,* his racing bike.

Dak has even made peace with his mother. They still seldom see each other, but now she sends him a present on his birthday, usually something hilariously inappropriate like a train set or a bicycle. He gives them to Toys for Tots. She isn't really a bad person, she just has no clue about how to be a mother.

Alicia . . . well, Alicia is still Alicia. She puts all her money into her own foundation, which runs drug and alcohol rehabilitation centers all over the South. She seems sublimely happy, except for one week every year just before her father comes up for a parole hearing. Ironically, without booze in him he's a model prisoner, so any year now he could get out. And start drinking again . . .

I figure that if Alicia lives as long as Mother Teresa she could win a Nobel Peace Prize, too.

* * *

MOM DIDN'T SELL the Blast-Off Motel, after all.

While we were away she and Maria sold tons of *Red Thunder* souvenirs. They had to set up a tent in the vacant lot across the street to handle the traffic. And from the day we lifted off, there has never been a vacancy. Now it's a good idea to reserve at least a year in advance. Except for the fantasylands of Orlando, we are the third most popular tourist attraction in central Florida, behind the 500 and the space center. Some years we even beat out Kennedy.

Two years after our return Daytona was hit by a late-season hurricane. The Golden Manatee suffered a lot of damage, some of which exposed foundations shoddy even by Florida standards. The city engineer said the wind from a passing butterfly's wings was apt to blow the thing over, which Mom and Maria and I wouldn't have minded if it fell toward the beach, which was where it was leaning, but it might have blown the other way and buried us. With her new clout at City Hall Mom managed to get it condemned, and two days later they blew it up. Before the dust had even settled Mom bought the land, which we turned into a parking lot and large restaurant/souvenir stand with a pedestrian bridge to give the Blast-Off easy beach access. We added a new wing, too. All the rooms have unobstructed ocean views.

Mom wanted no part of the business other than as a part owner. It turned out Aunt Maria actually liked the motel business, just didn't care for the physical labor. She hasn't made a bed since *Red Thunder* took off. She hired Bruce Carter, formerly of the Golden Manatee, to take care of all the hard work, leaving Maria to relax in the shade with her friends, playing dominoes and making sculptures of shell people landing on Mars. The Blast-Off maids are the best paid in Florida, with medical benefits and a pension plan.

Mom suddenly had free time, something she'd had almost none of from the moment of my birth. She was at loose ends for a while, but she soon found many things to fill her day, including volunteering at one of Alicia's dry-out academies.

She also spent several hours each week at the shooting range. Eventually she tried out for the Olympic team. She didn't do well at skeet but made it in fifty-meter rifle. Kelly and I and Dak went to Johannesburg, where she finished out of medal contention with a respectable eighth place. When she marched into that gigantic stadium with the American team on the first day, I thought I'd burst with pride.

THE HUGE BROUSSARD clan avoided all the publicity, except for Little Hallelujah, as the family called him, the youngest and shortest of Jubal's brothers. Hallelujah was the only child of Avery who was still deeply religious. He had followed in his father's footsteps, preaching in a little backwoods church. *Red Thunder*'s flight and his brother's unwanted fame was just the kick in the pants his ministry needed, and today he has a cable television show where he often connects Mars and Heaven in some manner only he really seems to understand. But he shouts, and he sweats, and he heals, and he doesn't handle snakes, so everybody seems happy.

TRAVIS JUST CELEBRATED nine years of sobriety. A year of appearances and hearings knocked him off the wagon once, but Alicia was there to help.

Travis stayed in the background as much as he could during the first, frantic weeks. He was content to let the media run with the story of the four kids who built a spaceship almost by themselves, armed only with the strange machine built by Jubal—the man of mystery in the early days—Travis being nothing more than a hired driver. We all tried to correct that impression in all our interviews, but the fact was that our adventure was much the sexier story. Travis's story concerned nothing more exciting than the possible destruction of human civilization. Can't sell papers with that.

But eventually, when the media blaze died down a bit, people did start to think about the evil side of the new technology.

Naturally the United Nations wanted to be in charge, from discussions to resolutions to implementation. They offered their meeting halls and their huge staff to facilitate matters. Travis turned them down, politely. Then he issued an invitation to all the countries of the world—except China. Travis was never going to forgive or forget that *somebody* in that government had ordered the destruction of Big Red and the death of her crew. The other nations were each to choose a delegation consisting of two scientists, two political leaders, and three ordinary citizens to assemble in three weeks at the Orange Bowl, in Miami, to meet with Travis and Jubal and the *Red Thunder* crew to determine what to do with the Squeezer drive.

A week later he invited the Chinese, too. It didn't have anything to do with the tremendous diplomatic uproar China's exclusion had caused. Travis really enjoyed that. He knew going in that you couldn't exclude one-sixth of the Earth's population. But you *could* slap their leaders in the face.

There were plenty of other things to howl about. Seven delegates from each country? Seven from India, and seven from Luxembourg? Does that make sense? "It does to me," Travis said. "And until Jubal and I stand up and speak our piece and then hand it over to you, it's our stadium, our ball, and our bat. Stay away if you don't like it."

Naturally, it was a zoo. The United States sent the President and the Senate leader from the other party. There had never been such an assembly of presidents, premiers, and prime ministers, and there may never be again. The Orange Bowl was surrounded with tanks and helicopter gunships.

Every imaginable pressure group was there. Some called the Squeezer drive a tool of Satan, or worse, of American Imperialism, Zionism, Racism, International Cartels, the World Trade Organization, Big Oil (which the Squeezer would soon put out of business, but nobody ever said a protester had to make sense), Communism, the United Nations, or those five space aliens who had come from Mars pretending to be human. On the streets, the *Red Thunder* crew was denounced for "despoiling the natural beauty" of Mars, polluting Earth's air with radiation on takeoff (a lie, but how do you prove that?), and "encouraging the consumer culture by sweeping Earth's garbage under the rug." Guilty on that count, I guess. The Squeezer was a mighty big rug to sweep trash under. In less than ten years every landfill and nuclear waste dump on Earth has been squeezed into a little silvery sphere and used to propel spaceships. This is bad?

They were all opposed to the newly christened International Power Administration and in favor of staying on a polluted and threatened Planet Earth, and many of them threw rocks and Molotov cocktails to prove how passionately they loved the Earth. Three cops died, and two protesters.

It bothered me, but Kelly scoffed at them. "The perpetual two percent of malcontents," she called them. "Honestly, if God showered manna from heaven on that bunch, they'd want to know if He used pesticides on it, or added any preservatives." I didn't point out that Alicia might be one asking those questions.

So they assembled, a thousand official delegates on the field, twenty thousand reporters clustered around the fifty yard line, the rest of the seats taken by people who had lined up since Travis announced the public was invited, first come, first served.

The first day was all Travis's show.

He brought a large metal suitcase. He opened it to reveal about a hundred dials, switches, and trac-ball controllers. We managed not to giggle when we realized this was the Beta Model of the Squeezer Jubal had built out of scraps lying around his workshop/laboratory. Travis's aim was to make the Squeezer look a lot more complicated than it really had to be, on the theory that it might get scientists looking in the wrong direction.

He put the Squeezer through its paces for the assembled delegates, expanding the bubbles, contracting them, making them go *boom!*, which they did with a mighty reverberation in that big arena with its brand new dome. He fitted a bubble into a toy rocket and flew it up to the dome, then brought it back and set it down.

Then he asked Kelly to try her hand at it. We five were the only ones who knew what would happen next. The giant Squeezer melted into slag in a chemical reaction too brilliant to look at.

"It didn't like the pattern of her retinas," Travis said. "The machine used a laser scanner to identify an authorized user. I was the only authorized one. If any of you had tried to use it, the same thing would have happened.

"You folks are going to have to figure out something like that. We are going to have to have more than one Squeezer to handle the demand, and we'll have to have people other than my cousin Jubal who know how to make more of them. But they *cannot* be allowed to fall into the wrong hands. These bubbles can be made as powerful as thermonuclear bombs, but the thing about H-bombs is that they're hard to make. The Squeezer is cheap.

"You've all got a terrible task ahead of you. I said, 'the wrong hands.' But who has the *right* hands? Who do we trust with that much responsibility? How do we identify someone who can be trusted not to steal the secret, sell the secret, or hand it over to his or her native country? I don't envy you, but now I gladly hand the burden over to you. Thank you for giving me this opportunity, and please, please, be wise."

And he walked out. The stunned delegates didn't know whether to applaud him or tackle him and start pulling out his fingernails.

SO THE IPA proposed and debated and approved and rejected and discussed and shouted at each other and got into fistfights, and in about a year produced a course of action. It didn't satisfy anybody, but was probably the best they could do. Some problems don't have easy or obvious solutions. Some have no solution at all.

The IPA could impose levies on its member nations, so it did, and bought the Falkland Islands, which contained 2,945 people, 700,000 sheep, and millions of Rockhopper, Magellanic, Gentoo, King, and Macaroni penguins. They moved the now-wealthy shepherds and their sheep to milder climates. The penguins they let stay. And there they built the most secure facility on Earth, the one place on Earth for the manufacture of the machines that produced Squeezer bubbles.

The manufacturing plants there on the cold, windy Falklands built Squeezer machines that would initiate, expand, or contract Squeezer bubbles. They didn't build many of them. These machines were sent to governments under strict handling rules, and with what Travis called "a million exploding cigars" built into them. Tamper with them, and you die. Every year some jerk thinks he's figured them out, and is burned alive.

THE TOUGHEST QUESTION facing the assembly in the Orange Bowl was this: Jubal can build machines that will create, expand, contract, and produce thrust from Squeezer bubbles—but not turn them off, that was forbidden—but Jubal won't live forever. Who will pick up the torch of unlimited power once Jubal is gone?

What the IPA eventually came up with was a lot like a priesthood, and a lot like a guild. The trade secrets or magical arcana of Squeezing would be conserved, used, and passed down by means of an elite scientist class. To be in this elite you had to be capable of understanding the physics and mathematics. This eliminated me, and Dak, and Travis. In fact, it narrowed the field to about one in a hundred million.

So beginning with this small pool, the IPA set up the most rigorous tests and examinations it could conceive, and started sifting. Before they were done, a candidate was pulled apart and put back together again. You could be eliminated for being too chauvinistic or patriotic, too wedded to one political or religious doctrine, too egotistical, or too just plain crazy. It was amazing how many physics Ph.D.'s fell into that category.

The popular press immediately dubbed these seven men and women the High Priests of Squeeze. They served for life, because even if they retired they had to be watched for the rest of their lives. They were not precisely *confined* to the Falkland Islands, but if they went anywhere they were constantly guarded, both from kidnapping and from passing the Squeezer secrets to somebody else.

These were the people who actually built the Prime Squeezers. These were the self-sacrificing saints who were let in on the whole secret of the Squeezer phenomenon, who agreed not to reveal it to anyone under pain of death, the wise ones who would chance partaking of the fruit of the Tree of Power. These were the poor schmucks who assumed the burden that had fallen on Jubal the day we lifted off in *Red Thunder.*

OF ALL OF us, the aftermath of the voyage has treated Jubal most cruelly. He lives on the Falklands. He is not a prisoner there, but if and when he leaves he is under enormous security. He hardly ever does leave these days.

Three months after our return, not long after Jubal came out of hiding, an attempt was made to kidnap him. It came very close to working, but ended up with eight dead would-be kidnappers and three dead Navy Seals, who had been assigned to guard him at Rancho Broussard. Travis believes the caper was planned and paid for in China, but Travis sees ChiCom Reds under every rock. Most of the eight criminals had Italian last names. "Chinese could have hired them," Travis said. Me, I thought about Squeezer bombs in the hands of the Mafia, and shuddered. Or Irish rebels, or Palestinians, or Zionists, or any other group of paranoid malcontents you want to name.

So Jubal doesn't tempt fate anymore. He hated the Falklands at first for its cold, windy climate, so different from the lands where he had spent all his life. The IPA does its best to make him happy. He has a fine house, a wonderful laboratory. All he has to do is ask for something and he gets it. All he's ever asked for is Krispy Kremes. A dozen are delivered every afternoon on the daily plane.

He does a lot of rowing in the many bays of the islands, he told me, but nowadays he's accompanied by a destroyer, part of the IPA's protective fleet. It is such a funny picture, and so sad.

He's become a world authority on penguins, like the Birdman of Alcatraz. Often you can find him sitting among them, completely accepted.

I asked him once how effective he thought the elaborate IPA system would be, in the long run.

"*Long* run, don' nothing work forever," he said. "Dey say ain't no Squeezer-buster gone *ever* be develop. Dat ain't nuttin' but swamp water. Dem seven smarties over yonder, dey done figgered out how to turn one off, oh yeah. If'n you understan' how to *make* dem bubbles, makin' 'em go 'way ain't too hard, no. Then, *boom!*

"Aside from dem smart boys and girls, somebody else apt to figger it out, jus' like I did. I jus' hope he don' need to get whomp upside de haid, like I did!" He laughed and rubbed the dent in his skull.

So there it is. You can't hide knowledge forever. The only encouraging thing I can think of about that is, we've had the atomic bomb for a long time now, and the last city we destroyed with it was in 1945. Maybe we can get by that long before somebody figures out how to make his own Squeezer.

WE TRY TO visit Jubal at least once a year. Sometimes it's a reunion with the whole happy family, sometimes just me and Kelly. The flight to Stanley, the capital, makes you feel the islands are almost as remote as Mars.

Six months after the return we got married as quietly as we could, not wanting to deal with shouting paparazzi and circling helicopters with long lenses. Two years later our daughter, Elizabeth, was born, and in another two years, our son, Ramon.

Kelly became more or less a full-time mother . . . but, being Kelly, still had time to handle a few projects on the side, little things like helping run our many business interests and serving for a term in the State Senate in Tallahassee, where she helped pass the first meaningful land-use laws Florida had ever seen.

Her father is currently between beauty queens, though he's been seen with a former Miss Maine on his arm. Kelly and I made up with him, as far as it is possible to make up with a conniving, back-stabbing, larcenous racist. We usually spend Thanksgiving with him, unless he's been too obnoxious the previous year. Even my grandparents, both sets, have decided that my being white, or Hispanic, doesn't matter too much if I'm rich and famous. After they had appeared on their local television stations crowing about how wonderful I was, they couldn't very well ignore me. We usually spend a stiffly polite Christmas Day with one or the other.

Travis was right. Both MIT and Cal Tech sent cordial invitations for me to continue my education there. But who was I trying to kid? I simply didn't have the kind of mind that would put me through either university without the kind of covert help they usually shower only on sports stars. And I'd be afraid that if I went, that's exactly what they'd do, graduate me still unable to extract a cube root. So I turned them down.

Instead, after all the fuss had died down, I went to Florida State, where I eventually earned an M.B.A., with a major in . . . hotel management.

I didn't give up my dream of going into space as a career, I just took a closer look at it. What did I want, exactly? Well, to be a spaceman. Wouldn't that be great?

Mom says that when I was seven she found an old telescope in a thrift store and bought it. Instantly, I decided I wanted to be an astronomer. Then I discovered that real astronomers hardly every actually *looked* through their telescopes. They took pictures with long exposures, they ran data through computers. Where's the fun in that? I went back to wanting to be a fireman.

Before *Red Thunder* there were basically four types of people who went into space: pilots, scientists/payload specialists, United States senators, and the occasional rich person willing to spend a million dollars or more for a week in space.

After *Red Thunder* . . . *everybody* could go into space. There may have been things that changed human civilization as radically as the Squeezer drive—fire, agriculture, the Industrial Revolution, the automobile, the computer—but nothing else changed it so *fast*. Suddenly, you could just buy a ticket and *go*. For a while there were even trips you could take to be the "first." One expedition took two hundred tourists to Uranus and those folks became the first to set foot on a dozen small moons. It was as if Lewis and Clark had pulled a Greyhound bus after them, full of folks in loud shirts, snapping pictures all the way to the Columbia River.

So managing a hotel made perfect sense for me . . . if it was a hotel on Mars. The Marineris Hyatt is about three months from completion on a site within an easy Bigfoot drive of *Red Thunder*'s first landing. I have been hired to manage it, and that's a job I can do well. After that . . .

Just as soon as it became possible to buy Squeezer bubbles to install in your homemade spaceship, there was an explosion of crazies—they seemed crazy to me, anyway—headed outward. Dozens of them, bound for all the nearest stars. The ones who aimed for Alpha Centauri should start arriving back at Sol System soon, those who lived, anyway. They will be only about a year older because most of the trip they will have traveled at nearly the speed of light. They will have the satisfaction of being the first to fly to another star and return, but progress has already overtaken them. They went hoping to find habitable planets, and we know Alpha Centauri has none. Gigantic telescopes on the far side of the moon have told us that. They have also discovered dozens of Earth-sized planets at the proper distance from the right kind of star, planets that show the signature of water in the spectrograph, all within thirty light-years.

Thirty light-years is an easy journey with a Squeezer drive. *Any* distance is easy, they all take about a year when you're going so fast time virtually stops.

Several very large starships are now being built. The one closest to completion will be ready to shove off in about five years. It is owned by Red Thunder, Inc., so Kelly and I have a reserved berth, if we want it.

If we go, I won't be driving the thing. I won't be in charge of the engines, I won't be in the landing party when we get there. But on the way, I can handle the human needs of the voyage very well. A starship is just a very large, very fast hotel, isn't it?

Kelly isn't sure yet. For that matter, neither am I. Elizabeth would be thirteen, Ramon would be eleven. Do we want to bring them up in a pioneer society with an alien sun in the sky, or on nice, safe, familiar Mars? There's plenty of time to decide.

Sometimes I think back, and I'm impressed how much of our lives are determined by chance.

What if we'd run over and killed Travis, that night on the beach? Our lives would have been very different. What if we'd missed seeing him entirely, just drove off into the night and the tide took him or he woke up in a sand dune with a hangover? I'm sure that every day opportunities pass us by and we never even know they were there.

Then again, we can see a chance, take it, and watch it all go sour. My father saw a chance, took it, and ended up with a bullet in his gut.

We of the *Red Thunder* had incredible luck, but we worked very hard to take advantage of it. Did we "deserve" to be the first on Mars? I'm sure there were worthier people, but the chance fell to us.

MY GOODNESS, THE stories we'll have to tell. I see Kelly and me, 110 years old, sitting in rocking chairs on a planet with two suns during the day and six moons at night, telling our great-great-grandchildren stories they probably won't believe.

How perilous it was to go just to Mars in those days.

How alien this new planet thirty light-years from home looked to us.

Alien? they will say. *This* is home, it's not alien. What's perilous about traveling to another star? And here they go again, about how they were the first. So what?

Yes, I know, it doesn't really mean anything. But the fact remains . . .

We were the first!